MW01485819

PRINT/AMAZON VERSION ONLY

Ebook/Print Cover: Carol Marques Design
Editing, Proofing, backgrounds, & Formatting: Dirty Sexy Words/ Storm shield Editing/Little Tailfeather Publishing
Cassandra /LTF logos: Pretty in Ink Creations/Artlogo
Goosebusters Alpha team: Kat Silver, Becky Ross, Erica Taryn
Duckhunters Proofers: Jackie H, Jaemi Serrano
Sensitivity Readers: Brit Mason, Gail Jericho
Legal Services: Joshua Farley, esq.
Representation: Laura Pink at SBR Media
Images/Fonts: Creative Fabrica, Depositphotos, Shutterstock, & Photoshop
Map: Cassandra Featherstone

No GenAI was used within this book. All errors and greatness are by an ADHD muppet.

Little Tailfeather Publishing

APEX ACADEMY
CAPERS

EAT
PREY
LOVE

INTERNATIONAL BESTSELLING AUTHOR
CASSANDRA FEATHERSTONE

Stalk Cassandra Featherstone in the Dark Corners of the Web

Join my Facebook group and follow me everywhere!

Want More?

Sign up for
my bi-weekly manifesto for a
free series sampler:

Join my Ream as a FREE follower or exclusive subscriber to get access to cover reveals, WIPs, Serial Stories, and personal chats from me!

GET A SECRET BONUS SCENE!

For a secret bonus scene that follows *In Prey We Trust* click the link below, sign up for my newsletter, and get your freebie.

Get your bonus scene from IPWT here!

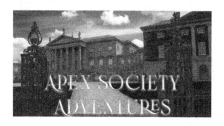

It is **HIGHLY** recommended you read this, plus the holiday novella, *O Holy Spite*, prior to this book.

Content
Information

FEATHERSTONE

This is a *paranormal whychoose romance with poly elements*—our FMC, Delores, will not have to choose between love interests.

There are many situations included that are intended for mature audiences (18+).

In this book, there may be instances/references (be they small or lengthy) that could trigger some individuals such as:

- liberal use of appropriate consent
- biting
- BDSM and intro to BDSM
- primal play
- raw sex
- shifted sex
- traumatic childhood
- MMF, MM, MFM, MF, MMFMM, and more
- super heinous puns (seriously, lots)
- underage drinking
- drug use

- unhealthy coping mechanisms
- body parts in jars
- neurospicy MMC
- death
- body modifications
- fancy genitalia
- mate knots/barbs
- unhinged MMC
- bullying (in person and on social media)
- PTSD
- blood
- emotional abuse from parents and friends
- alcohol abuse
- domestic violence
- death of a parent mentioned as off-page event
- implied child abuse
- body dysmorphia
- bad language
- fight clubs
- emotional manipulation
- power play
- adorable nicknames
- physical intimidation
- coercive emotional abuse by authority figures (not in poly group)
- voyeurism
- rough sex
- biting
- sex with wings and tails
- attempted/successful kidnappings
- therapeutic abuse (not sexual)
- marking
- lawyers (ugh.)
- professors/student (above 18+)
- age gap (from 17 yrs to almost 2000 yrs)

- use of sex toys
- family dysfunction
- betrayal (non-poly group)
- disabled side character
- absolute disrespect for shitty parents
- pop culture references (so many)
- brief mentions of non-body positive dieting culture
- discussion of disability & neurodivergence
- mention of drug sales and distribution
- very liberal re-imagining of history
- discussion of other species as lower
- official corruption
- name calling
- occasional misogyny
- inappropriate use of a library
- exhibitionism
- discussion of non-MC treating a side character with a disability poorly
- hand necklaces
- adult bullying
- magical kinks
- impact play
- sensory deprivation
- abusive bosses
- elitism
- bribery
- corpses
- fat shaming (not by MCs)
- drama
- physical threats to FMC and others
- species-ism
- discussion of shifter trafficking
- discussion of trafficking auctions
- suspicion of brainwashing

No sexual practices in this book should be taken as safe or appropriate for real life application.

Content information is important and I don't ever want to harm a reader with inaccurate information.

Author Ramblings

FEATHERSTONE

Readers,

I am so *overwhelmed* at the progress my bad ass bunny has made this year that I can hardly write this author note.

Not only did we overcome the shadows of the past and move on to a less damaging future, but Dolly is now headed to audio in December and translated into German. I cannot wait for the rest of the world to get to know our vulnerable then strong bunny who, like me, was beset on all sides by fake friends, vicious narcissists, and groups of minions willing to follow their mean girl leader until the end.

We've made it, y'all—the terrorists didn't win.

In *EPL*, Dolly will continue her quest to find out about her roots, deepen her relationships with her men and her allies, and really dig into the cause of the Fae attacking the schools. She won't find everything out, of course, because there's two more books, silly faces.

But she will learn new things, encounter enemies new and old, and gather her forces to continue fighting the nasty Council, her parents, hidden enemies, and maybe… the Fae?

(I mean, we're not sure, right?)

Her resilience and ability to keep going in the face of so many obstacles is part of how I'm able to keep going when the writing world gets tough. If numbers are lagging, I think about my FMCs and what they'd do—suck it up and push harder. (Not to the detriment of mental health, because my gals are smart cookies, yo.) Dolly's fortitude despite constant attacks from places she only finds out about third-hand or when something gets shown to her is a testament to our ability as women to break free from the abusive exes with self-healing, therapy, focus, and… well, in her case, a lot of smoking hot pred dick.

Sigh. Don't we all wish…

Anyway, my point is Dolly—like the IRL Dolly—inspires me a lot, despite her youth. She's the girl I wish I could have been at her age in terms of mental health and ability to heal, but I'm super glad I'm more similar to now. As you age, problems become more complex, but people remain unchanged. So learning to deal like she is has saved me and my writing—as have readers like you supporting me.

Enjoy the next installment in our bunny's life and find your inner bad ass along the way.

As Fitz would say, "Namaste, motherfuckers."

Blood and guts,

Cassandra Featherstone
QUEEN OF SMART, SASSY SPICE

Reader's Note

A few things you should know...

Come Out & Prey, Let Us Prey, In Prey We Trust, and O Holy Spite should be read *before* this book. The world in which our characters live is set up in those books and I also recommend reading all the bonus scenes as well.

This is a multi-book series, so *everything will not be revealed in the first book*. Some plot lines will continue through series in a larger arc and not get resolved until the last book. (There are six planned.)

I write lengthy books with intricate world building, strong character development, and *lots* of tiny threads that stretch throughout a series that may not always seem important at first glance. However, I promise nothing I put to paper and leave in the book is unimportant; it may simply become *more* important later on. There is no 'throwaway' detail in my worlds, so every scene will mean something eventually.

I promise it will all get tied up and have a HEA; don't worry!

Eat. Prey. Love. is a why choose/poly romance, which means our FMC will not have to choose.

I would consider it a medium burn, slow build family group. It has gotten spicier throughout the series. If you're looking for porn with little to no plot, no judgment, but this isn't the series for you. It's also not closed door or FTB, so I believe the spice was worth the wait. I realize spice scales are subjective and everyone has different opinions on it, so forgive me if mine and yours aren't totally aligned.

There are some characters and creatures that speak in other languages. I made the *translations clickable end of chapter notes* to help.

Just an FYI:

There are a *lot of puns*—they are intentionally bad at times and writing them made me giggle. If you don't like silly, world-specific humor like that, it may annoy you.

There are some words that are slang, jargon, or foreign that may seem to be spelled wrong—*please email the author or find her on social media rather than report to Amazon* if you find a typo. This has been proofed and edited *several* times since release; if you believe you found errors, you may not be correct. It could be a stylistic choice or a dialect choice. Please do not assume the two ARC teams, betas, alphas, and several proofers missed everything you believe is incorrect.

If you see this book *anywhere besides Kindle Unlimited in ebook format*, please reach out to me via social media or email. Pirating kills my ability to write full time and I am so grateful for your help.

Contact my team for typos or to report piracy: teamcassandra@cassandrafeatherstone.com

EAT. PREY. LOVE.
PLAYLISTS

CHAPTER TITLE SONGS

Eat. Prey. Love.Chapter Playlist

BONUS PLAYLIST

Dolly's Dance Warm-Up Playlist

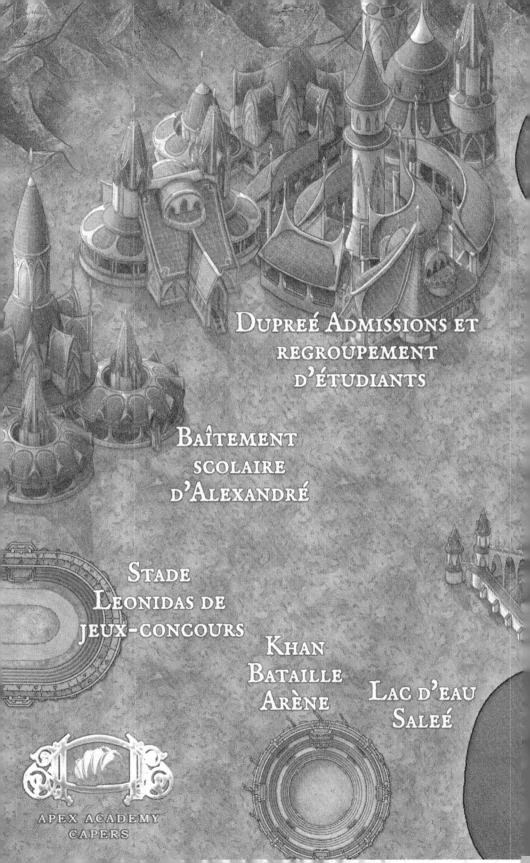

LAC D'EAU

CENTRE SHIRDAL
DES ARTS
PERFORMATIF

BIBLIOTHÉQUE ET
CENTRE DI
MEDITATION
DE KAVRIT

MAISON DES
DANSEURS

MAISON DES
ACTEURS

MAISON DES
MUSICIENS

MAISON DES
ARTISTES

Name:
Delores Diamond Drew
Semester: Winter 2024

CLASS SCHEDULE

All class schedules subject to administrative and professorial approval.

time	monday	tuesday	wednesday	thursday	friday
8:00 AM	TH 202 Theater History Bissonette	SHY 202 Shifter History A. KHAN	TH 201 Theater History Bissonette	SHY 202 Shifter History A. KHAN	COUNSELING CARINA ROCKLAND
9:00 AM	VOICE PRACTICUM ALEXANDRÈ	MODERN DANCE PRACTICUM ANTONOVICH	VOICE PRACTICUM ALEXANDRÈ	MODERN DANCE PRACTICUM ANTONOVICH	VOICE PRACTICUM ALEXANDRÈ
10:00 AM					
11:00 AM	BALLET 301 PRACTICUM FABRÉAUX	BREAK	BALLET 301 PRACTICUM FABRÉAUX	BREAK	BALLET 301 PRACTICUM FABRÉAUX
12:00 AM		TH 301-401 PRACTICUM WINTHROP		TH 301-401 PRACTICUM WINTHROP	
1:00 PM	BREAK		BREAK		BREAK
2:00 PM	TAP 301 PRACTICUM O' SHEA	PROJECT COORDINATOR JURY WORKSHOP STE JEAN	TAP 301 PRACTICUM O' SHEA	PROJECT COORDINATOR JURY WORKSHOP STE JEAN	STUDIO PRACTICUM & REHEARSAL BLOCK
3:00 PM					
4:00 PM	PGT 402 Pred Games		PGT 402 Pred Games		
5:00 PM	Team Practice Zhenga Leonidas	LIBRARY AIDE DRACONIS	Team Practice Zhenga Leonidas	LIBRARY AIDE DRACONIS	

This one is for all women who have been called villains...

You did it.

You survived.

No matter what, the emotional terrorist didn't win.

You are a bad ass.

Keep those boundaries tight and protect your peace, girl.

Nothing they say or do now will ever change that they lost.

Hold your head and your middle fingers high.

Every villain is a hero in their own mind.
~ Tom Hiddleston

WORLD & PRONUNCIATION GUIDE

Characters

Delores Diamond Drew (duh LOR es DIE mond Droo)

Lucille Rostoff Drew (lou SEAL ross TOV Droo) leopard, evil genius, Dolly's mother

Bruno Drew (Brew noh Droo)- crocodile, Dolly's father

Matilda/Mattie (mahTILduh/ mahTEE) Lucille's assistant, former nanny to Dolly, hawk shifter

Bruiser (Brew ZER)- komodo dragon, bodyguard for Drews

Heather Erickson (heh THUR AIR ick sun) aka Gold, bitchy ex-BFF, wolf

Heather Barrington (heh THUR BEAR ing tun) aka Pink, bitchy ex-BFF, jackal

Todd Birkshire (doosh BAHG)- hyena, former fiance to Dolly, asswad who took her v-card

Fitzgerald Khan/Fitz (FIH TZ jair uhl duh/ FIH TZ KAH N)-
comp sci, Pred Games, tiger

Felix Khan (FEE licks KAH N)- professor Shifter Studies 200,
tiger, twin of Fitz, exiled heir

Chester Khan (CHeh SS KAH N)- Apex Student Liaison, Guidance Assistant, cheetah, Fitz's consort and mate

Aubrey Draconis (AW BREE Drah CON iss)- Librarian and
Archivist, National Library, exiled King, dragon

Renard Laveaux (Rey NAR d LA Voh)- Guest Lecturer at Capital
and the Smithsonian, exiled King, gargoyle

Rufus McCoy (Roo fuss MICK OY)- honey badger, gangster, heir
to drug empire, Dolly's BFF

Cori Bouvier (kor E boo VEE ay) polar bear, Dolly's BFF

Raina (REY nuh) part of Captain's crew, has her own harem,
works in cafeteria

The Captain- pirate raccoon, heads crew, loyal to Renard

Banjo, Kirby, and Bowser (Ban JOE, Kir BEE, BOE zuhr) triplet
quokkas, part of Captain's crew, in Raina's harem

Holliday (Hohl IH day) armadillo, works in armory, part of
Captain's crew and Raina's harem, deaf

Percy (Purr see) skunk, works in laundry, part of Captain's crew
and Raina's harem, related to Argyle

Luc Growlvinchy (looKUH GR owl VAHN she) Dolly's boss at
design firm, (tiger)

Emile (ee MEAL) pangolin, head of pangolins who work for
Growlvinchy

Bettina (BEH tee nuh) school nurse, hedgehog

Clarice (Claire ees) school nurse, opossum

Argyle (ar-guy-ul) school nurse, skunk

Zhenga Leonidas (zen GUH lee oh nEYE diss)- shifter biology and Pred Games

Chisisi, Ramses, Asim Kavarit (ch IH see see, Rahm zen, aH seem Kah bah riht) owners of *Riddles & Rituals*

Farley McCoy (far-lee MICK-COY) honey badger lawyer for McCoy Mafia; Dolly's lawyer

Goliath (goh-lie-uhth) one of Farley's Postman

Monstro (mohn-stroh) one of Farley's Meessengers

Carina Raquel Rockland (CAH reenuh RAH kell Rahk land) Capital Preparatory Guidance Counselor & Cheer Squad Coach (vulture)

Titus Maclachlan (TIE-tuhs MACK-lock-lahn) father of Heather M. aka Yellow, Council member, tied to Khans tangentially, runs health care and hospital systems

Hannah Hopewell (HaN uh Hoh P weh l) mother of Heather H. aka Purple, Council member, tied to ministry and sketchy church with husband

Lief Erickson (Leaf AIR ik suhn) father of Heather E. aka Gold, Tech wizard, Council member

Oliver Barrington (AH-live-er Bear-ing-tuhn) father of Heather B. aka Pink, Council member, head of all media and social platforms

Kehinde Leonidas (Keh IN day Lee O nye duss) wastrel spare heir twin of Zhenga, runs all sports leagues for their father, involved in match fixing and cheating

Septimus Charles (SEHP tih muss CH-arl-zu) father of Heather C aka Silver, Council member, controls agro giant food industry

Bram Birkshire (Brahm Bur-K-shur) father of Todd, lower Council member, family runs low end banking for prey banks

Asani Khan (ah-SAH-nee Kah,N) cousin of Felix and Fitz, works on Bloodstone with their father, Delores' Shifter History teacher at *Academie*

Agathe Bisonette (ag-AH-th BEE-son-ET) exiled cassowary connected to Council; unsure of motives; Delores' Theater History teacher

Eulalie Alexandré (you-lah-lee AL-ex-AN-druh) related to Council family; snooty blue whale shifter; Voice Practicum professor

Marlène Fabreaux (mar-len Fab-ro) ex-prima ballerina; swan shifter; Ballet Professor

Rian O' Shea (ryan oh shay) Tap Instructor; Iberian lynx; delightful despite being related to a Council family

Nadia Antonovich (nah-dee-uh an-tone-oh-vich) professor of Modern Dance; wolf; related to Alpha Gregor killed at Apex

Brighton Winthrop (bry-ton win-thrup) professor of Theater Practicum; related to royalty; irreverent and fun; jaguar

Severine Ste Jean (sev-REEN SIN-jin) jury advisor for Delores; giant otter; likes to throw things at her students; mean as hell

Felicia O' Leary (fell-ee-shuh oh leer-ee) related to Council members, on Pred Games team, mean as hell, wolf shifter related to Alpha Gregor from Apex

Amity La Porte (am-IT-ee LUH POOR) related to Jacques LaPorte suspected Society member and French Council member

Cornelius, Amelia, and Aloysius Bathwaite- walrus researchers Aubrey knows from the Smithsonian

Locations

Apex Academy - college being repaired from magical bomb incident

Drew Mansion- Delores' home

House of Growlvinchy- designer fashion house she worked at

Khan Battle & Training Arena- training arena

Bloodstone Isle- Khans rule this island and reform school

Council Capital Headquarters- location of the Council formal business HQ and human liaison services

Riddles & Rituals- bookstore used by Cappie students in D.C. owned by Kavarits

Academie des crocs et griffes- The new academy the gang is sent to in Paris for the next part of the year

Capital Preperatory Academy- The academy the gang were at prior to the Yule attack

Zhuǎn xīng U&M- Asian Tech Academy

Suspected Society Members

Hannah Hopewell

Leif Erickson

Lucille Drew

Oliver Barrington

Septimus Charles

Bram Birkshire

Titus Maclachlan

Bronson Leonidas

Dmitri Rostoff

Taka Khan

Julius Draconis

Chantal Dupreé

Lysander Kavrit

Ryosuke Aung

Anton Bruce

Vera Hanson

Suki Morinaka

Aiko Rakoto

Oleg Brandenberg

Charlotte O'Leary

Ludmilla Faust

Claude Alexandré

Amelie Bouvier

Jacques La Porte

Rudy Blitzen

Liam Jameson

Annalise Janssen

Previously on In Prey We Trust...

At the end of *Let Us Prey*, Apex Academy lay in ruins, Chess was unconscious, and Dolly's group had successfully repelled a surprising magical invasion. As *IPWT* begins, Dolly is confined at her parents' estate for the summer, guarded by unpleasant body-guards while her parents gallivant across Europe. She's been unable to see her boyfriends except through video chats, which has made everyone stir-crazy. Her days are a tedious cycle of training in martial arts with Fitz's friend, working for Luc Growlvinchy, and trying not to lose her mind while being separated from her support system.

Things take a turn when Cori and Rufus call to reveal that Apex Academy will not reopen anytime soon, a fact Lucille and Bruno conveniently neglected to share. Initially panicking, Dolly is reassured when she learns her friends, boyfriends, and their motley crew of prey shifters will transfer with her to Capital Preparatory. Resigned to navigating an entirely new and treacherous social landscape, Dolly steels herself for the upcoming semester.

Meanwhile, Fitz, Felix, and Chess have been staying together during the summer, frequently video chatting with Dolly. Fitz, teetering on the edge of frustration, proposes they sneak into Capital Prep's perimeter to visit Aubrey and Renard, who are preparing their new library home. The trio heads to the library and finds Renard and Aubrey missing from the main living area. Fitz stumbles upon them in a compromising position in their bedroom, inadvertently discovering their secret relationship. Awkwardly retreating, Fitz fidgets through a group video call with Dolly, who immediately senses something is amiss. She subtly calms Fitz, promising him a reward for keeping quiet until they reunite.

Dolly spends her last days at home training and enduring her bodyguards' harassment, eagerly anticipating her departure. One night, she awakens to Fitz sneaking into her room through her window. Overjoyed, they spend the night together, though no one else knows Fitz has arrived early. The next morning, Renard calls to inform Dolly that Raina and the Captain will escort her to school, citing the troubling disappearance of predator students during transit. After packing her car and saying goodbye to her dull summer routine, Dolly and Fitz join Raina and the Captain for the journey to Capital Prep.

Their convoy is ambushed en route by faceless magical attackers. Forced into a brutal fight, Dolly and her companions fend off the mysterious foes. Dolly gets an up-close encounter with the attackers, who seem to be targeting her specifically. Upon arrival at Capital Prep, the group learns Fitz had been secretly streaming the battle via spy feeds to Aubrey and the others. Despite the invasive nature of Fitz's surveillance, Dolly dismisses their concerns, trusting his protective instincts.

Settling into her new surroundings, Dolly explores the dorms but quickly grows uneasy about living among other predators. The group devises a plan: Dolly will "fake" her presence in the dorm while moving into the library complex with Renard and Aubrey. Renard and Aubrey reveal the lavish accommodations they've prepared for her, complete with a room for her sandcat, Jinx. Overwhelmed, Dolly is delighted when the group officially welcomes her into their shared living space. That evening, Renard and Aubrey disclose their mating bond, which prompts celebrations and a sense of relief among their friends.

Dolly's schedule is packed with new classes, Pred Games practices, and a maze of social politics. At her first Pred Games practice with Zhenga, Dolly encounters haughty competitors and quickly grows frustrated with the social dynamics. The guys remind her that engaging in campus activities will help garner allies against her adversaries, particularly the "Heathers"—a group of snobby mean girls.

During a shopping trip for textbooks, uniforms, and essentials, Dolly and her group meet three triplet Sphinx shifters, who clash with Aubrey in a brief altercation. The day's adventures end with a stop at a sex shop, where the group lightens the mood with playful purchases. As the semester begins, Dolly adjusts to the reality that Apex has been destroyed, and many of her allies— including prey shifters—have transferred to Capital Prep for safety. The Captain and his crew establish a system to ensure Dolly is never alone, especially in dangerous areas like the underwater tunnel connecting the dorms to the main campus.

Dolly's troubles intensify when she discovers Lucille embedded RFID chips in her body during doctor's appointments. With Chess's help, she removes the chips, and Renard cleverly distributes them among kitchen staff to confuse anyone tracking her. Suspicion falls on Carina Rockland, Dolly's assigned counselor, whose nosy and inappropriate questions during sessions raise red flags. Aubrey uncovers disturbing information about Rockland, including her plans to write a book exploiting Dolly's relationships. The group rallies to involve Rufus's cousin Farley, a skilled badger lawyer, to counter Rockland's schemes.

The semester's social and academic pressures come to a head when Dolly's roommate, Kinsley, is found dead in their dorm room. Evidence links Kinsley to the poisonings at Apex, but her death leaves critical questions unanswered. The discovery prompts

Henrietta, Apex's former headmistress, to grant Dolly official permission to move into the library, alleviating her dorm-related worries.

As Dolly navigates classes and Pred Games matches, she strengthens bonds with her boyfriends and befriends Raina's eclectic group of prey escorts. She continues to face opposition from the Heathers, including escalating tensions during history class. Lucille's meddling complicates matters further as she pressures Dolly to excel in Pred Games and maintain the Drew family's reputation.

In one of Dolly's Pred Games matches, her opponent—a drug-enhanced canine shifter—nearly overwhelms her. Despite the unfair odds, Dolly's determination and training secure her victory. The aftermath leaves her injured but bolstered by the unwavering support of her boyfriends. Fitz and Chess comfort her, and her triumph sparks viral attention.

The group's investigations lead them to Apex's ruins, where they uncover hidden vaults containing Fae artifacts and evidence of Council family conspiracies. Clues point to the Society, a shadowy group of predator families whose influence permeates the schools. Among the vaults, they find genetically modified flora and documentation implicating the Charles family in crossbreeding Fae plants to amass their fortune.

Back at Capital Prep, Dolly faces Rockland's invasive scrutiny and discovers more troubling details about her plans. The group's list of enemies grows, and they work tirelessly to protect Dolly and uncover the larger conspiracy. During a Halloween party in a graveyard, magical attackers orchestrate a chaotic assault, resulting in multiple student abductions. The event shakes the campus, prompting heightened security measures and further lockdowns.

Despite the escalating danger, the group continues their investigations, exploring hidden tunnels beneath Capital Prep. They discover additional vaults tied to predator families, including the

MacLachlans, Kavarits, and Barringtons, each holding secrets that deepen the mystery. Among the findings are High Fae scrolls, which Renard reluctantly admits he can partially translate due to his childhood exposure to Fae culture.

The semester hurtles toward its conclusion with the Yule Ball looming. Lucille pressures Dolly to attend in perfect form, adding to the mounting tension. Fitz uncovers worrying chatter in online forums, and the group enlists a fox shifter to bolster campus security for the event. On the night of the Ball, Dolly and her friends make a grand entrance, drawing attention from the elite predator families. Lucille and Bruno attempt to provoke Dolly, but Aubrey intervenes, leveraging his mythical shifter status to silence them.

Chaos erupts when the Ball is attacked by magical invaders, including illusionists and Fae. Dolly and her group fight valiantly to protect the students, utilizing their unique abilities to fend off the attackers. Amid the battle, Renard confronts a taunting pixie illusionist who hints at a personal connection to him. A devastating magical blast incapacitates most attendees, leaving only Dolly, Aubrey, and Renard conscious. The trio's resilience underscores Dolly's growing power and her potential ties to the Fae.

Reeling from the attack, Dolly resolves to take the fight to the Fae and unravel the conspiracy threatening her world. With her loyal companions by her side, she prepares to confront the Society and their enigmatic motives, determined to protect her friends and uncover the truth behind the attacks.

Leaving on a Jet Plane

Delores

Looking around nervously, I lick my lips while I fight the urge to jiggle my knee. I'm nervous as fuck; this is the first time I've ever flown—that I can remember, at least—in an airplane. Lucille and Bruno never took me on their in-country trips, much less overseas. It doesn't matter that the guys are all familiar with this and have reassured me a million times.

When I fly with Aubrey, I know how his damn wings work and I can feel him.

This is a huge hunk of metal literally defying physics to rocket through the air in a controlled explosion—I don't fucking like it and that's that. Since I nixed flying on the Khan jet—for obvious reasons—Fitz figured out how to get us on a private jet that he and Rennie personally checked out before anything was loaded. Part of my fear wasn't illogical; this is a fantastic place to fucking kill me because I'm trapped a bazillion feet above a goddamn ocean. It seemed like tempting fate to even consider it, but the deadline for arrival at *Academie des crocs et griffes* didn't allow for a ship voyage.

Jinx hops up on my lap, batting the fingers digging into the joggers I borrowed from Fitz. I smile softly as I stroke my hand over her head. She's getting bigger, though she'll never be a large cat, and her attitude is twice as big as her physical size. "Hey, girl. This is pretty fancy, huh?"

"Top of the fucking line, Baby Girl. Only the best for you," the tiger himself says as he swaggers across the luxurious cabin with his drink. His brows waggle as he grins. "Ask me how I did it."

"How *you* did it?" Renard grumps from his spot sprawled over a large chair. "I think that's misleading."

A loud huff comes from the couch and I look up to see Aubrey cleaning his glasses. "A distinct distortion of the truth for certain. You didn't procure this flying tin can as much as ensure it wasn't messed with. There's a difference."

"Bro, tell them not to be mean," Fitz whines at Felix. His twin arches a brow before shaking his head to go back to reading the materials they were sent from the third school we've been at in two years. "Fine. Chessie, you tell them."

Chess pokes his head out of the galley, looking at Fitz with a sigh. "Baby, you helped. Isn't that enough? Our angel doesn't care who did what, only that we took care of her. Right?"

His gaze lands on me and I nod, giving him the best grin I can manage. "That's true. I'm just glad we didn't have to trust any of our families or ride in a big cramped plane with a ton of other people. My anxiety would have killed me before we got to France; I'm sure of it."

"Princess," Felix rumbles as he looks up from his reading again. "Are you feeling shaky again?"

"No," I lie as I pet Jinx carefully. I don't want them to see my hand shaking. I hate feeling weak and being afraid of this stupid flight makes my bunny furious. Unfortunately, no amount of breathing or visualization helps, so I don't have an option. "I'm good, babe."

"Liar, liar, pants on fire..." Fitz sing-songs as he gets up in my face. "We can smell fear, silly rabbit. You can too, and the fact that you forget this shit all the time is hysterical."

Goddamn it. Bruno and Lucille teaching me nothing *about being a shifter bites me in the ass again.*

Throwing my hands up, I pout. "Fine. *Fine.* I hate this. Nothing about it is natural and everything you told me only makes me question why anyone ever does this shit on a regular basis. I'm over-thinking it, but I can't help it."

Rennie sits up for a second, tilting his head as he grins wickedly. "What I'm hearing is you need to turn your brain off, *ma petite.*"

Jinx jumps off my lap in a snit, disliking the nervous energy damn near making me vibrate in my seat. I frown and wrinkle my nose as I suck in a deep breath and let it out slowly. "Yes. My brain is definitely in overdrive and I can't seem to stop it."

There's a moment when they all exchange their weird dude eyebrow thing and Felix puts down his tablet with a slow, heated grin. "Then we'll distract you, Princess."

I used to hate that damn nickname, but now, it makes my thighs clench.

His chair turns to face me and he leans his bare forearms on his knees as he smirks. "Gentlemen, get her more comfortable."

Before I can blink, Fitz has me lifted out of my chair, carrying me into the open space in the middle of the seating area. He plops on the ground with me on his lap, his hands tugging my tee-shirt up and over my head quickly. Rennie uncoils from his chair as well, stalking over to kneel beside us and rubs his cheek on my head. When Aubrey drops to his knees as well, my eyes widen.

Oh boy.

"We have you, snack size," he murmurs before ducking his head to kiss me roughly. My response is a low groan as desire unfurls in my gut, displacing the anxiety that was curled there. Big hands cup my face as his tongue sweeps through my mouth and I barely notice Fitz shucking my sweat pants to leave me almost naked.

A pleased rumble echoes in the room and when I pull away from my grumpy dragon, Fitz yanks my chin until I'm looking at him. "Baby Girl, what the holy fuck are you wearing under our baggy ass clothes?"

My cheeks flush. They destroy damn near every lingerie set I own on a daily basis, but my drawer never gets empty. I have no idea which one of them bought the naughty set I'm wearing today, only that it appeared in my drawer. "I don't buy it; I just put it on when it appears, Fitzy."

He laughs, nipping my ear as he arranges my body to lean against his with my thighs draped over his thick ones. "Which one of you kinky fucks bought this? Look at our girl all trussed up like an adorable fucking *snack*."

Felix's eyes roam over my heated skin first, taking in the tiny, pale pink panties trimmed in white lace with strings tied at the hips and a white bow. He can't see the little white bunny tail on the ass, but his gaze roams over my soft belly up to the bra with a pleased rumble. The bra is just as useless function-wise, but the ruffly pink and white lace triangles cover my nipples at least. It ties behind my neck and has criss-crossed straps over my boobs, making the exposed cleavage look even deeper. By the way his expression darkens, I guess leaving off the garter and choker that came with it was a good plan.

His expression is damn near feral.

"Ah, *mes amis*, look how adorable she is. It's no great feat to assume which one of us procured *this* masterpiece," Rennie says with a grin. He winks at me, pulling the hair tie off of his wrist to gather my long hair up for me as Fitz squeezes my tits. "She's a pretty pink bunny all trussed up for us."

I groan as Fitz sucks the cord of my neck until the skin definitely bruises. "I knew it was you, big guy. There's a poofy tail on back," I breathe out.

"How could I resist?" Aubrey smirks as he takes my foot in his hand, his large hands massaging it until my eyelids flutter. When I moan again, his lips curl up and Felix gapes at him. His chuckle is dark and he shrugs at the Raj. "She's a fucking rabbit; rubbing her feet makes her let out almost as good a sound as Chessie's desserts do."

My eyes pop open and I glare at them all for a second. "Just rubbing them. They hurt a lot from training. The first person to put their mouth anywhere near them is getting punted to France ahead of the plane."

That makes Fitz howl with laughter and I can feel him shake behind me. "Not a fan of footsie, eh, Baby Girl?"

I turn bright red, ducking my chin as I grumble. "I don't like feet. Ask the big guy how long it took me to let him do this without kicking him in face."

"So many tries," he mutters.

Rennie makes an 'ah-ha' sound and I turn to see him grinning like a madman. "The black eye last month… he said a book tumbled off a high shelf and caught him in the face. I *knew* that sounded like bullshit."

Swatting his arm, I grumble, "Shut *up*. I didn't *mean* to."

Aubrey chuckles and leans in to place a kiss on my knee cap. "Forgiven, lunchable. Now, can we please spread you wide and make you scream until you have to nap for the rest of this flight?"

Felix blinks in his seat, then smothers a laugh in his hand. "She's even got the goddamn dragon asking her to pretty please let him lick her pretty pink pussy. We're all doomed."

I bat my lashes at him as Fitz widens his legs to position mine. All the yoga we're doing is making us both pretty flexible, so it's not a full split, but it's close. "I have all the power, right, Sir?"

Now I've got him.

"That's right, Princess. You know your word, and you know what happens when you say it." Felix looks at Aubrey with a dark smile. "Pull those cute things off and see how wet our little bunny is for us. Fitz, keep her in place. Ren, release those beautiful breasts."

"What about… Chessie?" I manage as Rennie and Aubrey do as he says. My whole body is exposed in the middle of this flying deathtrap and I can't seem to give shit as their hands coast over me.

"He'll join in once he's got things settled in the kitchen, Princess. For now, I want you to keep count. If you lose track, we'll have to start again."

How is that a punishment?

The tickling sensation of Aubrey's tongue sliding up my thigh wipes that thought out of my mind and my head falls back on Fitz's shoulder. He dips his head and gnaws along my shoulder, making me shiver more. The combination of my big man heading straight for the flood of wetness between my spread legs and his pointed teeth on me is more than enough to put my fears out of my mind. But then Rennie dips his head and sucks my nipple into his mouth and I feel myself slipping into the warm, pleasure-filled head space they're aiming for.

"Fuck," I whisper as Fitz winds his arms around mine to keep me from moving or touching anyone.

"That's perfect, brother. Princess, you look exsquisite when you let everything go. Give me those pretty blue eyes while they make you whimper."

I raise my eyes to his, my breath coming in soft pants as my dragon tosses the untied panties over his shoulder and buries his face in my pussy. His tongue draws circles around my clit and I bite my lip hard as a whine echoes in the plane. Aubrey's hands are squeezing my thighs hard and I know that will leave bruises, too, but it doesn't make me scared—only hotter.

Being marked by them is so fucking hot and I can't get enough of it—it has to be the animal in me, right?

"Well, well. What the hell is going on in here?"

My eyes flutter as a thick finger slides inside of me and Rennie's teeth graze my nipple. The voice belongs to Chessie and he sounds more amused than upset, so I give him a dopey grin as pleasure spirals through me. "Come join us, my white knight..."

Fitz growls softly next to me ear and I can feel his dick twitch against my ass.

"Yeah, baby. Come join us."

EYES ON ME

CHESS

"WHERE DO YOU WANT ME, RAJ?" I LOOK AT FITZ, MY LIPS curving as he licks his lips in anticipation of my joining them. The scent of our girl is making him crazy, but he's content to do what his brother says if it helps Dolly relax.

Felix winks at me, his expression pure heat as Aubrey draws gasps and whimpers from the flushed bunny. "I think she and Fitz might enjoy tasting you together. Go stand by them, Chess."

Hell, yes, sir.

Walking over to the group, I tug my tee over my head with one hand, tossing it away. The gleam in Dolly's eyes makes my cock jerk, and I undo my pants slowly. Once I stand by their heads, I drop them, revealing that I didn't bother with boxers today. I knew we'd have playtime at some point during the trip; it seemed superfluous.

"Get that beautiful pierced dick closer, Chessie. I want to suck on it with our girl until you beg."

The growl in Fitz's voice triggers my submissive side and I move without thinking. In a blink, I feel warm lips and a wet tongue on either side of my cock. My eye rolls back and I moan softly. My tiger lets her arms go so she can hold my thigh, doing the same with his on the other side.

I probably need the help staying up if they're going to keep this shit up.

"Aubrey, how many is that?"

I laugh when the grumpy book dragon doesn't stop, only lifts one hand to show two fingers to the tiger running our little scene. My hand drops to stroke over her rainbow hair, murmuring, "Are you quivering, Angel? I bet you are."

Fitz's teeth scrape my shaft then he rumbles against my skin. "She's shivering like a leaf, baby. You will be, too, soon."

A snarky response dies on my lips when Dolly sucks the crown of my dick into her mouth, suckling while Fitz continues nibbling along my length. Blinking at the dual input, I dig my fingers into his hair as well. My teeth sink into my lower lip as my head falls back. Having both of them do this while the others get Dolly off is so hot that I'm afraid I'll come too quickly.

"Good girl, Princess. You're coming so hard for Aubrey and Ren. And you look gorgeous taking Chess's cock with my brother. It's perfect."

"Fuck, yeah, it is, Baby Girl," my tiger mutters as he nips me. "Do you feel how hard I am against your ass? I could fuck you senseless right now."

Felix laughs when she moans around me and I grunt. I'm trying not to thrust because I've been given orders, but holy hell. I can only take so much.

"Would you like that? Should Flames stop for a moment so we can get Fitzgerald buried inside of you, *ma petite?*"

Looking at the gargoyle through hooded eyes, I note Aubrey is stroking him while he's lavishing attention on our girl's perfect breasts. I have no idea how the two of them manage that, but maybe it's a dominant thing? Dolly and Fitz seem to be able to multi-task, too, and I'm just about brain dead with their teasing.

"Mmmmphhh," Dolly says and I gasp when the sound vibrates over me.

"I think that's a 'yes,' Raj," Ren says in an amused voice. "Shall we accommodate our good little bunny?"

Felix nods, leaning over to dig in his carry-on, then tosses a bottle of lube to our stony friend. "Aubrey, help Fitz get his pants off while Renard pours the lube. Princess, don't you dare come again until he's inside of you."

Her lips pop as she lifts off me and she looks up at me with a satisfied grin. "Bossy fucker, isn't he?"

I laugh first, but then Fitz and the other join me as they follow Felix's instructions. "It's so kind of you to let him direct, Angel. It's a shame he's stuck watching, though."

"If you two smart asses are done, I'll have you know I have plans for that," Felix rumbles as Aubrey yanks Fitz's pants down. "Just wait."

"Yes, Sir," Dolly mumbles before she ducks her head and swallows my dick like a fucking champ.

Aphrodite in a whorehouse… she's going to kill me.

"We are lucky our *petite lapin* is such a fast learner, mmm?" Renard winks at me and I nod jerkily. "Soft, curvy, and so very adventurous—that's our mate."

Fitz groans and I'm certain he's going to rail the hell out of her once he's settled. He holds his hand out for the gargoyle to pour, then growls as he slicks himself. His legs widen, pulling our girl's thighs open more as Aubrey lifts his glistening face to wink at me. The long, flickering dragon tongue makes my eyes widen and I suddenly understand why Fitz's joggers were soaked when he pulled them off.

Cheeky asshole. He's a lot less stodgy now that he's getting laid even more often.

"Don't fuck around, Fitz. Impale her so we can resume the count."

"Aye, aye Bossy Fucker!" He wraps his fist around his cock and lines up, pushing into my angel with a moan that's absolutely sinful.

Dolly's teeth scrape over me and I snarl, making Ren and Aubrey smirk. They look at one another, the dive back in to work their mouths over her breasts and pussy. I can feel her shuddering now, instantly pushed to the edge with all the sensation. But she's holding out until she's given permission and I can't help but be impressed.

"The count starts from four here…" Felix says with a feral grin. "She should be jell-o by the time we stop."

Well, it's one way to distract her from her plane anxiety.

"I THINK… I THINK… FIFTEEN IS A NEW RECORD…" DOLLY PANTS as she lies draped like a pretty pink starfish on top of my lover. "No more. I won't be able to walk when we get to Paris."

Felix stands, grinning proudly as he walks over to the bathroom, opening the door to fetch clean-up materials. "That was my plan, Princess."

Aubrey and Ren are slumped against the couch, also hazy eyed and I finally dropped to the ground at Fitz's feet. We're *all* spent as fuck—literally.

"You'd better be getting enough to go around, Raj. You're a goddamn task master when you're in charge," the dragon says on tired huff. "Even I'm tired."

Dolly lolls her head over to give him a satisfied smile. "I love when everyone is together, though. It's so… hot…"

Renard blows her kiss, his eyes dancing as he leans against his mate. "You are entirely correct, *ma petite*. Our family is perfectly matched."

A loud buzzing sound echoes off one of the panels and everyone groans. I roll my eyes over to where I think it's coming from, squinting. "It's yours, Angel."

"I'll grab it," Felix says as he comes out with wet cloths draped over his arm like the quintessential Dom. He pauses to hand me one, then picks up her phone before giving one to Aubrey and Ren. When he stops in front of our girl, he drops Fitz's on his face with a chuckle. "Do yourself, bro. I've got our girl."

She smiles at him like he hung the moon when he hands her the vibrating phone then kneels in front of her to rub the soothing warmth over her thighs and pussy. Her voice is breathy when she answers, "This is Dolly."

The sudden tension in her frame makes my hackles raise and I arch a brow at her as I get the remnants of our mini-orgy off me. "Who?" I whisper.

Pressing the mute button, she gives us a sad frown. "Farley. He has news about the relocation."

Oh, shit.

Growls echo all over the cabin as we tend to the mess while watching my angel for signs of what the badger is telling her. Her face is a myriad of expressions ranging from anger to worry, and I curse under my breath. This shit is never-ending and I fucking *hate* it. It's even made me wonder if the twins and I could broker some sort of deal with our asshole father to put a stop to it. I wouldn't, but I guarantee it's crossed their minds as well.

"I thought you said this was settled—or at least as much as we could." She frowns again then growls under her breath. "Can I put you on speaker? Okay, get ready for the guys, too."

"What I was sharing with the lovely Dolly is that our old nemesis is up to her bullshit again. The paper didn't make the splash she thought it would—it only circled the drain around the kind of fools that would align with an abusive bint like her. There are several *new* developments in the Rockland Bully Chronicles."

Fitz lets out a tiger yowl and we all jump. "I'm getting tired of this cunt. Felix, you'll back me up if I simply fucking rip her head off and piss down her filthy neck like I did Gregor, right?"

"I'd prefer to roast her slowly," Aubrey grumbles.

"I favor the rack. It's much more painful." Renard smirks at us as we stare. "We'll find one in Paris; after all, the Marquis was from there."

Dolly gives them a grateful smile, but shakes her head. "You guys are sexy as hell threatening to kill her for me, but we have to handle this the boring way. We know she's prone to spreading lies and bullshit through the social networks. Killing her won't stop that shit from continuing and who knows what the publishers will do with her trash book if they have control. The ones letting her spew hate and false shit are obviously as psychotic as her."

She's got a point—if you agree to publish shit you know for a fact is a legally questionable hit piece in your catalog, you're no better than a sleazy tabloid.

"What do we do then, Princess? Suggestions from the Country Counselor are appreciated." Felix crosses his arms over his chest, looking contemplative.

"I'm not sending a Postman or Messenger this time. Because she's managed to finagle a role at this new school through fuck only knows what…. Goliath, Monstro, and I will be arriving in Paris within the week. I'm handling this shit in person this time."

We all look at one another in shock. Rufus told my angel Farley only leaves their hollar to go to court and even then, it's brief and he's heavily guarded. His prowess in the legal business for the McCoys is vastly compensated for and he's never without protection because he's so valuable.

"You're… coming… to France?" Dolly squeaks. "Really?"

The badger sniffs into the phone. "Yes. I'm using the family plane and I'll be bringing my nephew, your friend, their shit, and some other fucking lovers. Apparently, I'm also a goddamn babysitter." I can practically *hear* him rolling his eyes. "You should note that I don't pull punches and I'm going to decimate that woman so thoroughly that she never recovers now. Making me come to that land of cheese-eating surrender monkeys is an offense that rivals spitting in my goddamn face."

Renard looks wholly offended, but Aubrey clamps his hand over his mouth before he shoots back a retort. I wink at the pouting Frenchman, and Fitz just grins like a lunatic. I have a *very* bad feeling about introducing Dolly's crazy-ass motherfucker lawyer to my psycho mate.

They're far too similar and that's a time bomb waiting to go off.

"Okay, Farley. We'll get settled when we arrive and if you can have Rufus text me the details as you travel, it will help a lot." Her lips curve up and she laughs. "I don't *know* how he convinced the triplets to close the store and take a sabbatical to study in Paris. He just told me they were coming and it was because their family is allowing them to travel around buying books for collections for the semester. As for Giselle? I think Fitzy sweet talked someone in admissions."

"I absolutely did. It didn't take much because the Captain's crew offered to come along to the school to attend to all the Igneous Iguana's fucking specifications. Since Betsy refused to fly, they're all now working for him and the ruffled Frenchman." My mate grins, stacking his hands behind his head as he looks pleased with himself.

"Excellent. You're going to need allies there, I fear. They aren't all looking to kill you like at Apex, nor are they all celebrity kids like Cappie. This is a school full of the artsiest, most snooty fruitcakes you've ever met according to our sources. And of course, just like you, people have arranged to follow you so they can keep harassing you."

Isn't that just fucking great? Non-hot stalkers following our girl for people we hate—perfect.

Hey Jealousy

Delores

We all take a turn in the bathroom of the jet before it lands in Paris. The damn flight was long enough that I even slept in short bursts. I woke up with a different guy curled around me each time and that helped my mistrust for airplane technology dissipate. I was a little shaky when we hit the ground, but now that we're descending the steps to the tarmac, I feel *much* better.

Good sex, food, and naps will do that, I suppose.

Pulling my sunglasses out of my bag, I squint at the two large SUVs here to pick us up. "Who sent these?"

Felix gives me a pleased expression, walking over to brush his lips on my temple. "Good question, Princess. This detail was arranged by your designer friend, Luc. He has a *lot* of contacts here, obviously, and Fitz emailed him when we found out we had to go here."

I blink, surprised they looked up my friend without me. "Luc? Is this his jet, then?"

"*Oui, ma petite*," Renard says with a wink. "My fellow countryman was eager to help, especially when Fitzgerald mentioned his concerns about using anything tied to either of your families. He did not think we were being paranoid at all."

Biting my lip, I feel tears sting my eyes. When I started at Apex over a year ago, I had almost no one in my corner but Mattie and Luc. Now I've got this whole army of boyfriends and besties who move heaven and earth to help me. They even risk the wrath of my parents and the other powerful Council fuckheads—something I wouldn't have thought possible. It's so humbling and it makes me feel all soft inside.

"Aw, Baby Girl, don't get teary! You're worth the risk every damn day and I know all your friends feel that way." Fitz comes up and takes Jinx's carrier off my shoulder, handing it to Chessie, then slings his arm over my shoulders. "Trust me… I've been tapping everyone we know to activate our little network. Even our prey friends have been running interference where they can."

"I didn't know you were this worried," I whisper as I look up at him.

His eyes narrow and he growls a little. "Our father has killed people no one should be able to get away with murdering. Your mother is leading a council of dicks who have been hoodwinking our entire society for centuries. I put absolutely *nothing* past them, even blowing up a plane."

I'm about to respond when a sharp gasp, followed by a roar of disbelief makes us all whip around. My eyes land on Aubrey, half-shifted and blowing smoke out of his nostrils as he holds up his phone. I wiggle out of Fitz's grasp, moving to his side and laying a hand on his arm. "Big guy, what's going on?"

He sucks in a deep breath and pins Fitz with wild eyes. "You were right to be so careful. I thought you were overreacting a little. But *son of a bitch* if you weren't right. Look at what just hit the news."

We all crowd around his phone to see one of the Barrington news feeds playing a video of a plane exploding over the landing strip at an airport. The ticker at the bottom says it's in Asia, and...

Oh my fucking goddess... It was Bruno's goddamn plane.

"N-no survivors...?" I read, my voice pitching up at the end. My chest gets tight and I freeze in place. I have *no idea* what to feel right now besides shock. Bruno's treated me like shit my entire life, so I don't know that I can feel sad, but... Feeling happy or relieved also seems like it's wrong, too. I chew my lower lip, trying to assimilate the information that he's dead while my emotions ping all over the place.

"Angel, it's okay if you don't know how to feel," Chessie says as he lays a hand on the small of my back. "He was your father—as far as you know—but he abused the hell out of you. That makes his death hard to come to terms with, especially in this situation."

I suck in a deep breath then blow it out, nodding. "Yes. That's exactly what I'm having trouble with, my knight. I don't know how to feel other than shocked. But I also *don't* feel shocked because it's kind of amazing Lucille didn't off him before now. You know?"

Felix and the others close the circle around me, all of them touching me in a different place. My tiger king leans in, murmuring in my ear, "Fitz and I are very aware of how difficult this is. Our father is an evil dickhead and I assume when he's dead, we'll struggle."

"I won't," Fitz says as he nips my ear. "Because I'm going to slice the motherfucker up and feed him to his captive pets while my Baby Girl watches. He's part of this bullshit and *no one* gets to hurt her without suffering at my hands before they die painfully."

Aubrey chuckles and shakes his head. "Eloquent as always, Fitz."

"Look, Tangy Tuatara, I'm telling it like it is. I don't give a flip flying *fuck* who it is, if they so much as make her frown, they'd better stay out of my reach."

I turn to him with a small smile, rubbing my nose on his cheek. "My hero."

Chess sits his chin on my shoulder and I can almost feel his amusement. "We all wanted him to feel real emotions and look at what it got us—SuperPsychoFitz."

"I don't mind. It's sexy when you're all growly." I pause for a minute then add, "But I can take care of my damn self, too, so you have to let me try. Don't let that go to any of your heads—bottom or top."

Fitz guffaws, wrapping his arms around me to squeeze me close. "That's our girl. Let's get in these cars and blow this popsicle stand. I'm feeling itchy about standing out in the open all of a sudden."

He has a point.

"If Lucille felt comfortable enough to take Bruno off the board, we should definitely get moving. Who knows what else she's up to?"

The guys nod, moving away to gather the rest of our things. Once everything is loaded into the cars, Felix divides us up between the two cars and we settle in for the drive to *Academie*.

Hopefully, this ride to school is less exciting than the one to Cappie.

"WOW," I BREATHE AS WE DRIVE AWAY FROM THE CITY INTO THE countryside. The school is about an hour away from the main metro and suburbs, so we can take trips in if we want, but the pastoral towns we're passing through are adorable. "This is… so freaking cool."

Renard grins as he squeezes my hand. "France has many beautiful areas, *ma petite*. We might explore with Flames sometime, *non?*"

I clap my hands and grin. "Hell yeah. I have no idea how intense this place is—rumor is that while Apex and Cappie are more intense in networking and social shit, *Academie* and *Zhuǎn xīng U&M* are much more program intensive. For all I know, I could be trapped under a pile of work forty feet high all semester."

My crazy tiger leans in, his voice growly as he replies, "Or you could be buried under horny shifters all semester. Either way, no shithead magic rebels or fuckwit Council people will be able to get their mitts on you. So we'll figure it out."

Le swoon, crazy pants.

"Fitz is right. As long as we keep you safe, everything else is maneuverable," Felix says from the front. He made Chess and Aubrey ride in the second car—a choice that was *not* appreciated by the dragon or the cheetah. "But we need to get your schedule as soon as we're settled in because he has to begin doing checks on your professors."

"You know, it'd be nice to not have to vet every person I encounter because they might be part of some secret society trying to kill me. Just once, I'd like to not look over my shoulder when I'm walking around." I frown, my brow furrowing as I think about having to figure out yet *another* embedded social hierarchy. It's getting tiresome as hell, and I'm over the bullshit.

My gargoyle boyfriend chuckles. "Don't worry, *petite lapin*. You'll have us and plenty of friends you don't have to background check on site. Everyone else will be on a case-by-case basis since *Academie* is damn tight-lipped about their school."

"Unfortunately, she'll also have to avoid Rockland, the remaining Heathers, and whatever clique is running this place," Fitz says as he pulls my feet into his lap. "But I have no problem putting on a show to corral the sheep. I'm sure we'll find *some* sort of fight club where I can flash my teeth."

"Guys, we have to at least *pretend* to get along with the new folks until we get a feel for this place. I can't keep adding enemies to my plate," I sigh. "Heather E. and Heather B. will do their damndest to fuck with me, and we know Rockland is gearing up to stick her stinky face in mine. No fights until we make sure there's no land-mines where we're stepping."

Felix gives me a pleased grin. "Good girl, Princess. Thinking strategically is a better approach, especially since we know Z is here with *one* goal: get *Academie*'s Pred Games team in shape so they draw better crowds to fill the Leonidas coffers. You'll likely be one of the best trained competitors there and that will make people take you seriously on your own merits."

I squint at him. "You're saying *I* need to terrify them first."

"Exactly. Show them you're formidable on the field *and* on the stage *and* in the classroom. If you rocket up the leaderboards in every arena, it will be hard for those snot-nosed bitches to gather minions." The exiled Raj looks at me smugly and I have to smile back.

Felix Khan never fails to give me room to rescue myself and I love him for it.

"They speak English here, right?" Fitz turns to me with wide eyes, as if the possibility that no one speaks his language *just* occurred to him. "Because the Frying Pan Frenchie didn't teach me any of his ooh-la-la. He's been teaching me to sign for the little prey guy, but not that. Holy shit, guys! How will people hear my fucking excellent zingers?"

Covering my mouth as the SUV turns onto a long drive, I giggle. Rennie just sighs and rolls his eyes to the ceiling as if asking for patience. Fitz keeps freaking out and finally, Felix takes pity on him. "Of *course* they speak English, you nitwit. Students from all over come here, so the instruction is in English. However, you may get cussed out in a wide variety of languages—which I'm excited to watch."

"Don't be such a hater, bro. Foreign chicks love me…" he pauses and looks at me with wide eyes. "Not that they can *have* me, Baby Girl. Cross my heart."

I give him an amused look, tilting my head as I pretend to think about it. "Well. I suppose if they get fresh, I'll just have to start taking body parts to deliver to *you* in jars, huh?"

He practically has cartoon hearts in his eyes as he looks at me. "Baby Girl, if you bring me body parts, you won't be walking straight for a *week*. I promise that on the most precious thing I have: my dick."

"For fuck's sake, Fitz," Felix growls.

I just grin at him, my eyes full of promise as I watch him bounce happily in place.

They think I'm kidding, but newsflash, sports fans… I'm not.

BIG GIRLS DON'T CRY

FELIX

ACADEMIE HAS A SPRAWLING CAMPUS—EVEN I'M A LITTLE impressed. The buildings are all in this fairy tale style architecture that makes it seem otherworldly. Their Pred Games facilities are much smaller than Apex or Cappie's, but I'm sure Z and my twin can work with it.

After all, it's not the size that matters.

Chuckling to myself, I look back to see the smug ass gargoyle watching our girl marvel at the towers and spires, her face bright with excitement. It kills me that her abusive parents kept her locked away like Rapunzel—it makes her seem far too innocent and naïve for her age and pedigree. Knowing that her lineage might have an aberration tells me *why* they did it, but it doesn't keep me from wanting to murder them with my bare hands.

Dolly is a smart, beautiful, talented girl who would have represented them well in all their Council related travel. Her mother's jealousy and fear of being found out caused her to be a sheltered, beaten down girl who let people run her life for her. Watching her blossom makes my heart do weird things and my dick hard as rock. Unfortunately, it also makes me want to keep her safe no matter how much she hates it and that's my biggest challenge.

I won't hold her captive like they did, but it scares the piss out of me to let her put herself in danger.

"The library is massive and there's *so* many places for you to brood, Rennie!" she gasps happily. "This place was almost *made* for you guys."

Ren leans in and kisses her jaw, his gaze fond as he, too, takes in her delight. "*Absolutement, ma petite.* I believe this school will accommodate all of our needs—though Fitzgerald looks a bit disappointed."

"The fucking arenas are so damn tiny," he mutters. "We're supposed to build this shit up and they have baby facilities. Z is going to *have* to reach out to her fuckwit brother; we have no option."

I shake my head, sighing as Fitz goes off on a tangent about what he thinks needs fixing before they can grow the program. He's not wrong, but I'm not sure I want to insist on inviting unknown contractors onto campus. There's too many variables here as it is.

A low growl echoes in the car, making it shake, and I whip my head around to see Renard staring out the window like he's going to shift and bust the vehicle to pieces. "What? What the fuck is going on, man?"

Dolly lays her hand on his shoulder soothingly, her voice soft. "Rennie, what's wrong? Tell us what's going on."

"There are beings on this campus that are not shifters." His voice is low, dark and scarier than I've ever heard before. In fact, I don't *ever* think I've seen our friend act like this.

"Okay, emo boy. Talk to us. Tell us what you scented." Dolly doesn't look the least bit perturbed despite Fitz's jaw hanging open. "We can't help if you're going 'grr' face."

Grr face? What the hell?

The gargoyle is stiff as a board, pressed to the glass as he breathes deeply. I gesture for the driver to crack his window, hoping that the scent will get stronger so he can identify it. Then we can plan for whatever the hell this shit is.

"This school has secrets," he spits. "Dangerous ones—and I don't mean whatever vaults it's hiding. There are beings we cannot trust here and they are not visiting. The scent is too strong; they live here."

"Ren, what the fuck kind of beings are you talking about?" I ask in exasperation.

"Ones that are not *allowed*," he grunts angrily. "They are abominations—it is *treason*."

I blink, looking at the typically laid back shifter as he struggles with a gamut of emotions. He finally tears his eyes away from the window and looks at Dolly with a tortured expression. She cups his jaw, nodding as she pulls him into her arms. Ren buries his face in the crook of her neck and her eyes meet mine. It's obvious she has no idea what the fuck is going on, but that doesn't make it any easier.

Something has triggered our friend badly and he's falling to pieces before our eyes.

"Get us to the goddamn library," I snarl at the driver. "We'll go to the main building later. And not a word about this to *anyone*."

The shifter nods, turning the wheel to steer away from the hulking main building to head over to the back entrance of the library complex. Luckily for us, the escorts have loyalty to their employers, not the school or Council, because we couldn't have guaranteed this outburst stays secret otherwise.

Once we're safely in the loading area, I hop out and knock on Fitz's window. He joins me, walking to the back of the SUV to grab our shit. His expression is full of confusion and I shrug—I truly don't know.

"Sulky Shakespeare never acts like that," he says after I close the trunk. "And I don't smell a fucking thing out of place. Is it a mythical thing, you think?"

I shake my head. "I don't know. Let's see what Aubrey says."

Chess and our dragon friend exit their vehicle, going to the back to get Jinx's carrier and their things. By the time they join us, I'm hiding my escalating concern. Dolly and Ren are still in the car, quietly sitting together and whispering.

"What happened?" Chess frowns as he tilts his head.

Fitz snorts. "We don't know, love. All of a sudden, the big guy went apeshit, saying he smelled non-supes on campus and then sort of crumbled like a cookie."

Aubrey's eyes widen and he sucks in a breath. "Shit. I don't know exactly *what* it is, but I know what it has to do with."

I arch a brow. "Do tell, Draconis."

"Guaranteed it has something to do with that fucking orchid and his fucking past. Looks like he's going to be forced to unlock some of those cages inside sooner rather than later."

Shit. That doesn't sound good at all.

WHILE THE REST OF US GET OUR SHIT INTO THE LIBRARIAN'S complex at the back of the library, Dolly sits with the gloomy gargoyle in the living area. We'll need to modify this place to fit our family, but I'm certain Chess can help get it done. Our girl's punky badger helped get Aubrey placed here through his boyfriends. They made some calls to the Kavarits and the long-time Sphinx working at this place went on an extended sabbatical.

Unfortunately, this place looks like a grandmother's tea room and the Pepto colored walls and doilies are everywhere. There are creepy ass sightless porcelain dolls on every surface—and I do mean *every*—which is when we all find out they scare my twin to death. He's zipping around with his hand shielding his eyes as he drags our shit in, muttering to himself about them 'coming to life at night to kill him.'

I'd be laughing, but we can only handle one person losing their marbles at a time—Ren is a much bigger concern.

"Get it together, bro," I rumble at him, adding an edge of alpha to it so he pays attention.

Fitz straightens, glaring at me for a moment before he sucks in a deep breath then blows it out. "In with the anxiety, out with the calm…"

"What the fuck are you talking about?" Aubrey snorts as he pushes past with Jinx's carrier. He sets it down on the frilly couch, wrinkling his nose before letting the tiny menace out. "Why is everyone going banana pants? Is there something in the fucking air here? Fucking French…"

That gets Ren's attention and he lifts his head, giving his mate a dirty look. "*Suce-moi la bite, garçon lézard.*[1]"

A laugh bursts free and even though I don't know what he said, I get the gist, especially when Aubrey smirks at him. "Only if you stop being a whiny little bitch, *mon coeur*. Good boys get treats."

Dolly's eyes glaze over and I watch her squirm against our friend. She gives Aubrey a matching irritated look before hissing, "*Sois gentil, mon grand. Il souffre vraiment.?*"

When the hell did she learn that much French? Son of a bitch.

"Oooooh. I *love* it when you *voulez-vous*, Baby Girl. It makes my dick do backflips." Fitz walks over, bending to nuzzle the other side of her neck until she moans softly. "Much better than when this fancy asshole does it."

"It *is* sexy," Aubrey muses as he grins at her. "I didn't know he was teaching you."

She frowns, her eyes narrowing. "He's *not*. I took French in high school and Luc helped me a little this summer. I can learn things on my own, too."

"Speaking of your designer friend, we should text him and let him know we've all arrived safely. His help was invaluable," Chess pipes up. "We did *not* want to transport our family on other people's jets, so lending us his made Felix calm down immensely."

I roll my eyes, but nod at his statement. "Princess, you handle that. Chester, this place is…" I pause, not having the words to describe the décor accurately.

"A nightmare. I'm on it," he says with a grin. "Maybe Ren could help? He enjoys it and it might be a good distraction until he's ready to talk about what happened."

The gargoyle lifts his head again and huffs. "Fine. But shut the hell up about my… issue… until I can gather my fucking thoughts. There are many things we need to discuss and they are important for both our current situation and the future. Some of them are not known outside of small circles and my story is known to almost no one."

"More bad shit? I swear to Cereberus' furry balls, I'm tired of all this secret shit biting us in the ass. Our parents and all the stuffed shirt asswads on the Council need to go." He grins crazily, looking at Dolly. "You'll get a part of every single one of those fuckers for your trophy shelf, Baby Girl. Cross my black heart."

How he plans on cutting off a piece of every Council member, I don't know, but when my twin makes a promise, you can bank on it.

"Thank you, Fitzy." She turns her head and kisses him lightly, her eyes dancing with the same brand of psycho I associate with my brother. I'll make space when we get this place settled."

"Great, there are *two* of them," Chess mutters as he tries not to laugh. "We're in such trouble."

Aubrey huffs a few smoke rings, his eyes glittering with his dragon. "I enjoy snack size's violent tendencies. She's turning into an excellent huntress, Chester. Let Fitzgerald encourage her."

"He's right," Renard says as he sits up, blowing a long breath out and closing his eyes for a moment. When he opens them, his easy calm is back and I know he's put that emotion away until later. "We have much to do now that we are here. There is no time for dwelling and certainly none for sympathy."

"Because of what you scented?" Dolly asks quietly.

"*Oui,*" he says with a decisive nod. "We know old enemies will descend upon this place soon enough and now we've discovered there's at least one unknown hiding amongst the staff and students. We don't know what else awaits us."

I look around, finding my bag and retrieving my phone. "First thing, Dolly will text Luc and you two work on making this place not abhorrent. Aubrey and I will go to the main building to check-in with the staff shit. We'll re-group afterward to talk about whatever sent Ren off the deep end."

"I have to check in with student services and Coach Z, too," Dolly reminds me. "I can do that once I get a hold of Luc."

Biting my tongue to keep from saying she can't go alone, I nod.

"Be careful. Have your phone and your knife handy. I don't trust anyone here we don't know."

"Sir, yes, Sir!" she chirps with a salute and I groan.

Great, now I'm going to this meeting with a raging hard-on. Par for the course today.

Run the World

Delores

I did not get to go find Coach Z alone.

"Baby Girl, you know I gotta see the pitch, too," Fitz says as he trots along at my side. He's pushed his growing locks into two crazy man buns that match mine and it's hard not to grin.

"You're mad as a hatter, you know that?" I reply as I grab his hand and squeeze it. "But it makes me smile, so don't even think about changing."

"Are you talking about my stylish 'do? 'Cause masculinity is not defined by bullshit gender expectations. I contain multitudes and so do you. Anyone who doesn't get it can fuck right off the side of the planet." He winks at me, then wags his brows. "I enjoy challenging people's image of me, especially if it gets back to dear old Dickhead Dad."

Chuckling, I look at the smaller arena in front of us critically. "Zhenga's probably already on the phone with her family. It's in okay condition, but she can't draw crowds with this place."

"Man, that chick likely has crews headed here as we speak. Z is a full-on nightmare when she's on a mission. She probably skipped her jackass brother and went right to Daddy Leonidas." Fitz lifts my hand to his lips, kissing it before letting go. "Go talk to her while I scope out the Khan contribution. Big bro might have to give our asshole patriarch a poke, too."

"Great," I groan as I huff. "We're here for a couple hours and drawing the attention of the stupid Council already. I was hoping we could fly under the radar for a little longer."

"Not a chance, Baby Girl. We were all *born* to be the stars of the show."

He blows me a kiss and turns on his heel, heading to the Battle Arena. Once he's far enough away, I face the stadium, looking for which door is open.

Hopefully, Coach Z isn't on a complete tear.

"THE FIRST MATCH ISN'T FOR A MONTH. I DON'T KNOW IF THEY told you, but they extended the school year by a month to compensate for the lockdown in January," Zhenga says as she rifles through the grungy *Academie* uniforms. Obviously, their team had so little support that they couldn't even get their kits cleaned. "So we have time for me to convince my father to invest in re-inventing this damn place."

I nod, stacking equipment into a usable and unusable pile. "I get all my news from friends and the TV. My mother hasn't spoken to me since Yule. I have no idea what she's up to—other than blowing my asshat father up."

Zhenga pauses, tilting her head as she studies me. "You're okay with that?"

"I would have preferred to deal with him myself. The guys would have, too." I frown and shrug as I go back to sorting. "This didn't give me any sense of closure, but I'm not surprised Lucille stole it from me. She's stolen everything she could since I was born. Why not my vengeance, too?"

"I knew I liked you," the lioness mutters. "I'm glad we figured out that mating shit. Honestly, I was clinging to the Raj as a way out. My family's easily as nuts as yours, but there are too many of them to get my revenge. I'd gotten attached to the idea of living well to spite them."

This is dangerous territory, but we're both adults, right? We should be able to get past this overdue talk.

Considering my words for a moment, I meet her gaze across the locker room. "We're good, Coach. The past is... the past, you know? You've been a pretty great sounding board and trainer, even if I hate you sometimes for it. And you deserve more than settling... you should have someone who treats you the way the guys treat me. Or someones, if that's your thing."

Her face lights up and she chucks a ripped jersey. "This is hopeless. These are old school, gross, and not salvageable—at least, not if we want to challenge the world's perception of the *Academie* team."

A thought strikes me and I scratch my chin. It could work if Zhenga is convincing enough. "What if we had a student redesign them as part of a school assignment? I guarantee that would make it special *and* save some dough. Your father would like that, I bet. He could run publicity around it."

"That's a *fantastic* idea," Coach beams as throws another destroyed kit away. "I suppose you have someone in mind?"

My lips curve up. "In fact, I do. Hopefully, she arrives in the next few hours with my other bestie and her girlfriend. We can arrange a tête-á-tête after they're settled. How's that?"

"Works for me." Once she finished with the grubby laundry, Z sits down and sighs. "What are we going to do to recruit? This place is so fucking arts centered—I bet they're going to be as picky as your professors were about you joining. I had to sign a million damned forms promising we'd handle your injuries with your dance career in mind at Cappie."

That's going to be a sticking point; I know it. Dancers and legs, musicians and artists' fingers…

"I'm not sure, honestly. It'll be an obstacle because so many of the students here are probably in the top of their chosen fields. None of them will want to risk it—except maybe some transfers and possibly those who are here not because they earned it, but because their parents demanded it."

Zhenga grins. "Legacy bullshit. That actually might help. There have to be folks who shouldn't be at this level and need something to succeed at."

"Yep. And that's who will be hungry to excel and make their parents shut up." I plop on the bench, sighing as I look around the poorly maintained room. "But we can't start unless you get this place upgraded. Snotty, elitest kids won't want to set foot in here."

"Agreed, despite it being not remotely predictive of a team's success." Slapping her thighs, Coach stands, putting her hands on her hips. "We're in this together, Dolly. If your friend needs help convincing a teacher to let them use this for a project, I'll run interference. Just let me know, okay?"

"Got it, Coach. Now let's go take notes on the field problems so I can get back home before they send in the clowns."

Laughing, Zhenga holds her hand out, tugging me to my feet. "Have I mentioned how much I enjoy seeing you take those grumpy asshats to their knees? If not, it's delicious."

She can't possibly enjoy it as much as I do, but I just wink at her as we head outside.

"THANK *FUCK* YOU'RE BACK," FELIX MUTTERS WHEN I WALK IN THE door. "Maybe you can wrangle them."

Walking up to my grumpy Raj, I kiss his jaw. "What's wrong?"

He arches a brow, then grabs my hand to drag me to the living area. My eyes widen as I see the entire place draped in clothes and taped as the Captain and his crew scurry around on ladders and stools to paint the walls a soothing azure. There are boxes everywhere, clearly filled with all the creepy ass dolls and old lady décor the room was overwhelmed by when we arrived. "It's Armageddon in here."

"I was only gone for like two hours," I gasp as I see Chess pop his head out from behind a sheet covered pile. He pushes his glasses up, smudging paint on his nose and my heart melts. "This is crazy."

Fitz barrels out of the hallway leading to the bedrooms, sweeping me off my feet and swinging me around. "They got rid of the Annabelle shit. My world is right again, Baby Girl."

"However, to do so, they've torn the gathering area to pieces," Felix grumbles as he moves past us towards the kitchen. He opens the cabinets, searching for a moment until he pulls out a bottle of brandy. His nose wrinkles, but he shrugs and uses a flowery tea cup to pour a hefty draft. "It's chaos in here."

"I see that," I reply when Fitz finally sits me on my feet. "Who started this?"

"*Him*," Aubrey growls as he walks in from the door that connects to the library. He hooks his thumb over his shoulder at Rennie, who doesn't look in the least bit perturbed. "He's overcompensating."

"I am doing no such thing, *mon ami*. You asked Chester and I to begin re-decorating and we did."

Giving the gargoyle a pointed expression, I walk over to where Raina is directing the triplets. "Hey, girl. Do you think you're all going to be done before it's time to head to bed?"

Her cheesy grin is huge as she turns to throw her small arms around me. "Leave it to me, Dolly. I'll whip these scallywags into shape. All you have to do is take the raging preds somewhere else so they'll focus on finishing rather than flinching."

I chuckle. The crew knows none of us are going to hurt them, but some instincts run deep and my guys are certainly worked up enough to unintentionally frighten them. "Got it. Remove the blustering boys and you'll let me know when this is… taken care of?"

"Yep. The furniture won't be here for a couple days, but we can handle moving all the boxes to storage and finishing the paint job tonight." Raina squints as she looks around. "Tomorrow, we'll work in the kitchen. Sounds good?"

"This chair be high, says I!" The Captain declares as he totters on a tall stool as he works on the edges of the windows.

Raina snorts. "Of course it is, you tool. You're too small to reach the damn ledges without it."

We share a look as the various men in our families fill the room with testosterone. I turn to Felix, tilting my head. "Well? Is there something we can do until we grab food in the mess? We need to get out of here if you want your space back."

Aubrey holds his finger up, cutting in before my tiger can answer. "We should probably walk through your schedule and tour the buildings. This place was definitely set up by artsy idiots who lacked common sense. It took us an inordinate amount of time to find the place we were supposed to be."

"Chessie? Are you coming with us or staying?"

My cheetah puts down his roller, walking over with a rueful smile. "Give me just a sec to get cleaned up."

Before I can answer, he speeds off and I blink. "Damn, he's fast."

"Only when he's running," Fitz crows as he comes up behind me and buries his face in my neck. "But that's for later, Baby Girl. Kitty sandwiches aren't appropriate when we have guests in the mansion."

"For fuck's sake, Fitz," Aubrey growls as he rolls his eyes. "Could you at least *attempt* to be normal?"

"Mmm mmm… nope." The tiger makes a face at him and I giggle. "Afraid I am who I am, Red-Hot Reptile. Good thing our girl loves me in original mint condition."

The dragon pinches the bridge of his nose, muttering about sanity and fireballs going places I know they definitely shouldn't. I wriggle out of Fitz's arms, moving to Aubrey with a soft look. "Hey, big guy. You know he's just playing. And Rennie only wanted to get this place feeling less like a bottle of Pepto. Raina promised the mess will be gone when we get back. Don't get all curmudgeonly."

"Bite size, I've torched people for less than this shit," he mutters.

Rennie nods. "That's true."

Save me from men with absolutely no training in emotional regulation.

"Well, that's not what we're doing today." I grab his hand and lace our fingers together. "Today, we're all adults and taking a nice walk around this weird place, then we'll eat like normies in the cafeteria because our place is full of paint fumes. Got it?"

My gaze narrows as I look at each one of them and they all mumble assent. "Now let's get out of their way before someone loses their bunny hugging privileges."

They don't have to know I'm full of shit on that count—I'd never give those up.

THE FIX IS IN

RENARD

THE TOUR PLAN GRANTS ME ANOTHER SMALL AMOUNT OF REPRIEVE from discussing what I scented on the way onto the campus. I know I need to share the secrets of my past, but the way gargoyles have always been raised is to protect the knowledge of our people and those we give protection to. Even after my world crumbled and I was exiled, I've never broken the oaths of my clutch. Telling my story and the mythos behind it will certainly edge that line, if not outright cross it. My gut churns when I think about; that's why I've never even been able to share this tale with Flames.

Why I still feel such loyalty to those who cast me aside for a youthful mistake, I don't know.

"Rennie... Yoo-hoo..." Dolly's hand waves in front of my face as she gestures at the door. "Chessie's ready. It's time for you guys to show me this crazy maze."

I chuckle, pushing my morose thoughts away for a moment. "The outside isn't labyrinthian, but the interior of the buildings is a challenge. That's what made it difficult for Felix and I."

"We should start with the Dupreé," the tiger says as he steers our group around the base of the lovely tower connected to the library. "That's where you can pick up your info, Princess. Unlike Cappie or Apex, *Academie* is definitely rooted in the past. Their shit is printed."

Her eyes narrow as she looks at him suspiciously. "For everyone or just me again?"

"What do you mean 'just for you again?' When did that happen?" My mate stops our progress towards the looming admin building as he faces our girl.

Dolly rolls her eyes and sighs heavily. "At Apex. They gave me all paper shit at first and I thought it was weird, but elite colleges can be that way, so I let it go. I didn't find out until the hyenas chased me all over Honeywell that I'd been bamboozled. You can thank the clinic prey gals for setting me straight before I got cornered again."

She never told us that.

"*Ma petite*, why didn't you mention this before?" I ask softly. It angers me to think people were handicapping her from the minute she stepped on campus, but I'm also proud she got around it.

"Because all the stupid little shit the idiots there did day-to-day wasn't as important as dead kids and secret ceremonies and staying alive." She shrugs, giving me a stubborn look. "I handled most of it until we all got closer; I'm a big bunny."

Aubrey raises her hand to his lips, kissing her knuckles. "You are, lunchable, but we would have enjoyed teaching the perpetrator a lesson."

"Word, Igneous Iguana. It would have been my pleasure to peel strips off their ass." Fitz's eyes darken with maniacal glee as he flexes claw tips on his fingers.

Felix rolls his eyes, but I can see the fury behind his mask of indifference. "They're right, but we're getting off track with the tour. Plus, it's done and most of the people responsible have been killed, kidnapped, or reassigned with the shit that went down in the past year and half."

"*C'est vrai,*[1]" I agree. Looking up at the huge Dupreé building, I gesture at the size. "We need to get this show on the road or we'll be wandering through the place far past dinner time, *mes amies.*"

"Thank hell." Dolly tugs on the dragon's hand, pulling him forward as she strides towards the front steps. "I hate talking about my stupid naïve first few months at Apex and how ridiculous people are. I refuse to let that shit live rent-free in my head."

"Good on you, Angel," Chess says as we climb the old stone staircase. "That's healthy—no thanks to that nasty body snatcher and her sessions."

The Raj steps to the front of the group, opening the door for us. "We'll deal with her once she arrives and not a second before. Farley is coming with the blustery badger and the bear, so we can discuss our least favorite carrion nibbler then."

"Do you think she's gotten me slated for her stupid sessions *again?*" Dolly says with a groan. "There's no way I'm going to have time to do the clue hunting, catch up to this place, spend time with you guys and my friends, revamp the team, *and* deal with her shit. That's a burnout waiting to happen. My eyes hurt just *thinking* about it."

I scratch my chin, considering her question for a moment. "She might if she knows about Bruno. The violent death of your father certainly gives her leverage, *petite lapin*. Getting her to back off will be a hard sell if she brings that into the conversation."

"Again, I suggest we kill the cunt," Fitz growls. "Two birds, one very satisfying torture session. I'll even let the rest of you help."

My mate pinches the bridge of his nose. "As much as I want to, Fitzgerald, we've discussed *ad nauseum* why we can't yet. That woman cannot be fully dealt with until we track down every damn sentence or recipient of that book in progress so she can't humiliate people from the grave."

Dolly wrinkles her nose, looking thoughtful as we walk into the grandiose atrium. "Maybe I should just get over that? I've already been the target of a social media smear and right now, I'm kind of riding on good PR from the Yule Ball Battle. If we kill her and someone releases what she's got, it'll only look silly. Right?"

"Depends on what she says and how your mother reacts," Chess reminds her. We walk down the long marble hallway to the double doors to the office—the one easily locatable room in the damn building—together as he continues. "If Lucille spins it poorly, you could end up being an even bigger pariah. It might make people come after you if she's done a good enough job spreading her filth everywhere."

Stopping at the doors, our girl leans into them and bonks her head on the wood. "Why me? I didn't do anything to this chick. She's just butt hurt that I declined her offer of friendship and guidance because I figured out she's fruitier than a nut cake. Surely I can't be the first person that's noticed her self-centered, lazy ass appropriation of others' lives or work in her books? I can't be the only one who got creeped out by her wanting to leech off of them?"

"You're fucking brilliant, Baby Girl!" Fitz yanks her away from the door and puts his hands on her cheeks as he looks at her. "We need more *victims* of her bad behavior. They have to be out there; you're right. I'll start searching, but we can tell the lawyer when he gets here, too."

The plan washes over me and I smack my forehead. "*Merde.* We should have thought of that by now. Instead of pushing her away and issuing threats, we needed to find more evidence of her destroying others for her own gain. Showing the world who she really is will make it impossible for her to refute your claim."

I'd do anything to keep the light that just went on in our bunny's eyes there forever.

"Watch out, Rockland. We're coming for you," she says with a bright smile.

Hell yes we are.

O<small>NCE</small> D<small>OLLY</small> <small>GOT HER BIG WELCOME BOX, SHE PULLED THE MOST</small> relevant things out—her schedule, the map, and the booklet with her assigned areas. As a triple threat sophomore, she has lockers in all the sections where she'll need them for class, access to private studios to practice, and a room in the Theater dorm. Her nose wrinkles at that, but she downright glares when she notes that there are two notes in the folder that are solely for transfers. The first is a typical welcome letter blathering about the college, but the second is a list of forms and releases she will have to fill out.

"This place needs a fucking tech upgrade in the worst way," she mutters as she looks at Fitz. "Everything I have to do is on paper. I'll die before I finish all this stupid shit."

He chuckles. "They have me focused on the Pred team and the comp sci program, Baby Girl. No one asked me to bring them out of the Dark Ages. Sorry."

"Damn," she grumbles. "Let's track down these classes, then we can head for the dining hall before I get hangry."

She hands me her schedule and I squint at it. They have her stuffed to the gills and this is going to be very difficult. "They have you packed from eight am to five pm almost every day—mostly in

Alexandré and Shirdal. Looks like the witch only snuck in one session, but my guess is she'll push for more."

Felix growls low, taking the schedule from me. "You're in all artsy classes, Princess. None of us have you as a student save the grumpy dragon for your work study period. I don't like it."

"Did you see it?" she asks me, her eyes still on the tiger as he looks over the document. "I'm waiting for him to—"

"*What the ass reaming fuck?!*" The Raj throws the paper at his brother as he roars. His tiger shimmers over him in fury and I blow out a slow breath.

I did *see it, but I was hoping we could avoid the topic until later—fat chance of that.*

"Holy shit! This dude is our fuckwit *cousin*," Fitz says as he grips the schedule in his fist. "He's a goddamn *creeper*."

"That explains the seven hundred pound problem we're about to have," Chess mutters. "Felix *hates* all of his male relatives. They're far too much like Taka— which was intended."

Aubrey blows two large smoke rings as his jaw locks. "You mean we got rid of the stupid MacLachlan girl *and* the Politics professor only to be saddled with yet another of your dad's shitty spies? It's like fucking Whack-A-Mole with that dick."

"I wish someone would whack his dick," Fitz mutters. We all stare at him and he waves his hand dismissively. "In the not fun way, of course."

Our girl giggles, shaking her head as she threads her arms through his. "I was *not* volunteering as tribute for that assignment. No fucking way."

Felix snarls from where he's still working to get his cat under control. "Never. *Never*."

"Duh," Fitz says as he gives us all a look like his twin is the crazy one. "No one touches our girl but us, *least* of all, our cockfaced father. Now, tell me, Baby Girl… which place are we going first? I'm tired of standing here like bait while shit pisses us off."

"We're in this damn place. Let's find out where the dead bird walking has her office so we know, then we'll go to Alexandré. Shirdal will be last, then we head back here for food."

Chess nods, jerking his head towards the bank of elevators. "The guide should be over there. I need to know where her stupid office is, too, so I second my Angel's plan."

"Coming, Felix?" I call as we turn to walk away.

The gold in his eyes flashes and he nods, but I know he's more beast than man at the moment.

"Chess, if she asks you one intrusive question this year, I want to know immediately." Felix looks at our girl, pausing before he adds, "And you need to record things. I'm sure Farley will agree. Nothing about your schedule is a coincidence—you have one of our cousins, a Council in-law, and several Council relative exiles as professors. Someone made sure you also didn't have classes with us. The fix is in, Princess, and we need to be on our toes from second one."

Now who's keeping secrets? Felix Khan knows something he's not saying and I want to know what it is.

THE SET UP

DELORES

THE GUYS WERE RIGHT ABOUT THIS BUILDING; IT'S NOT intuitively designed at all. Beautiful, maybe, but finding Rockland's office in the winding maze isn't easy, even with the map. None of us are pleased to find that it's on an underground floor, tucked in a corner where no one can hear you scream.

Ominous at best and frighteningly specific at worst.

"We might be overreacting," Chess says tentatively. "This might be the space they had or since she's a carrion-eater, the admin may have internal bias, so they stuck her in a hole. That's definitely possible."

I frown, looking at the door and hallway leading to it. I'm not looking forward to navigating this on my own; it reminds me of the places I ran through when the Heathers set those dingoes on me, but there's no escaping into the nurses' office. "I'm not coming here without someone escorting me. You won't have to coax me."

Felix gives me a smile that promises rewards. "Good girl, Princess. I think we're all in agreement about that assessment."

"Fuck that, I'll sit outside the door on the floor. This shit is dangerous," Fitz says as he glares at the dim lights and heavy décor. "It might look fancy, but it's like the haunted house level in a MMORPG."

"Did you pin the location, *ma petite?*" Renard asks. When I nod, he takes my elbow. "Then let's get the hell out of here. Flames and I are less than excited about being trapped in such an enclosed space, especially when it's under ground."

"Speak for yourself," Aubrey rumbles. "I *like* caves and hideaways. But this gives my dragon a weird feeling. He's not sure why, but he doesn't trust this space."

They don't have to ask me again. Rennie and I head down the hall to the elevator, waiting for the others before we all pack in. It's old timey, but big enough to fit—barely. Creaking and squeaking noises make my anxiety spike as we ascend and I wonder how often they do maintenance on it. I'd hate to get trapped here, especially if someone is after me. My eyes rove around the cramped interior, then up to the exposed shaft and I'm surprised to find myself calculating an escape route without meaning to.

Apparently, my bunny is none too fond of this fucking building, either.

IN COMPARISON, THE ALEXANDRÉ IS LAID OUT LIKE A MORE typical campus building. It has an interior map on the wall, letting know where the floors and sections are in bold fonts. Normal humanities classes are on the top floor, the arts classes are on the floor below, business below that, math and science next, and on the ground floor, there's a plethora of lecture halls. The underground levels are all labs for various classes from languages to sciences. It feels *much* safer than the Dupreé Compound and I breathe a sigh of relief.

I'm a bad ass bunny, but I'm not stupid.

When people truly want to hurt you, they'll find a way, whether it's straightforward or by subterfuge. Someone could pop in and use magic or simply catch me off-guard and spray me in the face with fucked up drug; just because I can defend myself doesn't mean I can't be incapacitated. Swallowing hard, I shake off the bad thoughts as I find the exact locations for my Shifter and Theater History classes. The former is in the middle of a hallway —not a fan of that—and the other is near a fire staircase. I can get away from there if I need to, but the first one requires a lot of focus to make sure I don't get pincer'd.

"Baby Girl, your brow is so furrowed you look like you're going to get a crease," Fitz murmurs as he comes up behind me and wraps his arms around my waist. His chin rests on my shoulder as he continues, "Why so glum, chum?"

"I don't like being in the middle. It's strategically shitty and I'll have to make certain I'm paying attention every time I come in or out. Plus, it's your damn cousin's class. Think that's a coincidence?"

The low snarl behind us tells me Felix *does not* think so. His tone is dark as he asks, "Do you want us to attempt to pull you from it?"

"No," I reply as I lean my cheek against his twin's. "That will only signal weakness to him *and* your father. They need to realize I'm not afraid of them. Sending spies to fuck with me will only result in finding out they're this much closer to being kicked out of that hellhole when we get to that portion of our new list."

Aubrey grins at me, looking pleased as hell. "Exactly, bite size. We don't back down—ever. It will send the message to everyone coming for you that we're serious."

Fitz snorts. "I'm *always* serious about carnage and anyone who thinks differently is delulu as fuck."

"Yes, we know you're crazy, love," Chess chuckles. "But let's save the rage for later? I'm getting hungry and we need to see these rooms, then the French version of the Shird."

His logic is flawless, so we get in the more modern elevator to go to the top floor. The bank has three cars and is on the end of the building closer to Dupreé. When we exit, I note the bulletin boards advertising various paid research projects, side hustles, and events coming up this spring. The public juries flyer makes my eyes widen—the arts classes don't have exams here. They must have year long projects that get presented at the end of the year for your final grade.

Motherfucker, I'm five months behind and so are my friends.

"What's wrong, *petite?*" Rennie asks as we head to the class number for Shifter History.

"They do juries. Rufus, Cori, and I will be almost half a year behind on large projects that get graded at the end. We could flunk out if we don't catch up and *fast*. It's going to make every- thing much harder, especially for me."

Felix shakes his head. "Fucking great. How is that not something that could have been communicated once they reassigned you? You could have been working from Cappie."

This stinks of Lucille, not going to lie.

"I'm sure they should have and shall we take bets on who might have neglected to inform me?" I give them all a wry grin. "It starts with a 'L' and ends with 'ucille,' if you ask me."

"Ra save us from the glut of enemies trying to fuck you over, lunchable. It's impossible to keep track of them all," the dragon mutters. "We can figure it out with your loud friends after we speak with the badger barrister. All we need is a plan."

"We need boards!" Chess says gleefully. "I'm on it."

Smiling softly, I turn to him and kiss him softly. "Yes, we do, my knight. You're in charge of organizing because you're so damn good at it."

He flushes bright red as Fitz gooses him playfully, bobbing his brows. "Look at that... a good boy *and* a good girl. We're on a roll, gentleman."

This time I turn red, so to hide it, I pull the door of the classroom labeled 'A. Khan' open to peek inside. "Shit."

Felix pushes through the group to stalk inside at my muttered curse, and he growls as he sees what it looks like. "I'm going to *murder* him. You can't stop me."

"I can," I say as I join him in the middle of the room. "And I will because it's not time yet, baby. I'm not sure why this place is set up like some jungle themed pleasure den for a fucking history class, but I'm sure he pulled strings we'll never be able to snip."

"It's like the room where..." he trails off and I feel the walls go up inside of him like a slap to the face. I know my fierce tiger doesn't mean to hurt anyone, but this is obviously a trauma he's never faced. The layout of this damn place is geared toward undermining his confidence and distract him.

Unfortunately, it's working.

"Bro," Fitz says as he strides over and shakes him. "Bro. Hey, Felix. Come back to reality, you dickhead. Don't let that old prick win. He can send Asani to mess with your head, but he *doesn't get to win.*"

Moving quickly, I sandwich Felix in between me and his twin, resting my cheek on his strong back. The others close the distance, too, surrounding him in a circle of quiet strength until he stops shaking. When he finally turns to look over his shoulder at me, I can see the pain in his eyes. There's a haunted expression that I haven't seen before—this is not about the woman he loved before betraying him.

This is something else entirely and he's too ashamed to talk about it.

"You don't have to talk about it," I murmur. "Not today and not now. We probably should so your cousin can't use it against us—just like needing to understand Rennie's past because of the magic people."

"Fuck," he groans as his eyes close. "You're right and I hate it."

Fitz clears his throat. "If it's easier, I could——"

"*No.*"

Aubrey arches a brow, and Rennie looks similarly grim. "The Raj obviously needs to deal with this himself, Fitzgerald," my dragon finally rumbles. "And we will allow him the time to figure out what that looks like for him. Right?"

Fitz rolls his head back on his shoulders and lets out a long suffering sigh. "*Why* won't any of you let me have any fun? I would be more than *happy* to peel this asshole like a banana and bring back his hide for the living room. In fact, I'm *begging* you to let me, Felix."

The tiger laughs a little, stepping back from his twin. "I promise you can when the time is right. Okay?"

I tilt my head, looking at them both before I speak. "I want that rug *and* his balls in a jar, Fitzy."

My crazy mate claps with glee and Rennie shudders. "*Merde, ma petite. C'est vicieux.*[1]"

"And sexy as hell," Chess mumbles. I wink at him playfully and the gargoyle frowns at my cheetah. "What? Obviously it's my thing; I'm mated to Fitz."

Taking one last look around the grossly decorated room, I shake my head. "I'll make sure I'm very careful here. I can make adjustments for this class in particular, much like I will for the Rockland sessions."

"Not to be a downer, but it's starting to feel like you're going to have to make concessions in *every* class, lunchable. That's also probably on purpose," Aubrey says with a grimace. "I assume you won't have many classes with your friends, either. Someone with a lot of pull arranged this shit."

"Lucille could have," I say thoughtfully. "But I'd bet she was busy working with Bruiser to arrange Bruno's splatter jet ride."

"Great," Felix growls as he prowls around the room for a moment. "Has another player entered the game?"

We look at one another, and no one has an answer. I can't stand here and let the fear of adding yet another plate to my stack, so I jerk my head at the doorway. Fitz grabs my arm, linking with me as we head down to the fire stairs. I'm pleased he figured out that I'd want to see what they look like and when he opens the door to the next floor down with a flourish, I giggle.

Fitz Khan is the best cure for the blues I've ever known.

"Let's get this done, Baby Girl. My focus is waning, and Chess is hungry. Felix is nearly falling off the edge of Furious Mountain. The mopey monster is still brooding. All we need now is the Saucy Skink to set the whole place on fire and we'll get kicked out on day one."

SHUT UP AND DANCE

AUBREY

FITZ ISN'T WRONG TO WONDER IF I'LL RAZE THIS CURSED PLACE. The buildings and set-up are perfect for men like Rennie and I— all focused on learning and art and beauty. But they've allowed corruption to seep in and despite the majestic outer layer at *Academie*, the core is rotten as they come. I despise seeing the least objectionable school in the private pred system turned into a weapon.

For that alone, I could justify burning it to the ground without a second thought.

Setting our delectable bunny up to fail or be harmed simply emphasizes the need for us to show these snooty dicks who they're messing with. Her smaller hand is tucked in mine as we walk across the manicured lawn towards the French version of the Shird. Fitz is discussing methods of dismemberment with Felix, who is seething like he used to before Dolly came to campus. His sore spot is his family and he needs to conceal it better. People will use it against him every time and all of us will suffer if he rises to the bait each time.

"What's on your mind, big guy?" Dolly asks as she squeezes my fingers with hers. "You're always quiet, but you seem simmery, too."

I smile as I look down at her. Perceptive as usual, the woman who has entranced my entire family never fails to make us communicate rather than letting sleeping dragons lie. "This campus is amazing, but they've tainted it with their evil. I hate that, and even more, I hate knowing that every time we remove someone from your gallery of goons, another steps forward. It's like some sadistic carnival game."

She snorts, covering her mouth with her free hand. "What do *you* know about carnival games, grumpy pants? I can't see you ever going to a crowded event with clowns and sugary shit and dangerous rides."

"You're not wrong, but alas, our mate has led me through some truly awful events in the past centuries. He enjoys studying humans and supes, finding new hobbies to amuse himself and dragging me alongside him." My gaze cuts to the gargoyle talking animatedly with Chess and I notice he's mimicking one of the stitches he's having trouble with.

How did I get so fucking lucky twice? Sweet Ra, I owe someone a boon.

"We're all enjoying your knitting lessons, you know," she grins and whispers conspiratorially. "Even Felix. I think it relaxes him and he doesn't realize it."

"Fitz's knots are pretty funny," I admit. "He's trying harder than I would have expected."

Dolly's expression turns smug as she lifts our hands to kiss my knuckles. "I told all of you that he's easy to teach if you adapt to how his brain works. Comparing the counts to lines of code was genius."

Her praise makes me flush and I huff a surprised chuckle. I don't know how she does it, honestly. Without even thinking about it, our girl is able to quell the raging fire in my dragon and the others' animals as well. It's completely effortless on her part and I'm baffled by the easy calm my fiery inner monster is bathed in now. "Do you think this place will be better or worse than Alexandré?"

"Who the fuck knows?" she groans. "I've gotten used to assuming the worst and being pleasantly surprised when I don't find some fucking cartoon character trap waiting for me. It's much easier on my anxiety than expecting people to act like they have any goddamn sense in their heads."

I squint at her, my lips curling up playfully. "You're awfully young to be so cynical, snack size."

"Oh, please. I've been hunted, shamed in front of the world, disowned, lied to, threatened, and attempts to poison or kill me are common. The bullshit in my life doesn't lend to being a ray of sunshine." She pauses and turns to look at me seriously. "But that doesn't mean I'm not happy with you guys. I truly am. It's the rest of the world who can get fucked."

"Even your band of merry shifters?" I tease. "Dolly Hood, the gatherer of misfits and rebels is a pretty good title for you."

Her giggle is delightful as we finally reach the broad archway of the fancy arts building. "I prefer Queen of Anarchy, thank you very much. Down with the system and all that shit."

Looking at the others as they approach, I shrug. "If you want to burn it all to the ground and rebuild, we'll all follow you to gates of Hell and back, Delores Drew. Just say the word." The look she gives me has a flash of her mother in it and it makes my dick stand at attention.

Our sweet little bunny is sexy as hell when she's plotting the downfall of the dictators.

"OH, *WOW*," DOLLY BREATHES AS SHE SPINS AROUND THE STAGE IN a flurry of ballet turns. Her excitement is even making Felix smile as she looks around *Academie*'s enormous theater in awe. "This even makes Apex's look small. It's swag as hell."

Rennie walks over to her, grabbing her hand to kiss it before bowing low.

Here it comes—Frenchie's going to dazzle her like a fucking Disney Prince.

"Rennie," she squeals as he clasps her fingers and sends her spinning outward, before bringing her back in close. "Can you do a merengue?"

He chuckles low, setting their hands in position before they start moving around the large proscenium in a quick step. The music must be in their heads because it's certainly not playing out loud. Regardless, the laughter makes my chest warm as they twirl around the stage like the couple in the dance movie they like to watch with ice cream. Before I can comment, Fitz rushes over, grabbing her hand when my mate spins her out again.

"My turn, my turn!" The tiger bounces like he's on an upper, leading her into a jaunty swing step. I blink when he holds her waist to swing her around his body and into the air like a pro.

When did we turn into an episode of 'Dancing with the Stars'?

"Fitzzzzzz," Dolly yells as he tosses her in the air to catch her then dip her low enough for her long hair to drag over the wood. "You've been practicing without me!"

Chess looks over at me and winks, telling me she's right. *I'll be damned.* Shaking my head, I walk over to the Raj, joining him as he watches from the edge. "That girl might be a miracle worker."

"You're telling me," he says fondly. "They'll have *us* taking dancing lessons next."

I blink, tilting my head as I smirk at him. "Who says I can't dance?"

His brow arches and he snorts. "Your entire personality?"

Prepare to eat your words, tiger.

Winking at him, I stride over to his twin and tap him on the shoulder. "May I?"

"Of course, Blistering Basilisk," he replies as he scoops Dolly up from the slide she did under his legs. "By all means, show us what you got."

The red faced bunny takes my hands with a bright smile before asking, "A waltz?"

I shake my head, yanking her close, then dipping her quickly. "Ready for a tango, lunchable?"

That gets her attention and her posture changes quickly, forming the necessary pose as we begin. It's been a very long time, so I'm not quick, but she's a skilled dancer. If I mis-step a bit, Dolly gets me back on track with small nudges as we dance around the stage. By the time she's winded, she's lost the somewhat jaded look in her eyes.

Maybe my mate had the right idea after all?

"Okay, okay. You've all had your fun," Felix grumbles good-naturedly. He looks less ready to maim someone, which is good. "Let's check out the studios and classrooms."

Fitz blows a raspberry at him as he pauses his jaunty dance with Chess. "Such a spoilsport, bro. Just admit you can't dance and be done with it."

The elder tiger gives him a cagey grin. "I'll do no such thing."

Looks like the Raj is keeping more secrets than we thought.

I'M SURPRISED TO FIND THE ARTS BUILDING IS LAID OUT IN A MUCH more functional manner. The lowest floor is underground two levels and it has the studios and workshops for all the majors. On the next floor, there's an enormous gym and the costume/stylist department. Dolly coos at the large doors to the costume storage, remarking that her polar bear friend is going to be in heaven. We bypass the ground floor since it's mostly occupied by the theater, dressing rooms, and a few offices. Floors two and three house the visual arts, architecture, and writing departments. Theater and dance take up the fourth floor and vocal/musical arts are on the fifth. Everything is brightly lit, clean, and looks state of the art— it's clear where the money goes in this place.

"Damn," Chess says as we finish touring and come down the main staircase. "Their shit is next level. I wonder if I can sit in on some of the art classes when I'm not stuck with the bitchy body snatcher? The 3D printer looks sick."

Fitz snorts as he slings an arm around both the cheetah and our girl. "If they tell you 'no,' I'll handle it, baby. If we have to spend the rest of the year here, I promise to make sure every single one of us has a chance to do shit that makes them happy."

"Even me?" I smirk at him as we exit the front doors.

"Why, Lord Draconis, I'm wounded. If you need more books to hump, I'll make it happen!"

Rennie has to cover his mouth to stifle the laugh threatening to escape and even Felix cracks a smile as he reaches over to whack his brother in the back of the head. The hyper tiger rubs the spot with a pout, no doubt hoping to gain sympathy from our girl. Too bad she's giggling along with his other mate—he might have had a chance.

"Seriously, guys! I mean it," Fitz grumbles. "There's so much shit to deal with—Baby Girl has the Games and catching up with work, we have random lesson plans we're not prepped for, there's psychos running around... We gotta take the good when we can."

"*C'est vrai, mon ami,*" Renard says with a sigh. "I'd hoped we could take time off campus to tour the wine region and Paris, but it appears we will have to wait until the spring or summer breaks."

Dolly's eyes widen and she lets go of the cats, running up to my mate with a look of pure adoration. "We can go tour the *Catacombs*??! Like in *Phantom*? Or see the *Moulin Rouge*? Oh my god, oh my god, oh my god..."

The entire group stops halfway to the library as she has what appears to be a spazz attack in the middle of the fucking green. Ren, however, is smiling so broadly his face might crack; he knew *exactly* what he was doing keeping that plan to himself until the right time.

"*Oui, ma chére.* We can even see Notre Dame, though it's not quite as majestic as—oof!"

A flash of rainbow nearly takes him off his feet as Dolly barrels towards him with a squeal of glee that might have called a herd of pigs. He catches her in his arms, lifting her to spin around again as she keeps making the ear-splitting girl noises. "I'm going to *kill* you for hiding this, you big meanie!"

Fitz tilts his head, looking at the rest of with a shrug. "I probably would have hid it, too, if I knew she was gonna lose it like this. Holy nerds, BatBoy."

"Shut it, Fitzy. There's soooo much cool shit we can do in Paris and I cannot *wait* to go." Dolly's feet finally touch the ground again and she pushes her hair out of her eyes as she glares at our fond expressions. "Don't patronize me. Now I have something to look forward to besides magical fuckwits and new mean girls."

Well, when she puts it that way....

Mine

Delores

It was hard to settle when we got home. The idea of seeing all the amazing things I've dreamed up when I was cooped up in Drew Manor while my parents ran around the globe makes all of this worth it.

Okay, not everything, because people have died and I'm being hunted but…

It made the stupid scary ass plane ride worth it, at least. But I was so worked up that even a big dinner and a snuggly pile of boyfriends barely kept me down. I woke up this morning with enough energy to hop all over the damn building and not even get winded. Fitz got assigned to help me wear off some of the jitters, so while they make breakfast, we're out in the pretty Zen garden in the middle of the open area in the middle of our complex.

"I've always wanted to visit exotic places, but Lucille said I'd embarrass them," I admit as I push into a headstand. "I guess I believed her. Stupid, huh?"

Fitz takes a moment to balance himself facing me before he responds, "Very, Baby Girl."

"Fitz!" I gasp, trying not to topple as I laugh. "You're not supposed to *agree* with me."

His face screws up as he focuses, his sexy muscles tightening as he slowly mimics my headstand. His yoga-fu is getting much better and I'm proud of him for really working to catch up. I love that he takes my hobbies seriously without batting a lash. "Why not? You're right. You used to let that nasty old witch get into your head and fuck you up. That's one hundred percent true. Now, you're stronger, smarter, and more confident... so you don't."

Well, when he puts it that way...

"You have a really good way of simplifying things, Mr. Khan." I suck in a deep breath, spreading my legs into an 'X' shape. Fitz follows my lead, but his legs aren't quite as straight so he looks a bit crazy. I smile as he furrows his brows and focuses on making the pose correct. "And you're really rocking this yoga stuff."

"Just remember that when anyone says I'm a psycho beefcake," he crows as he follows along when we switch to a different leg position. "Fitzgerald Khan is a shining example of transcending toxic masculinity... and I look hot as fuck doing it."

I almost topple over as I giggle, having to tighten every muscle in my core to prevent a domino effect. "I'll keep that in mind if someone dares to question your ally status, baby."

"So what has you hyper besides the tourist shit? That's cool as hell, but it's not enough for Felix to assign you to me for 'calm down' time." Bobbing his brows, Fitz licks his lips lasciviously. "Which we'll get to once we've stretched out properly."

Rolling my eyes, I give him a *look*. "That is not why we're doing yoga, buddy. Keep it in your sweats for now."

He pouts. "Fine, but I still want to know your answer."

"Cori and Rufus and all of them arrive later today—as long as everything stays on track. Plus, even if we're super behind and I'm stressing a bit, the art facilities here are even better than at Apex. If the teachers are, too, then I'll have a lot of opportunities to learn." I lower my legs, slowly moving out of the head stand so I don't tumble to the ground.

Instead of doing the same, Fitz tucks his chin and does a rough somersault grinning as he lays flat on his back. "Those are pretty good reasons, Baby Girl. And I like seeing you look so happy."

I crawl over to him, lifting a leg to straddle his waist. "There's too much bad shit going down constantly to let it ruin everything. And you... plus the others... and my friends... all make me happy."

Fitz gives me a pleased grin as his hands fall to grip my hips. "That's what I like to hear. Happy and satisfied is what we aim for."

"Mmmm. I feel that," I reply as I grind down on him. His dick is obviously in full agreement because it's hard as steel, poking into my thin yoga pants eagerly. "Do you plan to show me?"

"As a matter of fact," he growls before flipping us in a lightning fast move that puts me beneath him. "I do."

His hands come up to pin mine and his hips complete the domination as I look up at the crazy tiger with sparkling eyes. "Oooh. It's Cave-Fitzy. I'm at your mercy, baby."

That gets a dark snarl from him as he lowers his head to my neck. He sniffs along my shoulder for a moment and his body tenses as he inhales. This is the drive to mate from his tiger; I know enough from my talks with Coach Z to recognize it. Baring my throat and closing my eyes, I capitulate, letting his animal have the satisfaction of complete control. I don't do this often, but until I make the decision to go all the way with mating, it helps the inner beasts in my men to give them this occasionally.

Zhenga told me it would prevent 'accidents' and she's been right so far.

"You're thinking too hard," Fitz mumbles before he nips the juncture of my shoulder with blunt teeth. "I feel it, Baby Girl."

My hand comes up to cup the back of his head as he nibbles firmly over my skin. It makes me tingle from head to toe and my thighs frame his hips, pressing against them when they thrust. "Just thinking about how much I love you," I groan softly.

He pauses, lifting his head to beam at me with the gold of his tiger shining in his eyes. "I love you, too, Dolly Drew. I'll follow you into Hell and back with a wink and a smile."

The declaration hits me in the gut hard and I tug his mouth to mine, kissing him hard. From the moment I met Fitz Khan, he's treated me better than anyone has in my entire life. Anyone who didn't see the heart in this man is a fucking fool.

I'd step in front of a runaway train for him—no question.

A low rumble of pleasure vibrates over me as he lifts up just enough to grab the zipper on my sports bra and yank it down. Kneading roughly, his fingers twist my nipples and I gasp at the sting. Our mouths break apart when I bite his lower lip in retribution and he gives me a hungry expression. There's a tiny bit of blood on his lower lip, which he licks away.

"I thought you were being a good girl this morning," he tsks playfully.

My smirk deepens as I arch into his hands eagerly. "I never said that."

We both enjoy the battle for control and its resulting roughness—this is just foreplay.

Chuckling darkly, Fitz moves his hands to my pants, tugging them down and off. He turns his head to kiss my ankle, making me giggle when the light brush tickles. "You, my beautiful bunny, are going to behave so I can worship you."

"We'll see," I reply with a mischievous grin. "Do your worst, Crazypants."

He sits my feet on his shoulders, biting my left calf firmly. My body is singing with anticipation, so I probably shouldn't have poked the tiger with a teeny stick, but I'm a risk taker like that. The trail of bites, nips, and kisses moves up my leg until he reaches my now trembling thigh, but he stops. With a wink, he turns to the right side, starting at the ankle again as I groan in frustration. My pussy throbs at his teasing touches and I clench around an empty space inside.

Damn him and damn my big, fat mouth.

"Fitzyyyy," I moan as he spends time behind my knee on delicate skin. My fingers dig into the ground hard, clawing slipping out as my bunny demands he quit teasing. "Don't be an asshole."

"I'm not, Baby Girl." He lifts his head and looks at me hungrily. "This is getting you ready for my feast."

"Shit," I mutter as my back arches. When my psycho kitty wants to, he can edge the shit out of Chessie and I. That's what he's doing now and my body is dancing to his tune without a second thought. "I'll get you back for this."

"Oh, I hope so," he mumbles before sucking a big bruise on my inner thigh. "In fact, I'm counting on it."

When his breath finally hits my wet slit, I almost cry in relief. His fingertips trace the shape of me, gathering wetness to bring to his lips and growl as he tastes the fruits of his labor. A soft flick of his tongue makes me shiver in anticipation, but he doesn't touch me where I need it. Instead, he switches to the groove where my legs and pelvis meet, finally making me growl back in frustration. I can almost *feel* his grin against my skin; that's how smug the son of a bitch is.

"Say it," he rumbles against the skin he's marking it up. "Say you're mine, Baby Girl."

Shit. Possessive Fitz is fucking hot as Hades and twice as sexy.

"I'm… y-yours…" I pant when his mouth finally brushes over my apex. A warm swipe of his tongue makes my stomach clench and I'm shocked to feel the wave of pleasure sweep through me. Arching off the ground, I moan loudly as the orgasm wracks my frame with hardly any effort on his part. "S-Shit… Fitz…"

His hands push my thighs further apart as he settles between them, and the rough, flat tongue of his tiger laps at the juices flowing out of me greedily. It makes me shake more and I force my hands from the earth below me to bury in his long hair. Tugging on the silky strands, I feel the vibrations of his moan and manage to smile in satisfaction. He *loves* his hair pulled, but only when I do it. I hold on tightly, guiding him around my heat until he finally gives in to lick my clit.

The pleasure is so intense I come again with barely a whisper of pressure. That triggers him to work me over more aggressively, flicking and suckling on the sensitive spot until I scream and yank his hair *hard*. Another ripple of pleasure hits me and my eyes slam shut as my brain damn near fizzles out. My limbs tense as he gently cleans me up, waiting for me to loosen my grip on his hair before he pulls back to grin wickedly.

"Now, *that* is what I want to see. You're practically glowing." My tiger places one last kiss on my mound, then slinks up my body quickly, burying himself inside of me with one smooth thrust. I shudder as he fills me, gripping him inside as I groan low.

"Holy fuck." I don't have enough brain power to say more because the buzz of orgasms and the bunny inside me are taking up every available brain cell. When he moves, I feel the burst of a half-shift free my tail, ears, and fangs. A deep hunger claws at my gut, pushing at my consciousness until I growl again.

Fitz's hips swirl before he looks up at me and sucks in a breath. "Holy fuck is right, Baby Girl. You're bunnilicious right now."

"Can't... control... it," I grit out as I meet his slow thrusts. My nose twitches and I roll my eyes up to the sky as a powerful sensation coasts over my body. I don't know what the fuck is going on, but it's like everything inside of me is fighting to take the wheel.

His hips speed up, slamming into me and hitting the exact spot I need, forcing me to squeeze my eyes closed and moan again. "You're definitely fucking glowing and it's *sexy as hell*."

I raise my hand to touch him and suddenly, a loud roar echoes off the surrounding walls of the library. The sound makes a switch inside me flip and I dig my claws into his shoulders for purchase so I can meet the hard rhythm of his hips. We're fucking so hard it's going to hurt later, but I don't care. All the instincts inside of me are raging, prickling my skin as we get closer and closer to the edge.

"*Mine*," Fitz growls and I finally pry my eyes open again to look at the half-shifted tiger with golden eyes staring down at me possessively.

Oh shit.

"Fitz..."

"*Mine.*"

The second demand hooks into my gut like a punch and I surge forward as my thighs grip his. "No, *mine*."

That's when fangs flash and something like an explosion of heat hits me like a ton of bricks. Pain flares, and growls echo off the walls of the little alcove, then sparkles fill my eyes and my limbs start to go limp.

Uh-oh.

Bad Mamajama

Fitz

THE LIGHT IS FUCKING BRIGHT WHEN I OPEN MY EYES. IT TAKES ME a minute to realize I'm fully shifted and curled around a body, and I growl in frustration. Lifting a big paw, I rub it over my face in irritation and suddenly, everything comes back.

Holy fuck… we mated.

I look down, blinking big yellow eyes as I note my beloved bunny is *not* a tiny little rabbit as I would have expected from the full mating shift. She's tucked in a small ball, but Dolly is covered in the soft white fur of her bunny in a humanoid form. It's almost like she's only half-shifted, but from the big feet, cottontail, long ears and tiny pink nose… I know that's not true.

Since I'm not one of the three kings, I can't speak when I like this, so I push through the tiger until I'm a naked dude again. My hand reaches out to stroke her angora fur, chuckling when it comes back coated with some sort of sparkle. "What the actual *hell*, Baby Girl? What are you and how do we keep you safe?"

Her soft groan gets my attention and my eyes slide up to her face, trying not to preen at the fang marks gracing her neck. They'll heal slightly… enough to leave perfectly shaped scars to tell everyone who she belongs to. I watch as she stretches her limbs, slowly figuring out that she's not shaped like her normal self. Red eyes pop open to look at me with a shocked expression and I shrug.

"Fitz, what the fuck did we do?" I arch a brow at her and her bunny nose scrunches up even more adorably than her normal nose, delighting me. She huffs, rolling her eyes to the sky then back at me. "I *meant* why am I not a tiny flop-eared bunny in full shift instead of… this?"

"Hell if I know, Baby Girl." I think back for a second, furrowing my brow as it occurs to me this might have been predictable. "You know, Felix said you never fully shifted once in class the first year. He thought it was because you were afraid to become a small bunny that gave them a target. You always fight in the Games half-shifted. Have you ever done the full monte besides the one time after the prom?"

She frowns, her fangs chewing on her lower lip as she thinks. My dick perks up, liking her cute faces and sharp teeth. In fact, Captain One-Eye pretty much loves her and Chessie no matter how their bodies are shaped at any given moment, so I'm not surprised. A light smack on my chest brings me out of my head and I look at her. "What?"

"Did you just call your dick Captain One-Eye?" She's trying not to laugh, but I shrug. I have zero shame when it comes to my equipment. "Wait... how did I hear that?"

My face lights up in excitement as it comes to me. "Holy shit! We've got the 'ooh-wee-ooh' spooky shit going on. You can *hear* my thoughts like I can Felix if I want or the Flying Fruitcakes can! I thought it was only you could talk to *us*."

Dolly's eyes widen and she scrunches her face again as if concentrating hard. Suddenly, there's a loud shout of 'hello' in my brain and I burst out laughing. My new mate gives me a look that could gut a trout, but I can't stop snickering at her overcompensation.

"Baby Girl, you don't have to clench and shout. You can... just think in a normal voice. At least, I do with Felix," I finally manage to say when the laughter fades.

'Don't make fun of me," she pouts. "I don't know how the hell this shit works. Not that it's surprising, because I don't know how *anything* about me works or where it came from. I'm a fucking mystery even to other shifters and mythicals."

I snort, pulling her into my arms and breathing in the scent of her hair. "Who cares? I mean, I know you want to know and that's cool. But honestly none of us would care if you were descended from a damn Swamp Monster. I'd learn to love being slimy."

Her expression softens and the bunny attributes melt from her face and body until she's normal naked Dolly again. "People do *not* give you enough credit, Fitz Khan."

Laughing, I wink at her. "Why would I need credit? I'm an heir to the throne of Death Island. I'm set for life."

"*Ex*-heir, to be fair," she teases. "Just like I'm the *ex*-heir to the Drew shit."

Only if her dickhead mother and father did all the complex paperwork after she emerged and only if they made sure to have her sign it. Since she was an adult, they would have needed that and now that she brings it up, if they didn't, there's a new layer of danger added to her plate. Her mother killing off the idiot croc means everything from *both* sides of her family and her parents assets could pass to her.

That's absolutely fucking terrible news and I refuse to mention it until I talk to Smarty Salamander.

"We should probably go inside and clean up." I smile down at her, kissing her lips softly before I continue. "We have to share the news, plus getting all the grass off our asses before your friends arrive might be a good plan."

Her eyes widen as she looks around. "Damnit, Fitz! We're also in the middle of the damn courtyard and anyone on Earth could see."

I shrug, but her face turns bright red. "Don't worry. If I find out someone saw us, I'll pluck their eyes out and make you new jars."

"Ooh. I haven't gotten any surprise gifts from you in a while," she says as she stands up. Her hand comes out and she tugs me to my feet with a surprising ease.

"People keep dying before I can enact my vengeance." My grumble makes her giggle. "It's not satisfying when they're dead."

"You are a crazy bastard, Fitz… but you're *my* crazy bastard," Dolly says as she steps close to me and looks into my eyes. "I love every single bit of it… and you."

This might just be the best *motherfucking day* ever, *and I didn't even have to kill someone.*

EVERY EYE IN THE ROOM IS ON US AS WE WALK IN—PROBABLY because I'm starkers and thanks to her necklace, Baby Girl is clothed again.

That reminds me that I'm going to kick the moper's ass for not sharing whatever that gem is with the rest of us.

"Have fun, I assume?" Chessie calls from the kitchen.

I can imagine the face he's making while he works on something that smells fucking amazing. "About that…"

Before I can admit it, Dolly bounces into the middle of the room. "Fitz and I mated; isn't that great?"

Wincing, I look around, waiting for all the alphas to lose their shit. Instead, my twin comes up and claps me on the back, grinning broadly. "That's fantastic, bro."

Huh?

Chess comes out with a big plate of cheesy, greasy deliciousness, handing it to our girl with a broad smile. "I'm so happy for you both." Once she takes the food, plopping on the couch to dig in, he turns to me, cupping my face. "Truly, love."

Dolly points at me as she mumbles through a mouthful of food. "I fink he fought you all were goin to be mah."

I blink, tilting my head until Ren translates. "She said he thinks you thought we'd be mad. Judging from the look on your face, I'd say she's right. *Mais, mon ami,* you couldn't be more wrong. It's joyous news."

"It is?" I frown then shake my head. "I mean, I *know* it is, but why is it for *you?*"

Aubrey comes out of the kitchen with a scotch, shrugging. "Because if she's ready with you, she'll be ready for us eventually. Don't be dense."

Ohhhhh.

"I get it now," I say as I put my arm around my cheetah. He looks down pointedly and I realize I'm still flapping in the breeze. Moving behind the counter until I rectify that, I continue. "And you've all been busy here. The Captain is scary in his efficiency sometimes."

Felix rolls his eyes, but he comes over to sit at the other end of the huge piece of furniture. "Well, a bunch of money helps, too. But not having this room look like an eighty year old woman threw up in it is worth every penny. If they can get the other rooms done as quickly, we'll be set within the week."

"That would be great," Dolly says as she pauses eating then looks at us in confusion. "Is this ravenous feeling part of the bond thing? I think it is because I really feel like I could eat a water buffalo. I don't know if this will be enough."

Chess jumps up, bolting for the kitchen to join me. "Don't worry, Angel. I'll whip up some more stuff for you."

I smile fondly then look at her. "See? I told you it didn't matter what you needed or how you shift, Baby Girl."

"How does she shift?" Ren says as he drapes over a chair. "What do you mean by that?"

My grin widens. "I forgot to tell you. Baby Girl's full shift is like… a sexy sparkly bunny girl, not a teeny rabbit. She didn't even know, either."

Her face turns red again and she hides behind her long rainbow hair. "He's right; I didn't. The only time I ever shifted all the way was the night Todd and I…"

A chorus of growls fills the room and I chuckle. "Best move on from *that* subject, love."

Rolling her eyes, Dolly continues, "Well, it was dangerous because a bunch of people I trusted almost ate me. So I decided I wasn't going to do it again, especially not at Apex. It was easier to half-shift and I was stronger in that form. I didn't worry about it, really."

The gargoyle tilts his head, studying her for a moment. "Did your magic react to the mating?"

Now it's my turn to look sheepish. "I don't know about her, but something pretty big smacked into me and I was out like a light. I woke up next to her as a tiger, then I figured out she was a hottie bunny girl. I don't have a fucking clue what happened in between."

"He's right," Dolly says as she munches on another cheesy delight. "I woke up after Fitzy and was just as surprised. Welcome to my crazy life, as usual."

"That means we'll have to add it to the boards when they come in," Chess says. "Maybe you can search for alpha females with odd shifts, Aubrey?"

No one even reacts to the news that our girl doesn't shift like a normal pred or prey—we're becoming jaded as fuck about the weird shit that surrounds Dolly.

The dragon sighs, sipping his scotch slowly. "I can add it to the list, but you should be aware it's already unmanageable. I don't know how we'll be able to look into *all* of this while avoiding killers and poison, teaching, and the rest of it."

"Oh!" Everyone looks at me and I shrug. "I'm a tool for not thinking of it before. We need to… branch out. There's too much for us to do alone and we need help that won't question why we're looking right?"

Dolly tilts her head and I see her trying to gauge why I'm asking. "We do, Fitzy. What's your idea?"

"I have the least teaching shit in the room. I have the time to code a… gamified version of a scavenger hunt. I'll spread it through the nerd world of coders and shit, baiting them into doing some of this fucking legwork for us by tying it to some big mysterious prize they could win."

Felix scoffs as he shakes his head. "That will never work, Fitz.

None of your nerdy hackers will ever fall for it. These are smart people."

"So smart they're dumb, bro. Trust me. If I make this a big fucking secret, with a big secret prize and put pride as a gamer or hacker or whatever on the line? They'll bite big time." I grin as my girl looks proud. "And it might not get us the really juicy shit, but at least it could rule out some of the silly things."

"That's… actually kind of genius," Aubrey says begrudgingly. "You should do it, Fitz,"

I'm such a badass motherfucker that even the grumpy ass dragon had to call me smart—rock on, Fitz Khan.

Look What You Made Me Do

Delores

I can barely sit still as I wait for my friends to get here. It's been a while since I saw Rufus and Cori and coming with my charmingly aggressive lawyer makes their arrival even more exciting. Farley is the best solution to my Rockland problem, especially since it's followed me to yet another school. If he can keep her at bay while Fitz sources hackers to research dirt on her, we might be able to remove her from the board.

Removing obstacles rather than adding them is one of my fondest hopes at the moment.

"Baby Girl, you have to calm down. Your anxiety is making me hyper," Fitz says as he bounces on the couch cushions. He finally retrieved clothes while I ate lunch and while Aubrey and Ren took a flight to find hunting grounds, we kept pretending to watch TV.

As usual, my tiger and I are snuggled in with human shows on. Their media is far less likely to make me feel like an idiot when I stumble on shit I don't know and Fitz enjoys stealing shit that amuses him. It's a comfortable routine, and I'm impressed with his ability to sense I craved something familiar while I waited.

"I'm trying, but I missed them, Fitzy. And I'm not afraid of meeting the famous country litigator, but I *am* concerned about whatever info he has that made him hop on an international flight. Rufus told me last semester that Farley only leaves their lands for court or emergencies." Raking my teeth over my lower lip, I look up at him. "I've been trying to pretend I'm not worried, but I am."

Chess strides in from where he was working on cleaning up the kitchen and making lists for ordering, his hair in an adorable messy bun and donning an apron. "Angel, you know we can handle anything that nasty woman throws at us. We're a team, so we'll pull any strings and tap any favor we need to. But that's only if you need it, and you're a force to be reckoned with on your own."

His confidence makes me smile and I pat the seat next to me. I'd like to have them both close for a moment. While he's right —if I can handle Lucille's bullshit on the regular, I can definitely deal with the butthurt fake psychologist. Once Chessie joins us, I twine our fingers together and sigh. "You're right. I'm stronger and more powerful than ever before. I could definitely take her in a fight, but she won't come at me that way because she *knows* I can kick her ass. Rockland works in the background when she aims for people because she's an abusive bully and a coward."

"Sorry to interrupt y'all, but I most certainly agree."

My eyes widen and I pop off the couch to whirl around. Rufus is standing next to a short, stocky man with a neatly trimmed goatee and dark, glittering eyes. His gaze slices through me as he takes me in, and I shiver a little. Chess and Fitz leap up to stand beside me and my friend snorts in amusement.

"Dollypop, call off your kitties. Farley isn't going to bite *you*, no matter what it looks like." The grinning badger stalks over and lifts me up in a huge hug, making me squeal in alarm.

Even if my guys lift me with zero trouble, my psyche goes all panic, no disco when I think someone will figure out what I weigh... Thanks, Lucille.

"Rufus McCoy, put that darlin' young lady down before I tell Meemaw how rude you are." His words make my friend freeze for a second, then he lets me wiggle loose. "Miss Dolly Drew, it's a pleasure to make your acquaintance in person."

I watch in wonder as the muscled shifter in a sharply pressed, bespoke suit bursting with muscles bows.. *Do I....? I probably should.* Smiling, I nod and bend my legs into a curtsey with a sweep of my arms. "And you, Mister McCoy."

"For fuck's sake..." Felix mutters as he comes in from the office space. He was busy unpacking in there with Percy while Raina started cleaning out the main bedroom for me. "What is this, *Gone with the Wind?*"

Fitz beams at his twin, hopping over the furniture to give him a fist bump. "Nice ref, bro. You're learning."

My lawyer arches a brow at me, but I only wink. "Don't worry about our hobbies. You're here to help fuck this bitch up, right?"

"Indeed I am, Miss... may I call you, Dolly?" Farley says as he bustles over to the large armchair. "I know everyone does, but Rufus' Memaw and my mother would pitch a hissy with a tail on it if I didn't ask permission."

I didn't expect genteel manners from a dude who growls like a mafia boss on the phone, but it's kind of cute.

"Of course you may," I reply as I sit down primly, crossing my ankle as I look at him. "Just don't rat Ru-Ru out. I like him as he is —mouthy and fun."

Farley snorts, then lets out a boisterous laugh that brings three huge men into the room with narrowed eyes. I recognize the postman, Goliath, but the other one isn't familiar. The badger waves his hand and they back up to the doorway silently. "Don't be alarmed, sugar. Monstro is my most gifted messenger and his brother, Skelly, is one of my elite couriers. Skelly is busy at the moment, but they're all here to protect me while I'm stuck in this godforsaken land of long-legged amphibians."

Rufus groans and rubs his hand over his face as he takes the other end of the sofa. "Cuz, for the love of Boreas' frosty balls, can you *please* behave less like a bumpkin while you're here? If you run around insulting the French, we're going to have more problems than we started with."

"*C'est vrai, mon ami,*" Rennie says as he and Aubrey walk past the giant bodyguards. "My people are not so forgiving of those who take jabs at our heritage with no cause, even if you are saving our mate."

"Fine, fine," Farley grumbles as he opens his briefcase on the table. He pulls out a laptop, a pile of folders, and a sparkling gold pen before looking at each of us. "Now, before we begin, I need each of you to sign this binding non-disclosure agreement. The information we are going to share from now on may or may not come from legitimate sources and some may even be illegal. I don't know what my men will shake loose while we're here."

He hands out the paper and suddenly, it occurs to me that Cori isn't here. I feel like a total bitch, but there was a flurry of activity as the McCoys came in. She's usually a ray of sunshine and the lack of warmth in the room is partially because she's not here.

My eyes cut to my bestie and I clear my throat. "Shouldn't we *all* be signing this? Where's Coco, Rufus?" The sad expression on his face makes my entire body tense and I worry they've gathered everyone here to tell me something awful I'm the last to know. "*Where. Is. She?*"

"She's setting up our room in the Theater Dorm," he says softly. "While the triplets aren't here because they split off to get settled in their apartment in Paris, Giselle opted to stay at Cappie at the last moment. She broke it off with Cori by text as we hit the tarmac to board the plane."

"Fuck this, I need to go to her," I say as I leap to my feet. "My shit can wait."

Rufus shakes his head as he grabs my wrist. "She specifically asked for us to leave her alone for a little bit while she processes. You know how she was at Apex when there were break-ups, D. She slept on the plane ride most of the time and now she needs time to let it all out."

Frowning, I look at Farley suspiciously. "Did she sign hers on the plane? What about the triplets?"

His reassuring expression helps a bit as he finds more pens in the briefcase. "Everyone who might have direct knowledge of your situation has, including your design house friends, significant others, and once we're done, I'll make certain your personal helpers do as well. It's imperative that anyone close to you has something to lose if they speak with your counselor. I want them sweatin' like a whore in church at the thought of even mentioning your name in passing."

"Ugh, it's so intrusive," I grumble as I sign my copy. "I feel like I'm forcing everyone I know to put themselves on the line for me even though this part isn't their fight."

"Princess, anyone who truly loves or supports you won't hesitate for a second," Felix says in a confident tone. "Right, Farley?"

"Friends who refuse to protect you have the porch light on, but no one's home," he replies as the others hand in their form without even glancing at them. "Hopefully, this is the only paperwork y'all treat so cavalierly."

Aubrey stomps over, looking down at the burly lawyer with soft puffs of smoke escaping his nose. "We're trusting that our mate's best friend would not allow his family member to fuck over his friend. If that trust is misplaced, I'm sure Chester can find a delicious recipe for chicken-fried badger that will satisfy the whole family."

Oh, shit... pissed off dragon activated.

"Big guy, come join us. I can sit on your lap if the boys make room," I call with a sweet smile.

He rolls his eyes, arching a brow at me. "You think you can calm the fiery beast with an eyelash bat, snack size?"

Rennie gets there before me, mumbling, "She could do it with a finger crook, you squishy loving grump."

The librarian shoots him a death glare, but he trudges over and plops between Chess and Fitz, making the substandard couch groan. "This shit needs to be fixed before I break it all by accident."

My hand reaches up to ruffle his slightly messy hair. He thinks I don't realize he's the last one to start growing it out, but I have and I enjoy making his dragon almost purr when I play with the short strands. "Now, now. We've been here two days and the crew is working as fast as they can."

"As fascinating as this is to watch from a purely anthropological point of view..." Farley snarks, "...we definitely have to go over this material before I lose you to some private biological imperative."

"Watch it," Fitz says as he lays a hand on my thigh. "You can do your job with fewer fingers, I'm sure."

"I probably could, but pointless posturing won't get us anywhere." He opens a folder and turns it to face us. "This picture was taken less than a week ago."

The lanky frame and bird's nest hair tell me it's Rockland, but I don't know the other people she's sitting with. There's a squat, toadie looking woman with long hair, a dark haired woman dressed in athletic wear, a willowy blond woman, and a gorgeous man with familiar features. They're all at a table with the Eiffel Tower in the background and the amount of food and drink on their table tells a story about how long they met for.

"You know Rockland, but the people with her are cause for deep concern," my lawyer says. "Severine Ste Jean is the short one with glasses; she looks guileless on the surface much like her animal does, but she's meaner'n cat dirt. She's also your jury advisor, my sources say."

Mother. Fucker.

"This isn't good," Rennie murmurs as Farley points to the next person.

"Nadia Antonovich is a relative of the alpha wolf your boyfriend took out at Apex. She's your modern dance professor and word on the street is that she was very fond of her cousin." His fingers stabs at the last two people and he looks angry as fuck. "Marlène Fabreaux and of course the royals will recognize Asani Khan— they are also your professors."

Aubrey groans, leaning his forehead against my temple for a moment before he speaks. "The charlatan has made friends with those who would have already been our enemies by virtue of other circumstances. She's more clever than we thought."

"No way," I say as I shake my head. "Someone is helping her. You haven't heard the shit in her books. Rennie and I are struggling through them and…"

Farley tilts his head at me, waiting as I reach for words that aren't as harsh. "Go on, then, Dolly Drew. I dare you to find a nice way to say she's so dumb she could throw herself at the ground and miss."

My hand flies to my mouth as I cover the bark of laughter I can't stop. Felix chuckles, then Chessie, and soon, Fitz is howling. We needed a good laugh and apparently, Farley is as brutally witty as his cousin. "I was trying not to be mean simply because she's a bad person."

Rufus rolls his eyes then stares at the photo like he's memorizing the profiles. "Dollykins, some people are far too big for their britches. This chick was hired to fuck with your life despise having no beef with you and that's her own goddamn fault. We have every right to speak harshly of her when she spent all that time breaking you down to the nubs so she could control you."

"Amen to that," Farley says as he grins at Ru-Ru. "She better give her heart to her gods, because her ass is mine—and I don't miss."

All my guys grin in that hungry pred fashion and I shiver.

Carina Rockland is a dead woman walking and she doesn't know it yet.

PROTECTOR

Felix

I WAS SURPRISED WHEN THE IRASCIBLE BADGER SAID HE'D BE staying in the country for a bit while his goons worked on their shady tasks. Farley was obviously unhappy about being here, but despite his country rube persona, I smell the tinge of a predator who has the scent of his kill. He doesn't like Rockland defying his typical tactics; that's going to work in the Princess' favor. It means he'll sink his teeth in and not let go until she's dead enough to stink up the room.

I can respect that doggedness.

My entire ambush would love to lock her up and toy with her until she's begging to die, but we can't do that—yet. So I'll let the lawyer do his thing while I focus on figuring out what the motherfucking *shit* my asshole cousin is doing here. Obviously, the Raj sent him, and likely it's to torture me, but he'd be able to do that without taking on a class with our girl in it. No, this specific play was crafted for a reason beyond sending Fitz and I to the looney bin. It was plotted with multiple pawns placed to cause issues for my entire family.

"Felix?"

I blink, whipping my head around to see Dolly frowning at her hands. "What's wrong, Princess?"

"I want to go see Coco. I know Rufus said she needs time, but… I don't want her to be alone." She rises to her feet, looking up at me with big doe eyes. "Will you walk me over to the Theater Dorm so I can check on her?"

Hell no. We want you here where you're safe.

But I can't tell our soft-hearted girl that I won't help her. It's ridiculous and I'd kill anyone else who suggested it, but when she asks nicely, I'd do damn near anything without an argument. Walking over, I take her hands, tilting my head. "If it's important you go see her now, I will. But we have to come back before it's too dark. We don't know this place well enough yet to be taking chances."

She sniffs, but nods. "Okay. Thank you. I just… I can't get my head straight for anything else until I see that she's not doing anything stupid. Even if I didn't think Giselle was the one… Cori cared about her and she's my friend."

"Come on, then. Let's ease your worries so we can all snuggle up and watch a movie tonight." Her smile gets a little brighter as I tug her into the crook of my arm and lead her toward the door. "We can let you and Fitz pick. It's endlessly entertaining to watch the dragon throw a hissy fit about your selections."

She smacks my arm lightly, her voice soft as she chides me. "Felix Khan, don't be mean to Aubrey. He's doing really well with not being such a grouch. You wouldn't have learned that basket weave stitch if he hadn't been so patient with you."

"Would, too." I wrinkle my nose and make a face at her. "Khans never give up, and we never lose."

Giggling, she curls into my side. "Noted. But I'm told Drews don't either, so be prepared for lots of battles, Sir."

And just like that, I almost turn us around to go back inside for a different inspection.

THE DORMS ARE JUST AS FANCY AS THE ACADEMIC BUILDINGS, SO I'm mildly impressed as we make our way to the third floor where the juniors are housed. Everything looks clean and well-maintained, but even a cursory glance tells me security isn't fantastic. It's not surprising—the pred schools expect students to be able to defend themselves for better or worse. However, our girl has more than just shitty bullies or pranksters after her.

It makes me even more pleased she mated with my twin—we can use that as an excuse for adjusting her housing if need be.

"Princess, this dorm is nicer than Cappie or Apex… but I'm glad you're staying with us."

Dolly turns to look up at me with a tiny smirk. "Leave Chessie's cooking? Never."

"Ouch, Princess. Right in the heart with that one," I chuckle as I clutch my chest. "Good to know where your loyalties lie."

She giggles and squeezes me close, reminding me that less than two years ago, she looked like a lost kitten and I was torturing her for making me feel something. We've both come a long way from that point and as much as I hate to admit it, it's in large part to my crazy ass twin refusing to let any of us write her off.

That's why no one is surprised she chose him first—nor are they upset in the slightest. He was her first and only ally at Apex.

"You know, Cori is going to be sad. You can support her, but this will hurt for a while." I look down at her as we approach the door decked out with swag and sparkle that denotes the room she's sharing with my girl's fabulous badger buddy.

Dolly sighs and nods as she looks at the door for a moment. "I know, Felix. Todd was a first class fucknozzle and I was still hurt and upset by the betrayal. Giselle made her believe they had a chance and then yanked that away at the last minute—not even in person. Cori already feels isolated by her identity. This is very damaging for her self-esteem."

Tipping her chin up, I look into her eyes with a soft smile. "I know you can relate to that. It will help your friend, but remember, any feelings that come flooding back are the past. You are adored and accepted for who you are… even if your horrible taste in men extends to my twin."

"Felix!" She smacks my arm and I see the light in her eyes brighten a bit. "I know it'll dredge some stuff up, but I do want to be there for her. No one was for me when everything went down at prom and the only thing that kept me going over that summer was my job at Luc's, revenge, and Fitz's not-so-secret gifts."

I roll my eyes, but her admission makes me smile. My idiot brother's stalking actually made her feel wanted and I could kiss him for it now. *Not that I'll ever tell him that.* "Go on. Knock on the door and let her know you're here."

Our girl leans up and presses a kiss on my lips, then pulls away. I watch her curvy ass sway as she approaches the door, looking as delectable in her yoga pants and Aubrey's tee shirt tied at her waist as she does in couture. The silence hangs for a moment until the door cracks open and there's a heated whisper exchange through the crack. Dolly holds her ground, putting her hands on her hips as she speaks to the bear hiding in her room.

I'm oddly proud of her when the door finally opens and she turns to blow a kiss at me before she walks inside.

Delores Drew is a force to be reckoned with, even when it comes to the people she loves.

ONCE I'VE DROPPED DOLLY OFF, I CUT ACROSS THE CAMPUS TO the staff housing. As a visiting professor, it's marked on a special map in our materials that isn't available to the students. They have the pred staff in a special enclave north of the small mountain range and there's a weird tunnel thing connecting it campus.

Why do all the other academies have a thing for tunnel entryways? It's bizarre as fuck.

"It doesn't matter because we're not staying here, but I want to see if I can toss that fucker's room," I mutter as I slink around the admin building to the stairs leading down to passage.

"Fucking right, we're going to search it."

I whirl around, claws out and a snarl on my lips until Fitz's face registers. "By Apollo's stinky sneakers, Fitz! I could have maimed you. Scratch that, I *should* maim you for scaring the stripes off my ass. What are you doing here?"

He grins broadly, looking pleased with himself. "I know you took D to visit her sad friend, so I got Raina to keep an eye on the building. She'll text all of us through this emergency app I built on the plane if anything seems wrong. Whoever is close can rush over, but that leaves me free to fuck shit up with you."

Every word of that is new information.

"Fitz…" I give up on words and finally nod. "Fine. I don't know anything about whatever the hell you're talking about, but I assume it's good. Let's go find out why our shithead cousin is here."

"Besides our father being a fucking jizz stain?" I snort and he shrugs as we walk into the lighted, temperature control tunnel to the other side of the rocks. "Probably because he's working some angle behind Baby Girl's mom's spotted back. That fucker has sold out almost every relative and ally he's ever had since we were born, man."

I frown. "I don't like his sudden interest in her."

"Man, I don't like *anyone's* interest in our girl, but I don't know that Pop is the imminent threat."

Squinting at him for a second, I arch a brow. "Are you and Dolly reading spy novels now?"

"Why?"

"Because 'imminent threat' is pretty fancy for you, bro." I grin and wink at him. "And when you pick up new jargon, it's often from your shared reading time."

My twin shakes his head, groaning as he waves his hand. "I fucking *wish* we were reading spy novels. Ren and I are working through the corpse nibbler's shit with her word by painful word. Never in my life did I think sexy scenes could make my cock retreat into my fucking body but…"

"That bad?"

"Bro, her females are so damn ridiculous. They're supposed to be tough like our girl, but really? It's bullshit. They have all this power and let dudes treat them like dogshit. Queen D would plant a big ass thumper in any of our asses if we spent weeks or months calling her a bitch and other shitty names."

My eyebrows raise as I contemplate that and I find I agree with my brother. Dolly served our shit right back to us from the beginning, even if she was feeling unworthy. And to be honest, none of us would ever call someone we liked ugly names just to push them away. I was a bit of a dick, but I wasn't abusive and mean. I can't imagine that being sexy.

"No, no, wait. It gets *worse*," Fitz says as we walk out of the passageway. "Wait... it's two hundred and thirty steps—remember that. Now, as I was saying, it gets worse."

The fact that my hyper, ADHD twin could count and retain the number of steps end-to-end while conversing with me is nothing short of a damn miracle. That shit is *definitely* because of all our girl's work with him. He never would have been able to do that before. Hell, he could barely sit still or stay sober for a couple hours before.

"Two-thirty. Got it," I reply. We walk into the small staff village, pausing to find a scent. "What's worse than that?"

"The dude-on-dude stuff, duh." He looks at me seriously. "That woman has *never* seen two dudes or chicks together outside of porn. It's so incredibly bad. And it's... it makes me feel gross because it's not.... meant for bi or gay dudes. It's like... meant for women, like yaoi."

Once I pick up Asani's trail, I jerk my head in that direction and we move towards the section where his cabin must be. "So you feel objectified?"

"Ab-so-fucking-lutely, man." He shivers and shakes his head. "Not just me... the smoky-eyed granite man agreed. So did Chessie. Her stuff is definitely one-handed spank bank fodder and the bondage stuff is so bad I wish I had someone to report it to."

Giving him an angry look, I ask, "Is it bothering the Princess? She's had some unfortunate parental experiences with violence that damaged her. I don't want this claptrap traumatizing her."

Fitz waits until we're standing in front of the small building covered in our cousin's scent before he answers. "No, she's okay.

Baby Girl reads through it with us and has to stop because she's laughing so hard. It's adorable."

Clapping my hand on my brother's shoulder, I let out a slow breath as I process that. There are so many things vying to hurt our bunny that I find myself worrying like an old nanny goat sometimes. Knowing we're not making it worse with this task helps. And now that I know that, I'm ready to get into this cabin and find out what plans our cousin has.

That tangled mess of a counselor isn't the only villain targeting our girl on this campus.

My Friends

Delores

"Coco? It's me, Dolly."

There's no answer and everything is quiet, but I told Felix to go ahead and scoot. Cori is the most sensitive of my tiny friend group and I know she's been hurt more than a few times in the past. While the thought of two guys has filtered it's way through the echelons of pred society since I started high school, two women together is somehow still looked down on as weird or uncomfortable to witness. I don't get it because hot people are hot people and my girl Coco is a curvy goddess in supe form.

Frowning at the internalized homophobia that runs rampant in this world, I lick my lips. Maybe that schtick is why Cori is so upset… Giselle's exit is less about our affiliation with trouble and more about appearances. Rufus' explanation of her last minute change of heart seemed off to me. Not all pred parents are as nasty as Lucille and my departed father. They may not be awesome, but I can't believe that Cori's girlfriend wouldn't know their relationship would be a huge issue from the jump.

"Cori, you have to let me in. I'm worried about you. Ru-Ru is, too, and we're not going to let you go through this alone." The silence is deafening and I wrinkle my nose, deciding to use another tactic. "You can't leave me here in the hallway alone. I already sent Felix packing."

I'm not above being a little manipulative if it means I can check on my friend.

The door opens to a makeup-less, messy, miserable looking polar bear shifter who glares at me as if she'd like to skin me alive. "That was *not* fair."

I cringe. "I know, but it's true. I knew you'd let me in and I really did send him away a few minutes ago. If I texted one of them to come get me, you know how insane they'd get. This is a new place full of new and old enemies, Coco. None of us is safe, according to Farley."

She sniffles and nods, moving to the side as I come further into the room. It's obvious how upset she is by how barren the space is still. A room Cori and Rufus share should already be blindingly blinged out, piping in hot tracks while they dance to the beat. Instead, it's full of suitcases and boxes that have yet to be touched. The only sign Cori did anything is the blanket and pillow on her bed where she's been curled up with tissues.

Turning back to my friend, I gesture to the bed. "Come on, girl. Sit down and tell me what happened. Ru-Ru was annoyingly vague and Fitz made me promise to give him details so he can suitably punish the chick who stole your sunshine."

"No!" Cori shakes her head, curls bouncing around her reddened face. "I mean, I love that he wants to get vengeance for me, but... I can't send people to attack someone for a choice they had every right to make. It doesn't feel right."

I frown, not sure I agree with her statement. Giselle had ample time to tell Cori she wasn't coming along and she didn't woman up and say so. Instead, she strung her along until the last possible second and then refused to discuss it. That's not how healthy relationship work—at least, from what the guys have taught me—and I don't like cutting her slack. This wasn't about setting reasonable boundaries or some untenable core belief mismatch.

Cori's girlfriend chose the easy route, which makes her either a coward or a hypocrite.

"Coco, I get that you care about her and I respect that you want to be the bigger person." I give her a crooked smile. "But that doesn't always get you the closure you need. We know ignoring the Heathers unless they directly provoked me only gave them an entire year to torture me. I didn't want to stoop to their level of crazy and it almost got me kicked out of Apex."

Her eyes widen and her lower lip trembles. "You think Giselle might... strike out at me? Why would she do that? *She* broke it off with me. And it wasn't because I did anything wrong, except be a girl. At least, that's what I got out of what little she texted."

I'm going to kill the bitch myself if that's really why—that's a Drew promise and as Lucille says, 'our word is your blood.'

Taking in a slow, calming breath, I walk over to the bed and sit down. "She might if the whole 'I can't be gay or I'll get disowned' thing is a ruse. I just don't know her well enough to make assumptions. Did Rufus spend more time with you two or....?"

Cori's head dips and she shakes it again, wiping her nose on her sleeve. I hand her a tissue, waiting until she's ready to continue. Something about her attitude is making my gut churn, and I hate it. I know Cori would *never* do anything to hurt me or our rag-tag family, but she's far too kind hearted. She *might* have shared things she shouldn't have with a girl she thought was her endgame. The silence is deafening, but I hold my tongue as she figures out what she wants to say.

"Giselle was the first girlfriend I've had who I thought was 'real.' I trusted her, which is why she was allowed to be at our table during the Yule Ball, and why she was coming on Farley's plane." My friend pads over, sitting across from me on the bed as she looks at me with an earnest expression. "I didn't tell her anything *really* secret, but I definitely shared some things I worry about now."

Fury races through my veins at the defeated look in the bear's eyes and her wilted posture. Cori Bouvier has been the colorful light I needed from the minute I ran into her and Rufus again on my first official day at Apex. The possibility that some chick used her to get information on me and my men, then tossed her aside like a used Kleenex makes me want to take out a small city.

If this is true, she deserves a visit from Fitz as much as Todd did. Hell, I might even join him.

"Coco, what kind of things did you share with her?"

She shrugs and flops backward on the bed, looking up at the plain ceiling. "I don't know, D. That's the problem—it was such a whirl-wind and... everyone was busy. You were dodging killers and dealing with the professors. Rufus dove into the triplets like he wanted to get lost in their fucking ocean. I was lonely and Giselle was so... perfect."

"Too perfect?" I ask softly. I hate to make her doubt herself and everything in the world, but she's not wrong. This last minute escape screams 'set-up' and we need to figure who the fuck put her up to it. *Those* people I'll let my crazy tiger deal with, for sure. How we'll address Giselle is an issue for later when my friend isn't so raw from the heartache. She might change her mind after we do some digging.

Aubrey might enjoy a bar-be-que, come to think of it. We could have a violent family outing. Nice.

A long sigh echoes in the quiet and Cori whispers, "Maybe? I only had stupid closeted bitches to compare it to. My frame of reference isn't extensive and I was so damn excited."

"Okay," I say, scrambling internally to word my next question without making her cry. "When you told her things, was it just… normal conversations as you went about your day? Or maybe were all your secrets shared alone when you were…. intimate?"

Her eyes fill with tears and I wince. I really thought I'd asked as gently as I could, but knowing whether this girl was a honey trap depends heavily on how she got Cori talking. A fresh rounds of sobs shudder through her and I lean back on my elbow so I can pat her head gently. I wish Rufus was here; he'd ask things bluntly because he's a bitch. Cori would snark back, but she would know he wasn't being mean because they've been friends for a long time.

I just feel like a super fucking asshole and I'm sure I sound like one, too.

"Oh, Coco, I'm sorry," I murmur. "It's…. We need to know what happened and it won't be any easier later on. I'm trying not to rip the bandage off too hard."

"N-No… I j-j-just feel s-s-so stupid…," she sobs. "It's like I'm the w-w-weakest link and our bad guys knew it!"

I'm not going to tell her that's likely true. For one thing, it's not helpful, but I also don't want to rub her naivete in. She's having enough trouble simply admitting she might have made a grave error. "It's never stupid to love someone. Sometimes, we get blinded by an ideal—especially if we're looking to escape parts of our lives that we wish were different. That's how it was with my ex-douchebag. I didn't know it then, but I ignored the million red flags waving at me because I *needed* to. And it took me a while to forgive myself for it, too."

"But you have *five* hot ass dudes who are your mates now!"

I chuckle and shrug. "Exactly. It took Todd and the Heathers almost *eating* me at prom to get in the right place where I met them. I had to go through the bad shit before I found the good. Kicking myself in the ass for not listening to my gut about him or those vapid bitches all summer didn't fix the problem. That didn't happen until after I'd gone all the way through the grief cycle."

"That makes sense," she mumbles from under the arm thrown over her face. "At least you didn't fuck up your whole ass family for a piece of ass."

Smacking her leg lightly, I peer down at my friend until she lifts her arm to see me. "Absolutely not, woman. We all fuck up, and we'll continue to do so 'cause it's life. We have *way* too many people gunning for us to indulge in self-pity. Now tell me what the hell you think you spilled and we'll brainstorm some damage control."

Cori pushes up until she's leaning against the dorm wall and crosses her legs. "Well, obviously I mentioned the plane, destination, and who was taking us. And I think we talked about your troubles with the zombie licker."

Fuck. For a moment, I was going to assign blame for this to my mother without fail, but now…

"What kind of things about Rockland, Coco?"

She shrugs and closes her eyes, focusing for a second. "Um, how she was bugging you about what you and the boys get up to. How freaking goddamn gross it is for some cishet fruitcake to be writing salacious garbage she knows nothing about. There was some commiserating that we don't see enough of our preference in books and then she asked if we were going to be able to block her from publishing really badly written fanfic of your life."

Arching a brow, I try not let my friend know that my heart is racing. If she spilled Farley's plan to control Rockland, we have yet another thing to re-visit in light of the planted staff on campus. The villains in our lives might not be collaborating now, but evil knows evil. If they start helping one another out, my life will get a thousand percent more dangerous very quickly.

"That's... a lot."

"I know!" Cori wails as she thumps her head against the wall. "But I was so angry for you and so irritated by such a fake ass ally that I lost perspective. I mean... Rufus has probably told the triplets even more than I did Gracie. He's so damn pissed about that woman and he hides it really well."

Pinching the bridge of my nose, I groan softly. My friends have been amazing and they'd risk their necks for anyone in our little family, but right now... I have no idea how we're going to fix a leak as big as Cori's ex. I just have to hope Fitz's pick for my other flamboyant bestie was better than the one he selected for Cori.

Wait a tick.

Fitz picked Giselle out of his students. He's got good instincts, but he's a dude. Not only that, but he's a dude with a focus issue and a really good heart. If Giselle was placed there to lure him into doing *exactly* what he did, then it would have to be someone with access to class scheduling. Lucille could have someone do that for her, but it would leave more of a trail than she'd like. This probably wasn't my mother; she wouldn't assume a lowly polar bear was of any use.

That still leaves a shit ton of other assholes to clear.

It's going to be a long night in front of the computer, I fear. Fitz won't be able to sleep until he nails down what person put Giselle in his class and when.

I may need reinforcements.

What to Do

CHESS

When my angel called for a pickup at her friend's dorm, she looked both relieved and worried. She shook her head when I asked if everything was okay and it wasn't hard to suss out why when her eyes darted around us. She's worried the common areas around have been bugged. It's not an unreasonable thought, so I put it on my list to have Fitz do scans on his equipment to find whatever surveillance systems they have—both obvious and hidden.

"Cori is going to be hurting for a bit, but she'll survive," she says as we use our badges to get into the library. "That girl hit a deep rooted button about not being good enough or worthy. I'd skin her myself, but I'd rather do a little digging first."

My lips curve up. This is why she's perfect for my crazy tiger, but the empathy she feels for her best friend is part of why she's also perfect for me. "I understand her trauma a little, Angel. For a long time, I was afraid Fitz would be forced to choose and he'd have to let go of me for his duties."

"As if," she snorts. I grin, my cheeks flushing as we walk into the chaos of the Captain's crew working in the main area of the suite. "Fitzy would *never*, Chessie. His heart is too big and his love too ferocious. Plus, he hates being told what to do."

"Noooooot truuuuuuuue," my mate sing-songs as he rushes over to scoop her up, smacking her ass as she drapes over his shoulder. "I *love* when you order me around, Baby Girl. My dick's hard just thinking about it."

"Fitz, your dick gets hard thinking about garlic bread," Felix retorts from his spot at the counter.

The tiger shrugs, carrying our girl into the kitchen. "I can't resist the cheesy goodness and tangy flavor, man. Food gets our bunny going, too, you know. Give her a hard time."

"I'd be delighted," Felix mutters and I burst out laughing.

Fuck, it's good to see him so unbuttoned and relaxed again.

"Felix, tell him to put me down," Dolly grumbles as she wiggles. "We have lists to make."

I blink, grinning brightly as I hold up a finger. "No boards for a couple days, but I have notebooks. Back in a flash."

They're chuckling as I sprint to my room and dig out an unused notebook, labeling it 'Academie' in Sharpie. Finding a good pen, I ponder what else I'll need, but decide I can't get fancy with all the shit going on in our room right now. I head back to the kitchen, sitting next to the Raj and looking up at them.

"I'm ready. Let's get organized."

Aubrey comes out of the door to the library annex with Renard at exactly the right moment, arching his brow as he sees us. "Someone forget to summon us?"

I shake my head as I pull my hair back into a topknot. "Not at all. I just brought our girl back from Cori's and she wanted to sit down before it gets busy. I was going to text you shortly."

Renard slinks over and hops on the counter, looking disgruntled that he can't lounge in the chairs because of the work being done. "Good idea, *petite*. We should write everything we need to do as we think of it so Chess is able to create our workspace when all his things arrive"

"Now that we're all here…" Felix drawls in amusement. "We should get started."

"Fitz." Dolly thumps his back and he finally lets her down. She hops on the counter, sitting opposite Ren as she swings her feet. "So, when I was letting Cori hash out her pain, I thought about how it was lucky that Rufus' guys are legit."

"I picked them out," Fitz crows, then frowns. "Wait."

My angel nods, tapping her nose. "That's exactly the conclusion I came to, baby. You *also* picked Giselle out of your classes, and she was *new* to the program but very skilled."

"A plant," Aubrey says with a grimace. "We missed it entirely because of all the chaos at the time."

Covering my face with my palms, I scrub them over my features before picking up my pen again. I feel terrible that the cheery polar bear got hurt because we missed a step. Fitz will be off-the-chain that he was used, and I don't blame him. "She was so happy after the first date that we didn't vet her."

"That's a mistake we will not make again, eh, *mes amis*?" Renard says firmly. "No one new comes into our sphere, or the spheres of our friends, without being vetted down to their colonoscopies."

Dolly snickers, but sobers quickly. "Agreed. That includes the crew, my friends, Coach Z, Farley and his gang, Luc... anyone who is close enough to us to matter. I don't want to be responsible for broken hearts anymore."

"When I find out who sent her or who bribed her parents... or *whatever*..." Fitz's eyes flicker with his tiger and I know he's imagining doing things that would turn the stomach of most preds. "There won't be enough of them left to identify."

Felix gives him a nod. "And you will have your revenge, brother, but for now, we keep a low profile. You know we didn't find shit about us in our cousin's love shack and that means they expected us to toss it."

"Nothing? Damnit," Dolly pouts, kicking her heels against the counter in frustration. "I thought you said he's an idiot."

Fitz laughs, putting his hands on her thighs. "He is, Baby Girl. That means someone is running the show that's *not* an idiot and they have a tight grip on his leash."

I frown as I scribble notes about this. "How are we going to catch Asani if he's not behaving as we expect him to?"

Felix grins, and this time, it's full of sharp teeth. "I said we didn't find anything pertaining to us or our girl. But we didn't find nothing. He's still pulling shady shit with our father's accounts and messing around with preds he shouldn't. That evidence we snapped pictures of for later, but until we know what his game is here, we can't use it."

"I hate this crap," my angel says with a huff. "I know we have to be careful and smart, but I also just want to kill them like Fitz suggested, too."

Talk about bringing out the animal in each other... it's adorable.

"So what do we need to do so we're protected right off the bat, guys? That's the main concern for us to handle while D gets settled in her classes," I say, hoping to change the topic to one less charged with emotion.

Renard tilts his head, thinking for a moment, then holds up a finger. "Doorways and security. Theirs sucks and I'd like Fitzgerald to program our chips."

I write that down, glad he thought of it. It didn't even occur to me when I swiped us in the door earlier. "Okay, what else?"

"Deep background on that little shit who hurt Coco-cabana. I can't focus unless I can plan my vengeance for that."

Dolly smiles brightly, throwing her arms around his neck and squeezing. "Thank you for loving her as much as I do."

Fitz actually blushes and it gets a laugh out of us all. "Your people are my people, Baby Girl. Forever."

His twin clears his throat, looking at the clock. "Keep going. It's getting late and we have an early morning."

Remembering my earlier thought, I look at my mate. "Fitzy, we need you to make an app or something. We need to be able to get into all the security systems here, obvious and hidden, to know when it's safe to talk or do shit. Also, we need to know if people are watching or listening in places we wouldn't expect. Can you handle that while the background is running?"

He beams, making flirty eyes at me. "Anything for you, Chessie. Plus, I don't want anyone seeing our girl in places they shouldn't without losing their eyeballs."

"Agreed," the dragon snarls and the bunny in question hops off the counter to walk over and melt against him. "Snack size, that's cheating."

He doesn't let her go, though. I grin to myself and make notes about the proposed app, then look up at Felix. "What else?"

"We need to find out about the stony man's feeling as we drove in," Fitz says. "He said something about treason and we didn't push him on it."

The gargoyle's tail whips out immediately and whips back and forth like an angry cat. "We don't need to find out what they are —I *know* what they are, just not *why* they are here. Or who is allowing them to stay in the area."

Our girl pulls out of the dragon's arms, heading over to the agitated emo boy and looks up at him. "Rennie. Don't pout and be angry with us. It's clear this triggers you and if we don't know why, we can't help."

His voice is soft as he looks into her eyes. "Finding out the Fae are back is bad enough. But… I wasn't ready to come to our new home and scent vampires. They were supposed to be wiped out. Totally gone and dusted."

I'm sorry, what?

No one speaks for a moment and finally, the shock wears off so I can speak. "*Vampires?*"

"No way, rock man. They're not real, dude." Fitz crosses him arms over his chest and gives him a skeptical expression.

"Not true," Aubrey says quietly. "Again, we are far older than you, and we did not recieve the biased education given to shifters after the Treaty."

"Just fucking awesome," Dolly mutters as she tip her head back and looks at the ceiling in supplication. "How the hell did I piss off some supposedly extinct or non-existent supernatural *this* time?"

Renard shakes his head. "I don't know that they're here for you, but they *are* dangerous, unpredictable, and illegal to create or give refuge to."

The Raj scratches his chin, looking thoughtful. "Perhaps they were never extinct, much like the Fae were never fully contained in Faerie. Maybe they, too, went underground until the right moment dropped in their laps."

"Which means they're likely in cahoots with the winged rebels," Aubrey grumbles. "The two species make a very formidable team, especially if they're true allies, not just… convenient ones."

My angel stomps her foot looking at the ancient shifters with a pissed off expression. "Anything else you two want to share about things that go bump in the night and might pop up out of nowhere?"

They look at one another and shrug. Finally, Aubrey sighs as he shifts uncomfortably. "Since two beings we never expected to see again have appeared, I suppose it puts nearly anything on the table. There could be all manner of supernaturals thought to be gone that were hiding with the sparkly magic users. It's too numerous to list."

She lets out a shriek of fury, and I grin as her claws, ears, and tail pop free. "This is such *bullshit*. How am I supposed to get an education or you know, fuck my goddamn boyfriends, when the entire cast of *Supernatural* is after me?"

"Baby Girl…" Fitz's grin doesn't make her any less pissy, but she lets him grab her and wrap his arms around her. "It doesn't matter if we're trapped in a fucked up *Scooby-Doo* or even some fantasy show the Pouty Poet would love. We'll help protect you and we'll *definitely* fuck the shit out of you regardless."

"Seconded," the dragon rumbles as he shrugs. "I'm not afraid of creatures that can be killed with a pointy stick."

Ren rolls his eyes at his mate, his tail flicking again. "Flames, you *know* that's not how you kill them if you want them to *stay* dead."

"Don't be pedantic, Rennie, I—"

"Gentleman." Felix rises, giving us all a 'I'm in charge' look as as he runs his hand through his hair. "Squabbling and coddling doesn't fix the underlying issue. This vampire bullshit is *another* thing on our plate until we know differently, so Princess is right to be frustrated. We have too many things on our theoretical boards and some of it needs to go."

"Exactly," Dolly says as she looks up from Fitz's neck. "Lucille aced out Bruno, which helps, but now he's been replaced by stupid bloodsuckers. I can't win for losing."

I hate to admit it, but she's right.

I Don't Trust Anyone Anymore

Delores

This is the first morning of classes and I'm freaking out a little. I've got the *Academie* uniform on exactly as pictured in the handbook and my hair is behaving, but the butterflies in my stomach as I finish putting on the dusting of makeup won't quit.

I don't have the twins' cousin today, but I'm still worried since he was seen with other professors in Paris.

"You're fine, Dolly," I say as I stare in the mirror. "Last semester helped you get in touch with the bunny and you're working on the blue shit. Most of the ex-idiots aren't around, so now it's just new bullshit. You can handle that."

My reflection is only mouthing back the words I'm saying, so I take a deep breath and center myself. It's been hard to unlearn the shit Lucille drilled into me from a young age about my worthlessness. I have moments when I'm super confident and I feel like I can take on the entire world. Other times, I fall back into old habits and doubt myself, especially when I have to deal with new authority figures and possibly judgmental peers.

Progress is hard, no matter how much support you have in your circle.

A knock distracts me and the door opens to my poetic gargoyle smiling mischievously. Rennie whistles low and I grin, doing a little twirl for him. That makes him rumble softly as the skirt flares and again when I turn to walk over to my bed to grab my bags.

"*Perfectment, ma petite,*" he says and I have to squeeze my thighs together as the gravelly French I adore.

"You're biased," I reply as I stride over to him to plant a light kiss on his cheek. "But I'll take encouragement in any form."

"Get your cute butt in here and eat before Felix spanks it!"

I giggle, looking up at Rennie, who shrugs. "Fitzgerald is correct. You need to fuel up for classes today. There are many physical activities in your schedule."

"Ugh, I know. Hopefully, I won't be *too* far behind these folks. This place is entirely focused on arts and nowhere I've attended has had a program this intense."

Renard offers his arms, his eyes fond as he shakes his head at me. "None of that, *lapin*. I have learned you are capable of anything you put your mind to, and this will be no different."

I hope to hell he's right, or I'm going to drown here.

"*ECOUTEZ!*[1]"

My head jerks up immediately when the huge bird squawks her command in rough French. Madame Bissonette scares the living hell out of me already despite being an omnivore that eats things much smaller than me when her mood suits. I didn't know a damn thing about cassowary shifters before I walked into my Theater History class almost an hour ago, but I sure as fuck do now.

She made it *very* clear that they're the third largest bird in the world and will happily eat some smaller animals if they feel like it. I had to Google which ones when she wasn't looking, but I know I'm safe. Some of the reptilian and water preds might not be, depending on their size, especially since none of the other universities limit their student body to *apex* predators like my original school did.

"You will put down your pencils, styli, pens, or whatever you are using to complete your quizzes." Her dark, beady eyes glare until she sees everyone click off their tech or stop scratching on their pages. Oddly, she actually allows students to complete things in paper format, which I haven't seen since I was in primary school. "Now, as I stated earlier, this will determine whether I demand you be knocked back to re-take Theater History 101 or if you stay in this class for the semester. I refuse to catch up those who have not earned their place, even if it's due to a lack of curriculum vigor at other schools."

I don't look away as she glares at each of the transfer students like they've offended her ancestry. Giving her the power to make me cower isn't something I'm willing to do, even if she's fucking terrifying. Once she looks away from me, I dart my eyes around the room to see which people I know. We didn't get to do so when we entered the room earlier—the damn attack bird stopped each person at the door before either handing them a test book or a slip with a link on it. She made it clear we wouldn't have a second to spare if we wanted to pass the damn thing.

That's why I hippity-hopped in, dropped into a chair and got to work without watching anything else.

My gaze snags on the two Heathers who couldn't help but follow me like the weirdly obsessed stalkers they are. Since Todd and his bud went missing, their last bros and Heather C. have defected from the band of bullies. They stayed at Cappie as far as I can tell, but I have no idea how in the shit these dimwits got into this class with me. They're not even arts majors, so this is some sort of insane set-up to allow them to spy on or torture me.

"*Nique tes morts*[2]," I mutter under my breath. It's a vulgar as hell swear Rennie taught me, but even Fitz approves of this one. The dead bodies cinch it for him, I know, but I'm enjoying being able to mumble shit not everyone will understand if they hear me.

The stern avian professor gathers all the actual paper tests, then stands at the front of the room looking like she's going to charge anyone who argues. "You will sit silently for the next fifteen minutes until it is time to go to your next class or break. It is good for those wishing to command the attention of other preds to know how to be quiet and keep your power."

Fine with me. I don't want to engage with the people here, anyway.

MY VOICE PRACTICUM AND BALLET CLASS GO WELL, DESPITE MY immediate distrust of Madame Alexandré because of her Council ties. Fabreaux is no better, but I can definitely take the swan shifter no matter how rude and aggressive they are. A blue whale is simply enormous and I haven't a damn clue what the hell she can or can't do on land; that's why I'm putting Alexandré on my 'Sus List.'

You'd think when I felt like my 'Fuck 'Em Up, Sis' was mostly crossed off, I wouldn't have to do this shit anymore, but here we are.

I'm exhausted as hell when I head for the annex to grab my lunch. It's not a long break, so no funny business allowed. That's disappointing, but I don't want to piss off any professors by being late in addition to simply existing. My next class is Tap with Professor

O'Shea and I'll need the energy boost. I can't skip to explore or even to find Rufus and Cori.

"Yoo-hoo… anyone here?" I call as I swipe the temporary badge on the door to enter.

When no one answers, I trudge into the kitchen, dropping my bags on the floor. The fridge has a wrapped plate full of protein packed food with a post-it bearing my name and a cute little drawing on it. Chessie is my favorite for the moment, so I put my plate on the counter and find his pad to leave a matching note that I post on the outside of the appliance. Once I do that, I sit down and dig into my food.

The bad news from this morning—besides the staff and the Heathers—is that as expected, transfers will have to prepare jury performances by the end of the year despite the late start. It means I'll have to put together a five to ten minute fully fleshed out performance in Voice, Ballet, Tap, Modern, and Acting that includes every freaking piece to a real show. I'll have to see if Coco and Ru-Ru can help as part of *their* juries; otherwise, the costuming and directing will be big gaps. I can choreograph, pick pieces, record music, and the rest, but I'll never get those things done alongside the first two.

"Fucking bullshit if you ask me," I mutter around a huge bite of the salad with various nutrients shoved into it by my perfectionist cheetah. "And I hate fucking lettuce."

Ironic, I know, because… bunny. But I really do.

"Ah, but your diet must be balanced during training, bite size."

My head whips around and I arch a brow at the silent moving dragon. "Spying on me, big guy?"

"Just came to grab a snack of my own and here you were," Aubrey says as he comes closer and presses a kiss to my temple.

Pushing at his shoulder playfully, I snort. "It better not be me 'cause I have neither the time *nor* the cleanliness to allow that shit. I'm a sweaty mess from dance class."

He shrugs as he reads the note to Chessie, then opens the fridge. "As if I'd give a shit. But no, I have to get back before some lazy ass professor sends another full class of freshman to create all their log-ins and emails."

Frowning as I take another big bite of the stupid greens and chicken concoction, I wave my fork at him. "That's dumb. Why the fuck didn't the idiots do that before they got here?"

He gives me a wry look, then taps his nose as he pulls out a meaty charcuterie with his name on a note as well. "The oft asked and utterly unanswerable question, lunchable. I like to believe it's the entitlement of the students coming to private universities. They believe everything will be done for them and I have no interest in propagating that thought, even if it would make my life easier to have Betsy do it for the little shits."

I grin as he sits on the other side of me, tearing into the snack like he hasn't eaten in weeks. "You know, you're very well mannered most of the time, but when you're hungry, you're a straight up savage."

The dragon pauses his inhaling of the food to smirk at me. "I thought you didn't have time for that."

Swatting his arm as I flush, I stuff more of my vegetable-legume torture into my mouth before I say something that causes me to be late for class. He chuckles into his food, smugness wafting from his form like a perfume. We eat in silence for a few moments, then my librarian nudges me with his shoulder.

"Are your classes going well so far? Rennie is quite concerned about the professors, especially because of the…" Aubrey makes a face, using his fingers as fangs and I giggle.

"I haven't seen any vampires or even anyone as emo as him, so we're probably safe on that front." I sigh and tilt my head, thinking about what I've done so far with a more critical bent. "I don't know what side, if any, Bissonette is on. She's a holy terror, but that may simply be species stuff."

"Mmm. Good to know. We can have Fitz dig some more on her. Go on," he says as he bites into a big sausage.

Resisting the urge to snigger, I continue. "Alexandré is under suspicion because of Council ties. She was tough, but not overtly biased. It could be an act; it could be nothing. Fabreaux *does not* like me, but she seems to dislike everyone who is a transfer or not French. Hard to tell there."

Aubrey rumbles, his expression pleased as he leans in and squeezes me to his side. "A fair assessment, snack size. You're getting better at analyzing motives before you assign a designation."

"Uh-huh. What you really mean is 'that was very mature for your age, Dolly.' I'm not dim, buddy."

Laughing as he wipes his mouth with his free hand, my dragon nods. "I see your tongue is sharp today as well." I give him a wry expression and he shrugs. "Of course I meant you're maturing. It's not something to feel bad about. We all grow and change, and with that, maturity makes us see things differently than we did in the past. You are healing from a traumatic childhood and growing up so it's like a one-two punch."

"Whatever, old man," I snark as he looks aghast. "Just kiss me before I have to head out into the ugly world of intrigue and people who want me dead. I need that armor to keep me sane."

And I do, because I have no idea what I'm coming up against until Pred Games practice.

ADAGIO IN G MINOR

WHILE BEING IN ONE OF MY MANY HOMELANDS IS QUITE PLEASANT, I'm struggling not to take to the skies to hunt down the blood-suckers lurking somewhere on the campus. They are not students —the Council would never allow it—that doesn't change the fact that anyone old enough to remember their kind has to know they are here. When I was a child, they were prevalent as no one restricted their access to the humans and their numbers grew exponentially in some areas of the world. Vampires kept to them-selves other than feeding and their businesses—all geared toward the darker aspects of the psyche.

Supes may run sex clubs, gambling halls, and have their own mercenary groups, but it used to be the shadows where the fanged assholes thrived.

I'm not opposed to any of those things on principle; they all have their uses. But vampires see everyone as a potential meal, a recruit, or a target. They have a black and white view of the world and the powers to back up their claims. Since they disappeared with the Fae, information about them has disappeared from curriculum and family teachings. That means every student and staff member here is in danger with no knowledge of how to protect themselves.

"Such short-sighted morons in our leadership," I sigh as I rifle through the texts in the oldest part of my mate's library. "Hiding the past as if it will never come back to haunt them."

"Who are you talking to?"

My frown turns to a smile as the grumpy dragon returns from his lunch break. Jinx is following him and when he gets closer, I scent our girl on him. "Who were *you* talking to is the better question, *mon amour.*"

He gives me a rakish grin, running his hand through the shaggy locks he seems to be growing out like everyone else. I've never seen my dragon with hair this unkempt in our many years together, but it looks good. "Snack size dropped in for lunch just as I went up to forage for a bite. She gave me a run-down of her professors so far."

"Mmm," I reply as I flick through another folder full of documents. "Was it as bad as we feared?"

The heat of his body hits me as he joins me at the table. Aubrey runs warm because of his fire, so we all adapt to the lower temperatures needed to keep every room from being an oven. It's not a trial since many shifters run hot anyway, but he's on another level. Turning to face him, I wait for the information patiently as he compiles it in his mind.

"She said most of them ranged from downright rude to standoff-ish. There were two more sessions left on her day, but the last one is with Zhenga. They've patched up their differences since the sex ed bullshit, so that should be fine." The dragon frowns, grabbing my hand to pause my progress. "What's that map? Something about it looks different than the one we have."

I roll my eyes at him. "Other than the fact that it's like a hundred years old?"

"Yes, smart mouth," he replies as he squeezes my wrist. "Topography... I caught it out of the corner of my eye as you were flipping through. I'm not sure, but pull the damn thing out and let's look."

Despite needing glasses when he's not in dragon form, Aubrey's eye for detail is immaculate—when he gives a shit.

Pulling the delicate map out of the pile carefully, I spread it out on the table still in the protective covering. If I don't open it, we won't have to get out all his archivist shit. I enjoy having a bit of roleplay with the nerdy librarian at times, but having to take a thousand steps to view something is tedious. I'm surprised Dolly can bear it, except that she seems to have infinite patience for all of our hyper-fixations.

"See that?" Aubrey points to a section of the map beyond the main campus. "This isn't on our maps; they're designed to only show the main area. But I think this forest, these mountains, the graveyard, and this other lake are all part of the campus. They'd only stop making additions to avoid those places if there was no reason."

I frown, looking at the map, then tapping my lips to think about it. "We need to check property records to make certain they belong to *Academie*. If so, I fear you may be correct. All of those locations would be good for hiding things like secret vaults or vampires or whatever the fuck else they have up their sleeves."

Aubrey groans, rolling his eyes up to the ceiling. "You want the Smackbook."

"I do, *mon amour*. I don't know why you pretend to be so allergic to technology when you love what it can do for you."

He pushes back from the table, not answering as he huffs off to grab the laptop. I shake my head fondly as I go back to studying the sections of the map that we've identified. Much like the ritual space and vaults at Apex, they comprise the borders of the school. At Cappie, the secret shit was right underneath—though that could be because of their location and proximity to the tunnels in the Capital. I wish we'd gotten to explore that part of the city while we were living there, but we simply did not have the time.

Fucking Fae and asshole Council ruined a lovely tour through history; I'll suggest we go back when this is over.

"*Merde,*' I whisper to myself. "I cannot allow Dolly to miss the sights and rich beauty of Paris while we're here. Shadowy enemies be damned, we will visit the city I adore before we leave."

An idea forms and I grin broadly as the picture weaves in my head. I know exactly how to make sure that doesn't happen—I'll ask her on a date. We can go to the city and see the sights together on a starry night, as it should be experienced. None of us were able to take Dolly off campus last year and I think this is the perfect time to remedy that.

"Why are you smiling like a Cheshire Cat?" my mate says as he lumbers back in the room with his poor laptop. "No pranks in my library, Renard Laveaux."

"I wouldn't dare, Flames." Crossing my finger over my heart, I give him a solemn look. "At least, not in the archive room. I'm not Fitzgerald."

That distracts him as he hands me the computer while ranting about the tiger's ass and balls being rubbed all over his clean room at Apex. I knew it would, and as I click through the web to find where we can access property ownership rolls, my mind wanders to a perfect date set-up. It will have to be a long weekend, perhaps, or maybe the spring break time so we aren't constrained by activities so much.

"Rennie... Rennie..."

Whoops.

"*Oui?*" I ask innocently as I tune back into him. "I'm waiting for results."

"They appear to be ready," he replies, his brow arching as he studies me. "Though you were a million miles away for a moment."

Sighing, I click the link to pull up the map surveys of the area. "Fine. I had the brilliant idea to take *ma petite* on a date to Paris. It's one of my homes, and I'd love to see her experience it. Plus, none of us got to do a lot of wooing last year, and she deserves more than underground fights and vault thieving."

He ponders for a moment, then gives me a stern look. "Dolly enjoyed the hell out of her date to the fights with Felix, I believe. She also liked visiting my horde nearby, but I agree that we were limited in our ability to do such things once we were locked down. I think Fitz and Chess were disappointed as well. You should continue your plan, love. Your romantic aspirations will certainly appeal to her soft side."

"You're not mad?"

"Of course not. I want to take her on a hunt with us again, as that is our little thing together. I'm sure Chess and Fitz will have plans for her together and separately. Even the grumpy Raj might plot activities with everyone and privately. Our mate is always excited to do anything with any of us—even when it's Felix's blasted cardio runs."

I chuckle softly. She *hates* to run, but she goes with the surly tiger without much more than a few snarky barbs. "You're right, Flames. I was being silly by hiding it. Your input was valuable last time, if I remember correctly."

Aubrey beams and bumps my shoulder with his. "Now get to work. The map is almost downloaded."

The WiFi speed in this part of the library is almost untenable since it's underground, so I tap my fingers on the table as we wait for the last bit to hit our screen. When the map is revealed, I zoom in, checking the property lines and the borders carefully. Aubrey was correct—while the current maps don't list those areas as part of campus, they definitely belong to the school.

"Ten dollars says the fucking vampires are hiding in the—"

"Graveyard?" he smirks.

I roll my eyes at him. "No, don't be ridiculous. That's a human myth. Why the hell would they stay in the dirt? They're probably living on the lake edge. They don't like water, but there's ample room for structures on the far side, and they could build cool underground caves for their newly turned childer to cross over in."

The dragon scratches his chin. "They don't have sun issues once they've been turned for over a century, right?"

"Right, but they need places for the younger ones to hunker down until they age out. Depending on how large the horde is, they'll have normal looking houses where smaller sub-groups live together above ground."

"I'd think the forest is better for that," he says as he grabs the mouse and pans the map. "It's very dense, by the look of the drawings."

Swallowing hard, I shake my head. "It's not them I worry about inhabiting the forest, *mon ami*."

"Fucking Fae and their ilk," he snarls as he pushes back from the table. "That's who you think will hide there."

"Indeed. If they truly are larger in number and hiding all over the world, this would be a perfect place to infest to spy on our bunny." Squinting, I look at the massive amount of trees that stretches for miles. "And since it's so damn large, we'll have a shit time trying to pin point where they all are."

"Goddamn, I hate this. Dolly has enough to do to catch up here without worrying about rebel Fae or hungry vampires." Aubrey scrubs his hand down his face, looking annoyed and exhausted at the same time.

He's right, but we don't have an option.

"If we hunt down the bloodsuckers and they're benign, we can cross them off." My eyes close and I imagine Chess' list. "The ex boyfriend and most of her ex-bullies are done, thanks to the Fae kidnappers. We've got Farley helping with the corpse licker. The tigers are laser focused on the crooked staff." I tick things off my fingers, trying to re-group.

"Her bitch mother took her asshole father off the board permanently."

I growl softly. "That one was both helpful and irritating at the same time. I think we all wanted a piece of the brutish croc."

"Agreed. Though, he was nothing in terms of enemies. Her mother is the real problem." There's a slight pause as my mate thinks about his words before he says them. "Will we have to deal with your clutch here?"

I shake my head. "No. The last nests were in Bavaria. Notre Dame was rebuilt, but I cannot imagine the clutch returning to Paris even if it's just as magnificent as it's predecessor."

"You're certain?"

I nod. "I am, Flames. The gargoyles love the mountains and their home there. They would not return here, and definitely not without a word, even if I am exiled."

At least, I fucking hope they wouldn't.

Lose Yourself

Delores

Coach Z really put us through the paces at the practice today. By the time we finished, I was soaked in sweat and cursing under my breath. We spent most of the time working on endurance and cardio—something that I'll have to keep in mind since it follows my Tap Practicum two days a week. Professor O' Shea is energetic as *fuck* and he kept the steam rolling through the entire two hour block with very small breaks for water.

I feel like a limp noodle and I'm not in such bad shape that I should be panting.

"Alright, gather up!" Zhenga yells. She's eying the competitors who are much worse off than me with thinly veiled disgust. "You people, with very few exceptions, are the most poorly trained team I've ever worked with. The previous trainers should be drawn and quartered—it's no wonder the school withdrew before the finals last year."

"BITCH," A GIRL IN THE BACK MUTTERS AND MY HEAD WHIPS around. The girl is doubled over, her hands on her thighs as she struggles to stay upright. I don't know what her major is here, but she's got a long road to hoe if she wants to stay out of the hospital.

The lioness smirks, waiting for any other commentary before she continues. "You're right; I *am* a bitch. But that doesn't mean I'm wrong. I grew up in these games from being part of the Leonidas family as a child to competing in secondary school to competing in the male professional Games as an adult. None of you would survive my childhood coaching, much less the actual players in school. You're going to get hurt, but worse, you'll embarrass your families. We all know that's a much worse sin than ending up on crutches."

There's a lot of mumbled whispers and I wonder why the hell these people are even here if they don't want to be the best. It wouldn't have flown at Apex—not even for something as small as a newspaper position and Cappie was just as bad. *L'Academie*'s focus is so heavily on the arts that it seems like the students are completely indifferent to everything else in the world.

Would have been nice, but I wouldn't trade all the bad shit at Apex for my guys or my friends.

"Coach, what do we need to do before Wednesday?" I ask, hoping to cut this pity party off so I can trudge home and die in my own bed.

Zhenga grins toothily. "For those of you lacking, I'd suggest running the campus perimeter in the morning and once again at night for the next week. I have eyes everywhere, so I'll know who is taking me seriously."

This time, I join the groans. My schedule is packed and I already run with Felix in the morning, but I'll have to choose someone else for the evenings. I can't deal with his sporty pep twice in a day, that much I'm absolutely certain about. The circuit of the campus takes about thirty minutes at a good clip, I think, and I'm dreading the time he's going to make me set our alarm for.

"Now get your shit together and go carbo load. You need it, but don't skimp on the protein," she says as she turns her back to us.

I grab my bag quickly, hurrying to catch up to the woman I'm trying to make a decent relationship with. "You could have eased them into this, you know," I mumble.

"Dolly, you and I both know these shifters are going to get *smashed* in their first matches if they don't get their shit together. They don't have secret weapons like you."

My face flushes and I shrug. "Maybe not, but no one has ever taken the time to actually train them. This place is clearly only interested in the arts and I have no idea how you even have enough students for a team."

"Never underestimate the desire to be good at *something*, rather than *nothing*," Z chuckles as she stops mid-way to the locker rooms. "Why are you following me? Don't you have five men who are probably wearing a hole in your carpet?"

I snort, shaking my head. "Pretty sure Fitz is hanging about somewhere. I can feel him."

Her eyes widen and she grips my arm. "Holy shit, you did it. You really mated with the crazy motherfucker."

"Shhhhh!" I chastise as I look around to see if anyone is close by.

"We can't have that getting back to the wrong ears yet. But… yes."

Her smile is rueful as she studies me. "You will with Felix, too. And the rest."

"Duh." I roll my eyes. That's the dumbest statement I've heard all day and my classes have been *full* of weird shit. "But when we're ready. Fitzy and I were."

"Makes sense. He was obsessed with you first." Coach runs her hand over her hair, looking around with a wistful sigh. "Congrats, though. But I doubt that's why you're haunting me, Drew, so spit it out."

"My best friend Cori… you know, the polar bear?" I lick my lips, feeling nervous despite the fact that I don't think she'll say no. "She's having a hard time. And she's a fucking amazing designer who could probably integrate this into her end of year project, but um… I think she should design the uniforms."

There's a long pause and I meet her gaze, hoping my expression conveys how much this means to me. "She's a Bouvier, right?"

I nod. "Not happily connected, but yes."

"Hmmm." Z says as she scratches her chin. "That could work. An exiled Leonidas, running a re-vamped team with the exiled Drew heir, and the exiled Bouvier designing. It's like a 'fuck you' tour, huh?"

"It sure as fuck is." My smile is getting bigger and I almost remind her that having her design the boys uniforms since they're coached by the exiled Khans is a good plan, too. I need to make sure Cori can handle that before I dump thirty people on her.

"And the twins are exiled, too," Zhenga says. Her eyes dance as she grabs my hand. "You realize with this I can bug the dance idiots to put together cheerleaders. A full-on performance at half times… it would need a choreographer, a designer for effects… This is my way in."

"Way in to what?" I frown as she gets more excited, worrying that perhaps I've started something bigger than I intended. "What are you scheming about?"

"Dolly, I'm trying to help you and those malcontents. We need a way to get the staff to see me as one of them, not one of you. With this idea, I can appeal to their egos. They'll jump at the chance to be on the world stage with the league, especially if I hint it could get them a meeting with my asshole father."

Ohhhh. She wants to set a trap.

"Felix wants you to help keep an eye on his cousin, doesn't he?" I guess. Her smirk is answer enough, and I sigh. "He's really worried about this dude. Is he overreacting?"

Zhenga lets go of me, jerking her head toward the locker room. "Walk with me again. I don't want anyone overhearing."

Nodding, I walk alongside her, dying to know what she's so worried about. "Okay, spill."

"I can't spill all of it. It's not my story to tell and he never told me directly. This is all gossip, mind you. But…" Coach Z pauses for a moment before finishing, "…rumor has it that Asani was part of his exile. When the prey girl he loved chose the Raj's deal, Asani was who she was given to. No one's heard from her since."

I can't mask the look of horror on my face. "He *killed* her? I mean, I know that place is vicious and I know they're all terrible. But he took her just to off her? Why the fuck even bother?"

"I don't know, Dolly. This may not be the actual sequence of events, either. There was a lot of gossip when the Raj sent those boys packing to Apex. Felix and I were never close enough, nor was he *sober* enough, to ever discuss it."

My chest aches when I think of how betrayed he must have felt —by damn near everyone around him—and how sad he must have been when they got to Apex. Felix feels things just a strongly as his twin, but he's so much more reserved. I can't help but wonder if part of that comes from this awful piece of his past.

"Thank you for being honest with me. I won't push him about it, but I hope he shares with me someday. I get why he's having such an episode about Asani now, too."

And I do… he's terrified that Asani will hurt me.

"You know, I didn't think anyone could wrangle that group of grumpy ass misanthropes. I pretended I could deal to win Felix over, but deep down, I knew. I'm glad they have you; they're actually happy now." Her lips quirk as she adds, "But no less grumpy."

I chuckle, winking as we walk up to the door. "I don't think anything can fix that. They're determined to make the world think they're all going to tear them to pieces if they so much as speak to any of them. It's frustrating as hell."

"Go home, Dolly. I'll get cleaned up here and make a visit to the theater dorm to talk to your friend. I want to get this shit moving quickly."

"See you Wednesday, Coach." Saluting the lioness, I turn on my heel only to run into the girl who was damn near dying on the field. She's glaring at me like I offended her ancestors and I blink slowly.

"What were you discussing with her?" the girl demands as she puts her hands on her hips.

Uh, who the fuck are you to interrogate me?

I don't say that, though, because it's my first day and I'd like to have *less* enemies than I had at my previous two universities. "Nothing. Just team stuff."

"If you think you're going to use the fact that she was your coach before to get the captain spot, think again."

Squinting at her in confusion, I hold my hands up. "Whoa. We didn't have captains at Cappie. You guys have a captain?"

"Mon Dieu, tu es plus stupide que tu en as l'air.[1]*"*

Her face is a mask of disgust and I'm almost too shocked to answer. Unfortunately, mean girl antics are something I'm *far* too used to. "Look... whoever you are. We didn't have that position at my old school because we compete individually and honestly, I think it's stupid. You don't have to worry about me."

"You don't know who I *am?*" she practically screeches.

Hera, take the wheel because I am too tired for this shit.

"Nope," I say with a pop of sass. "No idea."

Straightening to her full height, the girl suddenly loses all appearance of being tired and wiped out. Her smile is wicked as she tilts her head and bats her lashes. "My name is Fellicia O' Leary."

I wrinkle my nose, giving her a blank stare. Even if I *knew* who the fuck that was, I'd never give her the satisfaction. She said it like she was announcing the Queen of England. "And?"

Her voice is a rough whisper when she stalks closer to me, pointing a semi-clawed finger in my direction. "Listen, you waste of space. My father talks, so I know who you are. Since those losers you date killed my exiled brother at the school you destroyed, I'm aware you have protection. But I won't let you take this from me—I specifically had my shit wiped so I could come here to be the fucking *star.*"

I tilt my head back, looking up at the sky for help, but as usual, no one strikes down the target of my rage with lightning. It's all such bullshit. When I look back at the wolf, my expression is bored as hell. "Look, Felina, I'm not here to take your spotlight. I'll compete because I like it and I'm good at it. If you win, you win. But I could give a shit less who your family is, especially the guy my boyfriend beheaded for threatening to rape me after he killed me. So do us both a favor and *fuck all the way off.*"

She snorts. "Gregor was weak after they exiled him. I'm stronger, especially now that I'm next in line. And it's *Fellicia.*"

Just fucking fabulous.

"Fine. You do you, boo. I'm going home to eat and catch up on the ungodly amount of work I have to do since I came here mid-semester. We're done here."

Before she can spit another insult, I reach inside, asking my bunny to help my speed off. Winking, I take off at a much faster speed than I showed on the track, headed for the library and the safety of my family.

Fitz is going to lose his mind.

FUNERAL PLANNING

Fitz

I'M GOING TO SKIN THAT BITCH AND MAKE A RUG OUT OF HER HIDE.

"Fitzy, calm down," our girl says as she strokes her fingers over my face. "I handled her. The Heathers have given me *years* of practice dealing with some deluded mean girl threatening me."

Growling low, my arms tighten around her as I bury my face in her neck. She doesn't understand; I know that. When I was stalking her or when we first got together, I already disarticulated fuckers who upset her. *Now*, she's my fucking *mate*. Fury is crawling through my veins like a fire out of control and I'm ready to rip the throat out of the first person who tempts me.

"Love, you have to take a breath. Remember what you did when we first..." Chess flushes and my posture relaxes a tiny bit. He's not wrong; I was touchy as fuck after I claimed him.

Probably time to make that confession...

"Chessie, I didn't control it as well as you think." Baby Girl arches her brow, looking at me suspiciously and I shrug, giving her a roguish smile. "I tore the pits up for weeks so I could control the anger that had me in a choke hold for the first couple... months-ish."

The cheetah shifter's jaw drops and he gives me a dirty look. "Fitzgerald Khan. The pits on Bloodstone are *dangerous*. People *die* in them several times an hour."

Felix walks in before I can answer, his expression smug. "Yes, he knows. For a while, they were calling him the Feral Tiger of the Dark Isle in the ambush."

"That was *you?!*" Chess gapes and my girl giggles—another reason I adore the living shit out of her.

My twin shrugs and drops onto the sofa next to me, his hand landing on Baby Girl's knee to squeeze it. "Who the fuck else did you think it was, Chester?"

"You."

I snort, shaking my head. "As if Dear Old Dad would allow his chosen heir to be in those hellholes unless it was some big show for the world. He's a sadist, but he isn't stupid. I'm the psycho, Felix is the prince. That's how it's always been and always will be, Chessie."

Dolly clears her throat, her big blue eyes serious. "And you said I'm the Queen, Fitz Khan, so you all have to let me rule my world how I see fit. I can handle this flea-bitten shithead and if I can't, I will *ask* for your help."

I love the confidence radiating from her, so I can't deny her the opportunity to prove herself.

"Fine, Baby Girl. I'll leave her processed hide in place… for now. But if she lays a single finger on you outside of practice, all bets are off. Got it?" My expression is as stern as I can make it because I'm fucking serious about this shit. I refuse to allow a repeat of the first year where those girls tortured her for no goddamn reason.

Felix leans in to press his nose against hers, blocking my view as he growls, "Your King says that's fair."

Chess snorts, leaning into my side as he mumbles, "There are three kings in this place. Who said you're the top cat?"

"No one," the dragon says, his voice tinged with amusement as he and Ren enter the living area. "The Raj is sorely mistaken if he thinks he's the one calling all the shots."

"Indeed," the gargoyle drawls as he flops onto the special chair his crew of rodents procured. It allows him to drape over the furniture in his favorite style and for a second, I ponder finding minions of my own. Those little prey shits are very useful and maybe I've slacked off on building an empire for myself.

"Excuse me," our girl says as she puts her hands on her hips. "The Queen has not consented to marry anyone, so none of your bullshit posturing counts. My rule is solo and you're all my royal courtesans."

My twin opens his mouth to argue and I put my hand over it quickly. "Don't argue with her you idiot. She's saying we're her sex bots and who the fuck wants to argue with that shit?"

His eyes widen and I feel the smirk under my palm. "You're right, bro. Being her courtesans sounds *much* more fun than politics."

"And it will be, but tonight, I'm so fucking sore that I want to die," she admits. "I'm hungry, sore, and I have two chapters of the stupid Theater History book to read because the big guy distracted me at lunch."

I snarl as my eyes narrow. "You what? No fair, Spicy Chameleon!"

Aubrey chuckles, shaking his head. "Not distracted in *that* way, though I'd be happy to do so anytime, snack size."

Pouting a bit for effect, I look at our girl. "Is that true, Baby Girl? No hanky panky for big and cranky?"

She holds up her hand like a Pred Scout, eyes wide. "I swear, Fitzy. We just talked about my classes and stuff. He didn't get a single article of clothing off. In fact, not one of you has today, which definitely disappoints me as much as you."

"Okay, good girl. Then Chessie is getting on dinner, and we're going to help you ease those sore muscles while you work. Frenchie, draw her a bath fit for a Queen after we finish eating. And I'll read you the chapter, then my stuffy brother will feed you dessert while Spicysaurus Rex gives you a massage. How does that sound?"

Her eyes turn into saucers and the shiver that runs through her makes my dick strain. "Yes. Yes, yes, yes, *fuck yes.*"

I groan, tipping my head back as I squeeze my eyes shut. "None of that, bad girl, or we'll lose all ability to follow the Queen's rules."

Not that I have great hopes for it, anyway.

"HOLY FUCKING SHIT CHESSIE," DOLLY GROANS AS SHE PATS HER food rounded belly. "That was so good I might marry it instead of you clowns."

My cheetah flushes happily and I lean in to kiss him before he gets too flustered. "You did good, baby."

Felix tosses back the end of his bourbon, wiping his mouth with the napkin and sighs happily. His eyes are fond as he looks at the whole table of full preds. The happiness in his expression comes from knowing his chosen ambush is well taken care of and it's one I hadn't seen in years until our girl hopped in our life. "Chess, buddy, you are turning into the best chef I know. You spoil the shit out of us."

"*C'est vrai, mon ami,*" Renard says as he leans back. "I'm impressed with how well you're learning as well. You could open your own restaurant eventually, I believe."

Chessie turns even redder, ducking his head, and Baby Girl tugs him over into her arms. "Your part in my relaxing evening was amazing, my knight. Thank you."

"Anything for you, Angel," he murmurs softly as their foreheads touch. "But I'm also pleased that the others like it as well. It makes me feel important."

I snort, squishing them together as I press into his back. "Baby, you're important in more ways than I can count. You keep us all functioning, especially me. Between organizing and food and snuggles, you're the backbone of our little family."

"Indeed, he is," Aubrey interjects. "Chester, without you, we'd be sitting on the floor with takeout right now."

"The Captain and his crew—"

"Oh, don't be modest, Chessie. You directed the mayhem." Dolly beams as she pulls back and looks around. "The rest of you are up to bat. I was promised a lovely bath, a massage, help reading, and desserts. Chop, chop."

Ren leaps up from his seat, walking over to take her hand and kiss it. "As you wish, *ma magnifique reine*. I'm off to create a beautiful, relaxing scene for you to absorb your history lesson in."

Cheating fancy pants Frenchie, I fucking swear.

Dolly melts a little and Aubrey snorts, shaking his head. "Such a fucking cheater. He knows what that does to everyone."

"I know, right?" I grumble as my arms tighten around our bunny. "I have too many things to learn to kick your ancient asses. It's very time consuming."

Felix puts his hand over his mouth, muffling his laughter, and I glare at him. "Fitz, you don't have to compete with them. Fuck, we *can't*, man. They have ridiculous amounts of time on us."

"Plus, I love you how you are, Crazypants," Baby Girl says as she wiggles. "You try everything and don't give a single shit if you're good at it or not. And your stalking might worry some people, but I like that you want to be with me all the time. It makes me feel… cherished."

"Good thing otherwise he'd end up in jail," the dragon mutters into his scotch. "He's almost attached to you like a damn shadow."

I shrug, grinning widely at them all. "Don't be jelly, guys. I keep eyes on you all, too. Can't have my bros-in-law and my other mate unsafe. I'm just less obvious with checking on you 'cause you don't dig it like our girl does."

The Hot-Headed Gila Monster glares at me, his expression cautious. "You spy on us all the time, too?"

"Don't get twisted, buddy. I still don't know what the fuck you two fuckers eat, and I didn't know about your little secret until you gave it up, did I?" My lashes bat as I look at him innocently. "I'm keeping tabs, but not that closely."

Chess finally pulls out of our grip, moving to clear the dishes. "Since I cooked, you assholes need to help me load up and clear this stuff. I'll pack up the leftovers in lunch bentos if you do."

Oooh. I love when he makes me care packages for later.

"Well, don't sit here like mold growing, guys. Who doesn't want Chessie's hot lunches for the rest of the week?" I clap my hands as I shoot to my feet, setting our girl on hers. "You go get ready for that bath, Baby Girl, and we'll help Chessie. I'll be in very soon."

She kisses my cheek, then hits up the other four, giggling when each of us grope her. "Thanks, Fitzy. I'll get my hair tied up and head for the bath with my stupid textbook."

I watch her skip off, then turn to the dragon, cheetah, and my brother with dark eyes. "Now that she's gone... We need to keep an eye out for that skank who threatened her. O' Learys are Council fuckers and they have pull. If that little wretch tells her parents who the competition is, I guarantee it will get back to Dolly's cuntfaced mother. She doesn't need any more problems."

"Agreed, Fitzgerald," Aubrey says as he lifts up the platter of meat to take it to the back counter. "I don't like her garnering another rival so well connected. Between the other problems at this school and this, our planner keeps filling. It will become unmanageable."

I grin fangily. "It won't if you all quit putting me on a fucking leash. I could clear players off before anyone even knew they were missing."

"That draws too much attention, Fitz. Threats and light maiming are working fine." Felix pauses for a moment. "Perhaps that would be a good choice if this O' Leary keeps bothering Princess. Take her claws one by one—it will hamper her in the games."

Excitement floods me as I look at my twin. "Seriously? No one will lose their shit and call me impulsive? Not that I care, but I don't like fucking up Chessie's planning."

My mate's chuckle is soft and I wink at him as he wraps up lunches and puts them in the fridge.

"I think the Raj is right, and I know Rennie will agree," Aubrey says grimly. "Show this girl we're not kidding around if need be, Fitz. And make it painful—we need her to believe it the first time."

Fuck yeah, she will. I know exactly what to do.

Friends

Delores

The rest of my night was actually as restful as promised—save one minor detail—and I fell asleep in the pile of my handsy boyfriends with no trouble at all. Breakfast was delicious, but the minor detail from last night made the guys brood like Cure fans. The upcoming day's one snag hung over us like the sword of Damocles, making me want to jabber until they all perked up, but I knew it wouldn't help.

Today is my first class with the twins' cousin and they're worried.

The argument last night was about who could hold their temper well enough to walk me to class. After seeing them all turn into obnoxious alphas as they tried to work it out, I texted Rufus and Coco to meet me outside the library. Raina volunteered to join me afterward when I headed back to Shird 3.0. Once that was settled, they calmed down and we were able to relax again. I know they're worried; hell, *I'm* worried. The way the twins dance around their past with Asani tells me he's not a good dude, and Felix's anger only highlights how bad the tiger must be. My Raj is pretty fair, and I don't think he's exaggerating.

"Dollypop!"

I turn to see Rufus rushing over with my other bestie in tow. The last time I saw Coco, she looked so dejected I was almost afraid to leave her alone, but today she looks… marginally better. She's got makeup and a colorful outfit on, even if her expression doesn't quite match her bright smile. "Hey guys. Thanks for coming with me. I didn't want to have to peel the guys off this creep if he looks at me sideways."

Ru-Ru grins as he hauls me into his arms and does an impromptu swing step with me, then sends me reeling into Cori. She catches me with a small chuckle, dipping me then letting me up. "You two are a bit much for eight in the morning. How much caffeine do you consume?"

I arch a brow at her. "As much as we always consume, Coco, don't worry. But… shhh. I snagged you a burrito." Beaming, I pull two wrapped breakfast burritos out of my satchel. The one in foil is salmon and the one in wax paper is meaty as fuck—Chessie helped me out since they agreed to help this morning. "Don't let any of the other guys know my cheetah and I hid them for you. Food doesn't last long in our kitchen."

There's a sentence I never thought I'd get to say with Lucille in my life.

"You spoil us," she says as she grabs hers. "But I'm glad we came, too. I didn't get to thank you for… you know."

Sighing, I slide a look at Rufus, whose lips curl up a bit. He's being awfully gentle this morning and I guess curbing his snark is his way of being kind to our friend. "You're my friends and the guys constantly remind me that we're allowed to spoil the people we care about."

"I'd *love* to be on the receiving end of *that* kind of spoiling," Rufus says and I shuffle into him purposefully, knocking him off balance as we head toward the Alexandré building. "Though truthfully—"

Cori rolls her eyes as she cuts him off. "Enough of that. You and those triplets are nauseating enough on your nightly video calls."

Oh, Ru-Ru. She's pretending to laugh, but you're probably killing her.

"She's right. There's enough innuendo at home. What I really want is… gossip." I look at them both, then scan our surroundings. "You haven't been around for our meetings yet, but I've got another 'raving fan.' Her name is Felicia O' Leary and she's definitely going to be a problem."

The polar bear frowns. "You draw crazies like flies to shit, girl. We've barely gotten rid of the first batch—and the F-A-E did most of that work for us."

"Very subtle, Coco," Rufus says as he rolls his eyes this time. "I'm sure our enemies are unable to spell, therefore will have *no* idea what that means."

Covering my mouth as I giggle, I squeeze my hands on my bag as the happiness of being with my friends flows through me. I'm sure other people are so used to this feeling that they don't appreciate it, but having them and the guys *still* gives me an electric jolt of giddy when I compare to how my life was before the bunny. "He's not wrong, but yeah. Oh! And I have another big WTF for you."

They walk closer, forming a tight group with me as Cori murmurs, "Is it bad?"

"Hell if I know, but it seems to be. The broody one won't give us *all* the deets yet, but there are *vampires* on this campus."

Rufus' eyes widened to saucers and for a second, I think he's glitching. "We. Are. Living. *Twilight*. And you *didn't tell me until now!"*

Cori groans, shaking her head. "Now you've done it. He's going to be absolutely interminable during film studies now."

It's hard to control my laughter as he starts prancing about, pretending to hyper-speed towards the academic building. "If he starts wearing tons of booty dust so he sparkles, Aubrey will ban him from our place. He's still mad at Fitz and I for the Christmas incident."

She grins and shrugs. "He has full access to all my cases; I make no promises."

Rufus zips by, his arms out as he pretends to have a cape flowing behind him and I roll my eyes. "Good thing we love that idiot— and that he's found the Kavarits, because this look is *not* sexy."

"Hey, are you the one that had Coach Z contact me about the uniforms?" Coco gives me a shy look and I nod. "Thanks. I'm actually pretty excited about it. It will be something besides all this fucking school work and… you know… *that*… to focus on."

Now it's my turn to blush and I shrug as I tuck a hair behind my ear. "I know a little something about being betrayed. And finding a purpose helped me make it through that summer before Apex. Luc's kindness, the prey staff… It's how I survived."

She gives me a wry look. "That and your vengeance list."

My eyes dance as Rufus finally stops running about and joins us again. "Well, yeah. Revenge on those that hurt me fueled me, too. It also helped me when I arrived at Apex knowing people were going to try to kill me. But you don't have that to worry about— not directly, anyway."

"We're *all* targets now, Dollybear, but you're worth it." Rufus' hair is sticking up all over and he's flushed, but his enthusiasm has taken the edge off my worry about this new supernatural. "But together, we're one hell of a Scooby team."

He's not wrong about that.

MY FRIENDS LEFT ONCE WE GOT TO THE CLASSROOM, AND I'VE been standing here ever since. The door is closed, but I can hear voices in the room. There's several people in class already, so I'm not worried about being caught unawares, but every time I reach for the knob, I remember the look on Felix's face and Fitz' fury. This tiger is *not* like mine and he definitely poses a danger to me and my family. I can't get out of this damn lecture, but I have to be extremely careful. I don't want to give this joker *any* reason to keep me behind.

"You are a badass bunny. Last year, you made the Pred Games your bitch. You're standing up to your bitch mom. No one gets to make you a victim ever again," I mutter to myself. The words don't quite do it, but I gather up the 'Drew' in me and straighten my shoulders. Even if this douchebag is dangerous, I can handle it.

After all, I am Delores Diamond Drew, the only predatory bunny with blue lightning magic I've ever heard of—this guy can bite me.

Grabbing the door handle, I yank it open and stride in with the determined gait I use on the Games pitch. Random shifters stare as I stomp past them to take a seat in the back where I can see the entire space. I'm close enough to the door to hoof it if needed, but not so close anyone will assume I'm afraid of what's coming. Just like Fitz says, location is everything when you're trying to intimidate your prey and I want to be certain Asani Khan knows he's the one being hunted, not me.

I've only settled in for a moment when the door blows open and a tall, dark-haired man bustles in. He definitely has the Khan 'looks,' but he's not nearly as hot as either of my tigers. I'm curious what kind of tiger he is given his bulkier frame, but I suppose it's better if I don't find out. Fitz' snowy white cat and Felix's fierce orange bengal coloring are gorgeous, but they'd lose their shit if I somehow ended up seeing this guy shift.

The whispers in the room increase as he moves to the standing desk, spreading his things out on the surface before he plugs a laptop in. "Settle, people. Once I have the presentation up and running, we'll dive into the first lesson. I'm going to assume that even our famous transfers are caught up to the point the previous professor stopped at before he was tragically killed on Yule."

Hell if I know. This asshole didn't preload a syllabi, and none of the past lessons were online because this place fucking hates tech that would make my life easier. They only seem to give a shit if it's about security and only the stuff *they* want locked up, and not a damn thing more. I look around, noting the obvious returning students opening their notes while a few others are frowning like me.

I watch as the bulky professor pulls a cord, raising the jungle-themed cover that was blocking a big ass TV. It surprises me because so much at *l'Academie* seems to be purposefully clinging to the past, but I suppose you can be some big wig in the Khan empire without being dialed into technology. He fusses with a remote for a second then turns to face us. "Good morning, class. As you know from your schedules, I'm Asani Khan—yes, *that* Khan, but you don't have to worry! I'm not feral or insane like *some* of my ilk."

His eyes cut to me then move back to the rest of the room. That move isn't missed by my classmates and I grip my tablet tightly to avoid reacting. If his game is to alienate me from the other students, he's two years too late for that bullshit. It's a rookie move, and one the Heathers wouldn't have bothered with. Anyone with real power doesn't have to actually have to gather the peons; they flock to them without being called.

"Your current seats can remain such for the semester, and you should be receiving your syllabi in..."he looks at the fancy watch on his wrist. "Right about now."

As if by magic, the chorus of dings fills the room as people's devices get the notification. It's a good trick, but again, amateur-hour. He spent plenty of time futzing with his shit to make that moment happen as planned. I'm not impressed, even if he is smirking like he's won the lottery. Groups of girls twitter amongst themselves as everyone opens the document, but I don't pay them any mind. So far, it's three for three on the hot teacher scale with Khans; it's not like it's a big surprise.

"Professor Khan, can I just say how excited I am to study the Magic Accords? Ridding the world of that scum was the *best* thing the Council ever did."

Oh, no. How did I miss that?

My old nemesis, Gold, is sitting on the other side of the classroom in a shadowy corner. I didn't have to see her witchy face once during the break, and I was hoping with the intense arts focus here I'd be able to avoid her and Pink. Silver got shipped to *Zhuǎn xīng U&M*, so she's off my plate, but these two are back to make my life miserable.

Asani smiles broadly, clicking his remote to reveal the syllabus on the screen as well. "I, too, look forward to that discussion, Miss...?"

"Erikson... Heather Erikson." She sits up straighter and despite her lack of groupies, I see the girl who tried to have me eaten shining through. "Our parents are *very* well acquainted, I believe."

"Indeed. The Khans use Erikson tech exclusively on Bloodstone Isle. It helps keep our more... feisty students in line without fail."

She grins wickedly and I have to suppress a shudder. I can only imagine what hellish shit the Eriksons have invented to punish reformatory students on an isle run by fucking psychos assholes with no oversight. The wolf's expression turns vicious for a second, then melts into a more normal one as she continues, "I'm certain you'll be my *favorite* professor in this ridiculous school. At least your subject is *useful*."

Gross. I hope this guy moves on or I'm going to heave all over his dumb tiki floor—guaranteed.

VERDIS QUO

AUBREY

"I don't like it."

My mate snorts as he lazes on top of a bookshelf, his tail flicking back and forth. "Shocker, *mon ami.*"

Whipping around to glare at him, I blow a smoke ring. The dragon is unsettled because our girl is in a classroom with the twins' shitty cousin—alone. He wants me to stomp over and force my way in like I did that time with the Nordic aquatic shifter, but I know I can't do that. We've barely arrived, for one, and our connections in this land aren't as strong as at home. Plus, Dolly needs to pave her own way and letting her stand up for herself from the beginning of our tenure here is a solid plan.

Doesn't mean I'm not fighting the lizard tooth-and-nail to keep from flipping a table.

"You know our *petit lapin* can handle herself." Rennie sits up, his expression far away for a moment before he continues. *"You may write me down in history/With your bitter, twisted lies,/You may trod me in the very dirt/But still, like dust, I'll rise.* [1]*"*

Lips quirking, I give him an amused look. "Maya Angelou?"

He shrugs, leaning on one hand as he continues lounging on my library furniture in a way I wouldn't allow anyone else to even dream of. *"Mais oui.* Not a comparable situation, but the sentiment is universal. Those held down are capable of casting off the bindings of their past, despite the opposition."

"You *would* be the one to practically sing 'One More Day' in support of Dolly." I turn back to my Smackbook, too tickled by my reference to let him ruin it for me. "It's the ooh-la-la in you, my love."

"We *are* an hour from Paris, Lord Draconis. It's entirely appropriate."

The ding of an email catches my attention before I can get annoyed with his refusal to let me have a good brood. Frowning, I scan the contents, tilting my head. "Ren, get down from there and come over here."

In a blink, he's rolled off the high case, flipping to the floor with the grace of a cat. Gargoyles are the oddest creatures—half lithe cat and half enormous rock monsters depending on which form they're in—and I'll never get used to it, even after centuries of time together. "What's the problem, Flames? You went from growly dragon to scowly librarian fast enough to give me whiplash."

"My contact from the Smithsonian has been looking over the pictures of all the artifacts and chambers from the schools I sent him. If you remember, I told you all that academics are as single-minded as that world-ending robot you made me watch. Aloysius just emailed about the connection to the prey exhibits Dolly's raccoon friend suggested we examine."

Grabbing a chair, my mate drags it over to look at the lengthy email from my walrus colleague. His brows furrow as he scrolls through it, his eyes scanning it quickly enough to make me grin. Renard's love of books is similar to mine and he speed reads like no one else I've ever met, even me. "He seems to believe that the stories *prior* to the Treaty that exiled the magic users paint a more integrated society for prey and preds in many parts of the world. They had control of the government and some industries, as well as representation with humans."

I sigh, thinking about it for a moment. He and I are the only ones here old enough to remember the times before the Treaty, but unfortunately, we're both unreliable witnesses. I was exiled young and came to this land only to hole up in my hordes and rarely venture out. When Apex opened, I came here and stayed until our gorgeous bunny's enemies blew it up. Ren grew up in Paris and then the mountains, but his kind are some of the most secretive, solitary shifter groups known to the world. His memories are probably faulty as well.

"Who are we going to get to talk to us about the time before? Everyone with families old enough to have personal records that might have avoided the cover-up is up to their neck in Council shit." The gargoyle leans back in his chair, tapping his fingers on the table. "And there's so much shit from those vaults, much of which is entirely useless for this purpose..."

He's right; we've found some incriminating stuff, but a lot of it won't help us with the Fae problem.

"True. Getting dirt on the Council to remove them from power is great, but until we can guarantee snack size's safety, it's not worth the paper it's scribbled on."

Ren crosses his arms over his chest, his face a mask of frustration. Something is brewing in his head that bothers him, so I wait for him to work through it. Hopefully, it's not going to send him into another brooding jag like the damn vampire thing did. After a few minutes, he finally sighs heavily.

"We'll need to put word out to the mythicals groups, and we have to find out what mythical is working or residing here. Whatever they are, they don't advertise their presence. You know as well as I do that every one of the schools have one or two exiles from the rare species."

"Damn it," I grunt. Now I know why he's so pouty—putting word out through the underground grapevine to dragon clashes, gargoyle clutches, griffin aeries, and all the other reclusive groups could go wrong in so many ways. "You know doing this might draw... the wrong eyes, right?"

His nose wrinkles and he makes a face so petulant that I lean in to kiss him lightly. "I do, and you can't sweet talk me out of the funk that possibility will put me in."

I can't tell him how ridiculously adorable he is right now.

"No, but I can remind you that unlike *my* parents, yours are almost *never* dialed into the world. The gargoyles are damn near invisible, except for the ones working on the shifter resorts. The likelihood that they'll find out you're on this continent again is very slim."

Nodding, he looks over at the email again, then up at the ceiling, and then over at me. "Fine. But only because it might help our future mate and if it brings the roaches out from under the cupboard, you have to help me deal with it."

"Always," I say softly before leaning in to kiss his temple. "Now help me with this blasted High Fae while you're here so we can keep our minds off parents and our woman in class with an evil Khan."

"Deal, *mon amour.*"

"SO FAR, THIS IS A BUST," REN MUTTERS AS HE SHAKES HIS HEAD. "It's fascinating history, and something tragically hidden from the shifter world, but I'm not seeing anything in the text that will help. It's much earlier than the Treaty and focuses on their royal succession."

I hold up a set of maps with gloved hands. "These are more telling. Notice all the territory boundaries and where they over-lap... then look at the next set. See how certain borders are shrinking over time?"

He frowns, taking them gingerly and tilting his head. "*Oui.* It appears the Fae lose land each time they're re-drawn. I wonder if there's some correlation to human politics or business..."

That's it—it has to be tied to major shifts in governments.

When he gives them back, I take the first map and pull up both a screen on the PredNet and the human internet done in the same time period. Slowly, I send both maps to the printer across the room, then move on to the next era. Once I've finished gathering all the dates for the maps at hand, Ren runs over to grab the print-outs and brings them to me. It only takes a few moments to confirm the humans don't have anything to do with this.

"You might try printing out the prey maps as well," my lover murmurs from behind me. "Raina wouldn't have mentioned that if it wasn't important."

I nod. "That's true. But even the pred maps don't seem to show a political gain other than more territory."

The gargoyle scratches his forehead, then snaps his fingers. "Timelines. Look up timelines, Flames. The border changes might have to do with resources, not governing bodies."

Frowning, I use the library's access to the Preynet to print hard copies of the maps he suggested. They don't appear to be hugely different for the first couple of periods, but the ones since the Treaty are *vastly* different. There's definitely something to this theory, and I'm beginning to realize it has nothing to do with dangerous species. That propels me to search the historical time-lines for all three, making sure to check boxes for events, innovations, and other notable moments.

"This is going to take a while," Rennie says as he watches the screens scroll by. "Going through centuries of history from all three species and ferreting out what might affect the land will be a grueling task."

"We need help."

"I believe so, *mon ami*. Perhaps Chester? He's not working in the office after twelve today. If we each tackle a group and highlight things around the times to go over together, we might even be able to finish today."

Taking off my glasses, I rub my eyes. "I've never been so grateful that it seems like no one in this damn college comes to my library."

"It's been *two* days, Flames." Rennie chuckles, his eyes dancing with humor. "Have you made a judgment about the entire student body in that time?"

"The books are so dusty Betsy had an allergy attack in the first hour," I retort. "And that was in the current fiction section. She had to don a dust mask to start the archives."

He laughs, shrugging as he grabs the shifter maps. "They focus on the arts pretty heavily here. I've never had students at Apex focus on poetry as intensely as my class yesterday. I was shocked to find they actually gave a damn about hidden meanings and literary devices. I'm sure you'll at least get the writing majors soon enough."

"Love, literacy and reading comprehension have been on the decline for decades. I know I bitch about PredNet and social media, but people just don't love books anymore." My expression is sad as I sigh. "As if that wasn't bad enough, research skills are abysmal. We're becoming even more outdated by the day—even at work."

The room is quiet for a moment, and then it fills with belly laughs. I blink at him, my jaw dropping as he continues to clutch his stomach and roll around in his chair. He wipes his eyes, shaking his head as I just stare at him. He finally takes a breath, trying to gather himself and I roll my eyes.

What the hell is so goddamn funny?

"What a sad sack declaration," he says when he's gotten control of himself. "We've lived far too long to worry about that kind of shit, Flames. Our kind both have extended life spans and that's not a new revelation. We're destined to watch other species and the world evolve—and it's not always for the better. No need to mope about because our passions aren't in vogue at any given moment."

"Well, I…"

He smirks at me as I bluster. "Plus, unlike most creatures that are damn close to immortal, *you* found *two* mates."

Flushing as I consider that, I make a face at him. "You're annoyingly accurate for someone I have to spend eternity with."

"It's a blessing and a curse." He pulls his phone out, winking before he texts Chess. "And you love me regardless… don't pretend otherwise."

I pinch the bridge of my nose as I watch him. "You're damned lucky I do, you pain in the ass."

"That's your job, big man. Now shut up and let me translate."

Ra save me from mouthy mates and their determination to drive me to drink.

ALONE TIME

DELORES

"So the entire class was that gigolo pontificating and the remaining Heathers simpering." I tell my raccoon friend as we walk toward the newest Shirdal building. "I might have to order barf bags in bulk to get through the semester."

Raina titters next to me. "I'll make sure the boys know to check that classroom a couple times a week."

I roll my eyes, smiling at her fondly. "If you do that, I'll make more work for them. You guys help us out enough as it is. I don't want to be a pain in the ass."

"Miss Dolly Drew!" She stops and looks at me, her tiny hands on her hips as she wags a finger at me. "Never say that. You are my friend and Monsieur Renard is the Captain's friend. This is what we do for one another, yes?"

Putting my hand over my mouth, I cover the giggle threatening to well up at her small body looking so deadly furious. Once I'm sure I've got it swallowed, I nod at the tiny prey animal. "Your family is part of mine, Raina. I can't tell you how glad I am you were the one to take my order in the cafeteria at Apex."

She flushes—I think—and turns towards the building so we can start walking again. "Dolly, you were the first pred outside of our gracious gargoyle to ever treat me so well. I knew the moment we met that you were special and I was right."

Well, shit, I'm going to cry if she doesn't stop that.

"Shhh, Raina! I can't go into the shark tank all weepy," I chuckle as I wipe the corner of my eye. "They'll eat me alive in Modern Dance."

Her laugh tinkles in the air as we finish the walk to the French version of the Shird.

Maybe I wasn't born under a bad sign, I just had to wait for the sun to shine on me.

"FASTER! YOU'RE ALL FAR TOO SLOW AND LACK CONTROL. HOW you got this far is beyond me," the huge female wolf growls as the lines of dancers move across the floor one after another.

My legs, arms, and feet are aching from the vigorous beating they're taking. For the first class, I'm pretty winded, and if this is how they're all going to be, I'm in trouble. Nadia Antonovidrovna doesn't like *anyone*, but she's definitely been sneering at me more than anyone else. I don't have a fucking clue why; I've never met the woman until today. So I've pushed myself as hard as possible, hoping to win her over with my effort.

Fat lot of good that's done—she just got harsher.

When the buzzer at the front of the room goes off, I lean on the barre, panting softly for a moment. I can feel the eyes on me; it's almost as bad as when I started at Apex. The arts focused people are cut throat here, so they see me as competition who didn't earn their spot. I've got professors who seem to want to string me up, and the few Heathers not kidnapped are starting their shit again.

"It's almost like I've done the fucking Time Warp," I mutter as I walk over to change my shoes. Spraying them so they don't stink up the entire bag, I pull on my socks and boots, then get up to tug my uniform skirt over my leotard. I'm not changing entirely for my short lunch break because I have theater practicum afterward. "Everyone is rewinding back to 2022."

"Your gear certainly is," one of the willowy dancers snarks as she walks by and I sigh.

For fuck's sake, I can't escape this rubber stamp mean girl shit no matter what I do.

"Yeah, yeah," I say as I wave her off. "Maybe I'll feel like serving you your ass next time, but today, I'm not in the mood."

She huffs, but at least she doesn't take that unintentional opening to insult my love life. Winging a prayer of thanks at the ceiling, and gathering my shit. I'm meeting Felix outside to go check out the salt water lake while we have a quick bite. I know he's really coming because he wants to know what the hell his cousin did in class, but that's okay. Indulging his worry makes him less over-the-top and I enjoy spending time with my guys no matter how I get it.

Once I have everything, I limp out to the front of the Shird, grinning broadly at the handsome Raj waiting for me. He frowns at my gait, and I move a little faster to get close enough to soothe his ire. "Difficult dance class, baby. Don't worry."

"Princess, you're hobbling like the Winged Weenies had you strung up last night."

There goes my focus...

His laugh glides over my skin and I make a face at him. "The professor for Modern is a real hard ass. I can't believe others didn't come out looking as wrecked as me."

"Were they working as hard as you? Somehow, I doubt it," the tiger says before turning to give me his back. "Come on, then. Hop on and we'll head for the lake before we waste all our time."

Recoiling, I shake my head. "Absolutely not."

Felix looks over his shoulder in exasperation. "Princess, you hop on my twin all the time. What's the problem?"

I snicker for a sec and he rolls his eyes as if chastising me for my immaturity. But then my feet start throbbing again from standing for so long and I give in. "Damn you for being right *and* knowing exactly what would happen if I refused. But you should note that I hop on *everyone* at home and this is the only time you've suggested it in public."

"Touché, love." He turns again, waiting for me to jump on, so I do. Once he has my thighs arranged on his waist, he grabs the picnic basket he must have gotten from Chessie in his other hand. "Now hang on..."

I wrap my arms around his neck, holding on as he takes off like a shot. It still amazes the hell out of me when they do stuff like this —I'm not a small bunny—but I've learned to swallow that ingrained fear. Lucille may have spent most of my childhood destroying my self-image, but the past few years have helped me stop cringing every time they haul me in their arms. "You know, you're very strong, Your Highness."

He rumbles a chuckle and I feel it against my chest. "Princess, if that's your way to cheat the rule about not picking on yourself... you're not fooling me."

Leaning in, I kiss his ear. "I could never trick you, Raj. You're far too smart for that."

"Oops too far, bunny rabbit. Now I *know* you're tugging the tiger tail." His hands pinch my legs and I wiggle with a gasp. "I don't respond to flattery nearly as well as my brother."

"Yes, *Sir*," I chirp as I squeeze him tighter. "Duly noted."

He groans as we approach the shore of the north lake, finally putting me down and spinning around to face me. "You're as bad as the gargoyle, Princess. You know exactly how to rile me up and how to perfectly stroke my fur to calm me down again."

I arch a brow at him. "Rennie is stroking your fur?"

"For the love of Apollo's sunburn, Princess, *no*. He does it to the grumpy dragon constantly." Felix gives me a wry look. "I'm still a bit irked that I missed it all those years."

Winking, I lower myself to the grass by the shore. "Your head was too far up your ass to see anything until I came into your life."

His jaw drops and he joins me, opening the basket to hand me a bento box that screams Chessie. "I take exception to that!"

"Do whatever you want, Felix Khan, but you know I'm right." I open my box and the water he gave me, taking a swig of the cold liquid before I wipe my mouth on my hand and look him in the eye. "And if you think you're any less obvious, don't think I missed you taking the lunch after my first class with your smooth-talking cousin."

His face flushes and he growls low, "Watch it, Princess."

I arch a brow at him, enjoying his discomfort enough to play with him a little. "I don't know if I could possibly talk about it with my feet aching so badly."

He rolls his eyes, yanking my shoe off first, then my sock, and starts working the aches out of my arch. "If anyone else in the universe tried to blackmail me this way, I'd slice open their guts and eat their liver."

Cupping my hand to my ear, I call out, "Fitz? Fitz, is that you? Oh, Fitzzzzz…"

"Who do you think taught him to be crazy?" Felix says as he wrings my toes through his strong fingers and I groan. "I am three minutes older than him, you know."

"Fine, fine. Okay, you win. Asani was pretty douche-y, though I could definitely see the relation." I take a bite of the wrap from my box, chewing it quickly before I continue. "But I also felt this… ugly streak I've never felt from you or Fitzy. It's like he has the perfect looks and suave delivery you guys do, but there's just a bad vibe coming from him."

He snorts. "You have *no* idea. "

Frowning, I look at him curiously. "He was making flirty faces at the Heathers. I have a pretty good idea of what an asshat he has to be."

"No, it's worse than consorting with a few bobble headed fools, I'm afraid. And that's probably why I'm so edgy about it." Felix licks his lips and looks out into the lake for a moment, then back at me. "Asani was my brother Titus' right hand. He helped make sure I was exiled and provided the evidence about my consort's betrayal."

Ohhhhhhhh, that explains—wait a minute.

"I'm going to kill that son of a bitch with my bare hands," I snarl as I drop my food. My eyes burn as they turn red and I feel the electricity shooting through my veins. "I'll even put his gonads in a jar for you."

"You are spending *way* too much time with my twin," he says with a soft smile. "But I wouldn't mind watching it; you're hot when you tear people to pieces, I hear."

"I'm hot when I do a lot of things," I pout and sparks jump from my arms to his as I think about how much I want to destroy the people who hurt my kind-hearted king. "Doesn't mean I'm not going to slice your asshole tiger relatives into black market steaks."

Felix laughs, scooting closer to cup my face in his hands. "Somehow, I'm a lot less worried about you having him in class two days a week and a lot more worried about what's going to happen when he inevitably pisses you off."

"Again, I'm considering fileting," I mumble. "Perhaps julienne."

A splash of water hits us both and we sputter in tandem, then look over to the lake. Standing on the back of a huge whale shifter is the Captain, grinning with his small raccoon features as he waves. Behind him, a comically small boat with Raina and a few other prey animals floats by as they toss food into water for the shifters.

"I suppose I deserved that for thinking you couldn't defend yourself to start with," Felix says as we wave back at our friends. "The Captain has impeccable timing; it's quite remarkable."

"Raina made me teary earlier."

He frowns. "Why?"

"Because she said something so sweet I could hardly stand it, and I was so happy. This time two years ago, I didn't think I'd survive the next month, much less have all of you and friends. And now we're in France on an adventure to solve a mystery... it's... overwhelming. Good, of course, but so different from what I thought was going to happen."

The Raj gives me a mischievous grin. "Do you think I had a clue two years ago that the girl my twin was stalking was anything more than one of his passing fancies? Hell no. We all thought he'd get in trouble and end up with another restraining order."

"Never."

"Delores Drew, you're the best thing that could have ever happened to us, and we don't give a fuck what anyone thinks. Don't let those girls back into your head." He gives me a stern look and I grin.

"Again, sir, yes, sir."

This time, it's definitely on purpose—a little torture never hurt anyone.

LONG DAY

CHESS

I spent most of yesterday morning helping Aubrey and Renard go through timelines from the past few centuries. It was tedious as hell, but their constant banter made it less cumbersome. I would have rather stayed with them to finish than go to my five hours of misery with the vulture, but alas, my presence on campus is tied to working as much as everyone else's. She didn't mention my angel the entire time, but no one who came in and out of her office looked better off. It worried me that students who seemed to need help exited looking worse for wear, but I couldn't do anything more than slip them a card with websites on the back.

Not enough, I fear, but at least an option that isn't harmful.

Reporting her to the administration didn't work at Cappie and I highly doubt it would here. Whoever her benefactor is, they have a good enough reach to keep the vile woman protected in her little bubble. At least, at work, anyway. Farley is making his moves in the background with his people and we have to trust he's getting shit done so we can focus on tracking down information on the bigger problems.

My family agreed with that assessment at dinner, but Ren and the twins promised to keep their eyes peeled for students who seem like they need assistance they aren't getting. Felix even said he'd give Zhenga a nudge, and our girl swore to enlist Rufus and Cori. That eased my guilt a bit, and we were able to clean up and relax while Dolly worked on her homework. She was exhausted from long, physically demanding classes and a mountain of work that seemed excessive for the first day of classes.

But no one asked me, and this place feels geared to weed out the weak with impossible tasks—much like Apex.

This morning, Fitz headed out with our girl after our family breakfast, laughing as she complained about Felix still waking her early to go for their run. I offered to go, but the Raj *hates* when I come and refused to allow it. He's still sore that I'm faster than him by a good bit, despite being told over and over that my animal is *made* for speed. Dolly pleaded with him to let me take her spot because of her aches, but he had us slather her with muscle cream and send her off anyway.

"Chess, you've drifted, man."

I blink, shaking my head for a second as my eyes refocus. "Shit. Sorry, Aubrey. I was thinking about last night and then Dolly whining this morning because Mr. Taskmaster wouldn't let her out of cardio."

Ren grins as he lazes in a big chair across the room. "The Raj is immovable about some things, it seems. I wouldn't have believed it until I saw it because she's so damn crafty. But he's determined to get her endurance at peak in case shit goes down."

I nod, straightening my files as I sigh. "His worry about her safety overrides the pouty lip and kinky nickname, I guess. I don't blame him; my time in that office yesterday was like walking around on glass barefoot. I had to think about every fucking question the bitch asked and weigh my words to make sure I wasn't giving her more material. I really wish we could excise that putrid, oozing boil."

Aubrey snorts as he rises to go to the printer again. "You have a way with words, Chester. It's disgusting, but it definitely got the point across."

"I've never understood shifters who spend their lives purposefully being cruel to others," I admit as I scribble a note on the timeline near 'opium' then look up. "Bloodstone was full of cats big and small who were so desperate for the old psycho's approval that they watched the abuse and illegal shit going on without a word. And I'm not talking about people who feared for their loved ones —like the twins—but shifters who had no skin in the game, yet allowed atrocities and harm to come to others so they could vicariously enjoy it."

"*Oui, mon chat,*" Renard says sadly. "I did not witness it in my clutch, but for one time, and I can empathize with your frustration and pain. It is hard to accept that there are beings whose greatest joy is seeing others fail or causing them to hurt. But it exists in all forms—humans, shifters, Fae, mythicals... None of us are exempt from rotten apples."

"Dragons aren't exempt, either. I don't remember as much from my clash, but the ones online are insufferable elitists and do nothing but suck up to the non-exiled royals." The librarian frowns for a second, pausing to notate something on one of his sheets before he continues. "And we know even the fucking students at these damn schools are barely more than mynahs for their parents' agendas. Snack size has avoided those idiots from freshman year as much as possible, yet they seek her out to pummel her emotionally every chance they get."

"*Really* wish we could deal with those girls. I'm not one for hitting a female, but I'd make an exception for that Erikson girl. She's got rancid meat where her heart and brains should be," I grumble as I tuck my legs under me. "Imagine telling everyone how damn talented and successful and busy you are, but spending inordinate amounts of time bullying someone who hasn't spoken to you in years. It's pathetic."

Ren grins, his eyes dancing as he looks at me in interest. "Chester Khan, I like this evil streak you're developing in regard to our woman. It's hot as hell and I volunteer to help you with any low-grade mischief you might want to get up to in regard to those *vaches*."

Uh-oh. I've started the chaos gremlin up; is this going to get me in trouble with Felix?

THE DAY GOES BY QUICKER THAN I WOULD HAVE EXPECTED, AND when the Raj gets home, he joins us in the library as we work. He's got lesson plans to deal with, but I like that he doesn't hole up in a dark room with bourbon alone anymore. Having the guy I've always seen as my big brother back makes my cheetah happy —something he's finally getting enough of. A purr rumbles in my chest as I sip the tea I went upstairs to make earlier, contentment filling me from head to toe as my tired eyes filter through the ridiculous amount of shit we're digging through.

"*Kowabunga!*" Fitz yells as he bounces into the room, leaping over a table to come skidding to a halt in front of me.

Aubrey whips his head around, glaring at my mate like he wants to incinerate him on the spot. *"Fitzgerald Khan, I will fricassee your ass.* Do not treat my library like a goddamn stadium."

Rennie chuckles, his tail flicking as he winks at me. "Now, Flames. He's like a puppy; you can't be angry when it gets excited and piddles on the rug occasionally."

"Yeah!" Fitz crows then scowls at the gargoyle. "Wait…. no. Fuck you, Stone Temple Poet. I'm all man and all feline—ask Chessie and our girl."

I blink at them, looking from the winged ancients to the amused king for a moment before I shrug. "I don't have any complaints. And… I'd rather not get the ick from you making him sound like some *Lolita-esque* grossness. Didn't my angel wag her finger at you guys for that already?"

"Chesssterrrrrr," the stone shifter groans as he flops out even more like one of us in his big chair. "Don't be such a buzz kill, *ami.* You're all *les enfants* to Flames and me; we pre-date the humans' landing on this continent. How do you think I feel, mmm?"

The dragon snorts and I smile when small smoke rings flitter through the air. "Rennie is correct. I pre-date so many things I'm having nostalgia flashbacks in every era I'm sifting through." He sighs, leaning back in the chair then sitting up again when it makes a suspicious sound. "I miss when the wealthy patronized the arts heavily; my best horde items are from those times. Now everything is made by mass production and it breaks so easily."

My gaze drops to his chair and he nods. "To be fair, you're a big guy, Aubrey. This furniture wasn't made for preds of your size."

"No shit," Felix mutters and the next death stare is focused on the tiger. "It's true, Draconis. Quit being cheap and have the Captain order you custom shit like you did at Apex. You'll never live it down if the damn things give out while you're working."

Fitz grins manically, leaning in to pat the surly librarian's head.

"He's right, Growly Gecko. Baby Girl and I will laugh until we have to shower off to save face. No cap, big guy."

"Fitz, what the actual fuck are you—"

"Anyone home down here? Yoo-hoo!"

We all grin at one another, the jabs forgotten when her voice echoes in the outer hallway. Dolly appears moments later clad in her Pred Games practice uniform, dirt, sweat, and the smell of blood. It's fucking delicious and the atmosphere in the room goes from joking to deadly serious within seconds.

"You smell good, Baby Girl," Fitz says as he moves to her side, sniffing her neck with a shudder. "I think our girl broke a piece off someone, guys."

She grins, her eyes flashing with the red of her bunny as she nods. "I took a chunk out of an ocelot. Coach Z tells us to pull our hits, but this chick refused to stop coming. I had to put her on the ground and do that… thing I do in the ring to make them fuck off."

Felix tilts his head, smirking. "You dominated her, Princess. The Alpha bunny made the tiny kitten its bitch."

Her nose wrinkles and Dolly shakes her head. "First, I don't like that phrase. I'm a bitch by most definitions, and that does *not* mean I'm going to let some jackass pin me down until I concede." A throat clears and she rolls her eyes. "In the bedroom is different because I'm *consenting* to giving up my power and that's even more powerful than domination. Everyone knows that, Tiger Prince."

The elder Khan chuckles, rising to join his twin in sandwiching her against him. "Very true, Princess. You're learning so well."

"Chess and I are aware of that fact, too," Ren says with a yawn. "You're not giving us praise."

"*You* don't need it," Aubrey mutters. "You've been a pain in the ass all day. At least Chester made lunch and afternoon tea. What have you done to earn your keep?"

"Boys," Dolly says as she pulls away from the Khans. "Don't bicker. It's been a hell of a day, and I could eat an entire hippopotamus then have room for dessert. Maybe we can order in while I shower? I'd like to get this yuck off of me."

Aubrey and Ren look at one another, then nod. The dragon gathers his papers, then takes Renard's, creating neat stacks on the table. I follow suit, putting my pile next to theirs and stretch up on my toes. Fitz comes over and grabs me, burying his face in my neck this time.

"Don't think I forgot you, love."

He puts on the scariest psycho mask for the rest of the world, but with the people he loves, Fitz Khan is as soft as a baby blanket.

"I don't get hugs," the gargoyle mumbles and his mate snorts.

"You've been here annoying me all day."

Dolly frowns at him, smacking the librarian's big arm before she walks over to snuggle Ren close. "I missed you, even if he's being a dick. I miss all of you when I have to venture out and deal with the rest of this damn campus. It's full of snobs and assholes, like home, but with prettier accents."

I can't fault her for that statement—I've had the same experience and I doubt it will get better as the year goes on.

KNOW YOUR ENEMY

DELORES

MY RUN WITH FELIX THIS MORNING IS BRUTAL AGAIN—I HAVE THE feeling that Tuesday/Thursday ones are going to kill me all semester long. He's grumpy as fuck about his sleazy cousin and while I get that he feels helpless, I'm going to be Usain Bolt by the time he's done with me. I don't say anything, though, because truthfully, having better speed and endurance is good for me when I'm being stalked by evil Fae and fuck knows who else.

Practicality is my new goal when it comes to secret enemies and I'm winning at it.

Cori and Rufus are waiting for me when I exit the library, their gazes hungry as they watch for me to pull out 'breakfast to go' from Chessie. When I do, Cori moans happily, taking her fishy concoction with a grateful expression and Rufus flashes his pointy teeth. My cheetah has life time devotees because of his thoughtfulness and it makes me smile as we walk towards the admin building in the early morning sunshine.

"You're never going to believe this, Dollypop," Rufus says around a huge bite of his burrito. "My fucking juries include year-long projects I only get this semester to complete. What a crock of hippo shit."

"Me, too," I sigh as I think about the routines I have to choreograph and practice for a final grade that could flunk me. "I have songs, dances, papers, scenes... and they all require the most ridiculous amount of full show shit. Like everyone else has already paired up with people to get this stuff done. What are transfers going to do?"

Cori swallows her bite and wipes her mouth, giving us both a look. "We team up, of course. I can do costumes for both of your stuff. It will help fulfill *my* requirements. We can all work on any sets, plus I bet the triplets could help procure props if you ask, Ru-Ru."

He nods, his expression thoughtful. "They can and that means we won't overload our girl's logistic cheetah."

Grimacing, I nod. "That would help because he's got food and organization in our fam. He's doing fine, but I don't want to swamp the poor guy. I'd feel bad."

"That means you two can model the costumes for me and everyone can star in the movies or scenes. I'm sure all of our friends will help. We just need to ask Raina." Cori grins and ducks her head, flushing for a moment. "My big project is Z's uniforms and thank fuck for Dolly suggesting it to her. It's perfect for making a big splash."

I arch my brow at her for a moment, sensing something off. She doesn't continue, though, so I move on. "Well, that's *your* biggest piece checked off. What's the big one you need help with Ru-Ru?"

He rolls his eyes to the sky and groans dramatically. "I have to make an entire short film! It's absolutely insane how much work that will take between shooting, scripting, editing, costumes... I feel like I'm going to *die* by the end."

Coco and I giggle as he rambles on for a minute, pulling his best Oscar-worthy histrionics, then she finally smacks him in the arm. "For the love of sparkly sequins, Rufus, calm down. We can all help with that. Come up with a premise and perhaps we can figure out how to cut some of the work out of the process. If it's unscripted, that will excise a huge amount of work, for example."

He blinks, tilting his head as we approach the doors to the Alexandré building. "Oh, shit, Coco! That's brilliant. Let me stew on it for a while and I'll get back to you when I have something suitably clever and avant garde."

"See? Team work makes the dream work, guys," I wink with a grin. "Now let me get inside to suffer through this asshole's pompous crap and Heathers' bullying so it's done for the week. Ciao!"

I have no idea what my bestie has brewing in his spiky head, but I guarantee it's going to be amazing—I can't wait.

"THE MAGIC ACCORDS WERE NECESSARY TO KEEP THE PEACE AND prevent humans from discovering our existence. However, Fae and the other magical folks are simply not as *evolved* as shifters, especially in terms of intelligence, so the factions ended up at war before they could be signed."

I roll my eyes as Asani drones on, weaving his shifter-loving fanfic to a rapt audience. He hasn't presented any actual *proof* this is how the history went—not one non-shifter written document, art piece, or even reference book that isn't distributed by the Councils. Yet everyone in this room—particularly my nemeses—are eating his bullshit up with spoons. I'm not typically so jaded, but... it's pretty obvious this isn't the whole picture.

You'd have to be exceptionally gullible and naive to accept that entire groups of people are sub-par because our glorious leaders say so.

Sighing as I scribble a few notes with my stylus, I use the time to study everyone in my classroom. I've caught names and I'm writing them down with little notations that help me remember what side I think they fall on. After finding out my roommate was a planted poisoner last year, I'm not taking chances with classmates. I want Fitzy including them in dark web searches and finding out their backgrounds and connections before I have to deal with them individually. Professors are insane and I can't guarantee one of them won't—

"And that will be the topic of your first group project this semester!"

Damn it. This is exactly what I was worried about.

I pull up the messaging screen, hastily firing off a group message to the guys.

> BabyGirl: Guys, your dick cousin is assigning group projects.

> TigerWoody: Never fear, BabyGirl, I'm on it. Gimme names.

> BabyGirl: I don't have them yet, but I will once I do.

> TigerKing: I don't like this.

> EmoBatman: I find this much too convenient, petite lapin.

LustyLibrarian: What will you do if he puts you with one of your ex-friends, lunchable?

BabyGirl: I don't know, big guy. If I complain, he'll know one of my weaknesses. If I don't, it will be Hell on earth.

TigerKing: Who says it won't be anyway? Group projects are rarely balanced in terms of effort, and the lack of participation can make or break grades of all involved. It feels like a trap to ensure your grades dip.

BabyGirl: Shit, I hadn't considered that, Felix. Thanks for making me even more nervous.

TigerKing: Sorry, Princess. I'm being realistic.

BabyGirl: It's okay. I have to tune back in now. Talk later, boys. Behave.

The rapid-fire exchange only took seconds, but I'm relieved to see both Heathers already have partners moving their seats to gather with them. It appears this is a duo project and my eyes flick around the room to see who's left. Hopefully, it's a female because honestly? I don't know if I can deal with some rando douche guy trying to skate off of me and Fitz might actually kill the dude when he finds out even if they don't flirt.

Priorities are important—no dead people, no panic attacks, and no slackers.

"Delores Drew, you will be paired with Amity LaPorte." Asani gives me a smug look as I recognize a girl from my Ballet class making a pissed off expression. "I expect great things from you, *cheries.*"

I have to swallow back barf as his use of French makes me want to hurl. When Rennie does it, it's lyrical and romantic which makes my thigh clench. This guy sounds like he's mimicking the chef from the Little Mermaid and it makes me dry as the Sahara. Sucking in a deep breath, I gather my things, moving from my seat to be next to Amity. She hasn't moved a muscle except to sneer as Asani continued on, so I don't have much choice.

"You're in my Ballet class, right?" I say as I sit down. My face is bright with my 'socializing' smile and I'm actively trying to project friendly vibes. This situation probably isn't salvageable, but at least I can say I didn't make it worse.

She sniffs, straightening her materials fussily before looking up at me with bright amber eyes. *"Peut-être que vous n'êtes pas aussi stupide que salope. Excellent.[1]"*

I blink at her, grinding my teeth so my jaw doesn't hit the ground at her bitchy response. "Excuse me?"

"Les Américains stupides ne parlent jamais la langue des pays qu'ils visitent. Très bien, je vais passer à l'anglais puisque tu es tellement... handicapé.[2]"

The bunny inside of me catches enough of her snooty insult to push at my skin in an effort to be let loose. I grit my jaw harder, keeping the snarl of anger in so I don't draw attention to myself. My eyes close, and I use the tricks Aubrey and I work on together to help keep our beasts from busting loose. After a few moments, I let out a long, slow breath, then look at the nasty girl with red eyes.

"I don't know what your problem is, LaPorte, but I don't allow *anyone* to speak to me that way. Show some goddamn respect or I'm skipping the professor to head for the Dean."

She gives me a saccharine smile, batting her lashes. "Ah, there's the *lapin en colère*[3] I've heard so much about. I wondered what it would take to get you riled and now I know."

Why the fuck does that matter?

"Look, if you don't like me, fine. You need better standards, but whatever. I don't let that shit bother me anymore." I tap my pencil on the desk, getting her eyes back to mine. "But I won't tolerate being called names, nor will I put up with you being nasty. Get it together and act like an adult or I promise, you'll regret it."

Her laugh tinkles as she shrugs. "I highly doubt that, Delores Drew. This is my third year at *l'Academie* and I have the connections to sway anyone I like to my side. You can do your worst, but it will not affect me in the slightest."

Great. Another one of those girls. Do they mass produce these bitches or something?

"Whatever. Look, I'll take the first half of this paper—the part about the build-up to the Accords, and you take the back half. We'll put them together and turn them in at the end after we read over it. Sound good?"

"As if my part would need you to proof it, you talentless plagiarist." Amity sniffs again and I narrow my gaze at her nostrils, suddenly wondering if her erratic behavior is a symptom of heavy Predstatsy use.

I frown at her, shaking my head. "What the hell are you talking about you crazy woman? I've never copied anything in my entire life. I don't need to. My grades are my own."

"Not what I hear. You were caught at the school you blew up. I assume you did it to cover your tracks as you moved to a new hunting ground." The feline shifter arches a brow. "If you think I will not ensure everyone knows of your proclivity, you are sorely mistaken."

Pinching the bridge of my nose, I close my eyes. I can guess who spread *that* gem around. Despite the *many* times they've been smacked down for slanderous bullshit, the stupid Heathers never seem to understand they're going to eventually lose it all when I unleash on them. When I open my eyes, my gaze cuts to them, noting their tandem smirks as they see my struggles. I have no idea where the fuck they're vomiting their bile—I blocked them and their cronies years ago on every platform possible. But it's happening again, and I need to address it before it gets out of hand.

"Fine. Do whatever on your part, Amity. I'll read it and give you notes, but you don't have to take them. If you can't take constructive criticism, that's your problem, not mine." Irritated beyond comparison, I grab my things and rise to my feet. "I'm going to the library to work for the rest of class."

I swear to every deity in the sky and all the ones below, one day, I'm going to punch those girls so hard their teeth end up in their colons.

PSYCHO

FITZ

SINCE MY TWIN GOT TO SNEAK IN TIME DURING HER LUNCH ON Tuesday, I cut loose as quickly as possible today so I can find her on library duty before anyone but the spicy salamander is home. Obviously, I can't kick him out of his *own* library—

Or can I? I am Fitz Khan, after all.

Grinning to myself as I imagine his rage when I tell him to scram, I almost skip to the Kavarit building we're living in. Our reptilian friend is doing much better than he used to now that we all have our girl and he's not hiding his skin slapping with the Frenchman.

That doesn't matter when it comes to his usual buttons, though, and winding him up is even more fun now that people try to calm him. In fact, it's one of my favorite things that don't involve death or my mates naked and wriggly.

"Fitz Khan, this is your life," I boom to myself as I head for the back door of the huge building, chuckling at my own joke. "Man, that's fucking classic. Too bad no one but me heard it. Wasteful."

I hold my arm up to the sensor, hoping like hell the flaky gargoyle has finally got this shit on lockdown. Keeping tracking of the fucking card is going to make me insane if he doesn't get it working— Oh. There it is. Hell yeah. I grab the handle and head inside, waiting until it closes completely before I stride toward the library.

Safety first, baby.

The suite is quiet, so I know no one but our girl and the winged weenie is home. Chessie will get home next, probably, and start a ridiculously tasty smelling dinner that everyone will inhale as if we haven't eaten in a year. Between him and the Onyx Chef, we're all going to have to join my big bro on that morning torture run eventually. I've avoided it so far because Felix deserves some alone time and he's most satisfied when he's in control—that means he has to run with a woody every day, which amuses the hell out me. Why interrupt *that* amazingly funny shit? I'm definitely going to get it on tape one day and that will let me watch my baby girl bounce all over the trail, too.

Win-win for Fitzy.

Yanking the door to the library open, I bounce in, looking around for the two of them eagerly. "It'ssssssss Fitzy!"

It takes a moment before the big ass dragon's head pops up from behind a large shelf, his expression guilty as hell. Sniffing the air, I point a shaky finger at him as I accuse, *"Youuuuuuuu!"*

The look on his face goes from guilty to sheepish and then to an unrepentant smirk when Baby Girl pops up next to him, her hair a tangled mess in back and skin flushed a pretty pink. "Fitzy, you're early."

Making an annoyed sound as I advance on the self-righteous dragon, I continue chastising him. "What happened to 'no sex in my fucking library,' you sanctimonious old prick? This is the *second* time I've caught you!"

He wipes his mouth on his sleeve, then picks up the glasses I missed on top of the shelf. The scent fills my nostrils and I glare at them both until he starts laughing. Baby Girl joins him, giggling as she moves around the corner in her uniform skirt that definitely has nothing but those sexy thigh-highs under it. "Aw, come on, Fitzy, baby. I had a hard day. Aubrey was… distracting me."

"I'll just bet he was," I grumble, but it's really for show. She snuggles up into my arms, and I press a kiss to her temple. "So who do I get to dismember with a spork? A spot of violence might calm my jealousy over Scaly Balls' being such a hypocrite."

"Hey!"

Ignoring his weak protest, Dolly looks up at me with a fond smile. "You can't kill your cousin yet; we've discussed this. And I don't think you can disappear anymore Council students without them flooding this place with more assholes to balance it out. I'll have to handle this snooty feline and your dickhead relative on my own."

My eyes flash amber with my tiger and I squeeze her closer. "I don't have to kill anyone. I'll just grab a little souvenir to remind them who they're dealing with."

"Fitzgerald, you can't—"

I arch a brow at the dragon, my expression amused. "Oh, Lord Draconis, you'll find I definitely *can* and certainly *will*. Give it time."

Baby Girl sighs, pulling back as she sighs. "Do what you must, baby, but *no killing yet*. Got it?"

I can live with that; she just gets me.

"Cross my heart and hope my asshole Father dies," I promise with a wink. "No killing until we're all in agreement——or perhaps, one of us loses it and then we have to deal with it on the fly."

Aubrey snorts. "At least he's honest, bite size."

"Through and through," I agree as I slap her pert ass and she squeals. "For better or for worse, I can't be bothered to make shit up. It's hard enough keeping track of real shit."

That makes Dolly smile and my heart flutters as she grabs my hand. She tugs me toward the tables on the other side of where she and the dragon have left a delicious smelling spot behind the bookcase. When I growl at her playfully, she laughs, wagging a finger at me. "Nope, break time is over. Come help Aubrey and me with the work they've been doing on timelines. We're almost through the twentieth century. Once we get everything highlighted, we are going to use one of the boards Chessie ordered to make comparison columns."

A damn good idea——the egghead trio have their shit together.

"I'll try, Baby Girl, but you know how hard it is for me to focus on shit like this," I reply as she yanks a chair out. "Maybe you should sit on my lap?"

The dragon snorts as he joins us. "I highly doubt that will allow for concentration, Fitzgerald. Nice try, though."

"You take this list of shifter events. Maybe something will spike in your memories? I'm taking the humans this time, and Aubrey has the Fae."

"You switch off?" I ask as I scratch my chin. "That's a pretty good plan. Seeing the same thing over and over makes your brain blur after a while."

"Indeed." Dolly takes the chair next to me, straightening her papers before she hands me a marker. "Use this color so we know where you started."

I blink, noting the bright orange highlighter. "You're even color coding it? This *definitely* has Chessie written all over it. Our boy is fucking baller at this kind of project."

"Chester has been invaluable in helping collate the research. He really should take some classes after we prevent this idiotic war; I think he's perfect for a library associate position."

"Noooo! Don't get rid of Betsy," Dolly says with a frown. "I like her. She's a scaredy cat, but I don't want any of the allies we've made to be sent elsewhere if we can avoid it."

"Lunchable, I would never get rid of Betsy. However, depending on where we end up, perhaps he could get a better spot than being an assistant for a nasty vulture woman trying to steal our lives for her shitty pulp fiction?"

He has a point; Chessie is such a jack-of-all-trades that landing the art position at Apex despite lack of credentials was a boon.

"I think it's a fabulous idea and I'll back you one hundred percent if you tell him, Charcoal Breath." I grin at him cheesily and he rolls his eyes, muttering what I assume is a 'thanks' under his breath.

All for one and one for all and shit.

"Fitz? What the hell are *you* doing down here?"

I look up, rubbing tired eyes as my twin walks in with Chessie and Moulin Huge in tow. "I'm hurt, bro. I'll have you know that I'm doing a fucking brilliant job at this nerdy shit. Ask our girl or Fire Pants."

They all look at the dragon inquisitively and I chuckle. Of course they won't trust our bunny not to sugarcoat things when it comes to me. *I'm* obviously her favorite, no matter what anyone else says. Aubrey sighs heavily, wincing like it's painful to admit. "He's actually been doing a good job and not distracting us too much."

Take that, butt munches.

"Really?" Felix gives both of my co-workers a suspicious look and Dolly narrows her eyes.

"Aubrey would *never* cover up for him, my grumpy King. Now come over here and kiss me, before I get mad about you picking on Fitzy."

My brows bob as my cheetah follows my twin, detouring to give me a rewarding smooch. "Thank you, baby. And thank you for defending me, Baby Girl. Hashtag blessed, that's me."

Renard rolls his eyes as he heads for the chair next to his mate. His eyes scan over the work we've done, and he whistles. "*Je serai damné.*[1] You have been working hard, *mes amis.*"

"We have and we're so fucking close to being current. Maybe after we get food, Chester can take earlier pages of one for his board and the twins can do the same? If we get the boards started, this will come together much faster."

Dolly groans and shakes her head. "You guys can, but I have to work on this fucking paper your asshat cousin gave me. I have a partner and she's a nasty witch—I don't trust her as far as I could throw her in the ring before I shift. I may have to do the entire thing and hold back the part she's responsible for until I see if she's actually going to do her part."

Felix's head whips around with a snarl. "*What?*"

Holding my hand up, I look at the other possessive alphas in the room. "Everyone calm down. Our Queen has asked that we let her handle this on her own. No killing, but I get to hunt her down for my trophy case once they hand it in."

"I never assign group projects," the gargoyle says as he flicks through the pages the dragon worked on in the Fae pile. "They never encourage cooperation and it's always a battle when grading because one person often pulls more weight than everyone else combined."

"*Exactly!*" Dolly says in exasperation. "And I've never met this chick before—just like the one in the Pred Games arena. But the two Heathers who haven't been volunteered as tributes yet seemed pretty smug about Asani's choice, so they may have had a hand in it. I've been pretending I was paranoid because that means I really need to be careful with this assignment. They always have plots going."

"I still think we could kill the two of them and blame the rebels," I mutter. "Not the new chicks, but the damn bitches who follow us like obsessed fans trying to fuck up your life because they have none of their own."

Baby Girl laughs, grabbing my hand and lacing our fingers together before she kisses them. "Never stop making me feel better with threats of violence against my cartoonish nemeses, Fitzy."

"Perish the thought," Ren says with a smirk. "How would we survive without Fitz' psycho tendencies?"

"You wouldn't."

Chess claps his hands, then flushes red as we all look at him. "Okay. If Angel has homework, we need to get food and drinks, then come down here to get our timeline finished while she works in the nook over there." He pauses sniffing for a moment, then gives Aubrey a wry look. "And possibly grab some air freshener since obviously people were taking a *break* earlier."

The big guy shrugs, and our girl laughs. Standing up, she lets go of me and goes to my mate. "I'm corrupting him very slowly. Sorry, not sorry."

Felix shakes his head, sighing as if we're the most trying thing in the universe. "Food. Air freshener. Homework. Research. We have our orders, you malcontents. Let's get moving or none of us will get '*breaks*' tonight."

Good one, big bro. Very nice.

Maniac

Delores

I can't keep my hands from trembling as Raina and the Captain walk me to what I *know* will be the worst hour of my first week at *l'Academie*. The guys wanted to accompany me, but even Coco and Rufus agreed that it would be a bad plan to show up with backup. I have to do this myself to show this vile woman I won't be cowed by her abuse, nor will I hide behind anyone's skirts to protect myself.

The raccoons look at me sympathetically as we trudge up the steps of the Alexandré building. Raina has been chirping cheery updates about my prey friends, their new duties, and the nicer lodgings they've been given here. I'm listening, but I think they both know how distracted my mind is. It's easy to know you could take someone in a physical fight—and I'd wipe the fucking floor with Rockland given the chance—but it's another to survive a mental and emotional beating once a week for a semester.

I should know; I grew up with Lucille for a mother.

Destruction of self-worth and hope is a long game that narcissists like my mother and this witch play well—it leaves damage that is difficult to heal, even with time. I was doing well despite Lucille and the Heathers' effort until Carina came along. Now I find myself struggling at the oddest moments, even though my brain knows the garbage she spewed isn't true. But I refuse to let her win, so I fight it with every fiber of my being and find joy in every one of my successes so she won't have the control over me she desperately craves.

"Dolly, are you okay?" Raina asks and I blink, looking down at her big, concerned eyes.

Sighing as the Captain opens the door to the building, I nod. "Mostly? I'm just fighting the bad stuff racing through my head and heart so I can show her who she's messing with. It's harder than you'd think."

The Captain squints at me with one eye as we walk past. "Listen up, lassie. I'm the last one to be blowin' smoke up yer arse, but... me matey is always right. This wench innit worth yer worries, nor the time o' day compared to ye. Walk the plank with yer head high and yer sword out."

I have to swallow a giggle; his pirate speak always makes me laugh, but the raccoon is deadly serious right now. Laughing would only take away from the very sweet message he's trying to convey. So I nod, give him a salute, and then smile at Raina. "I'll be okay to go down in the elevator alone. Fitz has the cameras... I don't even have to wonder about that."

"Are you sure?" she asks, wringing her hands together. "I would be very upset should harm come to you because we shirked our assigned duties."

"I'm sure." I wink at the Captain and he nods, taking his mate's arm. "Now go do your chores so you have time with your boys before the night shift. Give them my love?"

"Always, Dolly. Be careful and do not hesitate to call for us if you need!"

I wait for them to exit, and close my eyes briefly, drawing in a calming breath before I head for the elevator. When I get in, I punch the number for Rockland's floor, and blow a kiss at the camera on the ceiling. I wasn't kidding; I have zero doubt Fitzy is watching me ascend in this steel cage from somewhere close enough to get here within moments of trouble.

He's dependably crazy like that, though it makes me feel protected and cherished.

When the doors open, I take another breath and let it out slowly, then I square my shoulders and head down the hallway with a confident stride. All I have to do is keep my armor up, my Lucille face on, and give this woman zero to work with. I can and *will* do this because she is not my fucking supervisor, nor is she the arbiter of my worth. She doesn't even have the amount of malice in her whole body that my mother has in her dew claw on one foot. This will be a breeze.

"Miss Drew?"

The sound scares the holy hell out of me, but I clamp my lips together in a scowl to keep from shrieking. *No weakness*, I remind myself as I force my eyes to focus on the person who appeared out of nowhere. Once I do, I can't help but gape—there's simply no other option. Standing just inside the blind corner by Rockland's office is a honey badger so massive he makes Goliath and Monstro look tiny.

No way this dude isn't some kind of freakish science experiment.

"Uh… that's me…" I say as my eyes rove over the bulky guy that damn nears fills the width of the hallway and almost touches the ceiling. "Not to be rude, but who the hell are you?"

His laugh is a deep base, soothing like James Earl Jones, and his smile is reassuring as he slowly reaches into the front pocket of his impeccably tailored suit to hand me a card.

It says 'Skelly McCoy, Licensed, Bonded, & Deputized Arbitration/Negotiation Consultant, McCoy & Associates Inter-Species Attorneys-at-Law.' Blinking, I look at the mammoth dude, noting his suave, slicked back hair and clean shaven handsomeness. No wonder Farley made him one of the 'end of negotiations' guys. If this badger confronted me in a dark office, I'd definitely lose my shit, and he's not even *shifted* right now. People with less unsavory pasts than me must piss their pants when he comes knocking.

"Oh. Yes, um, Farley mentioned you traveled with him and the other… delivery men?" I have no idea what group moniker these dudes use, so I just wing it.

"We are negotiations specialists," he says with a grin full of sharp fucking teeth I didn't expect. "Our skills are similar but increase in intensity as you move through the ranks."

Good to know—that means this little session is going to be very interesting.

"The Boss would prefer you have legal representation present in every counseling session until he states otherwise. I will be recording them surreptitiously, and since this is a single party consent area, your permission will suffice for that activity." He pulls the pen out of his pocket, blowing on the end of it then saying, "Please state your full name and give full consent for recording these typically privacy protected sessions for use in your legal proceedings."

Eying the door nervously, I lick my lips. Before I do anything, I need to make *certain* this dude is who he claims to be. "Hold on just a moment, please."

I pull out my phone, suddenly thankful I gave myself plenty of time to arrive at my appointment. Rockland would use tardiness as a weapon, and I'm not saying *shit* on tape until I verify this guy is legit. It rings a few times, then a sleepy voice comes on the line, greeting me. "Hi, Farley, sorry to wake you, but I'm standing with a mountain of a shifter claiming to be Skelly, business card and all. He says he's to escort me into the session and I have to give consent for him to record it. Is that what you asked for?"

"Hell's bells, Dolly girl. This is the asscrack of dawn, and you're the rooster who won't stop crowing." I chuckle and he goes on, his accent getting thicker as he awakens. "Ask your friend what his favorite movie is—not the one he tells people, but the *real* one."

I look up at the big guy, covering the phone as I ask, "What is your favorite movie—the real one, not the fake one you tell people. Farley said I should ask."

Surprisingly, the enormous badger turns a beautiful shade of scarlet as he rubs the back of his neck and curses my lawyer. He finally gives in, muttering, "The Cutting Edge. And tell him he'll pay for that shit."

The laughter echoing out of my phone tells me this verification worked. "Fine. He's for real; I'll do the recording. Thanks for helping, Farley."

"Anytime, darlin'. I'm headed back to sleep after a very late night in Paris, but you take care. Tell Skelly his ass is mine if a single hair on your fluffy tail is harmed while in his charge."

The badger is rolling his eyes, so he obviously heard that. "Go back to bed, Boss. She's under control."

I click the end call button, nodding at his pocket as I wait for him to turn on the recorder again. He does and I clear my throat before saying, "I, Delores Diamond Drew, give permission for these sessions to be recorded exclusively for legal purposes pertaining to my case against Carina Rockland by McCoy &

Associates. Any other use of this material must be separately consented to in writing by me and no one else."

His grin gets wider. "Look at you, smarty pants. Very nice."

"I've got a maniac stealing my life story for profit, a bunch of mean girls who attack me online for funsies, and a reputation previously smeared by my own mother. I had to brush up on my knowledge just to survive the onslaught." Grabbing the knob, I warn him before we go in. "If you've got a temper, keep it frosty. She lives to rage bait and accuse others of what she's been doing to me."

"Oh, please let her try." The fangy grin he gives me is shiver-worthy, and I let him have his plotting as we head inside.

Chessie isn't working this morning—something I'm certain the corpse nibbler planned. She was hoping to corner me alone, as she has in the past, so there are no witnesses to her abusive and downright unethical behavior. Unfortunately for her, my lawyer is cunning and brash, with zero fucks to give when defending me. It must run in the family because he reminds me a lot of Rufus.

"Good morning, Delores. Come in and we'll start—" The spindly woman dressed in a silly looking Gothic-style dress blinks as she glares down her nose at my escort. "Excuse me, sir, but this is a private therapy session and you are not permitted to join Miss Drew."

Giving her a smarmy grin, Skelly reaches for another one of his cards, handing it over. "Good morning, ma'am. As a fully contracted Legal Consultant for the McCoy & Associates team, I have both my client's permission and a directive from my employer to observe this appointment. You'll find if you contact your own attorney, the Headmaster, or any other source that I'm legally required entry based on those requests."

Sniffing, Rockland looks from him to me, probably weighing the cost of arguing the point in the limited time she's been granted with me. "Fine. But you will remain silent as an observer should be."

I roll my eyes, following her and she does the awkward sashay to the office that I assume was meant to be sassy and sexy, but ends up looking like a knock-kneed stork swaying from foot to foot. This is going to be a painful hour, for sure.

The moment the door closes, Rockland looks up from her new desk, her hands adjusting the ridiculous decor on it for a second in a silent effort to command the power in the room. I stare back at her without a word, like Felix and Lucille have both taught me, waiting until she breaks. When she finally does, I notice a toothy smile from my bulky badger friend as he sits crammed into a stupidly small chair.

"Miss Drew, it seems you find yourself shunted to yet another institution under a cloud of scandal. I can't imagine why Capital Prep would not welcome you back, though I suspect the property damage, scandalous sexual escapades, and anti-social personality disorder are likely part of that decision."

Excuse, the fuck out of me?!

Before I can answer, Skelly holds his hand up for me to stop. "Miss Rockland, I'm afraid I must intervene on behalf of my client. This kind of rant is not only inaccurate, but unprofessional, slanderous, and legally actionable in terms of your ability to remain in your field. Perhaps you'd like to apologize and recon-sider your words?"

"I *said* you could observe *silently*!" she screeches as she jumps to her feet. "You will *not* interrupt my required sessions with your outrageous arrogance, Mr. McCoy. *I* am in charge in this room, and *I* am the one who decides what is and is not appropriate for this delinquent. She has made her own bed with her trashy behavior and is no longer welcome at the tables of the discerning elite."

Skelly stands, flexing his massive bulk as he gives her a slow, hungry look. His head tilts, studying her like all preds do their prey before he replies, "Carina Rockland, you are being officially warned. My client, Delores Diamond Drew, will no longer allow you to spew your petty jealousies and unfounded hatred for her in private or public arenas. Farley L. McCoy, Esquire, and his associates have served you with papers to that effect, but you seem incapable of respecting not only personal, but professional and legal boundaries. If you do not cease your abuse, libel, and slander in person and online, you will be sued to the fullest extent of civil law and when that's done, we will pursue criminal cyber-bullying and harassment charges in every country your poor judgment has been unleashed in. Do you understand?"

Holy fuck. This guy is terrifying. He looks like he's going to fucking devour her whole.

"You work for a shady strip mall lawyer that defends druggies. I'm not afraid of his thugs."

I wait for him to attack, but Skelly merely laughs at the hysterical woman. His voice is full of amusement as he shakes his head. "Apparently, you're not only too lazy to come up with your own ideas, but you're also too lazy to do research on the PredNet. The Boss didn't attend your slanted shifter schools in preparation for leading the legal department of our multi-species, international corporation, you idiot. He attended a *human* undergraduate school in a Southern Ivy league school, then reputable law schools in both the human and the shifter realm before he took over the practice his branch of our family runs. He was one of the youngest people ever in both worlds to present and win a case in front of the human Supreme Court and the Council Adjudicators of Merit."

"Well fuck," I mutter. I didn't know that, either.

"People often underestimate him because of his good ol' boy charm and the product our family distributes—legally, of course." Skelly smirks at me then turns to Rockland again. "But if we *were* also in charge of a secret drug cartel, not a pharmaceutical company on the up-and-up... what kind of fucking moron would come at our lawyer full blast and expect to survive with limbs intact? Just food for thought."

I'm too shocked by the blatant threat to even respond, so I just stare at the rat's nest on Rockland's head as thoughts go whirling through my mind.

"Miss Delores, let's go. I will walk you to your next class. I believe Ms. Rockland has some serious thinking to do."

I'll just fucking bet she does, Skelly. Five goddamn stars to you, man.

You Need To
Calm Down

Felix

"This girl is after her, Z. Keep your eyes on it."

The lioness looks at me in amusement, leaning back in her chair in the girls' Coach's office with her hands stacked behind her head. Unlike last year at Cappie, she's blinged out to the max here —it makes me wonder who she's hoping to impress. Zhenga hasn't been this obvious since our tenure at Apex, and I know she's moved on from me, but who the fuck has she set her sights on since we arrived? It had better not be my asshole cousin—not because I'm jealous, but because I *like* her when she's not harassing me.

Asani will chew her up and spit her out without a second thought.

"Felix, you worry like an old nanny goat. Your girl is coming into her own, which means she can defend herself. Of course I'd interfere if it was over the line, but you alpha morons need to keep your dicks in your pants. Dolly is capable and willing to fight her own battles—something we both know may be important in the future."

She's right and it annoys the fuck out of me. It's hard to explain how hard the tiger is riding me when it comes to the little family and friends we've gathered. It's my *responsibility* as the Raj to keep them safe and it's hard as hell when there are so many fucking enemies popping up out of nowhere. Our cheetah is keeping rigorous notes on them, but the amount of threats is becoming difficult to grasp simultaneously.

"I know she can, but that doesn't mean I'm not worried," I admit as I drop into the chair in front of her desk. I can't say this shit to the others without looking weak, but Zhenga understands how frustrating it is to not be able to protect those you feel responsible for. The good parts of the Leonidas pride are constant targets because of her brother and father—and she can't do a damn thing about it in exile. Being cut off from the evil families who spawned you is both a gift and curse that way.

She pushes forward, sitting up to put her elbows on her desk and look at me seriously. Again, I wonder who all the make-up and glam added to her coach gear is for, but I'm not going to ask if she doesn't volunteer the info. Zhenga's a grown woman and I'm not her keeper, just a friend. "You'd be a terrible fated mate if you didn't, Khan. Even when you were a bourbon soaked dickwaffle, I knew you were a good man, and it's why I pursued you. Not every eligible alpha leader is honorable and kind beneath their asshole exterior, you know."

Well, I'll be damned. She's being real with me.

"Then I'd be remiss if I didn't point out that others of my family do *not* have the same inclination as Fitz, Chess, and me. Be careful, Z."

Her eyes widen as realization spreads over her face and then she bursts out laughing hard enough to clutch her stomach. Tears are running down her cheeks as the amusement in her gets out, and it takes several minutes before she's able to take a gasping breath and regain composure. "Oh, Felix, you idiot."

"What?" I ask in puzzlement. I was pretty clear in my intent with that statement. Why is she acting like I told her to don a clown suit and give me a lap dance?

Zhenga shakes her head, then pulls a compact out of a drawer to check her face. A few quick swipes under her eyes with a tissue from the box on her desk seems to get her approval, then she looks at me again as she clicks the mirror shut. "Felix Ivan Nestor Khan... how could you *possibly* think I'd go anywhere *near* the rest of your degenerate ambush? I'm not *that* desperate to get into my father's good graces."

Ugh, the full name—she's serious as hell.

"You're becoming a good friend to my mate, Z, and you've been one to my little ambush even when I didn't realize it. I don't want to see you used up and discarded—or worse."

Her lips curve up, a satisfied smirk on forming slowly. "Such a softie now that you're getting laid on a regular basis. Don't worry; I won't spill the beans to anyone that your hardass image hides a squishy center."

"*Zhenga*," I chide, my expression dour. "I may be worried about you, but I'll happily kick your ass from here to Bloodstone in the ring any day, any time. Since we're in no way involved this time, I won't hold back."

"Oooh, I *like* the appearance of Danger!Khan again. Gives me those 'Mufasa' shivers." She pretends to shiver, clutching her arms around herself and I almost lose my temper.

Pinching the bridge of my nose, I suck in a deep breath to calm the beast inside. I know she's kidding, but fuck, I have such a hard time when it comes to my kin. "Z, having Asani around is making my tiger lose its mind. He's riding me hard and I'm struggling with my alpha tendencies more than I ever have since I was exiled."

Her expression turns sympathetic and she nods. "I don't blame you. Hell, I laughed because rumors of the shit that goes on at Bloodstone reaches every ear. You and your exiled bunch are the only good guys in that story, so *no*, I would *never* consider even looking at Asani Khan that way. I'd let someone skin me for a rug first."

Thank hell for that. I'd like to avoid a blood debt fight until it's absolutely necessary.

"Good. I've got enough issues dealing with Princess being in his class two times a week." For a moment, I let the exhaustion I've been hiding show. "My brain keeps replaying all the terrible things I saw him and the rest of the psychos who suck up to my father do before I was kicked to the curb."

Her brows furrow and she leans back again, looking up at the ceiling with a puff of air that feels as helpless as I do. "Felix, I'm doing everything I can to help your girl get stronger and more capable. You are, too. Your twin, whether he intends to or not, is honing her ferocity—I see it in her as she practices. The others are lending their strengths to her growth as a person and a predator. We can't predict if it will be enough if something bad happens, but we know she survived Lucille and Bruno Drew for eighteen years on her own. That took guts and moxie I don't know if I even have."

Chuckling, I nod. "Those two sadists give my father a run for his money, it's true. I was both grateful and furious when I heard the news about the nasty croc."

"How did your girl deal with it? She hasn't mentioned it to me," Zhenga asks curiously. "Mostly, she's just kicking ass and fending off that new girl giving her shit."

"Surprised, but not sad. Her reaction sort of spoke for itself." I shrug, not knowing what else to say. "The guys and I wanted to deal with him later, so there was disappointment, but not from her. She accepted it and moved on—even though it showcased how ruthless her mother is willing to be to stay on top."

"We all know how vicious the Council families are, Felix. My father is no joke, despite being ill, and the rest of them are as morally corrupt as her. She's just one of the top cats, so to speak." The lioness pauses for a moment, then adds, "And I heard Papa Rostoff showed his face in the States when Cappie was being destroyed. He hasn't come here since the Russian royals were alive."

What? Holy fucking shit. That old pimp never leaves his homeland; Z's right.

"That's... not good news." I frown, spinning the board around in my head again to look at the angles. Older Council members moving around when they are typically stationary and rule from afar feels even more serious than Fae showing their faces. "The biggest, most powerful elders must be taking notice of the Fae bullshit."

"Do you think they'll limit travel? That would fuck my whole plan for the Games teams here."

Thinking about it for a moment, I shake my head slowly. "No. The Games give a lot of those old coots good excuses to move around in ways they haven't in decades. It also provides cover for the current leaders to shuffle all over the globe."

"Sucks for figuring out what the fuck is going on, but I can't say that doesn't work for my strategy," Zhenga admits. "I hate to say that because I like your girl, too, but I also want to make this program work. The idiots here have neglected it for so long that most of my efforts are self-funded."

I make a face at her. "Jesus fuck, just ask Fitz to pull his weight. If you don't, I will. He probably doesn't even realize you're doing it because he's solely focused on the Princess and our family."

"Oh," she says. "Well, I will once my co-planner and I have everything hashed out completely. I don't want to bring anyone else in until we're totally ready." Her face flushes and I gape.

What the hell is that?!

"Z, I—"

Her phone rings and she holds a finger up as she answers it. Holding the phone to her ear, she smiles broadly. "Hi. No, I'm just in my office. Well, Felix is here. Yeah, he came to talk about—Yep. When? We'll probably be done soon, yeah. Okay, I'll meet you there. You, too. Okay, bye."

My eyes narrow at the tone in her voice and her posture as she talks to the mystery person. This is definitely whoever she's dressed up for—I remember what it looks like when my leonine friend is on the prowl. "On a deadline?"

She gives me a dirty look, then starts cleaning up the paperwork on her desk. "None of your business, Khan. As long as it's not Asani, you don't have to be worried, right?"

Putting my fingers on my temples, I growl softly. She's right, obviously, but I still don't want to see her harmed. "True, but—"

"No butts in *my* office, Felix." Her eyes dance and she winks playfully as she stands. "You need to scoot. I told you what you wanted to know and I'm not doing anything bad, so get back to skulking around or smacking your students when they say dumb shit. I have things to do."

Her sudden desire to leave makes my hackles raise, but Zhenga is an adult. I have too many things to manage as it is, and if she needs help, she's perfectly capable of letting me know. I grin to myself a little when I realize I'm actively ceding control in a situation—something that is definitely the Princess' influence. As much as we're helping her grow into the woman she wants to be, she's helping us be the men we should be, too.

"Don't be crude," I say with a grin. "But also, don't be a stranger if you need anything. Those of us cast aside by the idiots in charge for not being cruel and power hungry have to stick together."

Zhenga beams, nodding her head. "Absolute truth, buddy. Hell, if we weren't worried about the Fae slaughtering everyone responsible for their confinement, I'd say let them take over. It can't be any fucking worse than fuckwits we have running shit now."

I snort. "Preach, woman. I'd pay a pretty penny to see someone teach the Raj a lesson he sorely deserves, but then I won't get *my* vengeance and that can't happen. He's mine and Fitz's to deal with."

That's something I won't back off on—my father will die slowly and painfully by our hand for his sins, no matter what.

Swan Lake, Op 20, Act 1

Delores

I spent the rest of the day fighting off my fury and anxiety about my bitchy counselor. She didn't accomplish her goal of intimidating me, nor of making me doubt my extremely well-qualified attorney… but she did live rent-free in my head for a few hours. I hate that, but I'm just as capable of fear as any other being. My past still pinches when shit like this happens, so to distract myself, I focus solely on my singing and dancing. Despite the pecking of my professors, I got through it without incident and headed straight for my personal studio.

This little room is what all the students have for preparing their jury pieces and the size depends on what kind of specialty you are majoring in. It's supposed to be a haven for our creativity, but the relative emptiness of the hallways for theater and dance majors makes me suspicious. Pulling my bag up on my shoulder, I use my wrist to open the specially installed lock Fitzy and Rennie had the crew put in the minute they knew which one I was assigned. It clicks open and I enter, dropping my stuff on the big overstuffed chair in the corner. It has a sound system, a small upright piano, room to dance and a barre... but I can tell my guys have been inside, too.

The small fridge is likely stocked with food and drink, and definitely isn't university issue.

"Thank fuck for overbearing, adorable boyfriends," I murmur when my stomach growls. Technically my studio time doesn't start for an hour and I should be on lunch, but I wanted to get somewhere safe as soon as possible. I've felt like I'm being watched since Skelly and I left the admin building, and it's not my crazy tiger. At least, not only him—there's more than just a stalker mate trailing me around this campus.

Pressing my fingers to my eyes as I suck in a deep breath, I try to get my mind to focus. There are so many fucking things to deal with, but if I don't put that all aside to work on this *mountain* of school work, I'm going to flunk out. I plop down on the floor and make a pile for each class, plus the projects Ru-Ru, Coco, and I are collaborating on. Slowly, I take all the printouts, materials, and lists I've made for each one until the entire picture is spread out in front of me.

Hermes in a handcart, I am so screwed.

Blowing out another breath, I re-arrange the projects so they're in order of due date. That gives me a little relief as a great deal of them are farther out. If I work efficiently and plan carefully, I *should* be able to complete enough each week to stay on track. Obviously, I know there will be bumps in the road because the Universe laughs when I plan, but I think it's do-able without consuming so much caffeine I vibrate off the face of the Earth.

Since I've been pushing my voice and body in my previous classes, I grab the pile corresponding to the paper for the twins' asshole cousin, my laptop, and my food. Once I'm settled in the chair, I start my research on our topic.

The next few hours are going to suck.

AFTER TWO HOURS, MY LIMBS ARE CRAMPED, SO I PUT MY WORK aside and stretch. I might be able to get this damn thing done by the end of the weekend, then work on dividing it based on what I agreed to with my snooty partner. I'm going to do the entire damned thing just to be sure, and when she flakes out, I'll hand it in with a note to the knock-off Khan. I doubt he'll do anything about it since he's obviously out to get me; however, I have to try.

Frowning, I make sure to take pictures of my research that are date and time stamped, as well as shooting those and the draft to several cloud accounts, including Fitzy's, to make sure nothing weird happens to my work. After the bullshit at Apex, I'm more cautious about my work, especially in digital form. Heather E. is just egotistical enough to pull the same trick twice and I have to be prepared. The guys don't have the same connections as they did at Apex and Cappie, so I don't want to court disaster.

This shit is so fucking exhausting.

All these ridiculous people being jerks for whatever crazy reason they've made up in their minds are just noise; I know that. But it's hard not feel the strain of having to plan for random stealth attacks—whether vague or direct—when it's necessary every time I do anything. All my victories become fodder for their insanity and though I refuse to let them win by ducking my head and staying small, I have to watch for petty assholes to lob grenades in my happiness. They need to get a fucking life and move on, but I doubt that's ever going to happen.

"Just keep hopping, Dolly," I mumble to myself as I close my eyes. "Eventually, they'll find a new target and you won't be the sole focus of their ire."

I wish I believed that, but it's been almost three fucking years.

Taking a few minutes to calm my frayed nerves, I find the happy spot inside myself where I'm proud of the woman and pred I'm becoming. No matter what the Heathers or their ilk do, they cannot erase the hard work I've put in for my grades, my Games status, and in finding my real family. My mates—current and future—love me, flaws and all, even if all my exes never did. My life is my own, and I've dodged killers, social media mobs, and shitty parents to claim it.

"As Tay Tay would say, I'm aware and conscious of the path I've chosen and the one I didn't choose." Grinning as I open my eyes to look at my studio, I let out a calming breath and rise to my feet. "If they want to come at me, I'm ready for them."

I shed the outer layers I have over my dance clothes from ballet, then plop down on the floor again to pull on my pointe shoes. Once I'm laced and ready, I look at the rubric for my end of year project in that class. It tells me what Professor Fabreaux is looking for, so once I have that memorized, I grab my phone to scroll through music. I need to find that and once I do, I know the steps will come to me on the floor.

As I scroll, it comes to me a flash. This might be one of the most difficult roles in this genre, but her journey from victim of the evil Baron to victor who takes control of her life feels so viscerally real and... appropriate. The fouéttesare the end of the *pas de deux* will be hard as hell, but if I bust my cottontail like my girl, Baby... I can do it.

But who will I enlist to be the Prince?

Rufus' gift is *not* ballet, and neither is Cori's. I can't get them to do this with me because of the difficulty, but I also don't know who else to ask. Everyone in my stupid class already has partners if they want them and this is so last minute. My brows furrow and I curse under my breath, angry that yet again all the crap in my life forced the moving around which landed me here. Sighing, I stare at the screen of my Spotify playlist, knowing that even if that's all true, it doesn't change the fact that I need someone to do this shit with me.

It hits me like a bolt of my own blue magic shit. Renard can dance and he's fucking French—that's like, ballet in the genes, right? I snicker at my own silliness, as that's about as dumba assuming all us Americans play football. I sure as hell don't, but I *have* seen Rennie dance like a graceful cat on the big stage.

> BabyGirl: Rennie, I need you.

> EmoBatman: I am yours to command, petite.

> BabyGirl: It's a big favor, baby. Are you sure?

> EmoBatman: There is no favor too big, Dolly. Tell me what I can do.

> BabyGirl: I need you to dance with me for my project. We came in late and all the people have partners for the big jury projects and I don't…

> EmoBatman: Perfectement, mon amour. I would love to accompany you.

> BabyGirl: Can you come to my studio to work with me now? Or are you busy?

> EmoBatman: I shall wing my way to you shortly. Remember to use the code words.

My body sags in relief. If Rennie really can keep up, that will give me time to write up my proposal before my meeting with my sour-assed Jury Coordinator, Professor Ste Jean. I had diddly squat to discuss with her Tuesday and she read me the riot act about my lack of preparation—despite my lack of knowledge about this system until a day prior. Professors at *l'Academie* seem dead set against me or neutral at best, so I have to start pulling my weight quickly.

I plug my Pods in, using my notebook to sketch the dance playing in my head as I listen to the music. There's precedent for the dance—it's been around for almost one hundred and fifty years—but I want to give it my own spin. Squinting, I imagine a fusion of the haunting movement of the music mixed with a modern twist. My lips curve up and I continue using my choreography short-hand to mark the beats and moves.

Once I finish, I grin wickedly and sketch the costumes I'll need for it, leaving a lot to my sparkly bear's imagination. Cori will be able to bounce off this with little trouble, and I have no doubt her vision will match what I'm going to use the mixing software to achieve for my accompaniment. I may tap Aubrey for his opinion on that, and I know he's going to both love and *hate* this plan.

Suddenly, the world seems like it's full of possibilities again, and I shake my head. Focusing on the bad shit doesn't help anything and immersing myself in my passions makes it better every time. I leap to my feet, placing the phone on the charging pad on the table and connecting it to the bluetooth speakers.

The song I want is on loop, so I start by re-stretching my feet and limbs, getting my frame warm again after sitting for so long. By the time I'm ready, the music has played three times and I can feel it in my bones, taste it in my mouth, and see it in the air. Allowing myself to sink into the emotions surrounding me, I whirl and jump across the floor, following the movements in my sketches slowly to find transitions and highlights.

"You started without me, *ma petite.*"

I grin as I hear the gargoyle speaking outside the door, skidding to a stop in front of it to clear my throat. "Code word, please."

"To blave. It means to bet," he replies with a chuckle.

Pushing the button for the door, I grin as it opens to reveal my gargoyle in all black sweats, looking graceful as hell as he slinks into the room. "*Entrez-vous,* pouty boy."

Once he's sure the door is closed behind him, Renard listens to the music in the background and gives me a shrewd expression. "You're making a big gamble by asking me to dance one of the hardest *pas de deux* in ballet, *ma petite*."

I shrug, holding my hand out to him. "I believe in you, Rennie. Plus, you know… you're French, right? This is your people."

His bark of laughter startles me as he takes my hand. "Tchaikovsky was Russian. That's your scary relatives, if I'm not mistaken."

I can't argue that.

"Then we need to make them proud, Mr. Ooh-la-la. Let's get moving."

One down, a million more to go…

PEOPLE I LOVE

Aubrey

RENNIE WAS SO EXCITED I COULDN'T HELP BUT SMILE; THAT ALONE made me want to reward Snacksize for asking him to help her with her project. However, by the next morning, that changed when her best friends showed up to invade our space with *cameras*. The badger is filming some sort of avant garde documentary of daily life of arts students for *his* final project and he's using the giggly bear and our girl as his stars.

Ra, help me keep my dragon in check as he flits around filming for the next eight weeks.

"Dollybear, tell us about your jury for ballet. Since we've been left to our own devices as transfers, we all have to 'figure it out.' In layman's terms, that means completing year-long assignments that require partners despite all our fellow students being committed since the Fall. Correct?"

I arch a brow, not looking up from my tablet as I eat. That question is loaded, and it will be viewed by a hell of a lot of people, so I'm curious to hear what she says. When she started at Apex, she would have been politic to keep it from getting to her shitty parents. But now…?

"It's disgraceful, Rufus. None of the transfers had an option the first semester after Apex was destroyed, nor did they have one coming here this semester. We've been uprooted twice for 'security reasons,' yet we are being made to feel like intruders and set up to fail."

I'll be damned; listen to our girl go.

Cori nods, her rainbow curls bouncing as she holds up a pattern she's working on. "No one was sent to this hoity-toity arts school that didn't qualify for their majors, but the staff and students act as though we cheated to get a place. I find it both ridiculous and demeaning, especially for those of us who were attending *the* most elite college in the world previously."

My lips curve up as she sniffs, her affect completely different from her normal, down-to-earth persona. Rufus explained that he's filming this in bursts, creating small stories that seem like they're not related until the larger plot line ties together at the end. He wants to make it flow like that human crime movie, and while I think the idea has merit, 'Eleven Short Films About *l'Academie des crocs y griffes*' is probably going to ruffle feathers.

"Cut!" The badger pulls the camera back, looking gleefully wicked as he blows a kiss to the girls. "Perfect, my darlings. We're going to make those idiots *squirm* with this docu-drama. From exposé bits to pulling back the curtain, I'm sure it will get into indie festivals without a second thought."

"Rufus, are you *sure* you want them to sink on this thirty-five millimeter ship with you?" I chuckle as Felix snaps his paper down, his expression stern. "They could be flunked on their own performances and projects for being part of it."

"*Mais non, mon tigre*! Films go last in juries every year since forever —I checked. They want all the students to be the audience for them, so the other disciplines finish beforehand."

Fitz bounces in, his energy palpable as he looks at us. "You slowpokes are *killing* me. It's time for practice, Baby Girl. Z is gonna skin me if we don't hustle our buns to the field."

Dolly rolls to her feet gracefully, giving her shorter friend a hand to get out of the deeply cushioned couch. She walks over to the counter, kissing both Chess and Rennie on the cheek while they clean the cookware from breakfast. The cheetah pauses his work as she comes to Felix, murmuring in his ear and hugging him from behind. When she turns to come my way, Chess hands her a chilled water bottle and a handful of packed snack containers to shove in the big bag Fitz is checking.

"Hey, big guy," she says as I smile at her. "Crazypants is taking me to practice, but afterward, we can all meet and decide which lead to follow this afternoon. Keep them focused, mm?"

"Always," I rumble as she nuzzles my jaw. "Show those other preds who you are, lunchable. Just like you did in that statement earlier."

Her bright grin makes my chest flutter with love and she winks before she bounces away to hand Fitz the supplies from Chess. "Definitely. Coco, Ru-Ru? Let's blow this popsicle stand. I'm ready for my badass bunny close-up."

The badger gives me a feral grin. "Don't worry; I'll give you stuffed shirts a copy of the B-Reel of her taking some dumbass down. Free spank bank material, coming up."

Again, Ra save me from murdering my future mate's besties—she'd never forgive me.

ONCE THEY'RE GONE, I CLEAR THE REST OF THE COUNTER, helping Chess get the kitchen finished. He's whistling happily and it makes me realize that while we're all grumpy bastards still, we've definitely stopped being morose assholes. Felix was the most noticeable change, but even Rennie doesn't stay up in the tower brooding as much. We're functioning adults—mostly—and Dolly is the integral piece of that change.

"What's going on while our girl is at practice?" I ask them curiously. I know what we're doing when she returns—our first campus exploration based on whichever leads we choose from the research we've been translating.

Felix puts his documents down, scratching his chin. "Fitz has already broken into Asani and the birdie bitch's offices. He's got micro-cams placed, so we should work on finding out more about the other Council plants here."

"There's four of us, so we could split up," Chess says as he dries his hands. "I think it's important to check out the Voice teacher and probably the chick from her class with our moron cousin. They seem like the next imminent threats."

Nodding, I consider his suggestion. Dolly seemed most bothered by the Russian and the La Porte girl, but the wolf girl related to Gregor worries me as well. "I'm concerned about the canine from her Games team, too. Gregor was a sadistic bastard and everyone from his line of wolves and pack were taught to follow that path. He ended up at Apex simply to keep him in line when he ran afoul of the Council wolves."

"Aubrey is right about that, I believe. The O'Learys run the most dominant wolf line and their battles with Gregor's pack ended in his exile. I remember when he was sent to Apex, *mes amis*." Renard puts the last pot in the drying rack, joining our planning at the bar. "He was angry, violent, and many wolves still pledged their loyalty to him despite the O'Learys victory. Anyone still holding that torch after Fitz killed him is dangerously obsessed."

The Raj sighs, steepling his hands in front of his face for a moment while he thinks. Everything is quiet for a moment, then he blows out a breath. "Okay. Then I suggest Aubrey goes to the staff housing to see if he can snoop on Antonovich. No one expects him to be social, so they won't stop to chat. Chess, you will come with me to check out the Games wolf, and Renard, you can take the La Porte girl. Does that work?"

I ponder his split briefly, then nod. "Yes. I think I would stick out far too much in the student areas and my dragon despises small talk. You three will handle that much better than I."

"You're underestimating me again, Felix," Chess grumbles. "I don't need a protector."

"No, but everyone else needs one if they upset you, Chester," Rennie says with a smirk. "Dolly and Fitz would annihilate the entire campus if someone so much as broke one of your claw tips. We don't need them to go on a rampage, *oui?*"

He blushes a bright red, looking pleased and embarrassed at the same time. "I suppose that's true. We've seen what happens when her bunny is allowed to go completely feral."

"I'd prefer to avoid mass decapitations, yes," Felix retorts drily. "Not that the rest of us wouldn't be angry, but I shudder to think of what will happen when the 'Twisted Terrors' go full tilt. I'm not sure the world is ready for that, much less this cushy school."

Suddenly, it hits me and I burst out laughing. They all look at me as if I'm insane, and I wave my hand, unable to get control of the humor yet. It takes me a minute or two, but once I can speak again, I take off my glasses to wipe the tears off. "It's absolutely ridiculous and perfect."

"What is?" Rennie asks, his expression confused. "We don't get the joke, *mon amour*."

I shake my head, looking at them ruefully. "Your twin is a world renown psycho whose name is whispered to pred kids to scare them—even in exile."

"Uh, yeah, big guy. We know that." Felix waits, then adds, "Not new information and not hysterical laughter material, though."

"Despite being the exiled *Kings* and the twin of that guy... we all just agreed our twenty-year-old girlfriend is equally as terrifying as him and we worry about them going on a murderous rampage." I start laughing again as I imagine it. "And she has rainbow hair."

Chess blinks, then snickers softly, prompting Rennie to join and finally, Felix cracks a grin. "Princess may look like rainbow Barbie, but she's fierce as hell, and she gets it from that bitch who gave birth to her. I think she was pretty much *raised* to be Fitz's perfect rampage partner, Aubrey."

Snorting, I shrug. "I know, but... I mean, for fuck's sake. When people figure out she's not the fluffy bunny they expect her to be... It's going to be hysterical, Raj. Together, we span centuries of experience and savagery, but we're more afraid of her ire than the assholes running this joint."

"Gargoyles have a healthy fear of the females in our clutches, Flames. They are fierce, unyielding, and will destroy our enemies in swaths of rage. Perhaps the rest of you are simply catching on to our ways." Renard gives us a smug look, his eyes dancing as he flicks his tail in the air. "*Ma petite lapin* is formidable, but has retained her heart—something her disagreeable mother has not done. Whatever she chooses to do in this brewing war will be just; do not worry."

"Oh, I know that, Rennie," I reply. "But the people underestimating her have forgotten where she comes from because she's a rabbit. Fitz, for all his enormous faults, never gave a single shit about that. Keeping the people they like safe is extremely important if we want to keep the genie in the bottle."

"Agreed." Felix slaps his hands on his thighs, rising to his feet. "The best way to do that is to get whatever dirt or information we can on the people who publicly clash with Dolly. If we can rule them out as clout chasers, we can focus on the shit we *can't* see."

I look over at my lover pointedly. "Have you figured out where the nests are for certain?"

"*Oui,*" he says. "But they seem to be inactive at the moment."

"Inactive?" I frown. "I don't know much about the damn bloodsuckers, granted, but I've never heard of inactive nests that have a strong enough presence for you to feel them on the way into the school."

Rennie shrugs. "They certainly live in that forest area and their scents and marks are upon the building I believe they inhabit. However, they are not *in* the building now. Their coven may be traveling or hiding until we are no longer paying attention."

"Great, disappearing vampires," Chess groans. "Yet another bullshit problem that probably ties to the similarly disappearing Fae."

"When you sit at the top, Chester, there are always people waiting to knock you off the throne." He rolls his eyes at me, but I'm serious. "It's true. Felix, Rennie, and I are perfect examples of that theory. Our girl is poised to do or be something important; we know that from the interest the damn magic fuckers have in her. So there will be problems and all we can do is knock them off your board one by one, even if they keep coming."

That is, until Dolly comes into whatever greatness they expect, and then, all bets are off.

Don't Threaten Me With A Good Time

Delores

Coach Z ran us hard at practice and I was sore by the time it was over. My new Pred Games nemesis got in my face a few times, but since Coco and Ru-Ru were running around filming, it didn't last long. Rufus cleverly turned the camera in my direction every time O' Leary started up; it made her back off so her bullshit wouldn't get recorded.

He's a smart fucking badger and I'm a lucky bunny to have him as a friend.

Cori was sitting on the sidelines at a table where she did measurements and notes for the uniforms. Zhenga seemed really excited about it, getting distracted multiple times by checking in with my bestie as she worked. The bear smiled more in a few hours than I've seen for awhile, so I'm feeling pretty good about suggesting she do this for one of her juries.

"What's on the docket now, Dollypop?" Rufus asks as we head for the library. "I got a lot of footage at the practice, but I'll need *scads* of film to make this damn thing before the end of the semester. I'm practically sleeping with the fucking camera."

"Bet that makes the triplets cranky," I say with a grin. "I'm not saying my guys wouldn't enjoy fun with filming, but given my wretched luck and the people trying to destroy me, I'd never risk it. I'm already ping-ponging between famous and infamous daily.,"

Coco gives me a knowing look as we cross the open area. "Smart idea, babe. Even with your crazy mate locking down all the tech in your nest, that seems like a really bad proposition. Honestly, Rufus, you'd better not be doing that shit, either. We're all in the cross-hairs."

Which is entirely my fault and I hate it.

"Ah, ah…" the badger wags his finger at me. "No blaming yourself, Dollykins. I refuse to acknowledge bullshit self-pity. We are all strong and independent shifters who are making our own choices despite the ridiculous pressure put on us. Right?"

I look at the polar bear, and she nods before we chorus, "Right!"

"Then I ask again… what's on the schedule for today? I know your guys have some sneaky shit planned; the weekend is our only chance to work on clues."

"Felix and the others went to do sneaky shit while you were at practice, Baby Girl. They should be back soon," Fitz says as he catches up to us. "The grand poobahs will decide what's next based on whatever they find."

"They didn't include you in this mission? Hmm, I wonder why…" Cori gives him a mischievous look and Fitz gasps dramatically.

"Coco-cabana, I am *hurt*," he pouts. "You're doubting my integral role in this whole she-bang. *I* am protecting the most precious of cargo—the lovely and indefatigable Delores Drew and her snarky little friends."

Rufus almost chokes on his laughter as we finally get to the front of the library. "For fuck's sake, Khan. My hands are no cleaner than yours."

Fitz bobs his brows as he yanks me to his side. "Ahh, but if there are *two* of us, that means *both* of these ladies have a bodyguard, hillbilly. It's called *strategy.*"

"If you say so," the badger grumbles as we head to the back doors. "I think you just get off on watching her kick people's asses."

"That's a bonus, buddy, but thanks for noticing."

Giving them both withering looks, I hold my arm up to the sensor the Captain and his crew got installed. The door whooshes open and we all file into the hallway, heading for the main area. "Hel-looooo? Chessie? Aubrey? Rennie? Felix?"

No one answers, so I drop my practice bag in the spot Chess created for our on-the-go stuff. Kicking off my shoes, I nod at the others to do the same and head for the kitchen to get more water. Fitz follows me, pinching and tickling me as we go, and I giggle when my friends make exaggerated gagging sounds. Once I grab four bottles, I join them on the couches and toss the drinks to them one by one.

"Man, Coach Z worked us hard today."

Rufus looks around, tilting his head. "She did, but she also seemed very pleased with Coco's designs. You're going to ace this project for sure, girl."

Cori turns bright red and I arch a brow. She's not remotely shy about her design talent, so that reaction is weird. "I hope so. We have a lot of scheduled collab appointments for the uniforms and team merch. It would be a good start to a diversified brand portfolio for me."

I blink. "You want a sports line, not just high fashion? When did you decide that?"

"Zhenga said preds ignore sporty fashion and it's an untapped market. I like paving my own path and my parents would *never*."

"It's brilliant, really," Rufus says as he pulls his camera out again. "Gimme some of that biz talk for the film. I want to show all aspects of life here and how we're making our opportunities when the school isn't paying attention to the students who didn't start out here."

Man, he's really on a tear about this; hopefully, it doesn't bring more trouble to our door.

"I think the groups are good," Felix says as we all look at the board Chess wrote on.

Alphahole

Felix, Cori, Zhenga

Crazypants

Fitz, Dolly, Raina

Grumpy

Aubrey, Percy, Bowser

Pirate

Renard, Holliday, Banjo

Cinnamon Roll

Chess, Kirby, Captain

Chessie nods, tilting his head to look at the tiger with a pleased smile. "I think it's as balanced as can be. I didn't know Zhenga would be joining us, and I think maybe—"

"Nope. If I'm joining this weird ass quest, I pick where I go, little kitty."

Scratching my chin, I give my newest friend a suspicious look. "Coach, I trust you as much as I can at this juncture, but—"

The lioness rolls her eyes and sighs heavily. "Look, the current leaders aren't working out for me, obviously. You know I'm not after the royal dickhead, so stop worrying. I don't want this place to become a smoking hole in the ground they can't seem to rebuild, nor an unsafe cesspool like Cappie. I like having a place to live comfortably."

That's fair.

"Plus, any of us that share a Council-associated name should be worried about retribution if the magic people win whatever battles they're waging," Cori says quietly. "It won't matter if we're exiles or disowned—that's like Supervillain 101. You can't leave a Skywalker."

"*Nice* ref, Coco-cabana!" Fitz says, leaning over to fist bump her. "And very fucking true… look at our dickweed father. He'll regret his bullshit eventually."

"Yeah, okay Team Rocket," Rennie says drily as he looks at the board then signs for Holliday quickly. "Regardless, I think we're ready to explore the campus looking for the entrances to whatever hidden shit they have here."

"There are five teams, so I think maybe we will send the Pirates to the forest in the west. Then Alphahole goes to the north mountain and lake while Cinnamon heads for the east forest. Grumpy can take the southeast area with the lake leaving our team to scout the southwest by the arena," I say as I visualize the map in my head.

"That seems like a good plan, snack size," Aubrey says as he rises to his feet. "Let's get moving. I don't know what the hell we're going to find, but everyone needs to make certain they have both their phones and their earwigs in. We don't know where any of us will be, after all."

"Hopefully not dodging random enemies," Rennie says as he gives the dragon a pointed look.

I wrinkle my nose. "Yes, that's definitely on my 'no-no' list, babe. But if anyone gets in trouble, raise the alarm sooner rather than later. I don't want anyone to get hurt; I'd never forgive myself."

"Baby Girl, we're *all* going to be safe; stop worrying." Fitz stands and holds his hand out to me, pulling me to my feet. "Especially us because I'm in the mood to beat some ass to get the energy out."

Oh, fabulous. Good thing I'm with him.

"DOLLY, YOU DIDN'T HAVE TO LET ME DO THIS," RAINA SAYS AS she holds onto my back.

I chuckle, looking over my shoulder at the raccoon. "It's no big deal. You weigh almost nothing and until we find the right place to poke around, you'd have trouble keeping up."

Fitz pouts. "I'm still mad you didn't let me carry you both, Baby Girl."

"She has a point about that being a disadvantage if we run into trouble, Mr. Fitz." Raina's voice is thready, and I know she had to buck up the courage to say that to a big predator that isn't me.

"I know, little sunshine, but it doesn't mean I'm not mad her thighs aren't wrapped around mine right now."

The relief I feel seep from her small body as she holds onto me is palpable, and I have to stifle the urge to giggle. The two of them are going to be a very interesting group to explore with. "Fitzy, my thighs are wrapped around you damn near once a day. You'll get your chance when we're not looking for trouble."

"Some men have difficulty focusing when they aren't properly sated," Raina chirps. "Prey animals are all taught that by their mothers, Dolly." She pauses and I know she's thinking about my bitchy mother. "However, you did not have this education, it seems. Perhaps Miss Zhenga needs to give you another class?"

My face turns bright red and Fitz howls with laughter as we finally get to the arena. "Raina, I'm doing my best, but five of these dudes is hard, even for a rabbit. They're all horn dogs in spirit, if not in species."

The tittering giggle joins my tiger's laughter and he points to the covered walkway behind the columns on the outside of the competition stadium. "I think we should look for hidey-holes there first. It's big, old, and no one's done any upgrades in forever. Z complains all the time, but maybe there's a reason beyond disdain for sports."

I grin at him. "Solid logic, baby."

"Raccoons can get into openings of four or five inches, you know. If we find something small, I can likely get inside without much effort.

I did not know that, but it makes my team division feel even smarter.

"Awesome sauce," Fitz says, his eyes bright with excitement. "And I can smash things. So where do we start poking, Baby Girl?"

Raina hops down from my back as I eye the stadium. He's right about the walkway, but if we want to save time, starting at the best place on it will help. "I think... maybe the side facing the forest area? Rennie has been all pissy about something being out there —which is why I sent his team there—but if that's where weird shit is, then it tracks to start nearby, right?"

"I agree, Dolly. Preds think they are very clever when they hide things, but the prey staff always knows. At every school so far, we learn where the bodies are buried within a month or so."

I grimace, looking at her. "Unfortunately that metaphor is a bit on the nose, huh?"

Fitz snorts, gesturing for us to follow him around the stadium. "Don't even joke about that. I'm going to be pissed if we find a damn corpse now."

Raina frowns. "I believe Mr. Chess packed supplies for that in the bag, though."

"He probably did, knowing him," I say as I pat the messenger bag slung across my chest. "Chessie is becoming a regular Pred Scout. He runs our place better than a Higgins ever could."

Stopping in place, Fitz looks at me hungrily. "Holy fuck, Baby Girl, you just made a Magnum P.I. reference! My dick is going to burst out of my pants."

I wink at him. "Title of your sex tape."

His groan echoes off the stone walls as Raina and I walk away, heading towards the nooks and crannies to look for clues.

Operation Sexy Detective Bunny... locked and loaded.

Assassins

Renard

"Glorious gargoyle, this forest is very foreboding," Banjo says as we enter the dense treeline. "Are you certain we should be exploring it?"

Holliday rapidly signs his agreement and I give them an encouraging smile. "It's daylight, so we should be perfectly safe. I wouldn't endanger either of you—Raina would skin me for a floor rug."

That makes the quokka titter with amusement. "I cannot imagine such a thing, but Raina is quite fierce about her gaze. She would definitely make you regret it."

"Holliday, are you comfortable with my explanation?" The armadillo is a skilled lip reader, but I try to offer both options so I don't accidentally exclude him.

He nods, patting the scabbard on his right hip and then touching the fucking sniper rifle slung over his other shoulder. I'm not sure where they have smaller sized weaponry made, but working in the armory everywhere he goes must be part of it.

"Holliday could hit a gnat from miles away, Monsiuer Renard. He will help with long distance protection. Do not worry about him."

I chuckle as Banjo adjusts the bandolier of bullets across his chest, shaking my head. "I fear those weapons may not be as useful as you'd think. The predators I believe live in these woods won't be affected by them."

"They are when they've been painted with garlic and holy water," Holliday signs. "The Captain is quite thorough with his planning."

Shit. I didn't think he was paying attention when I was grumbling about the bloodsuckers.

"To be honest, I'm not sure what's fact and fiction, I'm afraid. It has been a very, very long time since these supernaturals have been encountered. Their kind have stayed as hidden as the magic users, so all I have to go on is a sketchy childhood memory and what has been written in various texts."

Banjo points to a tree, tilting his head. "That tree is marked by prey staff. It must be storage. Squirrels, I'd say."

"Huh. They didn't do that at Cappie or Apex. Is it because perhaps the preds here are less… threatening than at the American schools?" I'm genuinely curious, so I peek at the tree he pointed out, then continue on the path deeper into the woods.

Holliday answers again, his hands moving quickly as we walk, "The predators here seem very unconcerned with the staff. They are not kinder, but they are aloof and indifferent. Their permanent prey workers do not act terrified as they did at our previous jobs."

Interesting. Perhaps it's self-involved rich kid syndrome or maybe they have specific orders not to bother them.

We trudge deeper into the trees, and something pricks my senses. I stop, half shifting to enhance my predatory instincts. This scent is very familiar and it is *not* vampires. The two pirates watch me silently as I explore the area around us, trying to find the source of the memory-inducing smell. It takes a moment, but I find a very small faerie ring with offerings under some brush. It's been too long to remember *which* kind of ring this is, so I snap a picture with my phone for later.

"The magicals have been here. This was left for them," I murmur to them. "I don't know if it's the ones from the Cappie attack or others, but this doesn't seem elaborate enough to draw the truly powerful."

"It's very small, glorious one," Banjo says. "Fae who appeared on Yule were very large and intimidating, according to the staff in the event."

I nod, bending to look at the ring thoughtfully. "Indeed, but something this small creating a net of portals over the campus might explain how they got through all the security we placed at the entrances. I don't know enough about whether entries to the Veil can be daisy-chained like that."

Holliday frowns, then points across the forest floor with narrowed eyes. His kind has a keen sense of smell because they don't see well—and in his case, he can't hear—so I trust his nose. Rising, I walk to the area he indicated, rifling through the underbrush until I find yet another one of the rings. My brows furrow and I walk to the thickest tree nearby, digging my shifted claws into it as I climb upward to get a better vantage point. Looking down at the spots where I found the rings, I grin triumphantly.

If there are three more of them, it would form a star—bingo.

"I think they are getting in by connecting the small doorways to form a big one," I call down to Banjo. He relays that information to Holliday, who immediately starts sniffing out the other points. "I can't decide if we should damage one of them, all of them, or leave it as a trap."

"Perhaps we radio the others to see what they suggest?" The quokka looks up at me then his gaze-mate. "I think your clutch would be most helpful in this decision."

"You're right, Banjo." I grin ruefully as I leap down from the tree, shaking the ground as I land. Pushing the button on the earwig, I wait for it to activate before I speak. "Ahoy. Pirate Team with a report."

There's a scuffling sound and I hear our girl respond, "Team Crazypants is still searching. What do you have, Rennie?"

"Fairy rings and a theory about how they're getting onto the campuses."

"Team…Alphahole is surprisingly efficient this time," Felix says wryly. "But we haven't found any entrances in the mountain area yet. What's your theory, gargoyle?"

"Holliday is hunting down the other three, but I believe they are using the small rings where the pixies and smaller Fae receive offerings in a daisy-chain format to create a large portal spot in the middle. It would go unnoticed if no one was looking closely."

"The great one sensed a presence, so if no one had that ability, they would miss these tiny things!" Banjo adds and I hear my mate laughing quietly.

"Well, Team Grumpy finds the great one's theory credible enough," the dragon drawls. "Though his credentials are suspect."

"Oooh, smart guy burn," Fitz says. "Point to the Sizzling Serpent."

A heavy sigh comes on the line and I grin to myself. Chess has to endure quite a bit of our playful sniping while we are cooking, so I don't blame him. "Team Cinnamon Roll hasn't seen anything like that but to be honest, we have not been looking for things so small. Kirby and the Captain are fanning out now to help me search."

"Rennie, maybe you should tag the places you find these things... and anyone else, too. Then we can all figure out whether we want to use them as, like, traps or squash it for safety," Dolly says.

Always thinking ahead... she amazes me at times, but I'm sure it comes from trying to outwit her abusive parents.

"That's why I contacted everyone, *ma petite*. I wanted to make sure we are in agreement before we do anything to these miniature menaces."

"Princess is right, Ren. You and the crew mark the spots somehow, and we'll all do the same if we find anything suspicious. I'd prefer no one to run into a cave or whatever in such small groups, anyway. Feels like courting trouble."

"Aye, aye, Raj," I reply drily. "But your point is taken. Over and out."

I roll my eyes when I click the button on my ear and Banjo grins at me. "I find it hard not to remind them how much longer Aubrey and I have survived this world at times, eh?"

Holliday makes a snorting sound, then signs, "It's similar to when people speak slowly and make weird faces to try to 'assist' me with understanding them. Very annoying, but also amusing, that they believe being deaf makes me profoundly stupid."

"He's quite good at convincing people not to pay attention to him because of it," the quokka says. "Holliday is like a ninja because of dumb assumptions."

Laughing softly, I nod. "Yes, my stone form is useful that way as well. We are well matched, *mes amis*. Let's get these spots taken care of, then we will continue looking for the creature I sought to begin with."

Hopefully, I was right that they are not currently in their nests; I'd like to sneak around.

BY THE TIME WE REACH THE GRAVEYARD ON THE BACK EDGE OF the school, we've found three other star-shaped patterns. Four in this wood alone is concerning, but not nearly as concerning as the huge structure outside of the ancient burial grounds with buttoned-down windows. It looks as though it was created to house a groundskeeper, perhaps, but is now abandoned. However, the fact that its upkeep is pristine, and the wilderness around it is pruned back rather than taking over tells me there's life in this building.

Or something passing for it.

"This place is trying very hard to appear deserted," Holliday signs as he sniffs the air. "But it is not."

"You are correct, *mon ami*." I stand at the edge of the cemetery, looking at the structure analytically. "I think it is more than one level. Perhaps it has subterranean levels where the younger coven members live until they can join the elders."

Banjo frowns, which looks odd on the perpetually happy-looking quokka. "It is very dark. They've blocked every possible place for light to get in, Monsieur. How will we find out without entering? The Raj was very adamant."

I chuckle, winking at him. "What the puffed up tiger cub doesn't know won't hurt him."

My companions get sneaky looks on their faces and the spirit that got them to join up with a rogue like the Captain shines through. Banjo pulls his rifle, tucking it under his arm as he salutes me.

"I'm ready, Glorious One. Would you prefer Holliday to stay back for the long range cover?"

I nod at the armadillo, and he salutes, then scurries off to find a vantage point. "You know that will only help us if we get back outside, right?"

Banjo shakes his head. "Oh, no, Monsieur Renard. He has infrared scopes. He will have our backs above ground. We must be cautious below, though."

Damn these dudes are like having Sibbie SEALS along for the ride.

"The Captain takes shit more seriously than I knew," I mutter and Banjo chuckles. "Alright, let's head for the east side of the building since it's getting late in the afternoon. The sun will be brightest on the west side."

We slink out of the forest, keeping low as we move along the fence of the old graveyard toward the large cabin. Banjo follows without a word, obviously used to shit like this. It makes me wonder what the hell the Captain has them doing on the regular, but that's a conversation for later. Right now, we need to keep away from the sightline of the house. The windows are covered, but we have no idea if those coverings can be moved.

Hell, we don't even know for sure what powers these assholes might have.

"If anyone shows their face, Banjo, shoot first and haul ass, *oui*? I do not have enough information on what they are capable of to allow compassion."

"Aye, aye, Glorious One. No mercy."

When we reach the porch, I peek over the edge, noting it's immaculately clean. "Okay, we're going in."

Banjo and I move around the stairs, then up to the door. I pause to listen, gesturing for him to be ready when I open it. He stands with the gun in hand, looking like a caricature from a shifter war movie. Grabbing the knob, I turn it and swing the heavy wood out to reveal a dark, empty room.

"There's no one here, Monsieur."

Sighing, I nod as I walk inside with the quokka following behind me. The furniture is surprisingly modern and comfortable looking rather than Gothic and stereotypical. In fact, the entire room looks... annoyingly normal.

This place has to be hiding something; I just know it.

The Sleeping Beauty, Suite, Op. 66a, Rose Adagio

Delores

When everyone got back to the library, we used the map Chessie had made for the board to mark all the individual spots each team thought needed further exploration. It's a good list for next weekend, and since we're halfway through February as it is, we'll be able to focus on one spot going forward. The school year goes through the end of May and the Council decided not to extend it, so we know how to allocate our time. I'm worried about how we're going to get through all the fucking schoolwork, the spring break week, and the end of year juries without an incident, but that's because our new 'enemies' seem prone to attacking during the most vulnerable times.

Not fun Monday morning thoughts for certain, but such is the life of the unwilling 'chosen one,' I suppose.

"Madamoiselle Drew, *faites attention*[1]! Your *grande adage* is not crisp enough. Again!"

Biting the inside of my cheek to keep from spitting a retort back at *la prima*, I nod and return to the back of the line to do another pass. My *adages* were not messy, but the aging swan shifter was a world renown *prima* ballerina, so she's more demanding than almost every dance teacher I've ever had before. Her standards are so high *she* can't meet them anymore, and her family is well connected. They are not on our suspected Society list, but they definitely hang with the people who are.

Fabreaux's one redeeming feature is that she's earned her acclaim, and she doesn't give a shit that I'm prey-adjacent. No, she simply thinks everyone is shit compared to her and I can handle that. I'm fairly certain Lucille would also think her shit didn't stink if she wasn't a pred, too. My mother is pathologically narcissistic and my new ballet professor is as well. This is familiar ground for me; as long as she doesn't start smacking me with that stupid diamond encrusted cane, I'll survive.

One tap and it's on, though. No second chances is my motto this year.

"*Plus vif, plus rapide, mes petits hippopotames*[2]," the professor calls as she claps her hands and I grit my teeth.

There's virtually *no* dancers over a buck twenty-five except for me, so that's purposefully shitty. Again, nothing new in the bitchy woman playbook. I flex my feet, going up and down to keep warm as I ignore the hurtful bullshit. To be honest, the dance world is rife with this kind of body negativity and Fabreaux is nothing special with her insults. I want to throttle her by her long ass neck for it because not every dancer here will be able to ignore her. Many already succumb to unhealthy body dysphoria and the conditions that come with it, if the bathroom sounds are indicators—and they are. But I can't change dance culture as well as the entire phone book worth of shit I have to deal with right now and people have free will.

Sometimes, you have to expect people to take responsibility for their poor choices, and leave it at that.

I hate it, but it's another one of my areas of opportunity I'm working on. My heart wants to save the dance supes, Cori's ex, and a slew of others who bring pain on themselves. Unfortunately, closing the door on people who act against their own self-interest because they might hurt me or mine is necessary. My boundaries have gotten firmer every year since my big 'BFF break-up,' and it's helped me become a happier, more confident bunny. There's freedom in not letting abusive jackwagons continue to live rent-free in your head with their misery; I don't regret cutting them off for a second.

"And I'm no more or less popular without them, to be honest," I mutter to myself.

"Mlle Drew, did you have *une question?*"

My eyes widen and I turn to face the statue-esque swan with a brilliant, fake smile. "No, *La Prima.* I am merely counting to myself. Practicing mentally."

She looks surprised, then nods with a stern, but satisfied expression. "*Exactement*, Mlle Drew. This is how my dancers should be: focused, ever aware, and dedicated."

Whew. I don't need her crawling up my fluffy tailpipe, too.

"You got last year, Frenchie!"

Arching a brow, I wisely stay quiet as the guys argue about Valentine's Day. It's this Friday, and while I'm secretly giddy they all want to do something, I'm sure as fuck not weighing in on whether it's going to be a group or solo event. Fitz is right; Rennie did get to take me out last year on his own, but there were circumstances surrounding it. However, things are different now, and I can see why my crazypants tiger is being insistent.

He's a softie at heart when it comes to me and Chessie, so he's got passionate opinions.

"Fitzgerald, I think we all have been able to spend special times with Snacksize." Aubrey looks amused, especially since his time resulted in being amongst humans and giant bunny ears.

"That's true," Felix interjects. "Chess got New Year's, and the dragon got Easter. Fitz and I are the only ones who haven't had 'holiday' alone time."

Also true; good point, Raj.

"He got to mate first," Chess points out with a sly grin. The look he's giving the rest of them is pure trolling; I know he's not chuffed about it.

The exiled tiger king puffs up again, wagging his finger at his twin. "Ah-ha! I'm owed a special time."

"Aren't *all* our dates special, Sir?" I ask innocently, batting my lashes at him.

Sue me, now I'm kind of having fun.

"Don't start, brat," he grumbles before taking a bite of his huge sandwich. I know I've got him licked when he switches from Princess to brat; it's his tell.

Fitz comes over and wraps his arms around me, setting his chin on my shoulder to growl softly. "Every *second* with you is special. I don't give a red flying *fuck* what we're doing. You can be in the stupid bathroom, and I'm still glad to be on the other side of the door, Baby Girl."

"Ew, Fitz," I say as I laugh softly. "You're such a goddamn stalker. It's lucky I'm not easily scared off."

"It really is," Chessie agrees with a fond smile. "I grew up with his insanity; you're *choosing* it."

Felix even laughs this time, shaking his head. "Bro, I wonder how we came out of the same womb sometimes."

"It is fairly remarkable," Rennie says as he reaches over and heaps another thick slice of roast onto my plate with a stern expression. "He's almost your polar opposite, though that's common with twins, *non?*"

"Guys, I'm standing right here," Fitz whines as he pouts next to my face. "Stop talking about me like I'm a problem child."

Turning my head to press my nose against his, I grin. "You are, baby, but I *love* that about you. You make everything a thousand times more interesting and fun. They all know it, too."

"Fine," my dragon sighs as he rolls his eyes. "The psycho is amusing sometimes, and he makes you and our intrepid cheetah happy. That alone is worth the trouble."

High praise coming from the grumpy librarian.

"Aw, you *love* me; you really *love* me!" Fitz crows as he turns back to give them his best Sally Fields impression. "I feel *so* much better now. I think we should reward me with a group Sexy Day date."

"How did we get back here?" I mutter as I look at my plate. "Fucking one-track brains, that's how."

"Princess, if we didn't have people trying to murder us all the time, it would be so much worse. You know that, right?" Felix's teasing makes me glare at him playfully.

"I'd be hobbling to dance class, that much I'm certain of," I retort. "You horn dogs haven't even finished corrupting me yet according to those two." I hitch my thumb at Aubrey and Rennie who immediately do their pie-plate halo impressions of angels.

As if any of us believe that shit.

"I take offense at that, Baby Girl. The Winged Weenies have nothing on the Khan boys' swagger."

Choking on the bite I just took, I wait for my breath to come back then lean back to bite his earlobe firmly. "Stop saying that shit while I'm eating."

The others laugh as I grumble, clearly enjoying my discomfort. Finally, Felix is able to catch his breath, his dark eyes meeting mine. "I believe we should spend it together—as a family. We can plan lots of outings solo if we end up staying this summer. I know that's hoping no one blows this fucking place up and that's not guaranteed, but we have forever to do that. We only get one first family Valentine's."

I blink, dipping my head as emotion overcomes me. It's a present-based holiday and I've never cared about it… until now. The serious way my stern tiger king said that will make it impossible to ever call this day silly and frivolous again. "Felix Khan, you're going to make me leak, which I *hate* and I have to go to Tap class next. Damn you."

"Can't win for losing, eh, bro?" Fitz says with a wink. He lets go of me and strides over to the fridge, pulling out a pretty cupcake to hold up. "Look, Baby Girl. Chessie and the pouty poet made pretties."

My head pops up and I can't help but swoon. "Ooooh. Pretty sweets. I like that."

"See? Totally fixable," Chess chuckles as he pats a bewildered Felix on the shoulder. "Our girl is motivated by food, fucking, fury, and fancy shit. Just keep that in mind."

"She likes books," Aubrey adds. "And cute things."

"Music," Rennie sighs happily. "Plus, she's fond of a good cuddle."

I turn red, wrinkling my nose. "Stop listing my vices and give me that cupcake, you teases."

"Hmmm." The elder Khan arches a brow. "Food denial. That's a new kink, Princess."

"It is *not* a kink," I growl as I hold up my steak knife. "I'll stab you for real."

Fitz doubles over in howling laughter, barely managing to gasp, "I'm pretty sure she would, too."

"Don't test me," I grumble. "Cupcake. Now."

Chess grabs the sweet from his amused mate, walking over to hand it to me. "Here you go, Angel. I promise I'll try not to let them use treats to torture you."

"Try being the operative word," Aubrey smirks. "The idea has merit. She's wild when she's furious. The dragon likes it a lot."

Narrowing my eyes at him, I sink my teeth into the delicious, fruity concoction. They're definitely only half joking and I'm going to end up skewering someone who thinks they're slick. I'd better make sure Raina stocks first aid supplies in all the rooms. Can't hurt to be careful—we all have tempers and rather vicious tastes in vengeance.

"Uh-oh. She's plotting." The gargoyle tilts his head as he studies me, looking curious and turned on at the same time. "I enjoy her vengeful streak; it's hot."

Done chewing, I roll my eyes. "You know, I'm questioning why the hell I come home for lunch instead of packing and finding Coco or Rufus. That's sounding very appealing right now."

"Hell no!" Fitz comes over and grabs me again, holding me tight enough to make me grunt. "I love our lunch time fun, even when I don't get a blowie reward. Don't you test me, Baby Girl."

"The two of them..." Felix sighs, rubbing his temples. "It's a fucking full time job, I swear to Odin."

"He doesn't care, bro. He's missing an eye and has bad boys of his own to deal with. Dolly and I are *your* cosmic cross to bear; don't you forget it."

I grin prettily, then lick every speck of icing off the rest of the cake purposefully. "That's right, Sir. We're the punishment and pleasure you didn't know you needed."

Damn, I sounded pretty cool just then. Go me.

CRIMINALS

FELIX

Once Princess headed back to class, Fitz and I headed back to the staff housing. Our previous search of Asani and Antonovich's rooms yielded few leads, so this time, my twin and I are going to other dorms. The dragon isn't dumb by any stretch, but he's also nowhere near as skilled as us in this kind of subterfuge. Our father and his lackeys trained us to keep secrets all over Bloodstone to prevent outsiders and traitors from accessing the royal secrets. We're going to carefully search Fabreaux and Ste Jean's quarters since they were in the photo in Paris with the others.

I'd prefer to ransack Rockland's shit, but since neither Fitz nor Farley has located her 'nest,' this will have to do.

"Remote teaching is brilliant," Fitz says as we make a very wide loop around the campus to mislead anyone watching us. "I basically teach the little shits by logging in from anywhere, grading things or telling them to re-do it, and I don't have many time constraints. You should *definitely* do it, bro."

"Fitz," I sigh as I roll my eyes. "I can't remotely teach Shifter Studies. It's not conducive to online shit. Don't be dense."

He blinks, then grins. "True. Though I bet the weepy winged weenie is doing it that way for his lower level lectures. He hates having to deal with snarky shit-eating freshies. It makes his teeth grind and he pulls Batman when he has to."

"He doesn't do that as much anymore, though. Ren's been pretty fucking jolly—for him—since he and our girl got together. More so since the 'big secret' came out."

My brother thinks about that for a moment as we walk around the salt water lake on the south edge of the campus. "You're right. Cranky McFirepants has been much better, too. There's *nothing* my Baby Girl can't fix, I swear to Zeus' plentiful baby batter."

"Ew," is all I have to say as I watch the small pirate ship sail through the middle of the water. "I always wondered how they kept control of all these big ass shifters. That is, until I found out that the crew is full of some of the toughest prey animals I've ever seen."

Fitz grins broadly. "Did the emo bat boy tell you Holliday is a fucking *sniper*? I'm gonna get him to target practice with me sometime. That's a *real* challenge."

Rubbing my temples, I pause to gather my thoughts before I respond. I absolutely *do not* want my manic brother to have weapons more dangerous than himself, especially if it will definitely mean the Princess will want to go, too. However, I can't deny that with our lack of magic fighting capabilities, we're at a disadvantage in long range arenas.

How do I address that without involving goddamn guns?

It hits me, and I shrug at him, pretending that's not impressive. "Guns are what humans use. That's not real skill; now, Raina's bow… *that* takes true prowess."

A flicker of conflicting emotions comes over his face and I know my gambit is working. "Well… I bet the little sunshine would teach me. I'll have to get Chessie to order the right stuff. That's pretty specific, I think. Maybe Baby Girl can talk to Holliday since he works in the armory."

My grin widens when I realize I've successfully redirected his questionable desire to fire bullets at things. I don't doubt my twin could become good at it; he's ridiculously capable that way, but I really don't like giving him another method of murdering people. He's crazy enough as it is, and I refuse to add anything capable of blowing a hole through someone from miles away.

By the time he's finished his tangent on compound bows, we're back to the other side of the lake and heading for the stadiums. The staff housing is past that, tucked behind the arenas and the Dupreé building. We'll get there soon enough, but I simply don't trust the open spaces in this place. Something about the layout sets off my sensors and I can't put my finger on it. The student body being as stand-offish and rude doesn't help, either. Getting a bead on which people need to be watched is difficult, even with Fitz hacking and Ren translating.

Fucking Council bullshit allows this place to operate like it's harboring state secrets, not artsy rich preds.

"Hey, bro," Fitz says as bumps into me. "Look over there."

I turn my attention to the group of preds making their way across campus, noting they're heading for the staff housing. None of them look familiar, so they're not our girl's teachers. "Yeah, so?"

"If we mosey a little closer we might catch some gossip," he says with a smirk. "Everyone knows who we are, so they tend to avoid us. But this is out in the open, man."

"Good call," I admit as I pretend to be looking at the practice arena while we stop walking. "Just don't get insane if we hear something we don't like. I enjoy flying under the radar here."

He snorts, looking playfully offended. "*Moi? Je ne le ferais pas, mon frère!*[1]"

"I have *got* to stop that gargoyle. He's teaching you the most obnoxious shit when we're not looking. When did you start learning French?"

Fitz grins smugly as he shrugs. "I'm a true Renaissance tiger, bro. Once Baby Girl helped me figure out how I learn, I decided to pick up as much as possible. Truly, I am the superior Khan—admit it."

Arching my brow, I shake my head. "Never. Now shut up so we can follow these chicks."

We'll leave the miracles our girl has worked to later discussion; I'm on a mission now.

"FIND ANYTHING?" I CALL OUT AS I RUMMAGE THROUGH THE giant fucking closet the ballet prima has stuffed to the gills. It's as much a costume trunk as it is a functional closet and I can't imagine why the fuck she would need this stuff on hand at a school. Most of it is barely worn and zippered in protective, labeled bags, so I don't think she's passing on her legacy to the dancers here.

No, this suite is a monument to a giant ego that's no longer being stroked by adoring fans.

"I'm working on the laptop. Most of it is searching for shit about her performances and fan sites, but there's a hidden partition I'm prying open. You?"

"Swimming in satin and tulle, but not finding much. I'm trying to get behind everything, though, in case there are secret panels or boxes." I pull my head out of the pile of material, sucking in a breath of non-stale air as I survey the closet again. I didn't find a floor panel in the obvious places, but that doesn't mean she doesn't have a hidey-hole somewhere.

Fitz laughs, and I hear keys clicking rapidly. "We definitely need to watch this bitch with our girl. She's one hundred percent body dysmorphic and her web shit is filled with bad juju in that realm. Lucille was a bad enough influence; I don't want her hurt by some self-obsessed old biddy with an ax to grind."

"True. Maybe you should finagle cameras in the studio?" Grunting in irritation, I move to a free-standing shelving unit in the middle filled to the brim with ballet shoes in various conditions. Some have to be from shows—they have dates on the shelf —and some must be working equipment. There's a ton of colors and styles, but I don't know my ass from my elbow about this shit. The gargoyle probably would, and he's not here.

Maybe the display is showcasing more than her ego, though.

Pulling a pick kit out of my pocket, I get to work on the lock on this side of the fixture. It only takes a few moments for it to click open, and I gingerly push the glass aside with the tool. I don't want to leave prints on it, so I nudge it the rest of the way and look at the ten shelves towering in front of me. I don't know Fabreaux at all—only what her bio and info Fitz dug up say. But since she's obviously her own biggest fan, I assume anything important would be tucked into the rarest pairs.

"Any idea what the most famous ballerina roles are, bro?" I yell over my shoulder. He might not know, but he and Princess talk non-stop, so she might have mentioned this shit.

"Um… the 'G' one. Damn, she said this," Fitz hollers back. "Damn my brain. Gimme a sec and I'll have it…"

I grin as he fumbles, not growling because he's trying to recall something that's probably very obvious. Being more patient with my twin has made everything easier, and even though I could probably have Googled it by now, I'm letting him sift through the chaos instead.

"I got it!"

"The laptop?"

"No, damn it. The ballet is *Giselle*. You can't see me, but I'm doing the dance."

My lips curve as he continues to babble, adding a few other options now that he's on a roll. Fitz's victory dance is much more fun to watch in person, but I've got shoes to search. "Good job."

"Why the hell do you need to know anyway?"

I leave his question hanging for a minute as I carefully pull a pair of white shoes that seem like they're damn close to falling apart. The smell of sweat and blood emanates from inside and I rear back a bit as it hits me. It's one thing to have a cerebral knowledge of what happens to dancers' feet in their pointe shoes and quite another to have it invade your senses. Holding them gingerly, I use the pick tool to fish around inside to see if there's anything in the stinky things.

Holy shit.

I'm able to maneuver the pick until it catches on the ring, and I watch with baited breath as I carefully lift the keys out of the shoe. "I'll be damned."

"What?" Fitz yells.

"Nothing. I found something, but I have no idea what the fuck it goes to. Keep working on the computer."

He mutters an invective and I shake my head, sighing at his childish need to know everything immediately. I know it stems from his ADHD, but I need to get these things back in the case and check the other four ballets he rattled off before we get caught in this museum.

"Okay, *Nutcracker, Swan Lake, Giselle, Sleeping Beauty, and Romeo and Juliet*," I repeat to myself. "Where the hell would the rest of you be?"

A bright red pair of battered shoes near the top catch my eye and I grin when the tag says *Sleeping Beauty*. I set the *Giselle* pair back in their spot, then reach up to grab the red set. The shoes are all tucked one inside the other, with ribbons wrapped around them in the display, so I have poke around for a moment before I find the next treasure.

It's a flash drive on a key ring and I guarantee it's going to be a fucking bitch to deal with.

"Got a flash drive, man," I call out before I place the shoes in their spot. "I have three more places to check. I don't know if this is her only secret hiding place, though."

"Who is this chick, anyway? She's got military grade encryption on a machine she uses to troll other pro dancers on Instagrowl. Like, shit doesn't match," Fitz says with a grunt of annoyance. "And I do mean troll… because she's absolutely fucking brutal to people who should be her colleagues. It's gross as hell."

"That's on par with the level of ego in this closet." I think about it for a moment, and add, "We know the parents like all ours raise kids to think their shit doesn't stink. Fabreaux is a bit older than us, so she was probably put on this ridiculous pedestal and sees everyone as beneath her. I hate those people."

Fitz snorts, and I can almost see him shaking his head as I'm fishing in the *Nutcracker* shoes. "Nope. This woman literally hates herself; you can tell by this damn shrine. She needs everyone around her to worship at her feet. It's a pretty sure bet Asani is fucking her to keep her on his side. That's what she'd crave the most—the bad boy who thinks she's a bad girl."

Gross.

"Stop that shit. I do *not* want to think about that in the slightest." I shiver, feeling squicked by imagining my asshole cousin with anyone, especially this bird. "No need to analyze; we know she's a bad egg because she's in with him and his merry band of fools."

"True. But I'm planting a virus in this system now so we can work on cracking her shit from my real equipment. We'll know every dirty deed she's been part of soon enough."

Thank fuck. I'm tired of feeling up her nasty ass footwear.

FIGHT

DELORES

"BACK THE *FUCK* OFF, O' LEARY! YOU'RE DONE. TAP OUT."

The wolf refuses, struggling beneath me with her jaws snapping futilely. Scrimmages are always drawn from a hat at practice and just my luck, the pain in my ass chick got me today. I know it wasn't rigged; Coach Z almost re-assigned us until I shook my head at her. People can't show favoritism to me, even if they want to, because it will get around like wildfire. No one notices the professors doing the exact *opposite*, but they'll put favor on social media like it's going to buy them a new beach house.

Weak. Willed. Sycophants. Are. Fucking. Exhausting.

I sigh in irritation as I lock my thighs more tightly around her ribs, hoping to crack a few so she *has* to tap out. Not being able to breathe should do it, right? I'd think so, but I can't guarantee I'd let a rival win even if I was struggling to breathe. I understand the sentiment; it's about pride and stubbornness. But this chick is pushing the concept pretty far just to spite me and I won't look any better if I unleash on her in practice. It's totally deserved, but I'll end up the villain.

"I *said*, tap out, you fucking dumbass," I growl low. I hear booing from the stands and I roll my eyes.

To combat my friends and watchers, the damn lupine idiot has invited all her doggy friends to heckle me. Again, Zhenga was going to give them the boot, but I intervened. I don't need to close myself off to the assholes who are harassing me publicly to give myself a safe space. I have one amongst my family and friends as it is, and I'm not afraid to face these dipshits in a fair fight. O' Leary can't say that; she ducks and runs anytime we're not in the ring.

Felicia O' Leary is hiding behind bigger dogs while she works her nasty bullshit and that's not going to save her.

I vaguely hear Rufus and Cori shouting as I continue to put pressure on the girl, focusing on exactly how much I'm exerting so I don't get myself benched. She flails, then snaps, catching my arm in one of her jaws. The resulting bite hurts like a *bitch* and I snarl in pain, pulling my fist back and slamming it into her face until she finally goes limp. Panting, I relax my grip as I lean back and work to get control of the raging bunny monster inside of me. She's furious and she'd absolutely enjoy tearing this stupid fleabag into tiny shreds, but I can't. My veins hum with the weird power as I breathe, ignoring the shouts of people rushing over to our practice ring,

"You should have just fucking given up," I mutter absently.

Since I still don't know exactly how the blue lightning magic shit works, I had to be very careful. I know what the ramp up to its appearance feels like and that's how I'm working to keep it under wraps. This was really goddamn close, mostly because the idiot trash talked about everyone in my life prior to fully shifting. She's not an alpha, so luckily, she couldn't continue afterward. However, the initial effort did the job of getting me amped enough to have to plead with pieces of me that want her blood in retribution for this fucking bloody mark on my arm.

Zhenga gets to us first, shaking her head in irritation as the medic team joins her. "The spring is scrimmage and 'for show' matches. Why the hell is this girl going so hard in practice?"

I shrug, not wanting to admit I know why in front of the crowd of her acolytes and trying to keep my friends from getting to me. One of the mutts shoves Coco hard and she stumbles, falling back to her butt on the ground. I'm up like a flash, in the asshole's face with red eyes and a hunger for his death before I know it. "Watch what the fuck you're doing, assface."

Rufus appears at my side within seconds, shifted and looking like one of the hulking Messengers in his half-form. He's flashing his teeth as well, and before I can turn to tell him I have it, the roar of the lion stops everyone in their tracks. All eyes go to look at the display behind me, and I turn slowly to see what they're gaping at.

Zhenga is huge in her full lioness form, bigger than I remember from my pre-admission trip to Apex when I saw her and that bear fighting Felix. Her eyes are blazing with gold and amber fury as she prowls over to the two sides lined up on either side of my bestie. Cori is still on the ground, rubbing her ass grouchily as she waits for the fervor to die down. She's going to be waiting a bit, though, because Coach Z stalking into the mix with the grace of her animal radiating alpha vibes has the non-alphas frozen.

"I want everyone to move the *fuck* back *now!*" she roars and people scramble like puppets.

I feel the push in her tone, but it doesn't have the power to force me. I stay close to Coco, as does Rufus, and once the rest of the team and lookie-loos are dispersed, I get the nod. Reaching my hand down to our friend, I help the bear right herself. Ru-Ru starts checking her for injuries, but she swats him away, her face bright red with embarrassment.

"Stahhhhhhp," she mutters as she brushes the grass off herself. "I'm okay. I'll be bruised in body and spirit, but otherwise, it's fine."

The enraged lioness lets out another bone-chilling sound of anger, pushing the people back one more time. "There will be *no* violence against non-competitors in my practices, nor any scene like this again on my field. If anyone at this fucking school attempts to attack people when I am in charge, I will show them why I was a World Champion in the Pred Games. Is that understood?"

A chorus of assent comes from everyone in attendance and I look at the pack who made trouble, hoping to memorize their faces. I want to know who every single one of these fuckers is and who they're attached to. The act of bum-rushing the field wasn't about my friend and I need to know who we should watch.

Because they were without a doubt coming for me.

"Now *get the fuck* off my pitch and leave my players to cool down!"

Everyone but Rufus, Cori, and I scrambles, heading for the stands to grab their shit almost fast enough to leave fiery tracks in their wake. I chuckle, the tension seeping from my body as Cori continues to seem okay and Coach Z puts the fear of Sekhmet into those losers. Turning to look at the mess on the ground that I actually caused, I see the medics loading up Felicia on a stretcher.

"Well, shit," I grumble. "I knew she was going to make me hurt her."

Zhenga's half-shift is so smooth I don't know it's coming until she moves from four-legged jungle cat to two-legged humanoid shifter. She snorts and shakes her head ruefully. "You did what you could to avoid it, Dolly. I was watching, but as you kept signaling, I didn't intervene."

"I appreciate it. I can't have anyone see me being 'saved,' or we'll be fighting off random sneak attacks for the rest of the semester. This place has way too many places to hide for that," I reply as I shrug.

"Yeah, Dollypop, but there are going to be consequences for this shit beyond Coco's bruised hiney. You know that."

Giving Rufus a helpless shrug, I sigh. "What else was I going to do, Ru-Ru? The mangey bitch *bit* me and *broke the skin*. Do you *know* what's going to happen when I get home? Like, seriously."

Cori giggles, the first sign that she's not fudging her claim of being fine. "Man, your crazy ass mate is going to *lose his fucking mind.* That's before the others see it. *L'Academie* is going to bleed tonight if you can't get them under control."

My coach blinks, then starts laughing—hard. Before long, she's clutching her sides and wiping tears from her face as the three of us watch her in confusion. Zhenga slaps her thigh, looking every bit as silly as one would imagine in her furry, fanged, and tailed form losing her shit. I glance at Cori and Rufus, unsure what to say or do. She finally catches her breath, shaking her body as if to rid it of the amusement so she can focus.

"You young'uns have *no idea* how many times women tried to get *any* of those fuckers to give a shit about them over the decades I've been here. It's absolutely disgraceful, despite most of them not engaging in the slightest, and now this. I mean, all fucking five of those assholes are going to go on a goddamn rampage over a fair bite from a match… it's… I can't explain how sad and funny it is."

My confusion melts to empathy quickly because I know Zhenga was one of the poor saps who tried to get Felix to pay attention to her by hook or by crook. She's laughing at the irony, but also at her own stupidity, and that's to keep from feeling like shit. "Coach... I mean, Zhenga. It's not like I had any idea that—"

"Oh, don't apologize, Dolly. It's not like any of us were blind. Fitz was a player and Felix used sex for rage relief. The other three barely spoke to people, so they were even more off limits." The lioness wipes her face and gives me a sad smile. "No one had a chance, but they were the best options in a place with very few palatable ones. I haven't been interested in the Raj since I found out about the mates thing and we talked about that. It's just... so damned pathetic and humorous at the same time."

Rufus takes pity on her and tsks. "You were wasting that bod, Coach. You're made for sin and death like my bestie bunny, but differently. Who gives a fuck if your family is a bunch of crusty old misogynists? Do what you want, do it loudly, and rep it proudly. No one should get to decide who people love. I fought my way to the top of my hillbilly fuckhead relatives to earn my ability to do so. You can, too."

"He's right," Cori says softly as she looks at us with oddly soft eyes. "I got the boot from the main family because of politics, but being a sexual pescatarian didn't help. But I'm doing my thing, my way, and I'm going to teach those dicks a lesson, just like Dolly is. Together, we're all going to flip our stupid families on their asses. You should, too."

Zhenga tilts her head, smiling a little as she thinks about it. "You might be right. I've moved out of the pathetic 'debase myself for their approval' phase. Now I need to embrace the 'fuck you and your bullshit' phase like the badass I am." Her expression is still amused as she looks at me. "Delores Diamond Drew, you're a surprisingly good role model, even for me."

I snort. "The hell I am. I'm still a mess of childhood trauma, hurt and betrayal, and fury at everyone who put me in the state I was in when you all first met me. I'm not someone to emulate in the fucking slightest."

Rufus walks over, grabbing my hands to spin me around for a moment before he grins. "Feel that whirlwind, girl? That's what you did when you walked into our lives and I guarantee your men feel the same way. The breath of fresh air and the strength you seem to just dig deep until you find are just *some* of the shit we're learning from you. Own it, Dolly. You deserve the credit."

My face turns bright red and I have to turn away from them to pick up my shit at the outside of the ring before I get too over-wrought. Being with these people who care about me has been a gift from day one, and the stark contrast from what I had with former friends is sobering. But I struggle with praise, even from the guys, and I'm having trouble processing it.

Maybe one day I won't feel like such an imposter when people are nice, but it's not today, damn it.

KILLER

Fitz

I'M GOING TO SLICE THAT LITTLE BITCH INTO TINY PIECES AND HAVE the prey staff feed her to her pack in some fucking chili.

My Baby Girl came home with a dressed wound—it was pretty smart of Z to do that before she got here—from a goddamn mutt taking a shot at her when she should have submitted. Coco-cabana and the badger tried to downplay it with her, but Felix had the lioness on the phone before she could get half the story out. I'll admit, despite her vicious streak, Dolly made it sound like a basic scrap in the ring so no one would go flying out the door in a rage. She's got mad strategic skills and she knows how to keep us in line when need be. But this is a direct offense, and it must be answered for.

"Princess, the scene you are all describing and the one Zhenga has finally shared is quite different." Felix's arms are crossed over his chest as he looms over the three younger preds sitting on our couch looking mildly guilty. "Do any of you want to try again?"

"Gee, *Dad*, I don't know," Cori grumbles under her breath and we all give her a reproving look, especially the grouchy AF dragon. She juts her chin out defiantly, her eyes narrowed as she stays faithful to whatever promise our girl had her and the punk make before they arrive. "Will I be grounded if I don't?"

My arm flies out before Aubrey goes stomping over, blocking his path on instinct. He's not really mad at her, and he'd be sorry if his dragon pushed him to yell at her. The colorful bear is being loyal to our girl in the face of three kings, a beta, and another pissed off pred with decades to centuries on her. It's impressive even if it's not particularly bright. "Coco-cabana, we know the truth now. No need to keep up the pretense."

"No idea what you're talking about, Khan," Rufus says as he examines his manicure with a fangy grin. "We were all there."

"*Amis,*" Ren says cajolingly. "The gig, as they say, is up. Zhenga filled the Raj in and we know this was more than a practice scuffle. Why continue with the charade? It is pointless, *non?*"

Always the reasonable one, that gargoyle.

"I'm not sure *that's* an accurate statement," the bunny in question says mildly. "You bullied Z into giving you her side of the story, but it's no more reliably narrated than ours."

Aubrey sighs, cracking a smile then scowling at himself for doing it. "Lunchable, I don't get why you're downplaying something so serious. Help us understand and perhaps it won't be such a big deal."

She rolls her eyes, making Felix snarl dangerously, but it doesn't affect her. Our girl knows none of us would ever harm a hair on her head, nor her friends' heads, so it's more of a warning than a threat. "Look, I handled the situation. Yes, it was unfortunate, but we have too many unanswered questions about the *many* threats to go around offing every person who comes at me. It would be way too time consuming, for one, and it wouldn't solve anything, either."

Walking closer, I drop to my knees, pushing my fury into its cage as I look up at her. "Baby Girl, you're my *mate*. It's a whole other level of crazy that already filled my brains when I look at you. Seeing you injured without being able to do anything about it is making my tiger nuts—more so than normal. And since these jokers are intended mates as well—some with unstable beasts—it's riding them just as hard."

Huffing a bit as her posture relaxes, Dolly reaches out and takes my hands. "Fitzy, I'm not saying you guys can't do *anything*. But keeping this low-key was *supposed* to keep you all from *killing* someone who might be a good lead. I mean, I'd never met or heard of this fucking chick until I got here. Why the shit is she going for my throat like I fucked her dad at her sweet sixteen? Doesn't that merit some investigation?"

Rufus and Cori double over in laughter at her words, and I can't help it, my lips twitch in amusement. When our girl arrived at Apex two years ago, she *never* would have *thought* that simile, much less said it out loud in such a confidently sarcastic tone. The differ-ence in her is night and day, no matter how many times some things make her flush like a ripe peach. It's a beautiful thing, just like her ferocity, and it makes my heart thump just as hard.

"Baby Girl, I don't know how you expect me to take you seriously when you…" I trail off, shaking my head as the chuckles escape me.

Pretty soon, even the spicy salamander is snickering and the tension in the room drops by a million degrees. Her eyes sparkle with triumph and humor, letting me know she did that on purpose to get us all to focus on something besides our blood lust. Again, she's a goddamn smart cookie, and she knows how to play us like one of the dragon's expensive fiddles.

"Seriously, though. I really think it's important to milk these idiots for every drop of info we can get from them. And they're stupid, guys, because they make themselves known at every turn. Unlike the roommate chick I never met who flew under the radar, the Heathers and these new minions are painting targets on their own backs. Why *wouldn't* we use that to our advantage?"

Cori raises her hand, looking sheepish. "With the obvious people being so, um, obvious… doesn't it make you all worry that there's people being… less… obvious? Like, the big targets are there to draw your focus away like with magicians?"

Good fucking point, Coco-cabana.

"You're not wrong," the dragon says with a heavy sigh. "We are all concerned with the possible hidden enemies, Cori. That's why Fitz and Felix did a personal search of the *prima's* housing today while you were in class. She was the first on our list to dig more deeply into."

Dolly's eyes widen and she whips her head to look at my twin, who shrugs. "Princess, I told you we were going to get serious about the professors in that photo. It's better we did it than Farley sending his goons in. I'm fairly certain they're even more direct than us and with less concern about what effect it will have on your day-to-day life."

She chuckles, giving him a lop-sided grin. "You're saying they're a nuke to drive a nail, yeah?"

"*Exactement,*" Ren replies as he drops into his chair. "We should only ask your badger counsel to send his crew of enforcers when it is dire unless we want bigger messes to attend to."

"That's probably true," Rufus says as he scratches his chin. "My cousin is fucking brilliant at what he does, because he rarely gives a shit what size the blast radius is. He does what needs to be done, when it needs to be, and moves on. Fallout isn't his specialty, so he's actually being unusually graceful about how he's handling your issues."

"I'm special that way," Dolly says with a bright smile.

Inching closer on my knees, I look up at her. "You're special in every way to us, Baby Girl, and it's not surprising others think so as well. Do you know how many times Zhenga has lost her shit—like really lost it like today—in the years we've all known her?"

The bunny shifter shakes her head, looking at Rufus and Cori, who also shrug.

"Like three, Princess," Felix says seriously. "Today, once when her dad handed things he shouldn't to her brother, and once at a new professor who no longer breathes air on this planet. Her control is one of the things she's well known for—at least, when it comes to her temper. In other things, not so much."

Our girl snorts, muttering, "No shit, Sherlock." Her friends laugh, and even Felix cracks another grin. "But I didn't know that; you're right."

Chess finally speaks up from his spot in the kitchen and I'm surprised to see him toss back a bourbon. I was so caught up in wanting to murder the fucking wolf that I didn't notice he's been almost like a ghost in this situation. "Now that you've made up, it seems she's intent on being part of our extended family, Angel. So she's certainly going to stand up when she feels it's warranted. Zhenga has many flaws, and maybe she's finally coming to grips with those—that makes me happy for her. Being friends with you and the rest of the people you've taken in might be part of that. So of course, she told Felix the truth. She wanted him to know you weren't safe, but she helped."

"Here I thought she was tattling on us," the badger grumbles.

Coco shakes her head, the rainbow curls flying. "I don't think she wanted to impress Felix. That shit scared her; I could see it in her eyes with her fury. She didn't want anyone to get hurt."

Hmmm. Probably checks out, but what am I missing here? Only our girl was in the cross-fire.

"She's right," Rufus says as he leans back against the couch. "The Coach was definitely protecting people."

I let go of my girl's hand as she turns to give her friends an odd look, rising to my feet to head over and check on my cheetah. I'll get my vengeance for hurting my mate, though it won't be nearly as satisfying as killing the mangy dog. But now that I'm able to get my tiger to see that she's okay, I need to soothe my other troubled mate.

When I reach him, Chess lets me wrap around him from behind and set my chin on his shoulder. I murmur in a low tone, barely audible if no one's listening. "Your cat is giving you fits, my love."

I feel his sheepishness rather than see it on his face, as I keep my gaze trained on the three sitting on the couch having some sort of wordless argument about Zhenga. "Fitzy, I've never wanted to kill someone so much in my entire life, not even your father."

My chuckle is soft as I squeeze him in my arms. "Ah, Chessie. That's what happens when your inner pred is allowed to really stretch its paws. You've bottled him up for so long, afraid you'd upset me or cause a scene—but my Baby Girl freed him. Now you have to learn where to channel that energy."

"If you say in bed—"

Snorting, I rub my cheek on his chest. "Sometimes, baby, but that's not what I meant. You have to let the kitty have its say more often—not necessarily in the bedroom. You *like* being submissive there, but your cat wants to be more aggressive elsewhere. So stop putting yourself on a leash in *both* ways."

His amusement filters through our bond as he grumbles, "I've *never* let you put me on a leash, Fitzgerald Khan."

"Ahhhh, but you'd let Dolly do it, wouldn't you?" His shiver is answer enough and I laugh again, waiting for his soft purr to caress my skin. "Good to know. I'm always open to new experiences, especially when everyone involved is virginal."

"Gross," he mutters, but I know he likes the idea more than he's letting on.

Dolly's zeal for new experiences makes all of us get excited, even the ancient assholes, and not some weird cherry hound shit so much as seeing everything like it's new again.

"I know what I'm ordering for Pred Day on Amazon," I sing-song and he gives in, snickering softly. "I'll get Baby Girl all sorts of fun stuff. We're going to have so much fun, Chessie."

"Are you two over there gossiping?"

Aubrey's dry comment gets my attention and I look up, my brow arched. "No, making plans. We did agree that everyone is sharing Valentine's Day, right? And it's this weekend?"

"Shouldn't we all be part of that?" My twin asks with an amused look. "Not just you two clowns?"

I'd snap back with a saucy retort, but then he might ask me what we're discussing and I want that to be a surprise. So I wink at him while Dolly turns bright red on the couch and her friends giggle.

Baby Girl won't know what hit her—guaranteed.

EVIL WOMAN

DELORES

Tomorrow is Valentine's Day and the guys are being super secretive about their plans. I have to go see the evil bird bitch this morning, which is making my whole body rigid. Banjo is with me this morning, cheerily describing all the gifts he and the others have hidden for Raina in their new home. It makes me smile, especially because a grinning quokka is like a direct injection of happiness. His chatter is helping me calm my nerves, and by the time we get to the building, I feel like I can handle whatever she throws at me today.

It doesn't hurt that I know Skelly will be sitting in to keep things on track.

"Have a good morning, Dolly," the quokka says as he waves. "Don't forget that Mr. Skelly will escort you to your next destination."

I chuckle at the moniker, the image of a 'Mr. Skelly' in his suit and bowler hat invading my mind. "I won't forget. Have a good day and hug the others for me, Banjo."

"Aye, aye, Pirate Queen!"

My eyes widen at the new nickname and I head inside, hoping I'm not being promoted to royalty everywhere I go. I think I have enough shit to worry about at the moment without leading a prey revolution. "Just what I fucking need," I mutter.

Stepping into the elevator, I tap my foot until I get to my floor, then head out to see the badger in question waiting for me. His large frame fills the hallway, but he's smiling toothily as I approach. "Good morning, Miss Dolly. As agreed, I will be sitting in on your session once again. Are you ready for the shitshow?"

Laughing, I shake my head. "Not really, but I don't have a choice. How's Farley doing with the snooping?"

"The boss has all of our men on the ground working the trail. He's even got a few new digital bloodhounds working on the trail this woman left during her lifetime. We want to use her pattern of abusive behavior and public bullying to show that she's not who she claims to be." He pauses and shakes his head. "It's very frustrating to see so many people support someone this toxic. They are blind to the truth because they crave attention from online faux celebrities who don't give a shit about their loyalty unless they need them to attack for their cause."

"Even preds can be led like sheep, Skelly. I know that very well," I say softly. "I saw it when I was friends with the Heathers, and I didn't put a stop to their manipulations and horrid treatment of others. Some of this bad shit is my karma for that, I'm sure, and I deserve it. But the people who let them basically excommunicate me on nothing more than their word… those are the ones who scare me now."

Skelly tilts his head. "Why is that?"

"Because they still don't realize they were manipulated, and probably never will. Those are the kind of people who are following Rockland now, but likely even crazier. They'll do anything to please her, and that makes them dangerous." I bite my lower lip as I look at the door for a moment. "Even destroy the people around me for not shunning me like they do. So yeah, I worry about the blowback from that kind of mass indoctrination."

He shakes his head, putting his huge hand on the knob. "You're surrounded by allies, and those people always reveal themselves. No one in your life—your friends, your mates, your team—will let the morons get within a mile of you. Hold your head up and keep moving; trust the people who have your back."

I blow out a slow breath, straightening my spine and walking closer. "Okay. Let's do this."

"I THINK THERE'S MUCH TO BE SAID IN REGARDS TO KARMA, whether you believe in it or not, Miss Drew."

I arch my brow, pretending to consider Rockland's words as I lean back in the chair. "If I don't believe in it, how can it be of any importance to me?"

The truth is, I've been lying my ass off while Skelly watches the discussion, hoping to keep the crazy vulture from delving deeper into any topic. I don't want her to find any other 'gems' to use in her manuscript, nor do I want to admit to anything she can use to discredit me. I have to reply when forced, keep my cool, and let her hang herself on the tapes Skelly records during our sessions. Unfortunately for me, she's in prime form today; Rockland looks angry enough to rocket out of her chair into the atmosphere.

I wonder if someone is coaching her?

"Because *you* don't take responsibility for your actions, Delores." She leans back in her chair, a smug little smirk coming over her pointy face. Crossing her arms over her chest, her beady eyes bore into me as I look at her in confusion. "You sit there pretending to be innocent, but everyone knows better. That ridiculous badger and his mobbed-up cronies are no more than thugs-for-hire. Their maneuvers are stealing money from *my* pocket by holding up my publications and accusing me of spurious things like lying about the provenance of my works. Even the pieces not related to this are no longer selling as well as I'd prefer, despite my superior talent and skill, because you refuse to allow me to use my material."

Skelly opens his mouth, but I hold my hand up as I gather myself. This is the most direct Rockland has been, and like the nasty bullying of the Heathers online, it's still not quite enough to prove the vague defamation and libel being spread from them on social media. I need her to keep running her fat mouth so she digs a grave she can't get out of. I know she will; the remaining Heathers will, too. People with their mental illnesses *always* show themselves eventually.

"Ms. Rockland, I'm not doing anything to you. In fact, if you weren't *forcing* this contact with your stalker-ish behavior, you'd have no more space in my life or memory than a flea's fart." Her face screws up, but I continue, feeling the indignation rise in my gut. "But my team is doing their job—allowing me to live my life and not have the fruits of my emotional labor be locked in a cage by someone who does not own me or anything in my life."

"How *dare* you! I've trained at the best schools, worked at the edgiest institutions… I am a *best selling author with legions of fans*! What do you have? Nothing but exiled losers who pretend you have a shred of value to get in your pants. You'd be a star attached to my name, but without me, you're a no talent whore with rich parents."

My jaw drops and I just stare at the psycho sitting in front of me. She's gripping her desk with her claws, her head bobbing on her long neck so much that her ratty bun is falling askew. It's an image I'm never going to forget—a grown woman with so much unjustified ego and rage that she has to tear down another woman to feel better about herself. Someone so deluded about the reality she lives in that she's lost touch with what has happened in her head versus what's going on outside of it.

It's terrifying, and I'm used to Lucille, for fuck's sake.

"Ms. Rockland, this behavior is unacceptable." Skelly stands, moving in front of me before he continues. "Not only is it unprofessional and imminently reportable to the licensing board and administration of the school, but it's frankly pathetic."

"Oh shit," I mumble.

"Excuse me?!?"

The shriek makes my bunny ears hurt and I put my hands over them lightly just in case she's going to continue. Skelly is completely unruffled, and while I'm not scared she'll *physically* harm anyone, I have no idea what else this lunatic is going to do going forward.

"There's no excuse for people like you, Carina." The badger turns to wink me at me over his shoulder, then takes his jacket off, rolling up the sleeves of his oxford slowly. I'm unsure if he plans on beating Rockland's ass or is just being intimidating, so I scoot to the side a bit to watch. "You see, we can research, too. The boss's team got through all those secret layers someone built over your past."

Rockland's face turns white as a ghost, and a feeling of triumph zings through me. Whatever was hidden, she doesn't want anyone to know.

This is her Achilles' heel, and I cannot wait to hear what the fuck she's been hiding.

"You, Carina Rockland, are not the success you want this poor girl and everyone in your sphere to believe." Skelly gives her a sharp, fangy grin and she swallows hard. "No, you're the disappointment of your family, and that's why you're languishing at the schools rather than being lauded with praise publicly."

"That's a lie!"

He chuckles and shakes his head. "No, it's not. Your older sister is smarter, more accomplished, and your parents have always doted on her because of it—even as a child. The jealousy your mother engendered by making sure you knew you were second choice and would never measure up made you strive to be noticed, to be recognized, to be loved. But it never happened, no matter what school you attended or degrees and awards you received."

I wince, knowing what that feels like, but also realizing I've never used my trauma as an excuse to abuse others.

"I don't care what she thinks. She's a self-centered old bat," Rockland says, but her voice has a tremor that belies her words. "This session isn't about my mother, anyways. It's about your narcissistic, little bitch client."

"Ah, the real Carina comes out. Yes, our investigators found ample evidence in your past of how you reeled in friends, using them for whatever you could squeeze out of them, and then discarded them while trashing them by every method and in every place you could." Skelly smirks and shakes his head, picking up a book from her trophy shelf. "Like this book, where you cheaped out on your artist, stole their concept, and used it yourself to launch your first series. As usual, after a small amount of praise, you started leeching off others to get material for the next few books in the series, but pointed the finger publicly at anyone you thought was 'copying' your ideas."

Holy shit. Farley's outdone himself.

Before Rockland can retort, Skelly tosses the book and picks up another. "And this one, where you did almost none of the work and tried to blackmail the true writer into paying you extortion money. It's out of print now, but you continue to defame that poor shifter years later."

One by one, the badger goes through a litany of awful and unethical behavior, tossing the volumes on the ground until there are none left. I had no idea this chick was so prolifically awful to everyone she meets, but the facts the huge badger is spewing are obviously being hidden by some very careful PR campaigning. It's years of pervasive abuse and shady shit swept under the rug that would certainly destroy her careers if it becomes public knowledge.

"You can't prove *any* of this," she hisses.

"*Au contraire*, corpse licker. I can prove much of it and we've been compiling all the evidence very slowly to make our case. You'll give us what we need if we wait, and when you do, I'll be in the front row to witness you getting exactly what you deserve."

Rockland squawks, then shakes her head. "You'll never undo the damage I've done to her reputation. She will never be welcomed or invited at the tables of important people. My efforts won't be in vain."

I snort, shrugging a little. "I'm not aware of those 'tables,' and if they aren't big enough for me to know about them, I don't fucking care. Anyone who would exclude me based on *your* word is a fool I don't need to meet."

My giant bodyguard grins even wider. "Exactly. Plus, once we figure out who they are and what they've admitted—they'll simply join you in the penalty box. Problem solved."

Rising to my feet, I grab my bag and blow out a deep breath. "The loyalty you believe you have won't extend past being legally liable, I don't think. So be prepared to be ass out on that long branch by yourself."

And that's all I have to say about that.

Won't Say I'm in Love

RENARD

The incident yesterday put a pall over the plans for the evening, though luckily, it happened *before* our plans for Valentine's Day. While *ma petite* alternated between furious and outraged, she was able to vent that frustration playing Smash Preds with Fitz and Chess. She might be as dangerous to controllers as my mate —hers almost died several times during the marathon of fighting challenges in our living room.

Fitz, of course, reveled in her bloodthirsty competitiveness, and I saw the same kinship in Felix's expression. They were raised to identify targets, then systematically destroy the enemy when they grow tired of playing with their food. Flames and I hunt for sustenance and occasionally revenge, but not for sport. Watching our girl ping pong between the hurt, angry Dolly and the developing predator was interesting for everyone.

But it did not take away the desire to shred that disgusting flesh picker to ribbons while she screamed in agony.

Rockland is a gnat—an insignificant blip on our radar that stubbornly refuses to go away when there are bigger problems we should be focusing on. I believe she is being backed by Society members to keep our family from looking more closely into the sins of their past, but I cannot deny the effectiveness of her campaign of terror. She has cornered *ma petite lapin* by forcing her to attend the 'counseling sessions,' then using that time to wield what little power she has to provoke Dolly. If we could get someone to approve ditching the damn things, perhaps this would be easier to manage.

Unfortunately, that does not seem to be possible, so I am focused this morning on erasing that irritating event from her mind. Chester is working on gathering the food and supplies for dinner while I am mapping our space. The others have expressed jealousy over this kink and I think *ma petite* will be so distracted by her role that she will lose all thought of those who have tried to harm her this week. Aubrey and Felix are focused on other supplies, and Fitz was assigned to keep his eyes on her at Pred Games practice and then occupy her afterward so we can get ready for tonight.

Hopefully, he can keep his eyes on the prize and his mouth shut or he'll ruin the surprise.

Banking off the side of the mountains, I turn back towards the woods on the east side of the campus. The wind is light, but I'm able to glide over the treetops, peering down into the area the others said was fairly unoccupied. Since I didn't explore this section myself, I'm hoping anything unusual will spike my radar or at the very least, make my amulet pulse with the vibration of magical presence.

"This isn't the time of year for their shenanigans," I mutter as I think about our most dangerous foes—the Fae. "They will get more active as we head toward the spring equinox. Likely they are staying out of the spotlight after the lunar new year until it is time for renewal. Their powers will be greater then."

That would explain why we didn't hear about missing students between Yule and our trip to *l'Academie,* and it would also explain the lull in activity since. My knowledge of their cycles is based on old contact, so I'm not sure how closely the Fair folks will be following ancient traditions now. Being trapped outside of the Veil and in hiding for centuries may have forced them to behave in new ways to avoid being caught.

"The people we knew—*I* knew—were not this bitter or vengeful. Living the punishment their species was handed has made them petty and vindictive. I only remember beauty and moonlight tinged with rosy-hued glasses, I suppose."

I still haven't told the story of how I was exiled and I'm trying to work myself up to that admission slowly.

"Statues who have remained silent gatekeepers of the past for as long as I have are loath to speak about failures," I murmur as I coast past the easternmost edge of the forest. "But I cannot stand guard for my kind any longer. My family needs to understand how I know so much about our enemies."

But not tonight—tonight, we will all show our fated mate, the girl we were all waiting for, how loved and adored she is. It might not be in the sappy, Hallmark way humans would, but she will adore our plans. Together, we'll make Dolly feel all the love she's been denied in the past and she'll carry it with her whenever these assholes try to tear her down again.

Which they will... but not tonight.

MOONLIGHT FILTERS THROUGH THE CANOPY, CASTING SILVER shadows over the forest clearing. I perch on a branch high above, my onyx black skin almost indistinguishable from the velvety night. Below, Fitz and Felix, who only manage to work together this well when it's regarding our girl, guide Dolly through the underbrush with hushed tones of excitement.

"Come on, Baby Girl! You're gonna looooove this shit. Promise."

Dolly's soft laugh dances through the air as she holds onto them for balance. "Whatever it is, I hope it's worth almost breaking my neck trying to pull a Skywalker in a dark forest, oh Master Yoda."

"*Noice* reference, babe," Fitz says and Felix sighs heavily.

I had no idea how much a ridiculously mismatched family could fill my cup, as the humans say, until our bunny came along.

The clearing I chose is aglow with an ethereal luminescence that only the night can afford, and it's here we've laid out our Valentine's ambush for Dolly. My heart is pounding with anticipation—both for her reaction and the after dinner activity I've planned for us all.

"Are we there yet?" Dolly's voice dances up to me, light and melodic, betraying her eagerness. Her loose cotton capri pants brush against the foliage, and the slip-on shoes she wears make soft sounds against the earth—a stark contrast to her typical combat boots she stomps around in at l'Academie.

The moon acts as a spotlight, illuminating the vibrant ombre rainbow strands of her hair, making them shimmer like a kaleidoscope come to life. She's a vision, even in her casual attire; the crop top she made from Fitz's tee shirt allows glimpses of skin that I know all too well, smooth and warm to the touch.

"Almost," Fitz teases, his voice a low rumble of contained delight. "Keep those pretty eyes covered a little longer."

I watch from my vantage point as they reach the edge of the clearing. My gaze is drawn to Dolly's hands, fidgeting slightly with the hem of the blindfold, her fingers betraying the only sign of her impatience. It's a small gesture, but it speaks volumes about her playful nature—one of the many facets of her character that we've all come to adore.

The fact that she trusts us this much after the bullshit her ex pulled makes my poetic nature want to explode with verse—and it is the night for it.

"Patience is a virtue, Princess," Felix chides gently, though I can tell by the way his voice carries that he's smiling, probably wearing that smug grin that makes you want to punch him and hug him at the same time.

"Virtue, schmirtue. I want *food*, buddy," she retorts, but the giggle that follows is pure Dolly—unfettered and genuine.

They're close now, steps away from the blanket we spread earlier, a large blanket splayed out earlier in the night for our feast. Tonight is about more than just food and drink, though. It's about the connection that binds us, the shared affection we have for the woman who somehow brought us all together.

"Okay, stop here," Fitz instructs, as they reach her designated spot in the middle of the setup.

I silently leap down from my perch, landing with a grace that belies my statuesque form. The moment has come for the big reveal, and I can feel the energy of the night converging upon us, a silent witness to our peculiar courtship ritual.

"Ready?" Felix asks, his fingers ready to unveil the surprise.

"More than you know," Dolly replies, and I can almost hear the smile in her voice.

With a flourish, Fitz and Felix remove the blindfold, and Dolly blinks against the sudden glow of the moonlit forest. Her eyes adjust, and then widen with delight. In this moment, with her joy so palpable, I'm reminded why we've gone to such lengths—for the love of Dolly, our unexpected muse, our Valentine.

Aubrey ambles up beside me, his dragon forced to stay in his human guise for the occasion. The grin on his face is as wide as the wings he'll spread later. Despite the humor on his face being a rare sight when not nestled among leather-bound tomes and ancient manuscripts, tonight he's eager to show our bunny how much he loves her. His hands, usually reserved for flipping through pages with delicate care, now grip a wicker handle firmly. The picnic basket dangles from his grasp, its contents a mystery that only Chess knows. My mate's excitement is a tangible thing, wrapping around us like a warm shroud, and his eyes—those deep pools of knowledge—sparkle with pride over the moonlit soirée we've orchestrated.

"Brilliant, love," he rumbles in a voice that could easily be mistaken for the starting notes of a symphony, the timbre rich and comforting. "Under the stars, surrounded by nature's embrace—it's perfect."

As I nod my acknowledgement, Chess approaches, each step an exercise in balance and poise. I can't help but marvel at how his cheetah agility bears the weight of two coolers brimming with frosty beverages and treats. He maneuvers with feline grace, though the coolers swing like pendulums, testing his lithe strength. His expression is one of determined focus, which belies an underlying playfulness—like a cub pretending to be a full-grown hunter. It's a look that says he would shoulder any burden, no matter how heavy, to see Dolly smile.

And I know he would—just as he would for Fitz.

"Be careful, Chester," I call out, my voice a low rumble that dances with the night breeze. "The last thing we need is you spraining something before the main event."

He flashes a quick, toothy grin, his golden eyes catching the light as if they hold their own fragment of the moon within them.

"No chance, Ren. I'm all in for this," he says as he adjusts the straps of the coolers with a nimble twitch of his shoulders. Chess lowers the coolers to the earth, his slender muscles flexing beneath his fur, while I watch over Dolly carefully.

"Almost ready, *ma petite*," I assure her, my voice a thrum of excitement that matches her own.

Felix busies himself with the spread, arranging the finger foods Chess crafted with such devotion—each piece a love letter in edible form. He pops open our scotch, his claws deftly avoiding any mishaps, then pours out the crisp Dr. Pupper into a cup for our mate with an almost reverent focus.

"Good to go," he announces, stepping back to admire the feast laid out before us.

The moonlight catches in her rainbow-colored hair, setting it ablaze with vibrant hues. A gasp escapes her, a sound that wraps itself around my stone heart and squeezes with a warmth that threatens to soften even the hardest of gargoyles. She looks at everything, clapping her hands in delight as she takes in the spread.

"It's not... five-star fancy," Aubrey rumbles, scratching the back of his neck with a clawed finger, "but the best is yet to come."

Dolly's response is immediate; she whirls around, her arms flinging wide to encompass us all in her happiness. She plants kisses on each of us—a touch as light as a butterfly's wings—and then settles down amid the cushions and blankets, her gaze twinkling with mischief.

"Food, boys. You need to feed this B before I lose control," she declares, her voice laced with playful authority.

We all sit in a circle surrounding her with different foods to offer the girl who captured our hearts and changed our lives. The forest's symphony plays around us as I watch Dolly snatch and nibble on a golden-fried mozzarella stick, her eyes alight with pleasure. A laugh ripples from her lips, and it spreads through our group like wildfire, infecting us all with shared mirth. Her appetite is robust and infectious; she takes a bite here, a sip there, her delight in the simple feast evident.

"Take a bite of this, Princess," Felix insists, offering her a crispy onion, his eyes crinkling at the corners. "I promise you'll love it."

"Only if you have one too," Dolly counters, laughter lurking beneath her words. She feeds him in turn, their heads close together, an intimate exchange observed by the moon and stars.

I join in the merry dance, leaning forward to present her with a skewer of cheesy goodness, my fingers grazing hers. Our gazes lock for a moment, electric and charged, before she bites down, her lips brushing my fingertips. I can't help but shiver at the contact, feeling more alive than a man of stone should ever feel.

"Careful, Rennie," Aubrey teases, his deep voice resonant in the still evening air, "or you'll get too excited and we'll ruin the dessert."

His jest earns a round of chuckles, even as Dolly's hand finds mine, giving it a tender squeeze.

When the last of the food has been savored, and our laughter has woven into the tapestry of the night, we settle into a contented hush. That's when the gifts appear, each one adding another layer of emotion to the evening's tapestry.

Aubrey presents his first, the sparkling earrings that match the Dragon Empress Tiara glinting in the moonlight. Dolly's hands fly to her mouth, her eyes misting over as she admires their intricate design. She wasn't a fan of finding out who the crown belonged to, but she adores parading around in it when she thinks no one is looking.

My mate did a very good job packing these for our trip overseas; he, too, deserves a treat.

"Thank you, big guy," she whispers, reverence tainting her usually lively tone. "They're beautiful. I'm terrified of them, but I love them just the same."

The typically grumpy dragon's chest swells with pride, his grin stretching from scale to scale. "Of course, nothing less for our queen," he says with a wink.

Before the sentiment can linger too long, I pull out my own offering, the tickets gleaming like a promise of adventure yet to come. Dolly gasps, her eyes widening as she realizes what they are.

"Our adventure into Paris?" she squeals, pure joy radiating from her. "Rennie, this is perfect! I can't wait to see your city with you."

"*Oui, ma chérie.* I want to show you my home the way only someone who lived here when it was young can," I reply, my accent thicker on my tongue now that I'm basking in her excitement.

"Fucking French-fried show-off," Aubrey grumbles good-naturedly, but his smirk betrays his amusement.

"You know my people practically invented romance," I shoot back, sharing a conspiratorial glance with Dolly, who is still clutching the tickets as if they might take flight.

She leans in then, her kiss a sweet stamp of gratitude on my cheek, the scent of her happiness mingling with the earthiness of the forest around us. "I'm excited to have dinner and see the show, then tour the city, my *angel of music.*"

I roll my eyes and huff playfully, "*You're* the angel of music, *petite,* not me."

Dolly snorts. "I could totally be a mask-wearing stalker; I'm taking lessons from Fitzy."

The laughter of our family is a soft symphony of mirth as Chess steps forward, his sleek cheetah grace evident even with the coolers long set aside. He reaches into a side pocket and produces a worn canvas bag, which crinkles as he presents it to Dolly. She cocks her head, her rainbow hair shimmering in the moonlight, curiosity dancing in her eyes.

"Open it," Chess urges, his own eyes gleaming with a mix of pride and anticipation.

She dips her hand inside and pulls out a sweater, the fabric cascading over her fingers like a waterfall of colors that sing in harmony with her vibrant locks. The yarn is thick, soft, and full of love—every stitch a testament to Chess's dedication. Alongside the sweater are leg warmers, a perfect matching pair, their hues equally vivid and joyful.

"Chess, they're beautiful!" Dolly exclaims, holding them up against herself, the size just right for covering her dance garb on the chillier days.

"Knitting's become a bit of an obssession since we all decided to learn," Chess admits, scratching the back of his neck with a shy smile. "It relaxes me now that I've gotten better under Aubrey's tutelage."

Her eyes brim with tears, not from sadness but the overwhelming warmth of being cherished. "I can't even..." Her voice breaks, and she gestures for the bottle of scotch. Taking a hearty swig, she steadies herself before looking up at Felix, who now holds center stage.

Felix presents her with a box, its contents hidden within the dark leather confines. When Dolly opens it, the sight of the black leather collar studded with diamonds draws a collective intake of breath. At its center dangles a claw, pristine and menacing—one that has clearly been removed and treated, then blinged out.

It's that fucking alpha wolf's claw Fitz took with his finger the night he ripped the fucker's head off.

"I pilfered it from your jar. Sorry, not sorry," Felix explains with a grin that matches Dolly's wickedly arched eyebrow.

"Looks like someone has their big boy pants on tonight, *Sir*," Dolly teases, her voice sultry with promise.

Fitz laughs, stepping up beside Felix. "Not just him." He presents another, smaller collar, this one masculine and bearing a lock with two keys. With a mischievous bob of his eyebrows, he extends it towards Chess, eliciting a round of chuckles from the group.

"Thought you'd appreciate the leash that goes with it," Fitz says, winking at Chess, whose cheeks flame with a blush that could rival the setting sun.

"Fitz, for fuck's sake…" Chess protests, but it's no use; his embarrassment only adds fuel to their merriment.

Dolly delves deeper into the box, her hands exploring the treasures Fitz has packed. An array of adult toys, each more elaborate than the last, and a selection of lubes that promise a night of untamed pleasures. An impish laugh escapes her as she lifts a particularly audacious item, holding it aloft.

"Planning on keeping me entertained all night?" she asks, her gaze flitting between us as we look at her adoringly. "I can definitely get behind that, boys."

I walk over to her, tilting my head. "Are you ready for the rest of the surprise, *ma petite?*"

"Definitely."

Dolly's arms encircle me in a tight embrace, her warmth seeping into my stone-cool skin. She plants a soft kiss on my cheek, murmuring words of gratitude that hum through my core like the sweetest melody. She flutters to each of us, like a vibrant butterfly gracing flowers with her presence, her laughter mingling with the night air.

"Thank you, all of you," she beams, eyes glistening with unshed tears that are a testament to the joy we've etched onto her heart tonight.

She finally turns to face me again, her gaze expectant and filled with curiosity. The corner of my mouth twitches upward into a knowing smirk. "There's one more gift," I say, my voice as deep and resonant as the forest around us. "And this one is for all of us."

Dolly cocks her head, her rainbow hair catching the moonlight in a prismatic dance. "What is it?" she asks, excitement lacing her tone.

I stand taller, wings flexing behind me as I lock eyes with her. "You will shift," I declare, anticipation curling within me at the thought of the game ahead. "Then we *all* will hunt you through these woods."

Her eyes widen, a spark igniting within them—a blend of thrill and surprise. "All of you?"

"Every time one of us catches you," I continue, the smirk solidifying into a grin of raw, exhilarating challenge, "we get to decide our prize."

Dolly's lips part slightly, as if tasting the promise of the chase on her tongue. Her expression flickers, then settles into a fierce resolve that mirrors the wild spirit I've always admired in her. A shiver of excitement travels down my spine, the promise of the hunt enlivening every inch of my being.

"Game on," she whispers, her voice a sultry siren call that beckons us to the adventure that awaits.

This is going to be a very long and delicious night.

Run Rabbit Run

Delores

"Go!" Renard's gravelly voice shatters the stillness of the night, and I'm off like a shot, my heart hammering with exhilarating fear and desire. The woods become a blur as I dash through the underbrush, the cool night air whipping against my skin. My rainbow hair is a wild cascade around my shoulders until I yank it back, securing it with the elastic I've kept tucked in my pocket for this very moment.

Always be prepared like a good Pred Scout, that's my motto.

As I run, I don't dare look back, but I feel the heavy beats of Rennie's onyx wings and the rush of Aubrey's fiery breath as they take to the skies in half-shifted form. The thought sends a delicious shiver down my spine. They've done this with me before, I know how they work, what their path will be as they work together to track me. That gives me an edge from above, but this time, I have more than just my huge winged preds looking for me—I have the ground kitties as well.

I imagine Fitz and Felix's powerful tiger bodies slipping between the shadows while Chess's cheetah swiftness will help him close in on me—each movement calculated, each sense heightened in their animalistic forms. The three of them were raised on an island soaked in blood and they've probably had to hunt victims together before. I don't know because I haven't asked, not wanting to force them to re-live their trauma at the hands of their father anymore than I want to re-live mine. But now I wish I had, given that they are probably a dynamite team moving through the brush as one ambush waiting to scent me.

The soaked crotch of my capris giving them all a nice, strong smell to follow isn't doing me any favors, either.

Panting, I press my back against a thick tree trunk and listen. The forest is alive with nocturnal symphonies, but beneath that, I search for the distinct sounds of pursuit—the crack of a twig, the rustle of leaves, or the soft pad of paws against the earth. I tune into the bunny inside me, letting her prey instincts sharpen my hearing. The distant flap of wings sends a thrill through me, but it's too small to be either of my aerial mates.

I have to be clever, as much as my body thrums with the need to be caught, claimed, and ravished by them. I move again, quieter now, ears twitching at every sound, eyes scanning the dancing shadows. The woods are a playground, and I'm the coveted prize —a prize that craves the chase, the suspense of the hunt. But winning, for now, means staying one step ahead, being the elusive target that drives them wild with anticipation.

As much as I want them to find me and fuck me upside-down until I can't walk, the dark part of me where the red-eyed bunny and that blue lightning live refuses to make winning easy for them.

My legs move with a mind of their own, darting from tree to tree, the thrill of evading capture mixing potently with the growing need between my thighs. It's a dangerous dance, one where I'm both participant and prize, and I can't help the grin that spreads across my face.

"Ollie, ollie, oxen-free, boys," I whisper to the night, a taunting invitation to my lovers. A part of me wants to surrender, to feel the strength of their bodies pinning me down so badly that my cunt aches to be filled—but not when the chase is just as intoxicating as what comes after.

I press on, deeper into the thicket, my excitement building with every heartbeat. They're out there, my sexy, dangerous predators, and tonight, we play a game where everyone hungers for victory —and I'm eager to see who will claim their Valentine's prize first.

MOONLIGHT SLICES THROUGH THE LEAVES, CASTING A SILVER GLOW that I avoid like spotlights on a stage. I press my back against rough bark again, my heartbeat a frantic drummer in the quiet orchestra of the night. My breath is shallow, my senses on high alert as I use every ounce of my shifter instincts to become one with the shadows.

I feel their eyes scouring the forest, their ears tuned for any sign of my presence. But I'm careful, so very careful, slipping through the underbrush without so much as a rustle. The damp earth beneath my feet is cool and forgiving, silencing my steps as I weave between trees, deeper into the heart of the woods where the canopy shields me from prying eyes above.

The thrill of the hunt is electric, coursing through my veins and pooling at my core. I've played this game with Renard and Aubrey many times, their aerial advantage always adding an extra layer of excitement. But now, with Fitz, Felix, and Chess prowling below, the stakes feel deliciously higher.

I might be just a little twisted for enjoying the men who could literally eat me hunting me for sport, but who the fuck cares what anyone else thinks? No shame in the game, baby.

My laughter is a silent ripple in the air, amusement dancing in my chest at the thought of eluding all five of them. Kings and soldiers for their kind, but little old me, a cosmic mix of prey and pred that shouldn't exist, is leading them on a much more lengthy chase than should be possible. My victory is short-lived, though, as the pulsing need between my legs betrays another desire entirely—one that yearns for capture.

"Where are you, my fierce felines?" I murmur to myself, a playful taunt that only the trees can hear.

Suddenly, a rustle catches my ears. Not the whisper of leaves or the skittering of a small animal—it's something far more deliberate—a presence, fast and focused. Before I can react, I'm pinned against a tree, Chess's body a solid heat behind me.

"Gotcha, Angel," he purrs, his voice laced with victory as he shifts back to human form faster than a blink.

"Damn it, Chessie. You're so fucking fast," I gasp, but there's no real frustration in my voice—only a rising tide of arousal.

"Only when I'm hunting," he says with a dark smirk that's unlike him. His hands are on me in an instant, tearing away the fabric at my capris' crotch with a swift, practiced motion. The cool night air kisses my exposed skin, heightening the sensation as he drops to his knees. His breath is hot against my wetness, and I clamp my lips tight to stifle the moans threatening to spill forth.

I can't make a noise and have the others find us; I want to play some more.

Chess doesn't hesitate or ask like usual. This game has the possessive part of him raring to go and he's not going to worry about permission. His tongue lashes out, bold and demanding, while his fingers tease and plunge in a rhythm that has my entire body quaking. Every stroke, every suck sends me spiraling toward ecstasy, and I bite down hard on my lip, tasting blood.

"Keep it down, Angel, or they'll hear," he chuckles against my flesh, his voice a velvet taunt. "You don't want the others to join in too soon, do you?"

"Channeling Fitzy, my white knight?" I manage to mutter in between stifled moans of pleasure.

His laugh vibrates over my sensitive clit, and I detonate, shudders wracking my frame as the orgasm rips through me like lightning. Chess doesn't stop until I'm limp against the tree, spent and panting. His rough cheetah tongue is a goddamn delight, and I close my eyes as I try to unmelt my brain so I can speak.

"Alright, I'll give them a fair shot," he says, standing up and wiping his mouth with the back of his hand, a smirk playing on his lips. "But they better hurry, or I might just decide to claim another round."

As he saunters off toward the clearing we started in, I gather what's left of my composure and prepare to dart back into the darkness. The scent of my release lingers heavy in the air, a fragrant beacon for my remaining hunters.

"One went down, four to go" I whisper, the thrill of the chase reignited within me.

With a few deep breaths to steady my racing heart, I tug the remnants of my capris up around my hips, the torn fabric mocking me with its new purpose. The damp air of the forest clings to my skin, carrying the scent of my arousal like a tantalizing promise to my pursuers. I can't help but grin at the thought of what's coming—my body thrums with anticipation as much as the need to stay ahead.

For now.

I slip between the trees, my feet silent upon the leaf-strewn ground. Each step is a dance, a playful frolic that beckons them closer while moving farther away. My bunny senses are heightened by my time with Chess; I listen for the slightest shift in the forest's whispered secrets, the telltale signs of my hunters on the prowl.

Suddenly, a rustle above sends adrenaline spiking through my veins. Before I can dart away, an orange blur drops from the branches, and I'm met with the wild, gleaming eyes of Felix in cat form. His grin is all fang and triumph. I spin to flee, only to find myself ensnared by sinewy arms—the warm embrace of a half-shifted Fitz, his alabaster fur a stark contrast against the night.

They've caught me, their prey, and oh, how I've longed for this twin sandwich.

"Tsk, tsk, Princess," Felix rumbless, his voice a growl of delight. "Looks like you're trapped."

"You're ours now, Baby Girl," Fitz chimes in, his tone smug and victorious. His eyes are full of delight, flashing with hints of his big cat as he holds onto me tightly. "Time to pay the piper."

Their half-shifted forms are a sight to behold, primal and powerful. It ignites a fire within me, the heat of desire mingling with the thrill of being so thoroughly hunted. The twins tear at my shirt, shredding it down the front as if it were mere tissue, and I'm bared to the cool kiss of the night breeze. This is something we've haven't done yet, either—half-animal, half-men, and just the twins sharing me.

Best. Valentine's. Day. Ever. Motherfuckers.

Felix's rough tongue traces circles around my nipples, his fangs grazing tender flesh, sending jolts of pleasure-pain down to my core. Fitz's hands are on my hips, guiding me back against him, his erection pressing insistently at my entrance. Wet and wanting, I welcome him inside with a gasp, my body yielding to his invasion.

"Shhhh," Fitz whispers, his hot breath tickling my ear. "I'm not sharing with the winged weenies right now, only my bro. So keep that pretty mouth closed unless we occupy it, Baby Girl."

I bite back my moans as Felix enters me from the front, filling me completely. The sensation of being stretched, taken by both, is overwhelming. Together, they move in a rhythm that steals the breath from my lungs, their dual assault driving me toward a precipice I'm all too eager to tumble over.

"Princess, you're so damn wet it's like a waterfall," the elder twin says as his hands squeeze my breasts. Fitz is helping me stay upright, but Felix is definitely leading the charge in this menage.

Our climaxes crest quickly then crash in a silent symphony, waves of ecstasy that leave us shuddering in unison. They release me from their grasp, shifting back to human forms with a wink and a nudge to send me on my way. Legs trembling with the aftershocks of pleasure, I straighten and continue my flight, knowing full well the sky-bound pair won't be far behind.

How the fuck am I going to concentrate with my thighs covered in cum and my clothes in tatters?

My steps are less sure as I continue my path through the forest my body languid and sated, betraying my every attempt at silence. In my haze of bliss, I miss the gap in the treeline until it's too late. Renard looms before me, his hard onyx skin gleaming in the moonlight—a dark and fearsome sentinel. Beside him, Aubrey's scales catch the starlight, casting prisms across his imposing form.

"Goddamn it," I breathe out, eyeing their massive, half-shifted bodies. "You assholes were just *waiting*."

"Aren't we always?" Aubrey teases. "Hunting for dinner, then having you for dessert is one of our favorite activities, snack size."

"Uh-uh," I say, holding my hand up. "There's no way I can do this with you two... half-monsters. Not together. We've discussed this."

"Give us a tail, Dolly," Renard urges, his voice a low rumble of desire. "Your bunny changes everything; I promise, *ma petite*."

My romantic Frenchman would never fib to me about this, so he must be right.

Hesitant yet curious, I let the change take hold. Rabbit traits emerge, sharp and soft in equal measure—the length of my ears, the twitch of my nose, the fluff of my tail, the short, soft fur covering my limbs. Aubrey chuckles at the sight, his excitement at cuteness palpable, while Renard circles, admiring my feral allure.

When my amulet dissolves the last of my clothes, they strike. Caught between stone and scale, I'm lifted into the air, soaring high above the treetops. The sensations are magnified, the fearlessness of flight combining with the rawness of their touch. Renard fills me, stretching me in ways that draw a helpless cry from my lips, and then Aubrey joins, his unique texture sending sparks of heat through my core.

I'm not sure I won't break in half before we come, but man, what a fucking way to go.

Our skyward dance is fierce and brief, driven by the urgency of our shared hunt. The night becomes a blur of passion and pleasure, and when we finally descend to the clearing where it all began, my cries echo into the night, a testament to the hunt's thrilling end.

My legs give out when Rennie lets go of me, the forest floor spinning slightly as I try to find my footing. Fitz is there in an instant, his strong arms steadying me with a gentleness that belies his earlier ferocity. From the picnic basket, he retrieves a soft, plush robe, its fabric comforting against my sensitized skin. He drapes it over my shoulders and I can't help but lean into his embrace, the warmth of his body a stark contrast to the cool night air.

Always there to catch me, that's my crazypants mate.

"Seems our Princess had her fill," Felix teases, his voice laced with triumph as he begins gathering scattered utensils from the forest floor. "You're in charge of bunny wrangling, bro."

"More like she's been thoroughly hunted," Chess adds, his smirk audible even without seeing his face.

I crack an eye open to look at him, wondering if this bit of edge will lead to us mating next. His cocksure attitude tonight tells me it's possible, and that makes me smile drowsily, even though I want to snap back with something witty, but my words are slow, my brain languid and sated. "You guys suck," I manage, the attempted scold weak and unconvincing.

Rennie chuckles, his deep voice resonant in the quiet of the clearing. "Very well, from the looks of it, *ma petite.*"

Aubrey, wiping down a now empty platter, gives me a conspiratorial wink. "And we will again once you're ready, lunchable. Fitzgerald will attend to your aftercare when we get home, and once you rest, we will give it another go."

"Best... Valentine's... ever," I mumble, feeling my eyelids grow heavy. The praise is genuine, the experiences of the night engraved indelibly upon my memory.

"Time for sub-space bunnies to get home and cleaned up," Fitz murmurs, lifting me effortlessly into his arms. As they tidy up the last remnants of our celebration, I nestle against Fitz's chest, the steady beat of his heart lulling me towards oblivion.

"Thank you," I whisper, knowing my gratitude is felt by each one of them.

With that, I let the darkness take me, the journey back to the library nothing but a distant motion as I drift into sleep, cradled by the love of my men.

SCHOOL'S OUT FOR
THE SUMMER

AUBREY

THE GLOW OF THE COMPUTER SCREEN FLICKERS AGAINST THE lenses of my glasses, a soft hum of electricity whispering secrets in the quiet library. I tap a finger with deliberate care on the mousepad, opening an email that has just chimed into my inbox. My eyes scan the contents quickly, the words from my Smithsonian colleague igniting a flicker of excitement within my chest.

As much as I loathe tech some days, this application is quite useful.

"Examined documents from Apex and Capital Prep," I murmur to myself, digesting the implications. "Magic Accords... Society families... need more information…"

The message is detailed but tinged with frustration. My walrus counterpart at the huge hybrid library in D.C. believes we have located missing pieces in a puzzle that has long been scattered across the globe. Key documents elude them—documents unmarred by the Council's heavy-handed editing. History, raw and unfiltered, remains beyond our grasp, hidden away with purposeful intent.

"Of course, the Council would twist the truth," I grumble, smoke puffing from my nostrils as I consider the implications. The real story behind the Fae's banishment could change everything we know about the delicate balance between our worlds—and the tale we've all been told about why magic users have to be exiled or executed.

This only exacerbates my fear that we have inherited a problem that began with greed and will end in bloodshed.

I lean back in my chair, the ancient wood creaking beneath my weight, and gaze out the window at the stars peeking through the night sky. Somewhere out there lies the key to understanding, to unraveling the Council's deception, and I am determined to find it. Our mate is tangled in this mess somehow and though we don't know how, we have to protect her.

Flexing my talons, I fight the urge to smash things in response to our helplessness. Once I'm calm again, the talons recede and I feel the grooves of the keyboard beneath my fingertips as I compose a reply. The aquatic scholar's belief that more accurate documents are hidden somewhere in Asia sparks a flame of hope within me, but it's tempered by the reality of our situation.

"See if we can gain access from France," I type, my digits stabbing the keys as I type. "Electronic access would be ideal, though I suspect a personal touch may be required to uncover these truths."

Continuing my thought process, I type the information we've gathered in, giving only the most necessary details to my friend.

The email sent, I recline in my chair and let out a long breath, watching the digital words fly away into the void of cyberspace. Until summer, our wings are clipped by duty; Dolly's education chains us to *l'Academie* with an invisible yet unbreakable bond.

Fucking administrative garbage, if you ask me, but I don't get to make the decisions.

The door creaks open, and Dolly strides in, her lithe body still radiating the energy from her dance class. Her sweat glimmers like morning dew on her skin, and she tosses her hair back in a fluid motion that speaks of rhythm and grace. I can't help but admire her steadfast ability to keep going, even when there are obstacles at every turn. Her stubbornness is almost on par with my own, and that's saying something.

"We have a lead," I say as I stand to greet her. The words come out heavier than I intend, burdened by the weight of anticipation and frustration. "My colleague at the Smithsonian finally replied."

"Spill the tea," she insists, her eyes dancing as she plops onto the table. "I want to know *everything*."

Frowning, I ignore the tea comment so I don't have to admit that I have no idea what the hell it means. Instead, I pat her knee and smile indulgently. "He believes the academy in Asia may hold unaltered documents about the Magic Accords, but as you know, we're grounded until summer break."

"Fuck," she curses, the expletive sharp and sudden like a crack of thunder. "I hate being the reason we can't do shit. Being young is cool for a lot of reasons, but it's a pain in my ass sometimes and not in the good way like this weekend."

Snorting, I cover my mouth as the laughter shudders through me. Snack size's descent into Fitz-like innuendo is amusing as hell, and every time she spouts something like that off, it makes me grin. I didn't do that often before her arrival, and I like the change—despite thinking I wouldn't. "Well, non-pleasant ass play aside, we still can't go there to check it out for another two and half months."

Dolly hops off the table, pacing alongside the row of them in irritation. Her dancer's feet barely make a sound upon the floor as she moves, and it's obvious her mind is racing through possibilities. "Then we keep digging here. We found dirt at Cappie and Apex, right? There has to be more under our noses in this damn school."

She's right; the secrets of the Council could very well be entombed within these walls, just waiting for us to exhume them.

"Then we'll get back to it this weekend," I vow, the librarian in me eager to scour every shelf and shadow. "I'm sure the rest of the family will agree."

The library door swings open with a gust of wind that tousles the pages of the ancient tome on the other side of my Smackbook. Chess strides in, his cheetah grace barely contained within the human guise he wears. Dolly stops pacing, tilting her head to give him a bright smile as he enters. She never fails to look happy when any of us arrive or worried when we leave.

"Rockland didn't show today," he announces, his voice laced with a mix of concern and curiosity. "I finished the work she left, but her office was as empty at the end of my shift as it was when I arrived."

I raise an eyebrow. Rockland's absence is peculiar, especially after last week's explosive confrontation between our girl and the self-centered scavenger. It's odd for her to relinquish control or let her talons slip from any thread of power, even if she's smarting.

We need to keep an eye on this for certain.

"Perhaps she's finally taken the hint," Dolly muses, the corners of her mouth twitching upwards in a hopeful smile. We look at her skeptically and she sighs, kicking her foot over the carpet dejectedly. "Fine, it's probably too good to be true. A vulture doesn't just abandon her hunting grounds—not without plotting her return."

"Very true," I murmur, folding my hands together thoughtfully. "You'll have to make sure you stay on your toes despite her absence."

Before either of us can present further theories, the sound of heavy footfalls on the stairs punctuate the silence. Rennie enters, his lithe humanoid form slipping into the room with feline grace. He left earlier, wanting to glide over the campus as he does several times a day. He's certain the vampires will return and my mate cannot abide them coming back without us knowing the second they set foot on the grounds.

"Quiet out there," he grunts. "The forest is still devoid of magic users or bloodsuckers. I'm not sure what they *are* doing, but they are not here. At least, not right now."

"Let's hope it stays that way," I reply, feeling a temporary sense of relief at his report. Enemies are plenty, and one less emerging from the shadows grants us respite—however fleeting it may be. "We don't even know *how* to fight those assholes. Everything in the records might be completely false."

"We're going to continue our search here this weekend, regardless of what activity is going on in the trees," Dolly declares, her gaze fixed on some distant point only she can see. "If we run into shit we don't know how to handle, we use everything we have and worst case, we run."

"Excellent point, *ma petite*," Renard says as he hops onto the bookshelf behind me. "We cannot fret so much about things we do not know that we lose track of the things we must do."

Turning in my chair, I look up, grinning at him. He leans forward, his rough lips pressing against mine briefly. Dolly comes over, taking her kiss next. She gets a softer, more careful kiss than me, but that's not surprising. He is fine with being rough in the bedroom when she consents, but he turns into the romantic poet when we're not behind closed doors.

"Always the bearer of lyrical declarations," I say, my voice rumbling with appreciation.

"Someone has to be. You're about as poetic as a bathroom limerick," Rennie retorts. His humor is a shield—one he wields as deftly as any warrior with a sword. "And our feline friends, except for Chester, are no better.

Dolly's laughter dances in the air, a silver lining to the cloud of tension that lingers over us. "I think Fitz's limericks are very poetic. Not suitable for mixed company, but definitely full of rhymes and clever wording."

"Never tell him that," I groan. "He's bad enough as it is. You've spoiled that tiger so much that even his twin can't rein him in. We're just lucky he's focused on working on your Games training so he doesn't bounce all over my library like that cartoon tiger."

"Speaking of which..." Chess interjects. "Dolly, you need to fuel up for your afternoon classes. Let me snag you something that won't make your 'coach' have a fit."

"Ugh, fine," she groans melodramatically, but there's gratitude in her eyes. "Nothing too heavy, though. Dance and Games training are very different athletics, Chessie. I don't want to barf on someone's shoes."

Once Chess heads off on his culinary mission, we all turn our attention back to the ancient scrolls and digital archives scattered across the table. Our focus narrows to the task at hand—unveiling the intertwined history of the Fae exile and those Council families shrouded in deceit. Time slips by, marked only by the rustle of pages and the muted clicks of a keyboard until Chess returns, bearing a tray laden with carefully chosen snacks. Dolly picks at the assortment with a discerning eye, settling on the meats and fruits.

It's hysterical how much our bunny hates carrots, but I don't dare mention it, or she'll stomp away.

"Thanks, Chessie," she murmurs before taking a bite.

Pushing back from my table, I sigh as I look at my companions. "If my colleague is correct, finding anything unaltered by the Council in this mess will be impossible. Our best bet to figure out what the Fae want lies within the annals of the Asian shifter academy. There may be records untouched by Western tampering—chronicles that speak truth amidst the silence."

"True. But we have quite a bit of information to go through here still. That's not counting anything we find once we get into the hidden bunker here," Rennie murmurs, his gaze tracing the lines that span years and empires. "While I'd love to just wing it across the continent to look on my own, I doubt they'll appreciate an unknown gargoyle dropping in unannounced."

"None of us have contacts there," Chess adds, a note of frustration coloring his usually calm demeanor. "We can't risk reaching out blindly, not with stakes this high."

"No, we cannot trust people who are not long-time allies, I agree." I scrutinize the ancient timeline spread out before me, scales glittering faintly under the library's soft luminescence. My fingers trace over dates and events, a pattern emerging that sends a ripple of unease through my being. "Wait... look at this. These aren't just random occurrences."

Dolly comes closer, peering over my shoulder as I note the specific events in Asia on each of the three timelines, then point at the ones Rennie and Chess have put on the boards. She frowns, tilting her head. "I don't get it."

"The events are deliberate—spaced out across centuries. It's as if... as if magic users have been testing the waters, probing for the right moment to reemerge."

That stops all three of us in our tracks and we look at one another for a moment.

"You think they've been planning a return this whole time? Without anyone catching on?"

"Centuries of preparation," I reply, my voice grave. "It's not simply about returning—it's about choosing the perfect time—a convergence of circumstances that could be exploited."

Chess furrows his brow, his tail twitching in thought. "That means every historical event we've studied might contain a clue about their motives. If we can decipher their pattern..."

"Then we might anticipate their next move," Rennie interjects. "What we don't know is how Dolly fits into all this."

"Yes," I agree, feeling the weight of history pressing upon us. "The plot we're uncovering spans far beyond our immediate troubles. It's a tapestry woven throughout time, encompassing more than just the Fae exile or the Council's machinations."

"That suggests," Dolly says, her fists clenching in a mix of anger and anticipation, "that there are pred families, outside of the Council's influence, who may hold pieces of this puzzle."

"Exactly," I nod, meeting her gaze. "We must extend our search, seek alliances with those uninvolved with the Council—especially within the mythical shifter community."

"Uncovering allies among them will be crucial," Chess says softly. "Their histories might be untainted by the Council's censorship."

The weight of the cheetah's words settle over me like a shroud. "We'll need to converse with the gargoyles at some point." I glance around the room, my eyes landing on my mate, waiting for him to weigh in.

"We may have to seek out the dragons, as well," he replies with an arched brow.

I shift uncomfortably, looking at the pattern in the wood on the table. The thought of extending our inquiries to the families that exiled us makes my dragon angry. Neither of our previous families are known for their cooperation. And they sure as fuck haven't tried to contact either of us since we were released from our groups—except to facilitate our assignment to Apex.

At least, I think our families were involved. I can't imagine who else would have paved the way for it.

Dolly stops mid-reach for a parchment, her hand hovering in the air. "You mean we're actually going to meet—"

"Some of our relatives, yes." I can't meet her eyes, my own gaze drawn to a tapestry depicting the flight of dragons under an Eastern moon. "Most dragons dwell in Egypt, basking in its sun-baked sands. Except..."

"Except?" Chess prompts, tilting his head with feline curiosity.

"Except one," I finish. "One who chose silk over sand for her retirement—my grandmother, the former Empress."

Silence blankets the room. It's one thing to plan a journey to Asia, quite another to face the prospect of knocking on the lair of dragon royalty in voluntary exile.

"Will she see us?" Dolly asks, breaking the stillness.

"See us? Perhaps. Help us?" I exhale a puff of smoke, a nervous habit from centuries past. "That remains to be seen. She's... particular about her solitude."

"Then we must be equally particular about our approach," Rennie says, his tone firm.

"Indeed," I murmur, imagining the reunion.

The last time I saw her—a millennium ago—she'd imparted wisdom as ancient as the stars. With a heavy heart, I steel myself for the task ahead. Her knowledge could be the ember that ignites our hope—or the flame that consumes it.

Fuck, I hate the assholes who set up this bullshit rebellion and everyone else involved.

SECRET WEAPON

DELORES

MY MUSCLES PROTEST WITH EACH STEP I TAKE TOWARDS THE library, the aches reverberating throughout my body after the rigors of ballet class. Fabreaux definitely tried to kill us today, and I don't know if it was to make us better or to prove how good she is. Either way, exhaustion clings to me like a second skin, but there's a pressing need that fuels my weary legs. Rockland's absence gnaws at my thoughts, her last words echoing in my mind like a malevolent mantra.

I don't trust that woman not to pop up and cause trouble even if she wasn't at work today.

I push through the heavy doors of the admin building, looking at the map briefly to find the office my lawyer said he'd be waiting in. I don't know how he got someone to give him use of it and I refuse to ask; who knows what strings he pulled? When I get the elevator, I push two and wait impatiently as it ascends. It only takes a moment to find office two hundred sixty-nine, and I blow out a breath as I open the door. Farley is ensconced behind the huge wooden desk, glasses perched on his nose as he looks through a mountain of papers.

"Did you... commandeer an office on campus?" I ask in surprise.

Now that I've said it, I realize how on-brand that power move is for him.

He looks up, eyes sharp behind round spectacles, yet they soften when he sees it's me. "Miss Drew," he greets, closing the book in front of him with a gentle thud. "You look plumb tuckered out. What class has you so thoroughly wrung out?"

"Ballet. That woman has stamina like you wouldn't believe," I admit with a small smile, sinking into the chair opposite him. The wood creaks under my weight, as if sympathetic to my fatigue. "Any news on Rockland? I don't like thinking about her running around like a loaded gun."

Farley's expression tightens, a sure sign of concern. He taps a finger on the desk, a rhythmic and thoughtful gesture. "I've had everyone looking—Messengers, Postman, other couriers. They're combing the school and the cities nearby. Anything we find related to your case, you'll know immediately."

That's not exactly an answer, though, is it? Cagey old badger.

"I appreciate that." I lean back, closing my eyes for a moment, allowing myself this brief respite. Rockland's absence is as loud as her presence—a void filled with dread that I can't fill. Her shrieking in our last appointment still rings in my ears; accusations that stick to me no matter how hard I shake my head to dislodge them.

"Don't let that crazy bitch live rent-free in your head, darlin'. She's not going to do anything physical and the rest is my problem," Farley counsels, his voice steady and reassuring. "And I don't lose."

I nod, though the knot of anxiety in my stomach begs to differ. Opening my eyes, I meet Farley's gaze, grateful for his viciously fervent dedication to helping me defeat my adult bully. Many people would say I should simply work it out with her, but when the person holds enough power—real or perceived—you simply can not reason with them. They don't give a shit what line they're crossing if they think they have the high ground.

"What other updates do you have, if not where's she at right now?" I say softly. I'm not sure I want to know this, but I also can't stop myself from asking. I know his goal when we met last was to do more digging into the vulture's carefully curated resume. We all agreed it had to be fake as fuck, and knowing what levers to pull is another method of backing her off.

"After what happened in Skelly's presence last week, I sent my moles to do some digging," he informs me, his tone grave. "I have an entire team trained by kitsunes to navigate the digital spaces and ferret out information that isn't easily accessible."

"That's a reasonable response to that blow-up, I think," I reply, the image of the big badger's stern face flashing in my mind. "Rockland... she's losing it, Farley. She's not even trying to hide her crazy anymore."

He nods slowly. "As much as I hate to say it, that's not unexpected for her mental condition. Her renewed fearlessness suggests she has a new, powerful pred in her corner. That person is probably using her to get what they want, but it makes her even more of a wild card. It's worrisome."

Good to know her insanity is so obvious that it concerns someone as single-minded as my feral country mob lawyer.

A chill skitters down my spine at the thought of my next counseling session. "I'm scared it'll get worse. That she'll pry into parts... parts of my life that are private." Even saying it aloud makes my heart race—the kind of invasive questioning that could leave scars.

"I know," Farley says, his voice firm. "I've taken the liberty of filing injunctions against all publishers linked to her books globally. If we choke her finances, perhaps she'll reconsider her vendetta."

Snorting, I give him a wry look. "Those powerful people have money, too. I'm sure they'll finance her if she stays useful."

He's about to respond when a ding echoes in the mostly quiet room. "Speaking of Rockland..." Farley continues, tapping on his tablet with a smirk. "Thanks to your hacker tiger's GPS program, we just picked up her cell signal in Paris."

"Paris?" A flutter of surprise lifts the weight in my chest momentarily. "That's... oddly reassuring. Having her an hour away makes me feel a *lot* better."

"In theory, it should," he concedes, though his expression remains unreadable. "But she's had her phone off all morning and now it's on. I've got Skelly and Monstro heading for it to see what they find out. Just because she's not here doesn't mean she isn't making trouble, Dolly."

I nod, feeling the exhaustion flow through me again. "Yeah, I know. My mother excels at doing horrible shit from a long distance, so I'm not naive enough to think Rockland isn't similar."

"How is old Lucille? The scuttlebutt is she's living it up in Ibiza since your odious father got blown to smithereens."

Rubbing my temples, I shake my head. "Truthfully? I have no idea. I haven't heard one fucking *word* from her since I got here. That alone is weird as hell, but not getting a call gloating about getting rid of Bruno is even more bizarre. I've been too afraid to reach out to her because we all know what happens when you invite the vampires into your house."

"A lesson that may become important here, mm?"

How did he know?

Another ping from the DiePad gets his attention and he frowns at the screen. Holding it up, he swipes, bringing up a grainy image of a dimly lit bar. "She's with Asani Khan at some dive called *Le Renard Rouillé.*"

"Have your badgers seen anything useful yet?"

"Skelly and Monstro are on it," he replies, a sly twinkle in his eye. "Rockland may be cunning, but she's careless when she's amongst people she wants to impress."

I nod, comforted that they are close on her tail. "What about online? You know she's been spewing lies again, trying to paint herself as a martyr. How are you handling that?"

"Ah, that." Farley taps a few more times, pulling up charts and graphs that mean nothing to me. "Her traffic has spiked, alright. The increase in chatter seems like she's rallying her troops against imaginary 'haters' again—*ie*, you."

"But how do we stop her? If she keeps on distorting the truth..." I lick my lips, frowning. "It's hard enough having built in enemies everywhere I go because of the Heathers or my mother or..."

"Patience, Dolly." Farley points to another series of screenshots. "I told you earlier that we've been digging, too. My guys found a trail of abuse and bullying, stretching back years before she ever swooped into Capital Prep."

"No shit," I retort, rolling my eyes. "Color me shocked—shocked, I tell you!"

The badger chuckles, his eyes dancing as he looks at me seriously. "Ten assistants aren't nothing, Dolly. Ten young souls chewed up and spat out by her within the three years prior to her arrival at Capital Prep. Not to mention other authors she's terrorized into silence online with that devoted cult following of hers."

"Preying on the vulnerable is the specialty of cowards like that carrion eater," I murmur, feeling a surge of anger mixed with fatigue.

That behavior is classic Rockland—manipulative, self-serving, destructive.

"Exactly." Farley leans back, his chair creaking under his weight. "Once you peel back the layers of her so-called success, what's left is nothing but a narcissistic opportunist. She's been fired from every place that's had the misfortune of hiring her."

"Bad karma follows her like a wedding train on a runaway bride," I muse aloud, a faint smile touching my lips at the imagery.

"That's the country spirit, girl," Farley says, beaming proudly. "When the world sees her true colors, her halo will tarnish."

"Leaving her to deal with her own mess, hopefully."

"Exactly why exposing her is part of my strategy," Farley says with a conviction that stirs something defiant within me.

I nod slowly, my mind's eye picturing Rockland's halo disintegrating, piece by fraudulent piece. "So, instead of being on the offensive, she'll be too busy scrambling to pick up her own pieces?"

Farley's eyes glint with unrestrained glee. "She won't have the time or energy to focus on you."

A weary sigh escapes my lips as I think of the ceaseless barrage from Rockland. The desire to just breathe without the weight of her malice pressing down on me is overwhelming. "It's like she's this shadow, always looming. I'm just so tired, Farley—tired of looking over my shoulder for enemies, tired of defending myself against her lies."

"Understandable," he agrees, his voice softening. "You're carrying a huge burden for someone so young. Luckily you have a strong support system or I fear you might head the way of others I've known in the past."

The room seems to close in on me, the walls inching closer with every beat of my heart. It's not just the fear of Rockland's vendetta that gnaws at me; it's the struggle to maintain a semblance of normalcy amidst the chaos. School should be my sanctuary, yet now it feels like another battlefield.

"Even my degree..." I trail off, the words sticking in my throat. "It's hard to care about assignments and deadlines when it feels like your life's on the line."

"And I aim to lift as much of that as I can, though I'm sure your men and my ridiculous cousin are also trying to do so."

I sigh, feeling the tendrils of anxiety tighten around my chest. "The connection to the twins' family... it worries me."

"Rightly so," he agrees, his expression grim. "It's dangerous territory."

Farley's phone buzzes on the dark wood of his desk. With a quick glance at the caller ID, a change comes over him—a mixture of seriousness and an almost boyish mischief lighting up his eyes as he answers. "Monstro," he greets, his voice adopting a country lilt that reminds me of home. "What have you got for us?"

I listen, catching only Farley's side of the banter, but the gravity behind his light-hearted tone is unmistakable. They're discussing code words, something about Asani and Rockland's cryptic exchange in the bar. Scribbling notes furiously, Farley nods along to Monster's report.

This is the song that never ends... Maybe I should take Fitz's advice and just kill the bitch?

"Keep transcribing, we'll crack it later," he instructs before hanging up. Turning to me, his brows are knitted together. "They're up to something else. But the badgers can't get any closer without being noticed—the bar's too cramped."

"Will they follow her when she leaves?" My voice barely rises above a whisper.

"Like shadows," he confirms with a sharp edge of determination.

"Thank you, Farley," I say, the fatigue seeping into every syllable. With another glance at the clock, I realize time isn't on my side. I rise, hopeful for the first time in days. Farley's expertise was a weapon in itself—one I was lucky to have on my side. "I've got studio class soon."

"Keep your head high, Dolly," Farley calls after me as I retreat. "Remember, you're not alone in this."

I offer him a weary smile, my heart a little lighter for having shared the burden, even if just for these fleeting moments. With one last glance at Farley, the guardian of knowledge amidst his literary fortress, I turn and head out, ready to face the rest of the day's challenges.

"Keep your phone on, Dolly," he advises, his gaze stern yet kind. "Say hello to my crazy cousin for me, will you?"

"Will do, Farley." I grip my ballet shoes a little tighter, bolstered by the knowledge that Rockland's twisted web was beginning to unravel.

"Take care, bunny," he says as I head for the door, my spirit lighter than it's been since this whole ordeal began. "You need your strength for all the things coming."

Boy, howdy, he's right about that. My first match is this weekend.

Indiana Jones Theme

CHESS

My heart is a steady drum of excitement in my chest as I bound alongside Dolly and the twins. Every little noise from the rustling leaves to the distant chatter of students seems amplified as we head for the location of our newest clue. We're a motley crew this Saturday morning—the bunny shifter twitching at every sound, tiger twins with amber eyes scanning the shadows, the gargoyle whose cerulean gaze misses nothing as he slinks through the trees, and an irritable dragon who keeps snorting smoke when branches pull at his precious clothing.

That's my family—and I couldn't be happier about it.

"Seriously," Dolly mutters, her voice low but laced with a thrill, "it's like they think they're in a Tolkien movie or something." Her nose twitches comically as she peers around a thick tree trunk to grin as her besties, Cori and Rufus appear to join us.

Fitz chuckles, the sound deep and infectious. "Adventure is the spice of life, Baby Girl. We all know those tight-assed fuckers on the Council have so much money and influence that very little blows their skirts up anymore."

I can't help a smirk as retort, "Or raises their flag up the pole without a small blue pill." They all laugh and I pause in our walk to the area the crew said they'd rendez-vous with us at. "Check to make sure your earpiece is secure. The last thing we need is someone getting lost or ambushed because they couldn't hear a call for help."

"Good idea, Chessie," Dolly says and I flush. Her praise makes my cheetah happy as hell, and Fitz smirks at me, his eyes saying 'later' in response.

Felix's voice comes through the earpiece, all business now. "Everyone ready?"

"Over and out, Raj," I confirm, along with a chorus of replies from the others.

Once we're geared up, we finish our journey to the spot between the edge of the forest and the base of the mountain. The Captain, Raina, and the rest of their crew are waiting; they all look bright-eyed and bushy-tailed for such an early excursion. I flash a brief hello sign to Holliday, watching carefully to catch what he responds. The others do similar, though at various skill levels, and Renard peels off to greet his prey acolytes before we begin. They seem equally as enthralled with Dolly, which clearly delights her as she greets them, too.

Our bunny is hard not to love and it consistently amazes me that she has so many random enemies despite her inherent kindness.

After we all finish chatting, the group spreads out, our search pattern meticulous as we comb the north side of the campus. This place is perfect for hiding something important, to be honest. Renard has been keeping an eye on these woods since Valentine's Day because they felt too quiet and now we know why they seem deserted. Something is being hidden here and no one wants attention drawn to the area. Closer to the mountain crags, I understand why they would choose this spot—this terrain is tricky and it doesn't stand out as a place to hang out.

We comb through the rocky terrain, my feline eyes scanning for anomalies among the stones. Dolly pauses and tilts her head. "How did we even get wind of this place?" she asks, curiosity lighting up her face.

"Ah, that was all Holliday," Raina answers, pride evident in her voice. She gestures to the quiet armadillo shifter rummaging through his backpack. "He's good at reading lips; people tend to forget he's always watching because he's deaf."

Dolly's expression darkens with irritation, a surge of empathy for Holliday flashing across her features. She moves closer to him, signing an apology with swift, graceful movements of her hands. His response is a slow, deliberate mimicry, but his smile is genuine as he praises her growing skill.

My gaze shifts between them, noticing the red hue blossoming on Dolly's cheeks. Raina reaches out, patting Dolly's hand reassuringly. "You and your men, you're different from other preds. You've been nothing but kind to us prey."

"Because my Baby Girl is our beating heart," Fitz chimes in, wrapping an arm around her shoulders. "She's got the kindest soul of anyone I know." Dolly squirms, clearly battling a wave of embarrassment as a chorus of agreement echoes from our group.

"Flattery aside," I interject, my instincts prickling with suspicion. "Don't you think it was too easy getting this tip? It could be a trap."

Felix shakes his head, confident. "Underground vaults are a staple in places like these. They're here, and we'll find them."

Dolly nods, then bursts into laughter when Felix adds a word of caution. "And don't touch anything suspect or sound off any ancient alarms, please." Her laughter increases as he sends a pointed look at Fitz, the notoriously impulsive one of us.

"Who, me?" Fitz responds with feigned innocence, a smirk playing on his lips that betrays his act.

"Especially you," Felix retorts, and we delve deeper into the search, the air thick with anticipation and the weight of secrets waiting to be unearthed.

Crouched low, I scan the rocky terrain, my cheetah senses on high alert. The scent of salt and pine blends in the air as we approach the base of the craggy mountains where forest meets shore. There's a whisper of something ancient carried on the breeze, and it prickles at the back of my neck. We've been searching for hours, but it's Dolly who finally spots it—a series of enigmatic carvings etched deep into the stone.

"Over here!" she calls out, her voice tinged with excitement.

All the groups converge on the spot, every step careful and measured in case there are traps along the way. I can't help but think how much this feels like walking into a trap, but we have to seek the vault on this campus. The clues they all hold will lead us to the truth about the magic users and perhaps prevent a war.

Not to mention they might help us figure out why the hell our girl has that blue lightning.

There it is, almost blending in perfectly with its surroundings— a series of carvings. They're intricate, weaving around the rocks like ivy. It's no wonder we missed them from afar. I don't recognize anything about them; every one of the markings is a mystery to me, even after being in the other vaults.

This is fascinating and I know Aubrey is going to drool over it.

"It's been added to over the years," Rufus says, gesturing toward where the series of markings stretch into the distance.

"Never seen anything quite like this," Cori murmurs.

"Let's see what Rennie and Aubrey make of it," I suggest, nodding towards our winged comrades who are pushing through the underbrush to join us.

"Definitely not natural erosion. Too specific," Aubrey grumbles as he leans in closer. He pushes up his glasses, his expression tinged with a mix of irritation and curiosity. The librarian in him is just as excited as me, but he hates showing it, so he's defaulting to grumpy.

"Let's get more pictures before we do anything else," Renard suggests, his voice always calm, always rational.

Aubrey squints at the inscriptions, his dragon eyes flickering with an inner light, while Renard leans in close, tracing a finger lightly over the grooves. They exchange a look that speaks volumes of their shared history and knowledge.

"Good call," I say, taking out my phone. The prey pirate crew gathers around as everyone chimes in with their opinions on the markings. Dolly and her friends make up the other flank, examining some of the oldest, deepest ones with puzzled looks. "We have no idea what touching them or trying to read them might trigger."

"I've definitely never seen anything like it," Dolly admits, while Cori and Rufus nod in agreement. "Not in the vaults, or in anything Lucille had floating around, or even online. They'd make rocking tattoos, though. Look how intricate and delicate they are."

"Reminds me of tales my mom used to tell—like nursery rhymes for baby raccoons," Raina muses aloud, her gaze locked onto the carvings. The small raccoon frowns, and I smile as she closes her eyes. I've often wondered why she and her mates stay in a half-animal, half-humanoid shift when it would be easier to avoid preds looking like people, but it suits them, so I don't ask.

Plus, it'd be rude, wouldn't it?

Her casual remark earns her the group's attention, and even the Captain tips his hat in agreement, the gesture punctuating his pirate-like drawl. "Aye, lass, seems to tickle a memory in the old noggin."

Percy, Banjo, Holliday, Kirby, and Bowser shuffle forward for a closer look but then shrug collectively. "Doesn't ring any bells for us," Percy admits with a sheepish grin. "We're more about hammers and nails than dusty old books."

"They could be an ancient code of some sort," Cori muses. "The other vaults had weird shit like that, didn't they?"

"Looks to be a mishmash," Aubrey finally says, tapping at his DiePhone with growing frustration. "Some kind of pidgin between High Fae script and the vampire's tongue." His fingers fly across the screen, but each attempt at translation only deepens the furrow in his brow.

"Can't decipher it on the spot," Renard adds, his gravelly voice thoughtful. "Too many variations, some of these marks are centuries older than others."

I glance at Rennie and Aubrey, the weight of unspoken histories clouding their expressions. "You both realize what this might mean, right?" My voice is softer than I intend, tinted with concern.

Rennie sighs, rolling his eyes to the sky in supplication. "Yes, Chester," he grumbles. "We're digging up more than just dirt here. It will require... reconciliation."

Aubrey, usually so imposing, seems smaller somehow as he stares at the cryptic carvings. He lets out a low growl, the sound of boulders grinding together. "We'll both have to face the music eventually. Might as well start with your clutch since they're in Eastern Europe. It's... closer."

"Spring break?" I suggest tentatively, watching how the possibility settles on them like a shroud.

"We can make the trip easily in that timeframe, yes," Rennie confirms with a resigned nod.

Dolly steps in then, her delicate hand reaching up to touch Aubrey's arm. Her empathy shines like a beacon. "What about Egypt, Aubrey? Will we need to—"

"Later," he cuts in, smoke billowing from his nostrils as he turns away. His eyes are stormy seas, and Dolly's presence is the only lighthouse in sight. "Asia will be first... during the summer break. If I can avoid the African continent, I will."

Felix and Fitz share a loaded glance, the air thick with silent questions. They know that's where our shared family resides—or just off the coast—and we don't want to make a pitstop there, either. Fitz snarls, walking over to me and burying his face in my neck, "I'm with Senor Spicypants. Let's try to keep that entire portion of the world on the 'no-no' list if we can,"

Before the tension can suffocate us, Rufus breaks in with a loud cough. "What exactly is the dress code for meeting dragon royalty? I don't think my leather vests will cut it."

Laughter bubbles up unexpectedly, and even Dolly snorts, although she's quick to fire back. "I'm not wearing my damn crown in front of its prior owner."

Aubrey's response is immediate, and there's a flash of the old fire in his eyes. "Oh, but you will, Snacksize. It's not an option if we want her blessing."

"Blessing?" She blanches, reminding me of a rabbit caught in headlights, but the moment passes as quickly as it came. "Who said I need permission? I do what I want now, Aubrey Draconis, and your grandma had better just accept it."

"We should head back to start researching this shit," I say, hoping to get off the topic that will certainly be a bone of contention. "We don't want to trigger any traps or curses today."

"Or on any days, if I have my way," Dolly adds with a wry smile. "I like my cottontail attached exactly as it is."

"If we're right about this being the entrance to the council's vaults, we're sitting ducks out here." Felix finally says. "Chess is right; we should go. Take a few more shots and then we'll head back."

We snap a few more shots, ensuring we've captured every detail. The marks are worn, some new, some so old they're barely visible. There's a history here, secrets etched into the earth that speak of a time and knowledge long passed.

Once our task is done, we retreat, but I glance back at the crags, a shiver running down my spine.

What are we about to unearth?

HARD TIMES

DELORES

I FIDGET IN MY SEAT, GRIPPING MY TABLET AND THE FOLDER WITH the hard copy until it bites into my palms. My heart skips a beat every time the door to the classroom creaks open. I'm half-hoping, half-dreading it might be Amity, breezing in with some flimsy excuse clutched in her hands alongside her half of the work. But no, she's a ghost today, and as each new student enters, not one of them is her.

Not like I really believe she was going to do anything anyway, but it'd be nice to get proven wrong about a negative opinion for once.

"Settle down, everyone." Asani's voice cuts through the room like a blade. He stands with a predatory grace that belies his faux, designer academic attire, his sharp eyes scanning the class.

I resist the urge to shrink in my chair. Knowing he's my tiger twins' relative makes my skin prickle uncomfortably. He doesn't look *exactly* like them, but enough that it enhances the aura of malevolence he tries to hide under the guise of being a stern professor. This class makes my stomach churn with anxiety and disgust because I know the gross vibes that I get from their cousin must be what *all* the current Raj's acolytes feel like to my men. It's both sad and icky at the same time, but I can't focus on that right now.

Today is D-day—the dreaded day of our first project submission. As I said, I'm flying solo as expected. Amity, my supposed partner, has been MIA, leaving me stranded in a sea of unanswered emails and text messages. Not that I let her silence deter me; I've painstakingly completed the assignment on my own—ensuring every historical fact got checked and double-checked.

My take on the topic won't make a Council stooge like Asani happy, but he can't fault my methods, at least.

I settle back into my seat, the hard plastic somehow feeling more unwelcoming than usual. My ears itch, a physical manifestation of the unease that's gnawing at my bunny. Asani paces in front of the classroom, his steps measured and deliberate, as if he's the king of Bloodstone instead of a flunky of the king pretending to be a college history professor. My nerves buzz with anticipation and anxiety. It's not just about getting a grade for me—it's about proving I can handle whatever is thrown my way, even if that means tackling a two-person project alone.

"This project is a significant portion of your final grade," Asani announces, his tone almost gleeful, as though he finds pleasure in our collective student anxiety. I don't miss the way his gaze lingers on me a moment longer than necessary. "The quality of work you submit for this first assignment will make a very lasting impression on what success rate I anticipate for you in the class."

Does he know about Amity? and how I've been left to fend for myself?

I fight to keep my expression neutral, despite the desire to roll my eyes skyward. The nerve of him— acting like he's got some prophetic power to predict our academic future based on one shitty paper. I glance around, noting the anxious faces of my class-mates, their pens poised above notebooks, ready to scribble down every word as holy writ. It's all so unnecessarily dramatic for a ridiculous required general education course. Tuesdays and Thursdays are rapidly starting to rival the dread I reserve for Fridays, and that's because I have to suffer through Rockland.

"This should be a lesson in commitment," the pompous Khan continues, a smirk playing on his lips as he scans the room, "and the consequences of failing to uphold your responsibilities." His gaze lingers on the empty seat next to me, and though I feel a surge of anger at Amity's betrayal, I don't let it show. Instead, I focus on the clock, watching the seconds tick by, a silent mantra repeating in my head: dance classes, theater, stupid jury practice, then freedom.

My own fears would have me fretting more than I am, but there's quiet confidence soothing me from the inside. My secret weapon, Fitz, has kept copies of all my work in multiple formats, leaving a breadcrumb trail of documents scattered across various safe loca-tions. If push comes to shove, I can prove this project is solely my effort.

I refuse to let this new Regina wanna-be pull the shit the Heathers already failed to execute.

Squaring my shoulders, I rise from my seat when Asani calls for submissions, clutching my project in my white-knuckled fingers. This folder contains a paper fortress built on sleepless nights and relentless determination, but I did it despite all the other shit I had to deal with. My steps are steady as I approach his desk, the soft thud of my heart echoing the thump of my feet on the floor.

"Here you go, Professor," I say calmly, my voice betraying none of the turmoil inside as I hand over the fruits of my labor. "The complete project on the socio-political impact of the Shifter Accords."

"Very well, Miss Drew," he says with a sly smile, his gaze flickering to the empty seat beside me. "I'm thrilled you managed to make it to turn this in, unlike your partner."

"Solos are only awarded to the most skilled performers," I reply, mustering a smile that doesn't quite reach my eyes. With a small, satisfied grin, I turn and make my way back to my seat, feeling the weight of the project lift from my shoulders. That anxiety is replaced by a silent promise to myself that no matter what, I won't let Asani—or anyone—undermine my hard work with their bullshit.

Delores Drew gets knocked down, but she always gets back up, even if she's spitting out teeth.

Once he's collected the papers, the class topic shifts to a period of false harmony after the accords, when wealth supposedly rained down upon all. I listen, my heartbeat a staccato rhythm against my chest, as he paints a picture of prosperity and contentment that I know is a facade. My fingers clench into fists beneath the table—history has always been written by the victors, airbrushed to hide the grim reality.

"Everyone benefited from their Council's generosity," Asani declares, his voice dripping with self-assuredness. "The golden age for preds was a direct result of banishing the magic users and restructuring our society to reflect the appropriate roles of all shifters."

In my mind, I scoff at the blatant revisionism. I've seen through the gilded lies, and beneath my soft exterior lies a resolve as unyielding as steel. While the wealthiest preds rose to the top of the heap, many stayed the same or sunk below as the elite families used their Council positions to take control of industries. Men like Asani, who inherited their positions from those historical raiders, have no concept of what happened to other preds or Hera forbid, the prey species.

As Asani's lecture meanders through a maze of pred 'achievements,' I keep my eyes fixed on the whiteboard, my pencil dancing across the page in feigned attentiveness. My ears are alert, sifting through the grandiose claims for nuggets of truth—anything that could serve as a lead.

When he reaches the Rostoffs and their so-called empire of 'exports and luxuries,' my pulse quickens. The Rostoff name is what my mother clings to as her legacy of power, so this is important. I sit up straighter, ears perked despite my instincts screaming at me to stay off of his radar. This is the part of the lecture that might hold clues to the enigma of my ancestry, the missing pieces of a puzzle long since scattered.

"Damn it. Of course it involves Lucille," I murmur under my breath, the name leaving a bitter taste on my tongue. She's my only link to the history that seems to chase after me with the persistence of a shadow. The thought of calling her sets my nerves on edge; conversations with Lucille are rife with overt barbs and outrageous demands. Yet, the need to understand the obsession the Fae have with me and why I'm a bunny shifter propels me forward. It's a twisted curiosity, the kind that leads you down a path lined with thorns—you know it will hurt, but you can't resist the urge to know what lies at the end.

And much like many things in my life, I don't have a goddamned choice if I want to survive.

I scribble another note—a reminder to confront the venomous tangle of family history. Renard and Aubrey have to face their demons and so do I. After all, I can't ask them to stare down the families that cast them out so we can get the info to protect me if I'm not willing to expose myself in the same way, can I? No, I can face Lucille over the phone, and if I'm fortunate, she'll be too busy living it up with Bruiser and various cabana boys to consider why I put myself in the line of fire. With Bruno gone, her life *must* be easier, right? No more pretending, no more sneaking around, and power over everything in their domain. That *should* be enough to keep her from sniffing out my subterfuge... I think.

Turning my attention back to the lecture, I smooth down the pages of my notebook, each line a recorded testament to my solitary efforts. I can't let Asani's prowling eyes see the tremor in my hands; I have to be the image of a calm, yet dangerous pred shifter, not the prey he expects me to be.

"Moving on," Asani's voice cuts through the room, sharp and commanding, "we will now discuss the other titans of industry. These families also carved out their influence after the accords and their efforts are woven into the very fabric of our society."

Asani begins with the Eriksons, their tech empire glittering like a constellation of satellites in the night sky. I jot down notes, straining for mention of anything that resonates with the shit we found in the vaults at Apex or Cappie. But the way they simply invented tech that no one had ever seen before over and over— doesn't make sense. He transitions to the McLachlans, regaling tales of medical breakthroughs that seem more like miracles. I scribble furiously, each word a potential breadcrumb leading to the truth. We found a *lot* of Fae plants and herbs in their vault.

Perhaps that's the key to all the Council families' success—theft?

"The Barringtons," Asani gestures broadly, "masters of media, shaping opinions as sculptors shape clay."

My hand cramps as I take notes, but I push through, determined not to miss a syllable. Is it possible something the Barringtons are using is appropriated from the Fair Folks, too? How could they suddenly become gifted orators and news people, and the like? None of these people seemed to have any of this shit before the Treaty. But after? They rocket to the top as if propelled by missiles with zero information on *how* they achieved any of this innovation.

The Hopewells and their religious empires, the Charles' dominance in agriculture—I capture it all, a silent archivist of history both grand and terrifying in its scope. The Leonidas' sports empire, the Shirdals' contributions to the arts—each family carved out a piece of the world, molding it to their will. And as before, there's very little documentation about where all their skills and money to fund the path to the top came from.

Something is rotten in Denmark and it doesn't take Carmen Sandiego fluttering by in her red trench to get me to see it.

When Asani reaches the Drews, my father's family, I feel a spike of adrenaline. Exports and imports—could there be a link there? My pen dances across the paper, eager and anxious. Lucille and Bruno obviously married to connect their families' businesses and take the operation global. Bruno was from the American South and marrying Lucille connected him to the Rostoffs' European and Asian network. It makes sense, even though they were so dissimilar and obviously hated each other's guts and by proxy, me.

"Legal matters fall under the keen eye of the Birkshires," Asani continues, unperturbed by the weight of knowledge he dispenses.

I have to contain my snort at the thought of my ex taking over that empire someday and tangling with a skilled lawyer like Farley. My glee is short-lived, though, when I consider that he's among the missing and we have no fucking clue what's being done to them. Todd was a grade-A douchebag, but I don't think he deserves torture or weird experimentation. He just deserved to live out his life knowing what he missed out on and how stupid he was.

That, ladies and gents, is called growth.

Asani drones on about the Draconises, Kavarits, Alexandres, La Portes, and Blitzens so I catalog every detail and name. In this relentless stream of history, I'm searching for the one revelation that will help us figure out how to stop the killing and get the kidnapped students back without me dying in the interim. It feels like it should be easier to find the tricksy magicals motives, but this class has me considering if they only have one reason. If the predator shifters cast them out unfairly *and* stole all their shit to make themselves rich, it tracks that they would be planning their vengeance for a long, long time.

Though what the fuck I have to do with it—or any of the missing students—I can't tell you. Their methods are as opaque as their reasons, and that's why I'm still listening to the pompous fool pretending to teach.

My kingdom for a week without a bunch of stressful drama, I swear to hell.

As the bell signals the end of class, my notebook is packed with a ton of shit I want to look into with Aubrey. It's overwhelming; a deluge of facts and figures, but somewhere within the torrent of words, I sense the key to unlocking my story. With a deep breath, I tuck away my stuff, steeling myself for the future conversations it will undoubtedly provoke.

Knowledge is power, and armed with these insights, I am one step closer to facing Lucille, to braving the shadows of my lineage, and claiming my place in this court of shifters and intrigue.

That is, if I duck all the bullshit being flung at me from every direction along the way.

SUGAR, WE'RE GOING DOWN

FITZ

I TAP MY FOOT IMPATIENTLY, THE RESTLESSNESS CLAWING AT ME with sharpened nails. My ears twitch, catching the eager tone in Aubrey's voice as he relays the Smithsonian walrus's message, every word like a starting pistol to my already racing thoughts. I've been waiting for the spicy salamander to find something with his constant library time, and now it appears we *finally* have something to *act* upon.

Thank. Fuck.

"My counterpart believes it's a language related to a very underground sect that most preds thought was a myth," he says, his eyes scanning the screen again before landing on each of us in turn. "They are headquartered—coincidentally enough—in some sort of small museum between Paris and *l'Academie*."

A museum run by culty weirdos?

The tingle that races up my spine ignites a wildfire of excitement. Today is not just any day—it's Sunday. That place should be a ghost town, leaving a perfect empty stage for my *Mission Impossible* dream sequence. I bounce on the balls of my feet, barely containing the glee bubbling inside. "We're going today; no arguments. No one will be there and we get to be super spies," I declare with a grin that probably stretches too wide for my face.

Felix pinches the bridge of his nose, letting out a long-suffering groan. "With no preparation, Fitz? Really? We don't have the slightest damn clue what might be hiding in this secret headquarters."

"Come on, bro. No one will see us coming if we just show up and break in." I picture myself dangling from wires, sneaking in like the spy movies and it makes every cell of my body thrum with hyperactive pleasure.

I cannot fucking believe this is even a question.

Aubrey's frown deepens as if he's trying to calculate the probability of disaster. Chessie watches me bounce, amusement dancing in his gaze. He knows there's no stopping this train once it's left the station. Then there's Renard, whose chuckle rumbles through the air like thunder—soft but foreboding. He's a fellow lover of chaos, so he'll side with me, if need be. I just need to convince the stubborn fuckers in my family to indulge my desire to do something more dangerous than hack a security camera.

"Super spies, huh?" Dolly steps closer, her eyes glinting with shared mischief. "Count me in."

This is why I love this woman more than breath—she's all-in with zero hesitation.

"Even if we have to break in?" I ask, though my heart's already somersaulting with victory knowing she's on board. "It's a big gamble."

"Especially if we have to break in," she replies with a smirk. "I'm ready for some serious criminal shit, baby. Let's do it, Crazypants."

Her enthusiasm is the spark to my dynamite, and I can't help but feel invincible with her by my side. Walking over, I pick her up and spin us around with a happy growl. "You're the best Queen ever, Baby Girl."

"Fine," Felix mutters, resigned. "But I'm only doing this because I know you can get what we need before we leave, bro. And I get to call it anytime, do you all hear me?"

"Trust me, this will be epic," I assure my twin, clapping him on the back. My mind's already racing ahead—to gadgets, secret passages, and the thrill of the unknown.

"We're all in this together, Fitzy, so do your thing," Dolly says as she grins down at me.

Suddenly, I'm more alive than ever. We're about to dive headfirst into danger, and I wouldn't want anyone else by my side. Putting her down, I race over to the laptop I keep on the counter for situations just like this and pop it open. I have to get my shit going so we have the information we need or Felix won't hesitate to shut down my fun.

My fingers fly across the keyboard, a blur of motion as I unleash my digital hounds into the depths of Prednet. Lines of code cascade down the screen, my eyes tracking each one like the predator I am. The adrenaline is already there, tingling at my fingertips, an electric current of excitement. I need to set up a search spider that will gather blueprints and all the info available about this damn place, confirmed or not, before we leave this campus.

"Just a few minutes, and we'll have every scrap of info from the Prednet and beyond." The words burst from me as information continues to unfurl before my eyes—blueprints, security systems, even whispered rumors about this so-called museum. I spin on my heel, a grin splitting my face. "Now, where is my *super suit?*"

Dolly giggles, holding her hand out. "C'mon, baby. We're the two most bendy people, so they can't stop us from being the ones who break in. Chessie is fast, but he can't get around shit like a cat burglar and I can."

"I *knew* that yoga was gonna pay off," I crow as I look at the rest of them smugly.

Felix's eye-roll from where he's fiddling with some gadget isn't a surprise, nor is Chess's smirk. The Winged Weenies are looking at one another, doing that odd speechless conversation they like to do when they don't want the rest of us to hear their old dude grumbles. No arguments means I'm going to get my way, so I leave the laptop running and bound over to our girl.

"Time for our dance with danger," I announce, scooping Dolly into my arms before she can protest. Her laughter echoes through the room as we disappear to gear up. Groans and curses chase us, but they're music to my ears—the soundtrack to our impending caper.

This is going to be the most fun we can have outside of the bedroom and I can't fucking wait.

ONCE WE CHANGE, BABY GIRL AND I EMERGE FROM HER ROOM decked out in black thief gear that hugs our forms like shadows. I made sure we got lock picks and tech, but I'm more likely to use the former than her. We're yin and yang in terms of experience in this kind of shit, but regardless, we're ready to tango through lasers and leap over tripwires.

"Looking very Emma Peel," Aubrey says wryly, giving Dolly a once-over.

She looks lethal in her catsuit and high ponytail, and my cock does that twitch it always does when she's by my side. Dolly does a faux twirl for all the hungry eyes in the room, and I move in front of her before any of them decide to forget this excursion in pursuit of other fun.

"Don't want to keep the insane cult people waiting," she says to me, her eyes alight with that same wild spark that fuels my own fire.

"Could you two be any more dramatic?" Felix mutters, but I see the corner of his mouth twitching upward. He's not used to allowing so much democracy when it comes to planning, but our girl told us that she was in charge and he's doing his best to respect her confident statement.

My brother is almost like his old self now, and I couldn't be happier to see it.

The rest of our patchwork family picks up the stuff Chessie packed while our girl and I got suited up. Dolly grabs my hand, then takes our cheetah's, holding them as we all head out the back door and walk around to the front of the library.

"So how the hell are we going to—" I start, but the rumble of an engine cuts me off. A large SUV rolls up as if summoned by my voice. I blink, looking over my shoulder only to see the tricky gargoyle giving me a smug look.

Raina and the Captain jump out of the enormous thing, their entrance as grand as if they'd just docked a galleon instead of parking a car. The damn thing could hold like fifty raccoons of their size inside, so I'm baffled as to what they did to get it here on their own. "How?" I ask in amazement.

"Never underestimate the abilities of a pirate and his trusty first mate," the Captain replies with a roguish wink, his voice gravelly with that mock-pirate accent that could charm the gold from a treasure chest. When I continue gaping at him, the small prey rolls his eyes. "One at the helm, the other manning the rudders. Yer overthinkin' it, mate."

"Riiiiiight," I say as I shake my head. "Well, I think it's best if we take over from here, yeah?"

Dolly's eyes dance with amusement as she watches the two raccoons give me sarcastic looks. "Adventure awaits, Crazypants. Let's get moving."

"Hell yeah, it does, Baby Girl," I reply, my tiger purring with delight as Felix heads for the driver's side of the SUV. "And you and I are gonna grab it by the balls."

Dolly's giggle rings out like a silver bell, and she leans over to peck the raccoon pirates on their furry cheeks. "You two are brilliant," she says, her voice bubbling with mirth. "Thank you for all your help."

"Guess we're adding grand theft auto to our list of crimes today—or whatever they call it here," Aubrey mutters under his breath, but there's a reluctant smile tugging at the corners of his mouth. It's clear he's more worried about the potential for trouble than actually disapproving of our rogue escapade.

Chess opens the door to usher Dolly in with a gentle hand on her back. She slides across the seat with the grace of a cat, leaving space for me to squeeze in next to her. The leather upholstery is swanky, and I can't help but feel like a character from that heist movie Dolly adores. Chess settles beside me, his body a solid presence that brings an odd comfort despite the adrenaline already beginning to pump through my veins.

The two of them make my mind quiet a smidge, and I sigh as everything settles enough to ride in the car calmly.

"Everyone strapped in?" Felix calls from the driver's seat, glancing back at us with a mix of determination and concern etched into his features.

I roll my eyes playfully, clicking my seatbelt into place. "Like we're about to launch to the moon."

"Good." Felix's eyes meet mine in the rearview mirror, and there's silent communication there. We both know this is risky, maybe even reckless, but it's necessary. We have to find out what secrets lie behind those museum walls, and I'm not wrong about hitting these people before they know we're onto them.

I pull out my phone, tapping into the Prednet search results once more, sending the coordinates to Felix. The museum's security setup is no joke—a labyrinth of alarms and motion detectors that would make Fort Knox proud. A small, wry smile finds its way onto my lips. "They're either guarding the Holy Grail or something far more sinister with all this shit. You guys will have to keep a really close eye on our progress."

"Sinister is my bet," Renard chimes in, his eyes darkening as he looks at the info on his own device. "Places like this don't bother with subtlety unless they're hiding monsters in their closets, *mes amis*."

"Maybe it's vampires in their basements," Dolly jokes lightly. She's pretending it's a silly idea, but there's steel under her wisecrack. She knows that's a possibility.

"Either way, we get in, we take what we need, and we get out," I declare, meeting each of their gazes in turn. "Aubrey and Renard will get us to the roof without raising any red flags. Right?"

"Snack size is with me," Aubrey responds and I groan. He just smirks and jerks his thumb at Ren. "He will take you, Fitzgerald."

Felix clicks his tongue as he starts the engine. "Too bad for you, bro. Guess you don't get to ride the dragon tonight, either."

Glaring at him in the mirror, I move on without comment like a grown-up. "Meanwhile, Dolly will go vent-crawling, and I'll take the sky entrance. Felix and Chessie, you've got tech and lookout. Keep us updated as we infiltrate,"

"Absolutely, love." Chess's voice is calm, a sturdy anchor amidst the chaos of our operation.

My brother simply offers a thumbs-up, his attention already back on the road as he navigates us toward our target.

"If we work together, we'll get away clean and no one will be the wiser," I finish, locking eyes with my girl. Her response is a grin, fierce and fearless, and in that moment, I know we're ready for whatever awaits us inside that mysterious museum.

WITH THE GRACE OF MY TIGER HELPING ME BALANCE, I DESCEND from the skylight, my harness whispering against the cable. Below me, the museum—or whatever is masquerading as one—spreads out in shadowed silence. My heart thunders in my chest with each inch I lower toward the ground, the thrill of the heist flooding my veins with electric excitement.

This shit is the fucking tits and no one will ever convince me otherwise. It's almost as good as killing people.

"Easy does it," I murmur to myself, mimicking the cool demeanor of an action hero though my pulse races with the fervor of our clandestine escapade.

A glance through the glass below shows Dolly, twisting her lithe body through a maze of laser beams in a dance that would have gymnasts weeping in envy. Her movements are fluid, practiced— she's in her element, and it's as infectious as it is intoxicating. I want to leap down and fuck her senseless, but I know I can't—I have to focus on the task at hand.

"Show-off," I tease through the earpiece. "Guys, I think someone needs to plan a heist roleplay in the future. This shit is so hot my dick could sub for the diamond glass cutter."

"For fuck's sake…"

The dragon's irritation with me isn't unusual, so I ignore it as I look for my mark. My eyes fixate on the spot where I need to land and I reach down to grasp the release on my harness. Humming the theme song of the movie I'm copying, I release the rigging and land on the balls of my feet, poised and ready for the prowl.

"Fitz, we're trying not to trigger World War III here," Felix's voice crackles in my ear, a blend of exasperation and brotherly concern. "Don't set off shit by singing to yourself like an idiot."

"Relax, bro," I retort, "I'm as silent as the 'p' in psycho."

Who says you can't have fun when you're risking your ass? Not me, that's for damn sure.

The museum is eerily still, a stark contrast to the adrenaline that dances under my skin. Moving with exaggerated caution, I skirt around pressure-sensitive floors, my eyes scanning for any sign of tripwires or hidden cameras. The faint green glow of night vision goggles casts an otherworldly hue over everything, turning the mundane into something out of a spy flick.

"Find anything yet?" Dolly's breathless voice filters through, laced with the thrill of our mission.

"Working on it," I reply, spotting the glass case housing a book that reeks of ancient secrets. "Be patient, grasshoppers."

Its leather cover is cracked with age, and I swear I hear the whispers of the dark shit emanating from its pages. Carefully, I pull the cutter out of my side pocket despite my assertion about my cock. I use it to cut the case open, then lift the glass out. It takes a few more moments to determine that it doesn't have any other measures in place and once I know that, I lift the entire case off of it and set it aside.

"Fuck yeah, Tomb Raider Fitz," I mutter. There's a chorus of guffaws on the other end and I huff, slipping the book into the bag

I have strapped flat to my chest. "You guys can suck it; I have my prize."

"Jackpot," says the female voice on the comms. That confirms Dolly found whatever offices they have in the building and she's going to work on the computers. I can almost see her smirk as she plugs in the drive I gave her, the little gadget blinking to life as it copies files upon files of data that will no doubt unravel this enigma.

"Just be careful," Renard says softly. "We don't know if there are enemies within."

"You need to get out before they realize their hideout has been compromised either way," Chess advises. "So don't snoop more, Angel. Just download whatever you can and shake your cottontail."

"Guys, it's transferring," Dolly responds, and even through the static, I can tell she's pleased. "Stop motherhenning me to death."

My twin's voice comes over the line, worry obvious in his tone. "You guys haven't read all this shit Fitz found, but this place is not just a museum. The rumors are pretty dark, and if even half of them are true, it's definitely a cult headquarters. Get the hell out as soon as possible."

"This office is creepy as hell," Dolly replies. "It smells like death. Trust me, I'm not staying any longer than necessary. The drive is almost done, but I can't wait to find out what the hell this place is a front for. I mean, it's hiding in plain sight, you know?"

"Guess we'll find out soon enough," I muse, feeling the weight of the book against my side. "Especially since I've got the one book they thought needed to be put in a protective case."

Dolly sighs, and my heart stops thundering when she finally says, "Done. I'm headed out. You get moving, too, Fitzy. Time to go home and get some answers."

I walk over to the dangling line and hook the harness to it, grinning to myself.

No matter what info we managed to steal, getting to see Baby Girl in that catsuit was definitely worth the effort—no one will ever convince me otherwise.

Everybody Talks

Delores

My leotard clings to me like a second skin, damp with the effort of today's ballet class. The mirrored walls of the dance studio reflect a chorus of exhausted students, but I can't help noticing my own outline, slightly more rigid than the rest, as if I'm still on high alert. It's been a week since the museum heist—seven days of trying to blend back into the mundane rhythm of campus life.

But who could blame me for being tense? We stole shit from some unknown cult in a last minute raid.

"Come on, Dolly," Cori coaxes, her voice upbeat as she tugs at my arm, pulling me toward the admin building. "You can't avoid this place forever."

I hesitate, memories of snarling dingoes and their cruel laughter at Apex biting at the edges of my mind. My stomach tightens, not from hunger, but from the thought of walking into another potential ambush. If the ladies in the clinic hadn't helped me escape, I wouldn't be here right now. It's a sobering thought, despite the fact that I can defend myself now.

"It'll be fine," she insists, her eyes bright and reassuring. "Plus, Rufus needs to film some candid 'student day' stuff for his final project. He'll pout if we don't go."

Rufus is fiddling with his camera, lens cap dangling from his fingers as he smirks at me. I sigh, the weight of loyalty nudging me forward. My friends have been on board with all my crazy shit from day one, no matter how dangerous it was. It would be shitty to let my stupid trauma from Apex keep me from helping Ru-Ru get his shots done.

"Okay," I concede, my voice barely above a whisper. "I'll come along. It's time I got past this anyway, right? Todd's gone and none of his stupid dogs followed us here after Cappie. The cafeteria should be mostly mutt-free, unless that damn O' Leary chick is there."

A soft cough from my badger friend makes me turn and he shrugs. "There are other canines on campus, Dollypop. I want you to come so I can get you and Coco in my fabulous clips, but I'm not going to lie about what we might find there. It's a dick move."

Trust Rufus to be baldly honest with zero filter—it's part of why I adore him

"Fine. It might not be flea-bitten mongrel-free. Got it," I sigh as I grab my messenger bag. "At least I won't run into the remaining Heathers. They keep to themselves if they're not giving me shit in class."

"An important distinction," Cori agrees. "Only your *new* bullies might be in the place you don't want to go."

Thanks, Cori. That's super helpful.

DESCENDING THE STAIRWAY INTO THE ALEXANDRÉ BUILDING'S subterranean cafeteria, I can't help but grumble. "Why do they always put these places underground? It's like they're trying to hide us away or something."

"Probably because they don't want anyone seeing preds scarfing down their lunch," Cori quips with a smirk, her voice echoing slightly off the walls.

"Some of the prey work here, like Raina." I give them both a nod as we finally approach the entrance.

We push through the wide double doors of *l'Academie*'s cafeteria into a setting I've actively avoided since that first semester at Apex. I'm prepared for the scent of cooked vegetables and spices that doesn't quite mask the underlying odor of cleaning fluid and deep-fried resignation. I hear the distant clatter of cutlery and the murmur of student chatter, but here, there's an ornate host station blocking the entry to the dining area and the scent of roses.

What the hell is this?

"See? Not so bad," Cori says, her hand still on my back, gently guiding me to the stand. Apparently, this isn't a surprise to her, and I groan inwardly. If they've been here already, I look like the idiot who has no idea that she's not going to find a normal college cafeteria that would trigger my fear.

"You could have mentioned that this place is different," I reply calmly. My voice is steady, but my heart hasn't gotten the memo. It thunders in my chest like a drum, resonating with every step. "It might have made this excursion a little easier, guys."

"Welcome to *Le Jardin des Muses*," the willowy swan shifter at the desk says. "Reservations are closed today, but you may find open seating in the back. Your server will bring menus and water once you are settled."

Okay, this is insane. This place runs like a five-star restaurant!

The cavernous space is decked out like a museum rather than a place to eat. Murals loom large on the walls, depicting predators in various artistic poses, all gloss and glam. Gilded fixtures throw back the light in a show of unnecessary opulence.

"Are we sure this is a cafeteria?" I raise an eyebrow at Rufus and Cori as we weave our way between tables. "Looks more like they're preparing us for a five-star dining experience."

"We should find a spot away from prying eyes," Rufus suggests, scanning the ornate dining room with a filmmaker's eye. He's looking for the perfect shot, and I'm just looking to get through a meal without bolting.

"Good idea," I murmur, as I follow him to a spot in the back. My eyes skate around the room, taking in the sumptuous design, white napkins, and crystal barware. "This place is crazy. Who builds a cafeteria like this for college students?"

"Camille LaFragrasse," Cori supplies with a mischievous grin. "You know, the famous chef? This is the only cafeteria in the world with two Michelin stars. It's freaking amazing, which is why I wanted to bring you here. According to admissions staff, Camille herself stops in sometimes. She lives nearby."

As I sit, I press my feet firmly against the tiled floor, grounding myself in the present, in the company of friends who have no idea how deeply the scars of past ridicule run. Luckily, the opulence of this damn room and the information Cori just dropped on me are very distracting. I turn to her with an arched brow, my expression wry. "You wanted me to come here because it's swanky and nothing like Apex's space, right? Fancied yourself an armchair shrink?"

She flushes and shrugs. "Maybe. But I was right. You're not losing your shit and every little piece of you that you wrest back from those assholes is something the new enemies can't use against you, Dolly."

Shit. She's got me there.

Wrinkling my nose, I nod at her, letting her know I forgive the white lie. "Alright. Then let's film his shit before the waiter gets here so we can just hang out. I don't want to be doing taped stuff all throughout lunch. I like spending time with you guys."

"Ready when you are, Dolly," Rufus says, lifting his camera, a silent promise that he'll make this as painless as possible.

ONCE RUFUS GETS WHAT HE NEEDS FOR HIS 'MOCK-U-MENTARY,' our conversation inevitably steers towards more personal stuff—specifically, the triplets and Rufus. The details he crows about are risqué as hell, and I can't help the laughter that bubbles up despite my earlier anxieties. The badger has truly found men who make him happy—in more ways than I needed to know—and it's amazing to see him glow with that emotion.

However, our gossipy exchange is cut short when a capybara waiter approaches, menus in hand. His small stature is no match for his beaming smile as I greet him. "Hi, there. We're friends of Raina, and we wanted to check out the food here."

"Miss Dolly!" His excitement vibrates through the air. "Raina told us all about you. I'll make sure you're all taken care of; no need to even look at the menus."

"Uh, wait a sec..." I squint at the nametag before I continue, "Floyd. We aren't quite ready to order yet because we just got those..."

"Raina's instructions were very clear about what to serve should you visit. Leave it to me, Miss Dolly." With that, he scurries away, leaving us in a collective moment of bemusement.

"Great," I sigh, a touch of sarcasm tinging the word. "I hate being famous."

"Come on, it's not so bad," Rufus chuckles, clearly amused by the capybara's earnestness.

Rolling my eyes, I nudge Cori, bringing the conversation back around to something other than my fame. "Your turn, girl. What about those new Pred Games uniforms? Tell me all about your big project."

She hesitates, cheeks flushing with a secretive glow that speaks of more than just fabric and thread. Yet after a soft elbow jab, she relents, pulling out sketches from her bag. "Well, they're not quite done, but it's close."

"Wow, Cori... these are..." Words fail me as my eyes trace the black and silver designs meant for the Pred Games. They're sleek, intimidating, and positively dripping with style. "We're going to outshine everyone on the field."

"Exactly," Cori grins, finally riding the wave of pride in her creations. "That's the plan."

Rufus leans back in his chair, eyeing the uniform sketches spread across our table. The silver threads on black fabric gleam even in the dim light of the underground cafeteria. "These look amazing, Coco. But how long until Dolly can actually wear one? The spring scrimmage is this weekend."

The polar bear taps a pencil against her full lips, calculating. "I should have a prototype ready for Dolly to try since she's the captain. But we'll need to see it in action during practice before we outfit the whole team." Her eyes glitter with anticipation, clearly envisioning her designs in motion.

"Ugh, about that scrimmage..." I wrinkle my nose, folding my arms over my chest. "Facing off against the Cappie team won't be a walk in the park. They're still holding grudges from the fall. I know they'll be gunning for me now that I'm not a team mate."

"Plus," Rufus says with an arched brow, "the campus will be swarming with their team and the rest of their staff by Friday. Cappie snots and their hangers-on, here for days is a torture I'm not looking forward to."

Cori's grin doesn't fade. "All the more reason to stun them with your captain's swagger, right? Show them what real Pred Games royalty looks like."

"Royalty or not," I mumble, half-dreading the influx of visitors, "it's going to be a long weekend."

My friend's laughter bubbles up, light and infectious. "Hey, at least Rufus' 'supposed 'documentary crew' won't have to sneak him off campus with phony excuses for their booty calls. The gates will be wide open for the public," she says, nudging Rufus with her elbow.

"Yeah, it'll be one big happy family reunion," I say, sarcasm lacing my words. The sound of my forced laughter is hollow even to my own ears. My brain is picturing the throngs of visitors milling about as my ex-teammates make themselves at home on our new turf. My tail gives an involuntary twitch beneath the table, the escaping bunny betraying my annoyance.

Rufus raises his eyebrows, a smirk playing on his lips. "You love the spotlight when you're in your element, Dollykins. Don't pretend you're not looking forward to showing off your vicious skills in front of a crowd."

"Maybe," I concede, "but there's such a thing as too much company." I gaze past them, lost for a moment in the thought of the impending chaos. It's then that realization dawns, hitting me with the weight of a missed leap in ballet class.

"Guys," I interject, leaning forward, "we've been so wrapped up in chasing clues for this mystery that we forgot about the open campus. It's going to be a zoo out there." My mind races, thinking of all the preparations we'd need to consider.

This school has far less security than Cappie, and it's laid out with a million places to hide.

"We'll need to inform my cousin and his couriers what's coming their way," Rufus adds, reaching for his camera. He's always thinking a step ahead, ready to capture the next pivotal moment for his documentary. "He'll want to make certain that your various unwanted stalkers aren't hijacking your moment for their own gain."

"Not to mention simple safety," I say, tapping a finger on the table, feeling a sudden surge of anxiety. "We've got to plan for a fully open university. Security should be tight, but discreet. We can't let anything—or anyone—slip through the cracks. This would be a great moment for another Fae attack *or* another mass kidnapping."

My icy bear friend nods, her earlier mirth replaced by a look of determination. "Rufus can talk to Farley and I'll take the Captain's crew. You need to plan with your men, Dolly. They need to be on their toes with so many outsiders around."

"Thanks, Coco," I say, relieved to have her take the lead on this. I'm usually the leader, but with all the pressure of needing to call my mother and decode this shit from our heist, I'm swamped in extra work at the moment.

"All we can hope for is this scrimmage goes off without a lot of collateral damage," I add, trying to push aside the unease. "We know it won't be perfect, but if we can minimize the risk, that will have to be enough."

At least, I hope it will be.

SOMEBODY TOLD ME

FELIX

I PACE THE PERIMETER OF THE GARDEN GAZEBO, MY STEPS SILENT on the dew-kissed grass. The Pred Game scrimmage with Cappie looms over us like a storm cloud ready to burst, and my twin, Fitz, is knee-deep in prep mode with the men's team. As for me, I'm left to map out our defenses, my mind racing through strategies as sharp and varied as the stripes on my fur.

This scrimmage comes at the worst possible time, though I doubt there will be a better time later.

The morning sun filters through the lush greenery of the garden, casting a serene glow on Dolly's face as she stretches into an elegant cobra pose. I watch from a distance, admiring her flexibility in a way that isn't exactly innocent. Her deep breaths are in sync with the rise and fall of Rufus's chest as they move through their yoga routine, a tranquil island in the midst of our storm of preparations.

I'm glad she's got her friends to help her stay focused on her warm up and getting ready for the match. She doesn't need to be worried about the rest of this shit; that's for me and the rest of her family to handle while she is preparing. Walking over to the table again, I listen as she chats with the brash badger while they move through poses.

"Are you sure you're ready for this?" Rufus asks, his voice laced with concern.

"Who knows what competitor they'll throw at me," Dolly says as she reaches for her water bottle. She takes a long sip, her eyes scanning the horizon. "Grudges run deep with the famous girls at Cappie. Even if they don't do something shitty, there's the Fae or the Heathers... or even some of the professors who seem to hate me." Her tone hardens with the mention of the Council acolytes, but she shakes her head, refusing to let fear take root. "But I can't let it mess with my head."

"Zen, remember? Breathe in the calm, breathe out the anxiety," Rufus chides gently, and she offers him a small smile before returning to their routine.

"The gloomy gargoyle's crew did good with the biometrics," I mutter as I turn back to Zhenga. The lioness is standing by the table littered with blueprints of the academy with her arms crossed over her chest. I run my fingers lightly over the paper, tracing the pathways leading to the library and Dolly's studio— now secured fortresses amidst the unpredictable landscape of l'Academie. "But that only protects our personal spaces."

Nodding in agreement, Z points at the camera icons peppering the layout. "Aubrey's snarling push back with security paid off.

The new eyes will give us an edge." Her voice is steady, but there's a whetted edge to it, a readiness that mirrors my own tension.

"Chess has our food under lock and key," I continue, ticking off each completed task. The thought of anyone tampering with our sustenance makes my feline instincts bristle with distaste. "He's making enough to cover our household, but also her friends, the crew, and you. The lawyer is off campus, so he's got his own quality control."

Poison is a coward's weapon, and we're taking no chances with it this time.

"Raina and the Captain's secret cameras are in place, too," the lioness confirms, her finger hovering over the hidden spots only we know about. "They've swept the staff quarters to make sure there are no indications of prey animals being threatened or bribed to help with shenanigans. Raina had her stinky lover tell me when he came to fetch the locker room laundry."

"Good." I exhale, a low growl vibrating in my chest. There's something primal about protecting one's clan, and even as an exiled Raj, the drive to defend is ingrained deep within my bones. These people are all my ambush now, and I cannot fail them. My attention drifts back to my Princess, head tilting as I listen in again to see what she and the badger are talking about now.

"Farley will be with us today," Dolly says to him as she twists into an upside-down pose. "He'll be watching from the stands with you and Cori."

"Hell yeah. My cuz and his goon will definitely scare off any bitchy Cappie fans." Rufus grins then glances briefly in my direction, winking. "We'll all have eyes on you, Dollypop. You'll be safe as houses, girl."

"Speaking of keeping an eye on people," I interject, looking at both my bunny and her punky friend, "Fitz is going to be a challenge to keep in check if things get heated. Everyone has to be on notice."

"He's not wrong. Fitzy will go absolutely buggering nuts if he thinks someone is threatening me," Dolly snorts, transitioning to stretch her hamstrings. "At least you'll have the earpieces for quick communication if something goes down."

"Truthfully, it's Aubrey I'm more concerned about," I admit. "You know how he gets when his dragon flares up. He's more likely to raze the entire place if he gets provoked."

"Nothing a little sedation wouldn't fix," Rufus jokes, waggling his eyebrows suggestively. "I'm sure the crazy tiger has a little pred-stasy tucked somewhere. Why not use that?"

"Calm down, Dr. Feelgood," Dolly fires back with a smirk, not missing a beat. "I'd prefer not to drug our own team if possible. With Fitz, we know how he behaves in those situations. I can't fathom how the big guy would react, but if it isn't what you expect, it would only make shit worse."

Cori giggles as she comes out of the library with a basket and some water bottles, stepping carefully around Rufus's sprawled form. She kneels beside Dolly, inspecting the hem of the uniform shorts. "I got the water, but it seems like I came back at a really weird point in the conversation. Who's planning to drug a dragon? It sounds like a *really* risky idea."

"These look fantastic, by the way," Dolly praises, admiring the cut. "And the fabric moves really well with my body. You did a fabulous job, Coco."

"Isn't that kit a bit too sexy for the field?" Rufus can't resist poking fun, even as he appreciates the design. "I thought all the femi-nistas were decrying the sexy uniforms female athletes have to wear all the time."

"It's about choice, Ru-Ru," Cori retorts with a confident tilt of her chin. "Some of the Games gals might prefer these, but if they don't, I have several options they can choose from with different cuts and lengths. I'm empowering them to feel comfortable in their skin when they compete… on *their* terms."

"I see your point," Rufus concedes, eyeing the various uniforms laid out on the grass. "If Dollypop is comfy in this, she should be able to wear it, while someone else should be able to cover more without getting some ridiculous penalty. I like it, Coco."

"Thanks, babe," she responds as her fingers make meticulous adjustments to the fabric on my girl's uniform.

I'm staying the hell out of this conversation because I definitely do not *get to weigh in on it.*

Dolly stands, newly attired, looking every inch the fierce competitor she is. She swings her arms around, moving side to side, then winks at me before she does a backflip. Her smile is wide as the silver sparkle on the black glitters in the sunlight. "Yup. This is the shit, Cori. I'm going to rock this under the lights tonight, and I feel like a total badass."

"Ahem." Zhenga's voice pierces the morning calm, a sharp contrast to the playful atmosphere they've been indulging in. The urgency in her tone pulls my focus away from my Princess and her friends back to the security plans.

"There have to be eyes on Rufus and Cori at all times," Zhenga says, her hands flitting through the air as if she could physically place them under a protective shield. Her brows are knitted with worry, deepening with every mention of potential danger. "You and your dingbats can protect yourselves. Dolly is formidable after all her training. But these two aren't quite as well trained and they're a perfect target.

Huh? Where did this come from?

I lean back in my chair, studying her. "What makes you think they're at such risk?" I ask, trying to catch her eye. She pauses, glancing over at where Rufus is chuckling at something Cori says.

"Because," she exhales heavily, "vicious pred families like ours love snatching the innocent to leverage their position. If anything happened to them..." She doesn't need to finish; we both know how fiercely Dolly would react.

"It's a good thing the Kavarit triplets followed the badger here," I remind her, my voice even but firm. "Those sphinxes won't let anyone get within a whisker of Rufus and by extension, the giggly bear."

As if summoned, Rufus chimes in from his spot by the uniforms, clearly having eavesdropped on our conversation. "Don't sweat it, Coach," he says, a wry smile playing on his lips. "My triplets are fierce as *fuck*. If anyone tries anything, they will end up shredded like confetti before they can blink."

He's downplaying his own skill to allay her fears; I know that badger took on an entire family of drug dealers to win his spot as heir.

Zhenga nods, visibly relaxing. The tension slips from her shoulders, and I squint at her. I don't know if she's just grown attached to our girl as they've been working together or what, but she's very protective of Dolly's friends. It's nice... but weird. Then again, Z has never been normal, and I've never been able to figure out what the fuck is going on in her head accurately.

After a moment, I lower my voice and turn to Zhenga, hoping to understand her anxiety. "How about you? How's the team shaping up? I know the Princess is doing well, but what about the rest of them?"

She gives me a small, genuine smile—one that actually reaches her eyes. "It's going pretty well. I'm actually... happy. Building something new, making the decisions—it's liberating." A lightness infuses her words, a stark difference from the desperate lioness seeking a mate to get out of her exile I used to know. "The newbies are slowly learning; this will likely be a reckoning of sorts, but they need it. If they're going to be on the team, we will compete and they have to put the work in."

"And the Princess is helping?" I prod gently, aware of their budding relationship. "I'm glad she seems to be forming a friendship with you. She hasn't had a lot of stable people in her life before Apex."

"Having someone who's genuine and not just another rival in disguise... it means everything." There's a warmth in her tone, reassurance that this strange new world we've found ourselves in might just be better than the old. "Plus, she truly wants the others to get better. She doesn't sabotage them like other preds would."

"Good," I say simply, my heart lighter. "I'm glad to hear it."

Together, we turn back to the blueprints and notes on security merging into a map of safety and strategy. From the corner of my eye, I see Dolly transition into a warrior pose, strength and calm radiating from her. I leave her to her routine, her presence a silent anchor as we prepare for what lies ahead.

"I hope this is enough," I murmur, my gaze lingering on the determined set of Dolly's jaw. "We can't stop magical shit because we don't know what the fuck to do with it. This is what we *can* control, so it has to be as close to perfect as possible."

Zhenga's eyes meet mine. "We'll be ready for tonight, Raj. No one we care about will get hurt, other than the normal Games stuff. I promise."

Her confidence is a balm to the low thrum of unease that hasn't left me since Dolly came home and reminded me of the damn match. The headmistress's absence doesn't make things any easier; it's as if she's simply waiting for the chaos to unfold without her watchful eye.

Or maybe helping to orchestrate it, but that's a suspicion for another day.

"We've done everything we can," I reply, turning my gaze toward the horizon where the stadium gleams. "Everything else is up to Fate."

"I could pull some Tarot cards if you're worried! I won't even charge for my magnificent visions."

I roll my eyes as the badger mimics dealing cards and Dolly laughs. The levity helps, but I don't need him to use woo-woo fortune telling. What I need is for the dragon and the gargoyle to get back from their spins around the two wooded sections of campus. Once I know they've put their cameras in place, I know Fitz's system will have a view of the entire campus clear enough to see every possible entry point for an attack force.

Then, I might be able to relax for a minute or two—but not before.

VICTORIOUS

DELORES

THE SCENT OF SWEAT AND ANTICIPATION HANGS HEAVY IN THE Pred Games arena, a mixture that sends my rabbit instincts into overdrive. I was the bunny shifter they tried to send to her death, and now I'm the team captain of the competitive fighting team at a second school in two years. I no longer run like the trembling rabbit I was before; no, now I take the fight to my foes head on.

The predator within me defies the animal I emerged as and I love making them eat their words.

Lined up with my teammates, I feel Felicia O'Leary's glare boring into me like twin daggers. She's miffed, nostrils flaring at the sight of me leading the pack. Her ire isn't just because I'm at the front, but because I'm wearing Cori's masterpiece—a uniform so sleek and fabulous it looks like victory stitched into fabric. She wants to come after me, distract me, make me lose—but I don't have time for petty squabbles. My focus is razor-sharp on the matches ahead, and not letting this big event end in disaster.

Coach Zhenga steps forward, her presence commanding silence even among the restless murmurs of my fellow preds. Her eyes sweep across us, burning embers of determination igniting an inferno within each soul present. "This scrimmage," she begins, her voice echoing off the walls, "is where we start carving our legacy. We are not here to play nice or look pretty. We are here to work hard, earn our place under these lights, and claim the glory that comes with being a true competitor."

I nod, feeling her words like a war drum in my chest. This isn't just about today—it's about setting the tone for what's to come, showing every doubter and naysayer that *l'Academie* breeds winners, not wimps. This school has been relegated to a soft, frilly arts school for a long time, but we can show the world that's something to be reckoned with, not snorted at.

"Let them think you're just weak little artists," Zhenga's snarl cuts through the tension like a knife. "By next Fall, they'll know the truth. You are predators—fierce, relentless, and unstoppable."

A spark of pride flickers within me. Yes, we will take the championship, but today, today is where it all begins.

"Are you with me?" Our coach's voice crescendos, demanding an answer.

A chorus of roars erupts around me, a unified declaration of intent.

We are ready. We are hungry for the fight… especially me.

The moment we burst out of the tunnel, the stadium erupts—a cacophony of cheers and roars that could shake the stars from the sky. My heart hammers against my ribcage, a wild rabbit caught in the glare of an oncoming threat. The arena is a sea of faces, a perfect hunting ground for the Fae, a battleground where Council spies could be lurking, and all of their eyes boring into me from above.

But then I see my personal army of supporters, and something fierce and unyielding settles in my chest. Rows of Drew Fluffle jerseys stand out like a banner of loyalty amongst the crowd. Aubrey's glasses glint in the stadium lights, and Chess's top knot bounces as he claps. Fitz and Felix are a striking sight, as they stand together with a menacing yet proud look. Renard is smirking, enjoying the applause as he watches silently next to his mate.

Cori's larger-than-life diva-like presence draws a chuckle from me despite the tension, and Rufus, with his gangster swagger, seems ready to take on anyone who dares cross me. The Captain and Raina are next to Farley, whose sharp gaze sweeps over the scene. The crew and his couriers are all hidden around campus to help protect the space.

I can't help it—I flash them all a wide, fangy grin, a show of bravado. Midfield becomes my stage as I pause, striking a pose that screams confidence. It's not just for them; it's a reminder that I'm not just Delores Drew, the prey they sent to death two years ago. Now I'm Dolly, the predator bunny with five mates and a cadre of friends, fearless and indomitable in the face of danger. Cameras flash, videos roll, and for a moment, we're all immortalized in that surge of solidarity.

I can't fuck this up or I'll never live it down. Put up or shut up, Dolly.

After the team scatters to the sidelines, I'm rooted to the spot, watching my teammates engage in their own battles. Some dance through their opponents with grace and precision, others clash with the brute force of their animal spirits. But there are those who falter, who meet the ground with a thud that echoes the sinking feeling in my gut.

Cappie's team is no joke—they're trained, ruthless, and every hit they land whispers 'professional' in brutal arcs and calculated strikes. My turn looms at the end, the final act in this spectacle of tooth and claw. The announcer's voice booms across the arena, heralding my entrance with an edge that sends shivers down my spine.

"Prepare yourselves for the ferocity of *l'Academie*'s very own Delores 'The Destroyer' Drew!" His words hang heavy in the air, saturated with an expectation that feels like a weight around my neck.

That intro might have been a little much.

I know Cappie's tactics all too well. They've seen me grow, watched me evolve from prey to predator in their practice ring last Fall. Their new coach will have dissected my style, analyzed my every move, and now they'll send a ringer—one crafted to exploit every weakness they think they know. It's a chess game, and I'm the queen everyone's eager to topple.

A deep breath steadies my nerves, steeling my resolve. Let them come. I'll show them what it means to face a true predator, one who's learned to turn vulnerability into strength. The spotlight awaits, and beneath it, I will either shine or shatter, but one thing's for certain—I won't go down without a fight.

The stadium's energy crackles with anticipation, a live wire ready to ignite. Jaiyana Faez, the notorious saltwater crocodile shifter, emerges opposite me, her gaze as chilling as the legacy that trails behind her—her father was a Pred Games titan. I can taste the dread that name inspires, a bitter tang on my tongue. Worse yet, she's a croc, and last time I faced her I was stymied by the resemblance to my former abuser. But he's gone now and I'm burning to settle old scores with the likes of her kind.

If I can't beat the shit out of Bruno now, I can sure as fuck kick this chick's ass as a stand-in.

I plant my feet, feeling every inch the gladiatorial champion Cori envisioned me to be, clad in black and silver that gleams under the harsh lights. The crowd roars its approval, an ocean of sound that surges and swells around me. I let it wash over me—a baptism of noise before the battle. Then, my smirk cuts through the din like a blade; I raise my arms, commanding silence. It falls like a cloak, heavy and expectant.

With a wicked grin, I feed off their hunger for spectacle, and I give them one—a salute of twin middle fingers aimed at the shadowed boxes where our 'honored' Council guests probably lurk. Their outrage is my fuel; it burns hot and bright as I spin on my heel and stride into the ring, ready for war.

I'm no longer a pawn for my mother or any of these motherfuckers; I'm a free bunny.

Jaiyana wastes no time. Her strategy is clear: disconcert, unbalance, intimidate. She shifts seamlessly, human to crocodile, scales flashing dangerously. Each time she rolls, attempting to topple me with brute force, I realize there's an unnatural strength to her movements. This girl was *never* this fast, nor this strong before and gaining this much skill in the couple months since I fought her? The math isn't mathing, so whether it's magic or drugs, it doesn't matter. It's not normal, and it's not fair play.

My heart hammers a fierce rhythm as I half-shift. Bunny claws elongate, muscles coil tight with leporine agility. I dart and weave, a blur of motion that keeps me just out of reach of her snapping jaws. I need to strategize. My eyes scan hers, searching for the telltale signs of enhancement. No dilated pupils, but a darkness that doesn't seem natural.

I know what I have to do. The power lies within me—a cerulean reservoir of might I haven't tapped since Apex. But how can I unleash it here, without revealing my full hand to the stadium's prying eyes? The answer remains elusive, a puzzle to solve while parrying the relentless assault of a creature born from nightmares and honed by legacy.

No one said being the queen would be easy, and I'm on my own.

Sweat drips into my eyes, stinging them as I duck another vicious snap of Jaiyana's jaws. The crocodile girl is relentless, her strength inexplicably mounting with every lunge and strike. My muscles burn with the effort of constant motion—dodging, weaving, blocking, countering with rapid jabs that seem to do little more than irritate her.

"Come on, Dolly," I mutter to myself, breathless and desperate. "You've got more in you. You have to." I envision the bunny within, quick and cunning, but this fight demands more than animal instinct. It requires the part of me I have no idea how to control and call forward. I can't just knuckle my way through this one like I did with the drugged chick last year.

"*Please,*" I plead internally, directing my silent words to the well-spring of energy I know is buried inside me. I don't know if talking to it like I do my bunny will work, but I definitely have to try. "*I need you now. Not just for me, but for my mates and my friends. I can't let this girl get the chance to kill me in front of a zillion people.*"

The arena spins around us—a kaleidoscope of faces, cheers, and the pungent scent of bloodlust. The sight of my family—the one I chose—sharpens my resolve. They're counting on me, and the thought of letting them down tightens like a noose. I won't go down like the weak little rabbit my mother and all my ex-friends think I am.

I can do this; I just have to focus on getting that stupid lightning to listen to me.

"*Help me beat her without exposing my secret,*" I implore the enigmatic force, bargaining with a whisper of consciousness that feels both alien and intimate. "*Keep me safe and hidden, but alive. I have you for a reason and that's not clear yet, but it can't end right now.*"

It's a stalemate of evasion and assault until, suddenly, there's a response—an electric thrum that begins at my core and surges to my fingertips. As the power builds, it seeks an outlet, and I lash out with newfound potency. My hands connect with Jaiyana's scaled flesh, and the energy leaps from me to her—an invisible arc of crackling defiance. I'm almost too surprised to hold on, but I dig my fingertips in, making sure it all flows into her.

Jaiyana's eyes widen in shock, her body seizing up as if hit by a bolt of spring lightening—which I guess she was. She collapses in a heap of motionless predator on the grass field. The crowd falls into a stunned silence before erupting into a cacophony of awe and disbelief.

Ignoring the pain that racks my body and the blood that tastes like copper in my mouth, I stand tall amidst the chaos. With my legs trembling, I face the masses with my arms raised high again. The roar that meets me is deafening, a tidal wave of adoration washing over the arena.

I lock eyes with each member of my found family—their pride, their joy, their relief mingling with the wild exaltation of the crowd. Then, with a heart full of defiance, I cast a look towards the shadowed alcoves where the Council lurks, knowing full well the tremors of fear my victory sends through their ranks.

Dolly, you're more than a girl taking back her life. You're the storm they never saw coming.

THE PHOENIX

CHESS

PANTING, MY HEART POUNDS AGAINST MY RIBS AS I SKID INTO THE library, the scent of old books and dust hitting me like a physical wave. Thursdays are supposed to be uneventful for me, a day buried in paperwork in Rockland's office while I wish I was anywhere else in the world. But today is different—something is definitely afoot with the nasty corpse sniffer, so I paid as close attention as I could without drawing scrutiny. Afterward, my cheetah instincts screamed for urgency, but I had to take my leave for the day nonchalantly so she wouldn't suspect what I overheard.

Spy shit is a pain in my ass—my Angel and Fitzy can have the glory. I hate this kind of shit.

"Where are they?" I mutter under my breath, scanning the labyrinth of bookshelves for Aubrey and Renard. My gaze catches the usual corner where they huddle over texts and scrolls, but it's empty. I weave through the aisles, my breathing still uneven, and my ears twitch at every sound, hoping to pick up their voices and not faint grunting. Finding out they're a couple has made their occasional disappearances less like hide-and-seek and more like a coin flip as to what they'll be doing when they're found.

"Chester, why are you running in my *library*?" Finally, I spot Aubrey, his head popping out from behind a stack of ancient mythology volumes with a glare that could scare the tentacles off a kraken. "You *know* the rules about my—"

"Yes, yes. No fucking—except you and our girl or Ren, which is completely unfair. No running, no red food or drink. No unapproved food or drink. No rap music. No video games..."

He looks amused for a second, then goes back to scowling. "Fine. You know the rules and yet you are moving at a pace that may not be *cheetah* running, but on normal preds would be considered running."

Ra save me from the pedantic leanings of a librarian dragon in his element.

"Damn it, Aubrey." He blinks at my curse and I duck my head as a flush comes over me, then I have to shake it off. "I'm *hurrying*, not *running*, because I have news for you and Renard. Where is he, anyway?"

"Right here."

I scream like a girl when he backflips off the top of a shelf, landing in front of me with the grace of my kind and the silence of a ninja. "Holy fucking shit... How is it that garoyles are enormous, rock hard, winged giants when they shift, but in humanoid form they're like fucking panthers? It's really goddamn ridiculous."

Ren shrugs, giving me his very French, very *lassez-faire* smirk. "We are a very exotic species, *mon ami*. No one knows why we are the way we are, only that it serves our purpose well."

Great. I see we're feeling prone to riddles today.

"I still want to know why you were *hurrying* through the most delicate part of the archive with little care for anything you might damage, Chester."

Sucking in a slow breath, I try to calm my urgency a bit. These two are obviously in one of their contrary old fart moods and it won't help any of us for me to get them to dig in further. I need them to listen, after all, and when they go into Waldorf and Statler mode, it's impossible to get more than sarcasm. "I overheard some tidbits in the office today that I feel are important."

I watch the realization dawn on Aubrey's face, his eyes widening slightly. He gets the gravity of the situation without another snarky rejoinder and that's what I wanted. Any whisper from Rockland's lips could mean ripples of trouble or waves of disaster—but we have to prepare for both.

"Sit down, and we will talk about it," Ren says, pointing to the cluster of chairs in the corner. They added them so Dolly can do homework comfortably while they research, and I'm suddenly glad.

Nodding, I follow the two of them to the small sitting area and get situated. They look at me expectantly and I swallow nervously. I'm not entirely sure about what I heard and I may have just been completely overly dramatic. "Rockland's scheming, and it's all hush-hush. I'm not sure exactly what I heard and how it relates, but it feels like it's bad news. After Dolly's triumph at the Pred Games...and that therapy session win...the woman's got to be boiling over and ready to get revenge. She can't stand for our girl to be happy even if it has nothing to do with her."

Unspoken fears flit across Aubrey and Renard's faces. They know this chick is ten pounds of crazy in a two pound bag, just waiting to burst open and get her mess all over everyone. It's not a question of 'if' she goes nuclear, only 'when' she'll blow. The difficulty in cleaning up the fallout will be decided by how much we can protect our girl against the explosion.

"Get Fitz and Felix here." Aubrey grumbles. "We all need to hear this and then strategize from there."

My fingers fly over my phone screen, sending a summons into the digital ether.

> CSpot: We need you two back at the lair.

>> TigerWoody: I don't have time for a deep dicking for lunch, Chessie. I'm dick deep in these stupid projects.

> Tiger King: For fuck's SAKE, Fitz...

>> CSpot: That's not why. I have news about Rockland in her office today and Aubrey and Ren thought we should share.

I barely finish typing before I hear stomping. The twins materialize in the library with an urgency that mirrors my own. My eyes narrow at them, unclear on how they were able to thunder down the damn stairs that fast if Fitz was working on some projects.

"Why didn't you say it was this important, baby?" Fitz asks, his gaze scanning me as if he might find answers written on my skin. "I would have been here faster."

"You got here pretty damn fast," I reply drily. "One would think you two were up to something."

Felix arches a brow. "Even if we were, this is too precarious to put off. What do you know, Chess?"

"Whatever's coming has Rockland giddy. She was swanning around the office, humming to herself, and not being careful about her voice level. I picked up bits of her phone conversation and possibly some long-winded video blog speech she was making to her culty readers. She hinted that something is coming, and a narcissistic bitch would get what's coming to her."

"Could the vampires be returning?" Renard throws the theory into the ring, his brow furrowed. "Perhaps our museum heist activated the supes who run the place?"

"I doubt it," Felix interjects with a scoff, shaking his head. "Carina Rockland isn't the mastermind type. She's a low intelligence scammer peddling fetishizing fiction about shit she's never been within five feet of, not the queen bee of bloodsuckers."

After all, the same people who bitch about the 'wrongness' of Fitz and me—or Ren and Aubrey, for that matter—are the kind of people Rockland writes for.

Fitz, however, is already at work, fingers a blur over his laptop keyboard. He's hunting through camera feeds, scouring social media—anything that might give us a clue what Rockland is gloating about. My mate is channeling his rage into his work, and while I'm glad he can do that, I don't want him to lose his grip.

"If not vamps, then what could she be smirking about?" I press, feeling the coiled tension within the room. "Farley would have called if she's managed to wiggle through some loophole in the court case."

"Who knows with that fucking cunt," Felix murmurs, but his eyes are sharp, not missing a pixel on the screen as his twin works. "We have to take all her dipshittery seriously or we might miss the one important piece of bullshit she spews."

"Keep calm while I'm digging," Fitz mumbles. "I'll find it; it may just take a little time."

I squint at the monitor as Fitz's fingers dance across the keyboard like a maestro. This is something he's *very* good at, and because he excels at killing, people underestimate the intelligence of my hyperactive mate. But they shouldn't and it gives him an edge in situations like this. He won't stop until he's found every scintilla of information he can on the school's network.

"I trust you, baby."

That makes him grin at the screen and I didn't think it was possible, but he moves even faster. The digital labyrinth before us gives up its secrets one by one—a breadcrumb trail we're desperate to follow. A low growl echoes around the room when he hits something he believes is noteworthy and all the clacking of keys stops.

Aubrey leans over Fitz's shoulder, his eyes wide with concern, "Midori Aung is back," he whispers, as if saying it louder might summon the headmaster herself.

Frowning, I look at the rest of my family. "Why is that worthy of Rockland's glee?"

"She has meetings with Rockland, Asani, and... the IT department?" Felix reads from the screen, his voice laced with incredulity. "That doesn't seem like it's a herald of good tidings."

Fitz smirks without looking away from his screens. "The IT department here is about as cutting-edge as a blunt spoon. They wouldn't know a secure network if it bit them in the ass." He starts typing again, a sly smile playing on his lips. "Not to mention, Ren, the Captain's crew, and I have this place locked down tighter than Alcatraz. Midori would need a miracle to sneak into our system—and Erikson's lackies? They couldn't hack a paper bag in a real system."

"Her being here is cause for alarm. From everything I've heard from the staff, she's never around unless something's up," Felix says with a grimace. "I keep my ears perked when I'm in common spaces for gossip, and the other professors complain about her lack of care about this place all the time."

"Exactly what the crew has reported," Ren adds, turning towards Fitz, who's now leaning back in his chair, arms crossed over his chest. "We cannot forget how Dolly humiliated Kyaw Aung during the Pred Games at Cappie. Kyaw is her niece."

"Kyaw Aung," Fitz repeats, his relaxed posture gone as he sits up straighter, a growl building in his throat. "Goddamn. I almost forgot about that little witch. Zhenga had trouble with her and her mean girl group at Cappie, but they mostly squared off with Baby Girl's ex-BFFs, so we didn't focus on them. Now I wish I'd made a statement so they'd remember what happens when you come for my mate."

"Easy, love" I say, placing a hand on Fitz's shoulder. His muscles are coiled tight, ready to spring. "Remember… you tracked down La Porte after she ditched Dolly for that project. You've got that trophy waiting to be plucked. Focus on that instead of the Aung mess."

A low rumble escapes Fitz's lips, but his shoulders relax under my touch. I can feel the storm within him abate, even if only slightly. "Yeah, the Laporte girl," he mutters, almost to himself. "I'll take care of that first. She really pissed me off with her shit. And Baby Girl doesn't have a toe yet."

Fuck he's crazy when it comes to people he loves. I adore it, but sometimes…

"That sounds like a plan, baby," I reply, giving him a reassuring squeeze. "We'll handle the Aung puzzle together, then make a move when we have a better idea of what's actually going on."

But Fitz jumps to his feet, pacing like the caged predator he is. "I'm tired, Chessie. Tired of them thinking they can play games with Dolly and get away with it. Tired of holding back to solve riddles and find clues. This shit just keeps getting bigger, and the boards get fuller. When can we all just have a fucking break?" His voice is a snarl, barely contained fury lacing every syllable.

My voice is calm and steady to counteract his rage. "We all are, Fitzy. But we can't risk putting Dolly or our friends in danger because we're too impetuous. Right, guys?"

Felix nods, then Aubrey and Ren. The dragon looks at the hyper tiger with a stern expression. "You know Chester is correct, Fitzgerald. There are too many moving pieces to simply blast everyone with my dragon fire—or I'd be doing it. I, too, despise our inability to sweep the board to keep her safe."

"I'm going to the Shird to wait for Baby Girl. I can't sit here and do this right now," Fitz announces gruffly, stalking off with purpose in his stride, leaving the rest of us to untangle the web of deceit that's been cast over *l'Academie*.

With Fitz's departure still hanging heavy in the air, I shift my focus back to Aubrey, Ren, and Felix. There's no time for us to dwell on frustrations or personal vendettas; we've got bigger prey to chase. He'll work it out with our girl, and they'll come back with my tiger in a much lighter mood. His pout fits have always been short-lived since Dolly arrived.

"Don't worry about him. My Angel will sort him out," I say with a shake of my head.. "For now, we can't let our guard down because he's pouting. I think we need to crack that stash of shit from the museum before Spring Break. Whatever secrets are locked away inside that vault might be key to fending off the Fae or standing up to the Council."

Aubrey nods, his sharp eyes reflecting determination. "I'll pour over every document, but we need more help with decoding the odd language to complete the work. I'm going to reach out to my trusted contacts to see if we can figure out how to translate it."

Renard gives a firm nod in agreement from his perch. "Perhaps I should… initiate contact with some of my kind. There may be clutches that are not part of my family who have members old enough to recall the time before. I'd hoped to avoid it so I wouldn't activate the gargoyle grapevine, but… *c'est la vie*. My destiny is to meet them again whether I want to or not, it seems."

Felix exhales slowly, and then fixes me with a resolute gaze. "Chess, I'll talk some sense into my brother when he gets back, even if the Princess has calmed him down. We're a team, and we tackle these obstacles together. He has to respect that."

"Thank you, brother," I reply softly. "I empathize with his fury, as do the rest of you, I'm sure. But the solutions that worked on Bloodstone or even at Apex before Dolly are not the ones that will be successful with such widespread enemies."

The Raj sighs, nodding. "I know. And while he's doing much better at focusing and working through methods other than his killing sprees… he still aches to mete out justice the way he was raised to. He's as much a product of our dickhead father as I am."

Tilting my head, I smile wryly. "Felix, we're *all* a product of our upbringing, even our girl. When she turns on the 'Lucille' act, it makes my balls shrivel up and hide inside my body. None of us are safe from the past."

He laughs, then Ren and Aubrey join him, but I'm serious.

I have a distinct feeling that none of us will get through this without reconciling our past traumas and they need to get used to the idea sooner rather than later.

BROKEN

DELORES

FITZ'S SCOWL DEEPENS WITH EVERY SECOND, HIS EYES DARK POOLS of unresolved anger. I'm holding the jar with a pinky toe that's definitely female—I can tell by the fancy pedicure—but I haven't asked who he took this trophy from. I know his small retributions make him feel less out of control in the face of enemies we can't simply meet head on, and I adore that he wants me to know those who mistreat me are paying, even in this macabre fashion.

Everyone else looks grossed out, but I treasure Fitzy's body part tributes; it feels fitting to me.

"Fitzy," I start, my voice a soft lilt that usually calms him down. His gifts normally make him cool off, but he hasn't quite gotten to a stable mindset yet. That's worrying Felix and Chess, which is making me anxious. His hyperactivity and snap decision making activate when he's like this—something we definitely do not need with so many balls in the air.

"No," he cuts me off sharply, the single word slicing through the heavy atmosphere. His determination is a tangible thing, a force that won't be swayed by distractions or offers of physical comfort. It's one of the things I admire about him, but today it's grating on my already thin nerves.

I watch as he paces frenetically. Felix watches his twin like a silent sentinel, his loyalty to Fitz as unwavering as the north star. They exchange a look, and without a word, they're set into motion. "Where are you going?"

"Don't fret, Princess," Felix says as he winks at me over his shoulder. "We're going to do some recon—probably in the staff housing again. My brother needs to feel like he's *doing* something right now. I won't let him go off the ranch."

Resisting the urge to press him for more information, I sigh heavily. I know when Fitz is hell-bent on accomplishing a task he's better off without us holding him back. So I stay put, feeling my nose twitch, an anxious tick that betrays my own unease.

Those two going off on their own without a solid plan was not on the agenda for today.

The headmistress' secret meetings have cast a shadow over us all, and Fitz won't rest until we know exactly what that slippery serpent has planned. None of us are fond of the unknown and there's not a lot of information on Midori other than PR blurbs and the occasional puff piece in educational journals. It's infuriating and almost certainly orchestrated by whoever is working on their tech—an Erikson lackey, most likely.

I didn't need another reason to hate Heather E.; however, her family is ass-deep in this conspiracy, so I have one.

THE MUSTY SCENT OF OLD PAPER AND INK FILLS MY NOSTRILS AS I flip through the yellowed pages of the book with a delicate touch. Renard hovers nearby, his sharp eyes scanning the cryptic symbols as if he might divine their meaning through sheer will. Aubrey's fingers dance across the screen of his phone, pausing only to zoom in on a particularly gnarled drawing before snapping a picture to send off.

"These colleagues of yours," I muse aloud, "they're all predators, right?"

Aubrey nods without looking up, too engrossed in his task. "Yeah, top of their field in ancient cultures and shifter histories."

I nibble on my lower lip, recalling Raina's whispered confidences during a late-night study session. "We need to reach out to someone from prey academia, too. As I mentioned before, Raina told me what we learn about the Magic Accords isn't the whole story. The prey perspective is less... glorified. And it might reference the Fae because their archives aren't controlled by Council lackeys."

"That seems like something we should investigate further." Aubrey pauses, considering it for a moment. He tilts his head, a spark of curiosity lighting his gaze. "Their data could be a game changer if it's not been redacted. I know you mentioned it, but I got so involved in working on this new stuff from the museum that I forgot."

Chess looks up from his book with a smirk. "It's not like we haven't had distractions, big guy."

"No shit," I say, feeling a small surge of pride when they jump on board immediately. "Raina says their stories are like shadows—

always there but rarely acknowledged by those who don't need to hide."

"Shadows can reveal much about the truth of an object," Rennie chimes in, his voice low and thoughtful. "I will speak to Raina and the Captain about who we can contact to explore this lead. They will be able to point us in the right direction for certain."

Aubrey nods, already drafting a new message on his phone. I watch him work, a flurry of focused energy, and feel the library's silence settle around us once more—dense with secrets waiting to be unearthed. "Their assistance will be much appreciated, love. Let me know when you get their contact information."

My gargoyle leaps to his feet, pacing between towering bookshelves, tail flicking in agitation. "I never considered that they were sitting on a treasure trove of truth, undistorted by predator bias. We could have been further along with all of this timeline shit if I had been paying more attention. I apologize, *ma petite.*"

"Like Chessie said, we've been distracted by a lot of shit," I say, hopping off the table where I was perched. "Predator narratives are loud—they claim to be the only truth and we've all been taught that. it's easy to forget our smaller friends don't grow up in that noisy din."

"*Exactement,*" Renard nods, his expression softening as he stops pacing. "We must look further than our own belly buttons for the answers we seek. Very good, *petite lapin.* Once Flames has their information, we will work to expand our timeline with new data and perhaps that will lead us to someone who can translate the things we stole."

Meanwhile, Aubrey's fingers fly across the keyboard of his laptop, the click-clack of keys punctuating the silence that hangs heavy around us. He's back to work, having accepted the idea of using outside sources, and now he's moved on. His focus is impressive, and I smile as I walk over to wrap my arms around his shoulders.

"You work harder than anyone, big guy. Thank you for taking care of us."

"It's my job, lunchable—all of our jobs, really, but this is where I am most useful," Aubrey grunts, a corner of his mouth lifting in a wry smile. "Outside of burning everyone to ash, which my dragon would happily do at any time. But much like Fitzgerald, I know he is simply overreacting to the danger by wanting to eliminate everything without considering the consequences. Your gift for listening to your friends is what will help us in the end, I believe."

"Who knew my big ears were good for more than just eavesdropping?" I quip, trying to ease the tension in the room. It works, as both Renard and Aubrey chuckle, and I stand up, stretching my arms above my head. "Now I have to go eat or my stomach is going to cave in. Coming, Chessie?"

My cheetah drops his book and shoots to his feet, making me smile softly. "With you? Anytime, Angel. Let's get you fed and then we'll come back to help."

LATER, WE'RE HUDDLED AROUND THE ANCIENT TOME, ITS PAGES splayed open like wings of a moth. I can't help but feel the weight of centuries beneath my gloved fingertips. The symbols etched into the parchment seem to dance before my eyes—whispers of a hidden language that's just beyond my grasp. I feel like I should be able to read it for some reason and I don't know why. Ever since Fitz swiped it, the damn thing has been taunting all of us and I want to scream every time I look at it.

Why is this book calling to me like a siren? Ugh!

"Whatever secrets it holds are important," I muse aloud. "But until we figure out what fucking language it's in, we can't do anything with it. However, Fitz's software is much closer to unlocking the flash drive, so that's what we need to focus on." My voice hangs in the air, a taut string vibrating with our imminent discovery. Progress of any kind is better than spinning our wheels.

Aubrey nods, his gaze not leaving the page as he carefully extracts a few delicate samples from the old book with tweezers. "That data is crucial, but he needs a clear head to tackle it." He places each fragment into a small, sterile vial. "For now, we're going to get these samples prepped to go to the Louvre where my friend works."

Renard's hands are steady as he assists Aubrey, sealing the vials with a methodical precision. "Farley's guys will ensure everything reaches the Louvre without interference. Their brawn and quick wit should prevent any interference."

I'll say… Monstro and Skelly would twist an attacker into a pretzel without a second thought.

"Okay," I say, leaning back in my chair, the leather creaking softly under my weight. "The last thing we need is more variables to fuck up our plans. The board is too full as it is."

Chess packs the vials into a padded container, a miniature vault for the fragments of history that might soon unfold an entirely new narrative. Then Aubrey affixes a label, his handwriting meticulous and unreadable to anyone who doesn't know him well. Once they're done, Rennie takes the box, placing it on the top of a shelf carefully. Leaning back in my chair, I let out a slow breath as I think about what comes next.

"The Louvre is in Paris," I blurt out, a sudden burst of excitement surging through me. "We could go during spring break to check out what your friends find out about the samples."

It's a tantalizing thought—for more reasons than just the results.

Renard leans against a bookshelf, crossing his arms with a thoughtful tilt of his head. "That's not a bad idea," he admits. "I'll take you. I've been dying to show you my city; it's a date."

"Ooh la la, that sounds fancy," Aubrey quips, a smirk playing on his lips as he closes his laptop with a satisfying snap. "Will you be visiting the Tower to brood?"

"Only if you *têtes de noeud* refuse to leave us alone," Renard retorts, his playful smirk mirroring Aubrey's.

I can't suppress my grin at their banter, especially knowing I'll finally get to see the famous city. "Don't listen to him, Rennie. I'd love to go on a date to your former home. You can show me all the amazing, beautiful sights since we won't get a real break like everyone else."

Chess frowns. "What does that mean, Angel?"

"I have so much work to do that I'll spend most of my time practicing for the next scrimmage, finishing my homework, and going on whatever secret squirrel missions we have. Vacation isn't in the cards for me."

Aubrey snorts, shaking his head. "That won't do, bite size. You need to rest, too. Our romantically inclined mate can take you on his fancy date, but we will all plan a few distractions here as well. You may have a lot to do, but you can't push yourself until you break. That won't help at all."

"I agree with him," Chess says as he gives me a concerned look. "We can help with your work, too. All you have to do is tell us what you need. Plus, I can make anything you want to keep you fed and happy."

My lips curve as I look at the three of them with my heart damn near bursting from my chest. Whatever I did to deserve these wonderful men that everyone else discarded, I'd do it a million times over to ensure I never have to be without them. "Alright. We'll tackle it all as a family... but remember, you asked for this."

They have no idea what they just got themselves into and I'm going to enjoy every second of it.

MASQUERADE

I PACE AROUND THE NARROW CONFINES OF THE ROOM WE ALL SHARE when we're with our girl, each step feeling like a thunderous echo against the hardwood. My wings twitch with anticipation; tonight is a culmination of centuries, a night when I can share the city of lights with *mon amour*.

I've wanted to do this for a long time and eventually, I want Aubrey to come along to see it as well.

The bathroom door creaks open, and she steps out like a vision from an Impressionist's dream. The dress clings to her curves, a cascade of silk that mirrors the Seine under moonlight. Her hair, a storm of colors, frames her face in a way that would make the aurora borealis envious. Sparkling jewels catch the artificial light, casting prismatic dances across the walls.

"*Mon Dieu...*" The words slip from me, soft as the Parisian breeze.

"Too much?" she teases, her voice lilting with that familiar snark that sets my heart ablaze.

"*Parfait*," I insist, catching myself before I flit across the room to her side.

Restraint, Renard. You're a creature of old world charm tonight, not an animal. She deserves romance and escape.

"Good thing you wore that sleek suit, love. Can't have you look shabby next to snack size, now can we?" Aubrey mutters from the corner, his grumpy tone belied by the affectionate glint in his eye.

I offer him a wry smile, knowing his barbs are rooted in love. "It's not possible for me to look shabby, *mon ami*. Gargoyles are timeless creatures of elegance and grace."

"Mmmmhmmm," Aubrey hums, flipping through a magazine with disinterest. "Just remember you have to pick up our results, love. You're buzzing around like a moth in a lamp shop, and I'm concerned you're turning into Fitzgerald."

"Never." I scoff as I watch Dolly put on her jewelry. "Paris holds so much of my past. Sharing it with our mate is everything."

"Then don't keep the lady waiting," Aubrey says with a smirk. "Get your poetic ass in gear and head out before you decide not to go anywhere. Or worse... before Fitz decides you're not going."

Taking a deep breath, I extend my elbow to Dolly. "Shall we?"

She links her arm in mine, her laughter the melody that has scored my life since I met her. We leave the room, stepping into the night, and I feel the weight of centuries lift off my shoulders. Tonight, I am her romantic guide through the city that pulses in my veins, the city I once watched over from Notre Dame's highest tower.

"Lead the way, *mon* gargoyle," Dolly says, her eyes sparkling with excitement.

"Prepare to fall in love with Paris," I promise, and we head into the evening, the stars above winking their approval at our grand adventure.

Hopefully, she loves it even half as much as I love her

We walk to the front of the library where the fancy sports car the Captain procured awaits, gleaming under the streetlights like a predator at rest. I help Dolly into the passenger seat before sliding into the driver's side, feeling the leather hug my frame. The engine purrs to life, a symphony of mechanical precision that sends a thrill through me.

As we weave through the streets of Paris, the city unfurls before us, a tapestry of lights and shadows. Dolly leans back, her eyes roaming over the buildings as if trying to stitch together the story of my past from their facades.

"Tell me about when you lived here as a wee gargoyle," she urges, her voice awed as she looks around.

"During the 1400s, Paris was..." I begin, and the words flow from me, painting a vivid picture of a city wracked by plague and war. "The Hundred Years War was not just about humans, *ma petite*. Shifters and mages played their parts in the shadows, tipping scales and weaving spells."

"One of those books we've been reading said that Joan of Arc was a lion shifter?" Dolly interjects with a raised eyebrow, her tone skeptical. "I don't know how they hid that in battle. It seems like it would be really hard with all those humans around."

"*Oui*, she was." I nod, feeling the familiar ache of old memories. "She fought valiantly to restore balance when the mage and shifter territory battle threatened the humans. They said her roar was as fierce as her conviction, but I never met her."

"Learning the truth about history is kind of a bummer," she sighs, shaking her head. "I feel like the bad guy by association. We're lying to the humans—that's not such a big deal. But the prey animals have been relegated to a servant class and magic users were locked in a prison—so to speak. It feels icky as hell."

I give her a wry smile. "The truth is often uncomfortable, Dolly. While I knew the magical beings probably got a raw deal, I was sent away young like Flames. We lost the power to affect change when our families cut us out—though it's not really an excuse, I suppose. We were too damaged to do anything but wallow in seclusion."

"Rennie, you were kids." Her hand covers mine and she smiles softly. "That's like saying I should have been doing something radical when I was trapped with Lucille and Bruno. Feeling guilty about the past doesn't help anyone—what are we doing now? *That* will help people."

My eyes dance as I squeeze her fingers for a moment, then return to shifting. "Always keeping us from self-centered brooding, that's you, *lapin*. You're not quite sunshine, but you do keep the clouds away."

Our conversation turns, dancing between epochs and legends until the Louvre looms before us, majestic even in the dark. We're guided to a discreet back entrance where a figure larger than life waits. Dolly's breath catches as the gorilla shifter greets us with a nod, his size eclipsing the doorway.

"Got your results," he rumbles, handing me the envelope. His hand engulfs mine briefly, the exchange grounding in its brevity. "Aubrey said it was important so I muscled the samples through the red tape and line. He owes me one; it wasn't easy."

"*Merci,*" I say, tucking the envelope away. "We will examine them later with our complete family. Aubrey and the others will provide a myriad of viewpoints that will help us interpret your data."

"Makes sense," the gorilla shifter agrees. "Have the dragon contact me if he needs more assistance. *Au revoir et bonne chance*[1]."

I've never seen a pred as big as that meld into the shadows, but this guy damn near disappears as we head back to the car. "Everyone Flames knows is so fucking weird. It's mind boggling."

Dolly pulls out her phone, fingers dancing over the screen as she texts the group. "As opposed to those he loves?

She's got me there.

> BabyGirl: Samples secured, guys.

> TigerKing: Are you headed home?

> EmoBatman: Of course not, Raj. We have a date to go on.

> TigerKing: I don't like the thought of you leaving them in a car while you prance about Paris.

> TigerWoody: What if they don't prance? What if they just mosey?

> LustyLibrarian: For fuck's sake, Fitz...

> BabyGirl: You guys should put that on a tee-shirt. You say it enough.

> LustyLibrarian: He MAKES us say it, lunchable. And he does it on purpose.

> EmoBatman: ...

> TigerWoody: You'd better not be texting while you're driving my Baby Girl, you winged wanker! That's dangerous as fuck.

> TigerKing: For once, I agree.

BabyGirl: You all need to calm down.
Rennie is driving fine; I have his phone to
transcribe. Stop motherhenning me. We'll
be fine and he just said to tell Felix that the
trunk has some sort of lock box he can put
the stuff in.

I chuckle as she clicks her phone screen off and puts both of our devices in her purse. "Just like that, hmm?"

"Absolutely," she says with a wink. "This is our date now, and I don't want them intruding, no matter how well-intentioned."

Fuck she's hot when she's taking charge.

THE PARISIAN SKY PEELS BACK ITS COVER, REVEALING A TAPESTRY of stars as we sit beneath the gaping roof of *L'Étoile Ouverte*. The clink of fine china and the murmur of conversation harmonize with the sweet serenade of a violin player tucked in the corner of the terrace. It's an ambiance that breathes romance, the perfect setting for a night steeped in history and amour.

"Can you imagine," I say to Dolly, my voice barely above a whisper, "the artists who walked these streets? The poets and musicians who spilled their hearts into the Seine?"

She leans forward, the candlelight dancing in her rainbow-hued hair, casting prismatic shadows on the tablecloth. "You don't have to, Rennie. You *lived* it. Tell me about the 1500s now…about your Paris."

I smile, savoring the coq au vin that melts on my tongue like a savory memory. "*C'était une époque de renaissance*[2]," I begin, describing the revival of art and beauty that bloomed even as the old world crumbled. I tell her of hidden salons where preds and prey gathered to discuss philosophy and sculpture, where we debated under the moonlight, animated by the magic of the city.

"Sounds enchanting," she sighs, her eyes reflecting the constellations above us.

"Paris has always been magical, *mon amour*," I reply, reaching across the table to squeeze her hand.

As the final note from the nearby violin trembles into silence, I can hardly contain my excitement for the next surprise. "Dolly, are you ready for the *pièce de résistance* of our evening?"

Her grin is all the answer I need.

WE LEAVE THE RESTAURANT, THE COOL NIGHT AIR WRAPPING around us like a cloak. I lead her down cobblestone alleys until the distant echo of an organ fills the air. A shiver of anticipation courses through me. This surprise is one I had to use the hyperactive tiger to dig up, and I know she will adore it. I quietly made certain that we were both dressed for the occasion by nudging her polar bear friend and acquiring my own attire from the city via Captain's special delivery.

And she has not sensed it in the slightest, which means she'll be completely taken aback.

"Where are we?" Dolly asks, her voice laced with curiosity. "I didn't expect to be wandering around this part of the city, to be honest. I thought you'd take me to see your bells, or maybe to the *Moulin Rouge*."

My smile is mysterious and she huffs a bit until we happen upon the back alley door. I knock three times, and it opens, revealing an elegant waiting room. She arches a brow, her expression curious.

"We're going to a cathouse?"

Chuckling, I shake my head. "Welcome to the Phantom's lair." Handing her a delicate white mask, feathers fluttering at its edges, I grin, then take mine out of my inside jacket pocket.

Her eyes sparkle as she takes in my all-black suit, the stark contrast of my newly donned Phantom mask. "Rennie... what did you do?"

"I found an escape, no matter how brief, from the pressures of the world we're living in. Come with me, my Angel of Music." My eyes dance at the reference and she squeals, then slaps her hand over her mouth when the other people in the foyer give her amused looks.

We enter the grand ballroom, already alive with masked figures swirling in time to the haunting melody of *Masquerade*. Taking her hand, I draw her into the dance, our movements fluid, as if the music itself guides us. Laughter bubbles from her lips, and the sound is more intoxicating than the finest champagne.

"*Je t'adore*," I whisper against her ear as we spin, her dress fanning out like the wings of a vibrant butterfly.

"*Je t'adore plus*," she responds, her voice a playful challenge.

This will be one of the best memories I've made since I left my clutch, and I'm going to savor every minute of it.

THE MUSIC FADES TO A DISTANT THRUM IN MY EARS AS I GUIDE Dolly away from the pulsing heart of the ballroom. Our steps are unsteady, betraying our tipsy state, but there's an urgency that sobers my thoughts. A side room looms ahead—a sanctuary veiled in shadows and secrecy.

"Rennie..." she breathes out as I close the door. Her voice is husky, laced with desire and the sweet burn of champagne.

She's even more beautiful when she's unencumbered by the bullshit of reality.

"*Oui, mon amour*," I reply, my words barely a whisper over the sound of our racing hearts.

My back presses against the cold, stone wall, pulling her to me with a hunger that has been simmering beneath the surface all evening. Her rainbow hair cascades around us, a riot of color against my black suit. In the dim light, her curves are accentuated by the tight embrace of her dress, and I trace the outline of her body with hands eager to explore.

"Your wings," she gasps, as I allow the gargoyle out and they unfurl. They brush against her skin with a touch as soft as moon-light, and she looks up at me with the red-tinted eyes of her bunny.

"*Et tes oreilles,*" I murmur in reply, reaching up to caress the velvet texture of her bunny ears. They twitch with every pulse of excite-ment, which is adorable and sexy as hell. My tail coils around her leg, an additional caress that draws a shiver from her lips.

The last time we were alone like this, I chased her and we were rough, but this time, I want to be soft.

"Renard," she sighs, the sound spurring me on.

I lean forward, my lips finding hers in a kiss that speaks of centuries of longing. The taste of her is intoxicating, more potent than any spirit we've imbibed tonight. Her hands roam over my form, finding the horns that adorn my head, her touch sending jolts of pleasure through me. We still have our masks on, but I don't care because no matter what she looks like, Delores Drew is my mate.

She is ours—together.

"*Je t'aime,*" she whispers against my mouth, her breath mingling with mine.

"*Je t'aime tant,*" I confess, the words tumbling out amidst the tangle of emotions that she inspires within me. "Finding you after I'd already found him... I never thought I could be that lucky twice, but here we are. And I will do anything... face *anything*... to protect the family we've made."

Her lips curve up and the firm tone of her voice says everything when she replies, "I will burn the entire world down to save any one of you, Renard. If it comes down to saving the preds or my family? I will channel the ruthlessness in my DNA without blinking an eye to keep my mates and my friends safe. Can you live with that?"

Brushing a wisp of hair off of her face, I laugh. "*Ma petite*, none of us would expect any less. Between you and Fitzgerald, I don't even know if Flames would get to use his fire before you razed the entire battlefield."

"Good. Because you're right—Fitz and I have a very similar thought process when it comes to those we love. That's why his stalking doesn't bother me."

I wrap my arms and wings around her tightly, flipping us around so her back is against the wall. "Are we done talking about your other lovers or…?"

She lets out a husky laugh, then reaches up to touch her amulet. Her clothes disappear and I know that's her answer. I do the same, leaving us naked but for the masks and her sparkly jewelry. "Time for another dance, my broody gargoyle."

Within moments, our bodies are synchronized in a primal rhythm. Her nails graze my skin as she holds on, each stroke igniting sparks that threaten to consume us both. The room blurs into a tapestry of sensation: the softness of her lips against mine, the heady perfume of her hair, and the warmth of her skin against the chill of my onyx hide.

"Rennie," she moans, her voice crescendoing as our pace speeds up. "Staying quiet is getting hard."

I can feel her heartbeat, rapid and wild against my chest, as we rocket towards orgasm. A symphony of whispered endearments and ragged breaths fills the room, our very beings entwined in the most intimate of duets. "You promised, *mon cœur*. We don't want to be discovered in this state."

"Why the hell do I care?" she growls as her hands sink into my hair, tugging on my horns in a way she knows drives me crazy.

The rumble of my laughter doesn't stop our coupling, but I growl back at her. "We're shifted, *petite*. There are… humans in this place."

"Always in the fucking way of fun," she mutters. She darts forward to bite my lower lip, then licks it. "Take me to the stars, my poetic gargoyle, and then we'll head home where I can scream as loud as I want."

That is the best plan I've heard all night.

All Star

Delores

I TWIRL A STRAND OF MY HAIR, WATCHING RUFUS SLOUCH INTO the plush couch across from me, his eyes alight with the thrill of recounting his spring break adventures. Cori perches on the armrest, her usual chatty self replaced by a quiet, zipped lip behavior that's weird as hell considering she, too, left campus during the break. The main room of our suite hums with the energy of our reunited trio having a last days of break slumber party on this chilly spring night, and I couldn't be happier to huddle in with them for tea time.

"Spring break was amazing," I sigh, leaning back in the cushy furniture. "But I missed the hell out of you, even if you were having fun jaunts off-campus."

Rufus smirks, the corners of his lips twitching upwards as he leans back, arms outstretched as if embracing the memories. "The Kavarit triplets are a handful, but you know me—never one to shy away from a challenge." He wiggles his eyebrows suggestively, and I can't help but laugh. His innuendo about his three Sphinx men doesn't just border on scandalous—it gleefully leaps over the line.

"Triple the fun, huh?" I tease, joining in on the playful banter. "I bet they kept all of your… attentions busy."

His laughter fills the room, a rich sound that always makes me smile. "Oh, Dollypop, you're getting better at this! But the break wasn't just playtime, unfortunately. I got some epic B roll for the documentary. The scenery was almost as breathtaking as the company."

"Almost?" I arch a brow, earning another chuckle from him. "I highly doubt that."

Cori remains unusually tight-lipped, her gaze fixed on her brightly colored nails. It's unlike her to be this quiet, especially when there's gossip to share. "And what about you, Coco? Your silence is louder than Rufus' crowing about his sex-capades."

She shrugs noncommittally, a flicker of something crossing her face before she schools it back into neutrality. "Just sorting things out for the uniforms and getting all this damn work done," she says. Her nose wrinkles and she waves her hand. "Since we were all dumped into the frying pan with the end of year projects, I feel like that's all we can do outside of a few social things. You know?"

"You didn't have any fun?" I press as my radar goes off when she tries to wiggle out of specifics again.

What's going on with her? Is she still mourning Giselle?

"It's a lot, D," she says with a sigh. "I've been finalizing the uniforms for the entire Pred Games team, and there's a lot of logistics involved in making sure they're up to quality standards when I can't just make them all myself. I have to make sure they don't damage the brand I'm building."

"Isn't Zhenga helping?," I ask with a frown. "If not, I'll talk to her. She's supposed to make this easy for you since you're doing her a massive favor with the rebranding of the team."

Her eyes widen and she shakes her pastel, rainbow curls. "No, no! She is helping, but you know how I am. And I have to make sure I can compete with my family in the public eye. It's daunting."

"Okay, now that you've Spanish Inquisitioned Coco, spill it. Your turn to share more spring break shenanigans," Rufus prods, his eyebrows wiggling with mischief. "That will lighten up this party because you have *five* hunks of man meat."

I grin, leaning back into the plush cushions of my suite's main room. "Well, I had some luxurious times and some blah times, just like you, Ru-Ru. It was pretty amazing, especially since no F-A-E tried to ruin our vacay. I'd even say... transformative."

"Transformative? That's a big word for 'I got some tail, Dollykins, " Cori teases, her eyes sparkling with amusement.

This switch flipping with her is really weird and I have to get Rufus alone to talk about it. She's worrying me.

"Ha," I snort, intentionally ignoring her pun. "Fitz brought me something to balance out the scales—literally. Someone will be regretting their bullshit when they hobble across campus missing one of their piggies."

Rufus howls with laughter, "I'm picturing that chick trying to sashay her way around the green with a bandaged foot and it's *delicious.*"

"After that, his brother took his turn—and not *that* way, pervs," I say quickly. "Felix had me training hard for the next scrimmage every morning. He's relentless when it comes to making me faster and able to last longer if I need to run."

"Well, you do have to work off all the yummy stuff your cheetah makes. Speaking of Chess, what did he do besides try to make us all roll to the bed later with this food?" Cori grins a little and I feel that pit in my stomach knot more. She's definitely hiding something.

"Chessie joined Fitz and me for yoga sessions that twisted me into knots I didn't know existed. Plus, he cooked up a storm—his paremesan garlic fries are to die for."

"Sounds tasty and hot at the same time," Rufus says as he reaches for the cheesy delights on the table. "I'd love to watch those boys wrestling into yoga poses with their muscles—"

"Rufus! It wasn't a hot oil wrestling match. Just realxing, mediatative yoga," I say, chuckling. "Since I have so much work, we tried to keep most of the time very low-key and low effort. We were all knitting together at one point. You should have seen the guys struggling with their needles.

"Knitting?" Rufus gasps, feigning shock before letting out a deep, rumbling laugh. "Oh, to be a fly on that wall."

"Hey, they're not half bad. Aubrey and Chessie are really good at it," I defend, a smile tugging at my lips. "And of course, they were lifesavers when it came to researching papers and studying for tests—even Fitzy."

"Speaking of life-changing experiences," Rufus leans in, his eyes squinting at me as if he's been waiting to ask. "Tell me about that date with the emo gargoyle."

"It was... enchanting," I say dreamily, then snap out of it as I catch Rufus' expectant look. "He took me to Paris for a lovely dinner and then to a *Phantom* ball! We danced until my feet hurt.. but the real magic happened once we got home." I glance around conspiratorially before pulling down my shirt just enough to reveal an impressive bite mark above my breast, still tinged with purple and blue.

"Damn, girl!" Cori exclaims, while Rufus simply whistles low. "Two down, three to go."

"Don't be weird about it." I smack her playfully on the arm, but I can't help the blush creeping up my cheeks. "This is normal with mates. Everyone says so."

Rufus arches a brow. "I suppose if you're lucky enough to *have* fated mates, it is. Not all of us are so fortunate, even if we *have* found the people we might stick with."

Cori nods, looking less confident than before. "Not that some non-fated mates don't... you know. Bite for marking purposes. Because they do... I'm told."

What the hell is that about?

Rufus shrugs when I look at him and then sighs dramatically. "If only. I'm *such* a bite whore. It cranks my engine like no other."

"Alright, that's enough sex talk," I say when I see Cori's expression. I pick up a bottle of nail polish. "Since this is officially a slumber party, what color am I going with tonight?"

"Something bright and loud," Cori suggests as she looks through the selection on the table. "I still want to know which guy is next, by the way. Who'll be lucky mate number three?"

I consider her question, painting a perfect stroke of magenta on my nails. "I'll know when it's time," I reply confidently. "My bunny instincts haven't steered me wrong yet."

"Speaking of knowing when it's time," Rufus chimes in, "what's the scoop with your voice practicum song? We told you ours and you haven't shared."

I know he's changing the topic again because Cori is being weird, and I'm grateful for it, even if I'm not ready to answer this yet. "That's under wraps. It's going to be a surprise."

"Fine, keep your secrets," Rufus says, feigning annoyance. "But you owe me a sneak peek before the big day."

"Maybe, maybe not," I tease as Cori takes the polish to start on my nails.

Laughter and chatter fill the room, the air thick with the scent of fried sweets and the warmth of friendship. It's a comfortable bubble until the shrill ring of the phone punctures it.

"Who the hell is that at nine p.m. on a Saturday?" Cori muses, cocking her head.

I reach for the receiver, the playful banter fading into silence. The moment I hear the voice on the other end, my heart stutters, a chill running down my spine. The laughter and warmth of moments ago evaporate like mist as I stare at the faces of my friends, their expressions turning to concern. "Good evening, Lucille."

"You *are* alive. Who would have known?" The voice drips with venom and I have to steel myself for how this conversation will likely go. Her words slither through the phone line as she adds, "You've been quite the disappointment—again."

Blood drains from my face, leaving a sickly pallor. I haven't spoken to her since the Yule break. I knew I've needed to call her since Bruno's explosive departure from this world—not that I mourn him—but I've been putting it off.

This is exactly why, despite my confidence upgrade and successes on the playing field.

"What seems to be the problem, Lucille? I can't imagine what 'problem' you're referencing."

"Acting as if you're clueless again?" she hisses. "Don't make me laugh. You will fix this mess you've made, or I will find a way to do it for you—and you won't like it."

I glance at Rufus and Cori, shrugging in confusion. They know enough about Lucille to understand the danger she presents, but it's a fool's errand to guess without any context. *Fix what?* I think frantically, but keep my tone steady. "Perhaps you could enlighten me? I've been very busy with school—trying to catch up—and my grades are excellent. I don't know what you need me to address."

"Your behavior reflects poorly on our family. Actions have consequences, Delores Diamond Drew. Dire ones, if you don't get it together quickly."

Is she drunk and alone with no one to berate since Bruno's pushing up daisies? I have no idea what the fuck she means.

"Lucille," I say, my voice steady despite the ice slithering down my spine, "I'm doing well here; I promise."

"Fine?" Lucille's laugh crackles through the phone, a sound devoid of any genuine mirth. "Is that what you call your... spectacle? You need a firmer hand, Delores, and if you don't start showing some respect for our name, then I'll send someone to ensure you do."

That veiled threat sends a shiver through me. The last thing I need on top of everything else is her enforcer, turning up to put me in line. I take a deep breath, trying to keep my voice level. "There's no need for that; I will make sure everything is taken care of."

"You'd better. This embarrassment you're causing us needs to be dealt with." Her tone sharpens like claws unsheathing. "And it will be, one way or another."

Her threat hangs heavy in the air, a noose waiting to tighten. Part of me wants to lash out, to demand she stop speaking in riddles, but that would only send her spiraling further into rage. Instead, I take a different tack. Much like Rufus, I'm going to change the fucking topic—fast.

"Speaking of family, I have to do a Shifter History paper and I'd love for you to give me some information on your family from Russia. How are they, anyway?"

I don't know shit about her family other than a brief memory of her talking about her father, but if this gets her off my ass and gives me info for our reasearch, I'll say whatever I need to.

"Ah, darling, they thrive as always," Lucille replies, the pride in her tone unmistakable. Yet, she reveals nothing substantial, no tidbits of information I can use. It's all smoke and mirrors with her. "I'm afraid I don't have time to discuss the old country, though. I have other things to attend to."

At nine at night on Saturday? I don't even want to know.

"Perhaps on another call then," I reply, trying to keep the eagerness out of my voice. The guys and I believe knowing about her family history might give me a clue about my... exceptional circumstances, but if Lucille knows I *want* to know something she will work her hardest to make sure I don't get the info out of pure spite.

"Perhaps," Lucille says, her tone deceptively soft. "Now, I must go. Remember: I'll be watching you."

The line goes dead, leaving a silence that roars in my ears. I set the receiver down slowly, my hand trembling slightly. The uncertainty of Lucille's words wraps around me like a shroud, and I can't shrug off the unease that settles in my bones. I *really* don't want her to do something rash—like send Bruiser to France to trail after me.

"Are you okay?" Rufus asks, his voice low and concerned. "That sounded rough."

"As much as I can be," I groan. "Just typical Lucille bluster, I'm sure. I'm just frustrated I wasn't able to get anything out of her about her family. We're running into brick walls trying on our own."

When I glance at Cori and Rufus, their faces painted with concern, I can't help but wonder why Lucille didn't mention my Pred Games victory.

That was worth boasting about, right? It's aggressive, assertive—exactly her style. So why the silence on that front?

"Maybe she's upset about you calling out the Council," Cori offers tentatively, as if reading my thoughts.

"That's possible," I reply, but the suggestion doesn't sit right. Calling them out was bold—precisely the sort of move Lucille would eat up with pride. No, it has to be something else.

I feel it—an itch under my skin, a restlessness in my bones. Lucille isn't one for empty threats. Whatever scheme she's concocting, whatever ace she's hiding up her designer sleeves, it's clear she's playing a game whose rules I haven't yet deciphered.

I have to find out what the fucking hell she thinks I did to embarrass her before this blows up in my face.

"Hey, let's not worry about that now," Rufus says, trying to lift the mood. "We've got sweet things to eat and nails to paint. Let's enjoy our slumber party while we still can, girl."

"Right," I force a smile, letting my friends' laughter pull me back from the precipice of my fears. But as I join in, my mind races, trying to piece together the puzzle of Lucille's demands.

What the hell does she know that I don't?

COOL KIDS

AUBREY

THE MORNING LIGHT SEEPS THROUGH THE WINDOWS OF MY LIBRARY and I grunt in irritation. It's Monday—back to the grind after spring break and the world of academia feels particularly burdensome today. I stretch my limbs, each one popping in protest, as I sit at my massive desk and get ready for the day. The digital chime from my phone is insistent, so with a groan that rumbles deep from within my chest—a dragon's growl muted by human form—I reach for the device. I fucking hate this thing as much as I love its usefulness.

Dragons are complicated.

My screen lights up with a flurry of notifications, but two school-wide emails leap out at me. Their subject lines glare like a pair of eyes I'd rather not meet so soon after breakfast. The first proclaims 'an enhanced plagiarism policy', and the second heralds the arrival of 'new tech' to sniff out academic dishonesty. I can almost hear the hackles on my neck raise as I consider why this is happening here and now.

"New tech, my scaly ass. Fitz didn't install shit, so this was implemented without the actual IT deperment," I mutter under my breath as my dragon snorts in derision. He doesn't like this kind of shit anymore than I do because we're creatures of old magic and ancient knowledge. Technology always seems to bristle against our scales. A sense of unease coils in my gut; this initiative isn't just about maintaining integrity in essays and term papers.

There's a whiff of something else in the air—something foul and intended to cause maximum damage.,

My nails tap against the screen of my DiePhone as I fire off a group text to Chess, Rennie, Felix, and Fitz. I don't include our girl yet because right now, I have nothing but suspicion and no evidence. She needs to be able to focus on her classes to finish out this year strong.

> LustyLibrarian: Did you see the emails?

I wait for responses, knowing some of our family don't look at their phones often. Felix, the cool-headed strategist, will be plotting three steps ahead. Rennie will share my concern about the true intent behind these emails. Chess, ever the organizer, will be raring to add these things to our boards so we can get our steps in place. And Fitz... well, Fitz isn't likely to have read the messages due to the disdain he reserves for most of the administration. Once he does, he'll be ready to seperate spines if it affects our mate.

My scales itch beneath my skin, a sure sign that my dragon is agitated. I know I can't *stop* whatever this shit is leading up to, but he reminds me that I can absolutely destroy whomever is involved with very little effort. That's the kind of response I try to avoid, so I sit my DiePhone on the desk, taking a deep breath as I locate one of my squishies. All I need to do is keep my temper from flaring and then we can handle whatever is going to happen.

"Bring it on, assholes. I'm ready," I growl to myself.

MY PHONE FINALLY BUZZES AGAIN AFTER A HALF HOUR OF excruciating waiting. It's odd for the others to take so long, but they must have been in their own classes or absorbed in some scheme.

> CSpot: I don't like this one bit.

> TigerWoody: I had nothing to do with this shit. I need to do a full system scan to figure out what the fuck they installed. There are a lot of bullshit programs out there and some of them are going to give false positives that will impact a lot of students.

> TigerKing: This is definitely a problem.

> EmoBatman: I believe we have discovered why the Aung woman returned to campus.

> LustyLibrarian: I'm going to find bite size. The more I stay here and wait for the shoe to drop, the more anxious my dragon becomes.

> TigerWoody: Tell us when you have Baby Girl, Saucy Skink. I can't focus when I worry about her—and we all know what happens when I get antsy.

Getting up, I head for the back exit of our suite with a sense of urgency that has my heart thundering in my chest. Dolly should be in the Shirdal Arts building for her dance class, so as soon as I clear the doors, I head in that direction. I'm too close to the edge to half-shift and fly, which would be faster, so I speed up my stride.

Yanking the gilded doors open, I stomp into the fancy ass foyer of the building and sneer at the ridiculously overdone bronze of an eagle swooping down to grasp a raccoon. It occurs to me that Rennie's prey friends have to pass this eyesore daily and it makes me want to smash it. But I don't have time today because Dolly's in here somewhere. I look at the directory on the wall, then head down the hallway to the right. She'll be amongst the flurry of dancers and the echo of pointe shoes against hardwood floors, so I poke my head in every single studio door.

She should be here—except she's not.

My gut clenches as I rush back into the atrium, spotting her unmistakable hair and leotard-clad form being escorted none too gently by two shifters dressed in security uniforms. Their smirks are as clear as day, and they exude a smugness that sets my scales to itching beneath my human facade. They have no idea that they're risking their limbs by laying even a single digit on her— much less five—when Fitz finds out about this nonsense.

"Fuck," I mutter under my breath, quickening my pace until I'm almost jogging. Dolly's posture is relaxed, head held high with that trademark defiance that runs in her blood. I whip out my phone, fingers flying over the keys with an unusual precision born of fury and fear. Farley, our girl's honey badger lawyer with the reputation for being as tenacious as his animal namesake, needs to know about this yesterday.

LordDraconis: 911. Dolly's being taken to Headmistress Midori's office by school security. Looks serious and follows two emails about plagiarism and school policy on misconduct that came out of nowhere this a.m. Send your goons immediately.

The message flies through the digital ether, and the response is almost instantaneous.

CornbreadCounselor: Team is leaving now. Will crash the gates myself if I have to; I'm tired of this shit. Keep me posted.

The cryptic anger Dolly's toxic mother expressed on the phone this weekend now makes a sick sort of sense. Whatever this is, it's got the sticky fingerprints of someone powerful all over it and Lucille Drew fits the bill. But then... so do her ex-friends, the Khan cousin, the shitty counselor, the Irish Pred Games bitch, and a host of other enemies who have it out for our girl.

Dolly has too many hostiles gunning for her; we have to pare it down.

I pause long enough to send another rapid-fire text to the guys, wanting to ensure there are cooler heads than mine here as we wait for the badger couriers. My dragon is restless, wanting vengeance on the people who are hurting our mate. The bad part is that right now? I don't want to stop him.

LustyLibrarian: Admin building. ASAP.

This is risky, but I'm teetering on the edge as I storm across the green behind the goons and our girl. Dolly may be calm, but inside, my dragon roars for battle. Fitz alone brings the wrath of a psychotic enforcer trained to kill his enemies without batting a lash and they've taken his mate. I'm not sure what will happen when his royally inclined brother, his other mate, and my romantic gargoyle get involved, but it's likely going to get messy.

Muscles tense, I shove my way through a phalanx of security guards, their attempts to block me as effective as tissue paper against a torrent. The door swings open under the force of my push, almost flying off its hinges—a premonition of things to come. I barge into the administrative sanctum, my dragon nature clawing beneath my skin, demanding retribution, breathing silent threats of fire and destruction.

The office is a tableau of self-satisfied smirks and bureaucratic intimidation. Headmistress Midori, flanked by Asani Khan and Carina Rockland, who can barely contain their glee, turns her reptilian gaze on Dolly. My snack sized mate is perched on a chair in the center of the room, her expression a mask of nonchalance that mocks their authority. They're all circling her like carrion birds confident in their kill, not just Rockland.

"Ms. Drew," Midori Aung begins in a voice as brittle as ice shards, "the allegations against you are severe. This is no laughing matter."

I glance at Dolly, smiling as she channels Lucille's insufferable arrogance, and exudes an eerie calm. The Headmistress turns away from her, looking at me with an arched brow. "And what are *you* doing here, Mr. Draconis? This doesn't involve you or your family, pathetic as they are."

The serpent inside of me roars and I have to bite the inside of my mouth to keep my cool. My family has endured a lot of flack since my… childhood accident, but the Aungs are no saints, either. When I think I can respond without flaming the entire room, I open my mouth, but suddenly, the door flies open behind me.

Felix, Rennie, Fitz, and Chess burst in, ready to stand sentinel beside Dolly. Felix is blocking his twin from leaping into the fray without thinking, and oddly, Chess is doing his best to stand in front of an onyx-skinned, half-shifted gargoyle.

Perhaps I underestimated how unbalanced we might be now that two of us have completed the mating process.

"Headmistress Aung," I cut in, hoping to stem the tide of protective fury from the others, "this student has legal counsel. Continuing this inquisition is a violation of her rights, especially since you have been informed of this on multiple occasions."

Midori dismisses me with a wave, her yellow, snake eyes never leaving Dolly. "This is a school matter, not a legal battle. That is inconsequential."

"Like hell it is," Fitz growls, his voice a dangerous rumble. Felix stands in front of him like a living barricade, holding back his brother with a firm grip on his shoulder. "This is a bullshit con job pulled by those idiots next to you."

The standoff is cut short by an almighty crash as the door, now completely unhinged, topples to the floor. Skelly and Monstro stride in, their intimidating presence commanding immediate attention. They radiate power and unyielding resolve as well fury, and they focus on the anaconda shifter commanding this kangaroo court.

"Enough!" Skelly roars. "You will cease this illegitimate interrogation immediately."

Monstro steps forward, his eyes scanning the room as if marking targets. "We advise you to acquaint yourselves with the concept of due process before we educate you in a more... lasting manner."

"Explain to me in explicit detail," Skelly demands, fixing Midori with a stare that could turn lesser beings to stone, "what precisely are these baseless accusations about?"

Midori watches the two badgers carefully, then moves to her desk. "We recieved a signed statement from both Professor Khan—the one who *isn't* exiled by his entire family—and his student, Amity LaPorte. Both families are of high standing with the Council, so as Headmistress, I sought out evidence of their claims. Once they were confirmed as true, I amended our school policy to address this issue and sent for the guilty party to adjudicate her punishment. You'll find that I've documented that process meticulously. This is all above board."

"Amity's accusations are quite credible," Asani declares, his sneer as sharp as the talons I keep hidden beneath my human facade. "She claims Miss Drew plagiarized what work she shared, then used AI tools to fabricate the rest when Amity refused to complete the entire project on her own. Based on my own observations in class, the work handed in, and the technology acquired by our gracious Headmistress, her story is true."

I can't help but snort, my breaths coming in puffs of smoke as the dragon within me flares its disdain. The very notion of our girl cheating at school reeks of desperation, but it also reeks of a lack of originality. This is a scheme her ex-best friends tried at Apex—unsuccessfully—and we squashed it like a roach *before* Dolly had Farley and his team on retainer. Only two washed up pretenders would re-use a failed plot to ensnare their prey again.

And I'm looking at them right now.

Rockland chimes in, nodding her head with an eagerness that sends her messy topknot bobbing grotesquely. "Absolutely," she crows, "as a best selling author, I can spot AI-generated text a mile away. It's high time we expelled the talentless hacks who resort to such trickery. They make the rest of us brilliant creatives look bad."

Dolly, cool as the marble floors of this very institution, raises an eyebrow and examines Rockland with a critical eye. "One would think," she says dryly, "that someone standing here accusing others of theft wouldn't dare copy the person they are accusing so blatantly. But you've never been smart enough to know when to back off, have you, Carina?"

The room falls silent for a heartbeat as realization dawns on all of us. Rockland's hair, once an unremarkable brunette shade, now sports a colorful array that's a sad caricature of Dolly's signature look. We were all so focused on saving our darling bunny that we didn't even register the full-on makeover the woman must have given herself since the last time any of us saw her.

It's almost too ironic to be believed—that woman trying to mimic the style of our whip smart, fashionable mate while she cries about being plagiarized.

Fitz can't contain himself; his laughter erupts, filling the room like thunder. I join in the mockery, puffing out smoke rings that rise lazily towards the ceiling. Rennie's lips curl into a sneer, Chess stifles his chuckles behind a hand, and Felix, with a predatory focus, skewers Rockland with his gaze.

"Just because you can legally copy a more talented artist doesn't make you appear less pathetic than you do right now," he says, the contempt dripping from each word. "You're a joke and if you didn't have duped cult members trailing along behind you, you would have been kicked to the curb long before now, Rockland."

"Imitation is the sincerest form of flattery that mediocrity can pay to greatness," Dolly says, unfazed by the spectacle around her. She leans back in her chair, still the picture of poise in her ballet leotard and pointe shoes. "I suppose I should be grateful, but instead, I'm nauseated."

Rennie nods in approval. "Well quoted, *ma petite*. Oscar Wilde is always a good choice."

The administrators and professors bristle, their faces mottled with indignation as they attempt to compose themselves, but the damage is done. The absurdity of the situation is laid bare, and our unity is unshakable. Even Farley's bruisers are waiting to see what will happen next.

I lean forward, my voice a low growl as I address the room. "You've all been duped by nothing more than schoolyard whispers and baseless accusations," I say, locking eyes with the Headmistress, who recoils ever so slightly under my scrutiny. "Weak preds," I practically spit out the words, "have conspired to sway your judgment with gossip and innuendo, akin to trolls spewing venom from behind the safety of their screens."

My dragon bristles beneath the surface, irked by the injustice of it all and I fight to calm him before I continue.

"Fitz," I nod towards him, "has compiled a comprehensive digital and paper trail. It unequivocally proves that this paper is Dolly's work. It is original and untainted by any artificial intelligence or theft of ideas. Miss Drew came up with the entire thing and composed it all herself because she had to. As for Amity La Porte? Much like these two grifters, she's done nothing but ride on the coattails of others' efforts for a long time. We have proof of that as well."

Skelly, a hulking shadow of composure, steps up with his own brand of cold confidence. "Our boss is already en route with third-party authentication and techonological experts," he informs them with a razor-sharp grin. "If you even think of taking action against our client without due process, the consequences will be... severe. Farley doesn't play games. He'll sue you into the Stone Age, make no mistake about that."

There's a collective intake of breath, and the tension ratchets up a notch. Out of the corner of my eye, I see Fitz clenching his fists, his hunger for retribution barely restrained. The rest of us share a silent agreement; we're ready for whatever comes next.

"You will let her leave with us and back off," Skelly demands, and they have no choice but to comply.

Dolly rises gracefully, flanked by our motley crew. "Thank you, gentlemen. As for you, Carina? You can shove your bottom of the bargain bin leftovers and your obsession with me straight up your ass. Once I get free of your stalker shit, I promise you... there will be nowhere you can hide and no one who can save you. You can take that to the bank."

I grin as she takes my arm, proud of her for standing up to the abusive woman who is trying to control her. "You realize she'll come for you even harder now, right, little bit?"

Her lips curve up as she winks at me. "Big guy... I'm counting on it. The angrier she is, the more likely she'll make bigger and bigger mistakes. When she does...."

"That's when you have her."

"Yep."

This skirmish may be over, but the war has just begun.

TROUBLEMAKER

DELORES

I SPRAWL ACROSS THE COUCH, LEGS KICKED UP ON THE ARMREST, laptop balanced precariously on my knees. The cursor blinks in a taunting rhythm, daring me to find the words that will clear my name. The living room around me buzzes with a tense energy, the air a mix of determination and pizza—the latter courtesy of Chess' new obsession with creating themed food nights.

As much as I want that cheesy goodness to fix my problems, it can't.

"Focus, Dolly," I mutter to myself, squinting at the screen. "You were prepared for this. All you have to do is put everything together to show that bitch she's wrong."

The data stares back at me, a digital mosaic of my innocence. There it is, displayed in stark contrast: the vocabulary, the syntax, the soul of my writing plastered on the slides I'm cobbling together. My work has always had a particular flair—a certain snark that software can't mimic and Amity sure as hell can't replicate.

Aubrey leans over from his perch on the edge of the coffee table, peering at my laptop with an approving nod. "Nice. Those new plagiarism checker results are gold." He'd outdone himself, wrangling a program so precise it could probably tell you what brand of caffeine fueled any given all-nighter.

It helps to have friendly colleagues at every university in the world, even the human ones.

"Of course they are," I reply, a smirk playing on my lips. It's hard not to feel a rush of vindication. The checker slices through Amity's web of deceit like claws through tissue paper—something I'd love to do to her myself for dragging my name through the mud again. I'm so fucking tired of having to defend myself because these idiots can't just leave me the hell alone.

Fitz plops down beside me, his eyes flickering with the thrill of another successful hack. He spins his own laptop around to face me, revealing a scatter plot of Amity's academic history. Her papers are a flatline compared to the Everest of mine. "This shows the reading level of her work, the complexity of sentence structure, overused words, and every tiny detail that proves the paper my dumbshit cousin received couldn't have been written by that girl."

"Her stuff reads like it was written for grade schoolers," I scoff, pointing at the glaring discrepancy. "We're in college, for fuck's sake. Can't she even fake looking like she understands the topics?"

I'm being an intellectual snob, I know, but this snotty little shit tried to say the paper I worked on for weeks to perfect was hers when she barely contributed anything after the class sessions.

"Her vocabulary is quite elementary, my dear Dolly," Fitz quips with a grin. I roll my eyes but can't suppress a chuckle. Trust Fitz to bring Sherlock into this—he's been obsessed with the ferret-y looking human since we started the series last month. "Maybe even preschool."

"Let's add your comparisons to the slide deck," I suggest, already dragging graphs and charts into the presentation. "Everyone loves a colorful visual aid, you know?"

"Stop it, you two. You're making me want to vomit," Aubrey mutters as he sits with Chess and helps gather more proof to shoot over to us. "Besides, Fitz would *never* be Holmes. Obviously, that would be me with my stony Watson over there. Felix might serve as Mycroft, and perhaps Chester could be one of his Irregulars."

"Does that make me Irene?" I ask, giving him a playful look. "I could handle that. She was a better opponent for Holmes than Moriarty, for sure."

"Then *I* get to be the Crown Prince of Crime!" Fitz yells as he waves his hands. "Kneel before me, humble good guys."

"You are *not* Moriarty," Felix says as he shakes his head. "Not even close. Perhaps Lestrade."

Fitz pouts, slouching as he continues typing. "Not cool, bro. Not cool at all."

This is going to cause a snark fight and we have to focus—time to change the subject, Dolly.

"Who knew being accused of plagiarism would require so much actual work?" I grumble loudly. I'm actually serious, because though there's a fire in my belly, stoked by righteous indignation, I'm pissed that I'm doing even more work to dispute the charges. "It's bullshit."

"If they wanted to take you down, they should've picked some-thing less... provable," Aubrey says with a thoughtful look. "This is recycled content as a scheme, anyway. It didn't work last time."

"Lazy ass unoriginal fuckwads," I say, shaking my head. "That's what they are."

"Guys. Stop bickering." Chess's sudden exclamation is like a shot of adrenaline. I watch him pop up from behind his laptop, a wild excitement in his eyes that tells me he's onto something big. We all pivot toward him, our own work forgotten, as he beckons us closer with a manic wave.

Felix leans in, looking at the cheetah seriously. "What did you find?"

"Something very interesting" Chess says, his voice barely containing the thrill. The screen before him displays the analysis results of a novella Amity turned in for a writing class. "This doesn't match any of her previous stuff; it's not even close."

We all exchange glances, our confusion palpable. Rennie pads over to Chess, leans down, and murmurs something too low for my ears. I'm on pins and needles, watching the cheetah's fingers fly across the keyboard after whatever Ren whispered has sparked an idea.

"What's the big deal?" Fitz asks, unable to hide his growing irritation. "We know she's a liar, so she's probably a cheater, too."

"Ren thinks he knows who wrote this." Chess doesn't look away from the screen, but the corners of his mouth twitch upward. A chime fills the room, signaling a match. He lets out a victorious cackle. "Bingo! It's an exact match with Rockland's writing samples."

Oh. My. Lanta.

The room explodes into chatter, but I can only stare, dumbfounded. They cooked up this whole plagiarism accusation while they were the ones doing it? The irony would be delicious if it wasn't so infuriating.

"That conniving, hypocritical, death chewer," I mutter under my breath. The pieces click together, forming an ugly picture of deceit.

"Get all this proof together," Felix says as he gives Chessie a grim look. "We're calling Farley."

"HE'S SENDING COURIERS," AUBREY ANNOUNCES AFTER A BRIEF conversation, and I can't help but snort at the absurdity. We have a mountain of digital evidence against Amity and Rockland—enough to get them both sent packing—but even my lawyer feels he needs to send the enforcers.

You can't trust a snake, nor a shifter that's for all intents and purposes a garbage removal system with wings.

"Can you believe the sheer audacity?" I grumble. "They accuse me of plagiarism when they struck a deal to submit fraudulent academic work? If it weren't so insidious, I'd think they were using the plot of a bad cop show or something."

"Arrogance makes preds blind, Princess," Felix replies, leaning back with a knowing smirk. "They never think they'll get caught because they're so enraptured with their brilliant self that it's not even a possibility in their minds."

"Speaking of thinking you're too smart to get caught..." Fitz interjects, his face darkening as he recalls a memory. "It's exactly what our douchebag brother, Titus, did. His grand plan to oust Felix was so perfect in his scrambled brain that he thought we'd never find out. Buying into your own PR will get you every time."

"Ah, yes, dear brother Titus," Felix says with a snarl. "He encouraged dear old dad to kick me out over my refusal. He believed it would earn him the throne, but the Raj was never going to give it up. Now look where he stands—not on the throne and quietly awaiting death on our vengeance list."

"I'll help," I chime in with a wicked grin. "I have a few words for that sneaky motherfucker, too."

"Too bad we can't tie any of this to Asani," Felix muses, his disdain evident. "That tiger's got a knack for keeping clean, even when he's knee-deep in the muck, but I guarantee he was part of this plan."

"His time will come for helping your brother," I assure my tiger, though my thoughts are already racing ahead to the next move. "For now, we have to focus on clearing my name and taking down those who dared to challenge us."

"As soon as the badgers arrive, we're marching over to Midori's office to show her how stupid she's been."

I can definitely get behind that shit.

WE MARCH INTO MIDORI AUNG'S OFFICE AS A UNITED FRONT OF indignation and confidence. The gigantic badgers arrived a few minutes before, and together, we all headed straight for this building. It's time to lay our cards on the table, and hope that it gets this woman to back the hell off. My fingers grip the laptop tighter, the weight of my defense secured in its digital confines.

"Headmistress Aung," Skelly announces, his voice carrying the authority of Farley himself. "A member of your own tech department and your librarian have assembled information pertaining to this spurious accusation against our client. We are here to present this documentation in the hopes that you will rescind the charges."

Midori's gaze is as cold as the scales that sheath her body. "Miss Drew remains a stain upon this institution. I am uncertain that your 'proof' will change that," she hisses, her disdain for me venomous and clear.

What in the hell did I do to this chick? I'd never even met her until yesterday!

"I am hardly a stain on this school. You have much bigger concerns than me if you're worried about its sterling reputation," I retort, my lips curling into a smirk.

Goliath steps forward, countering her attack by holding up his tablet. "Records show you've been here for only five days since the semester started, Headmistress. You're hardly qualified to judge her character or contributions."

Monstro looms beside me, his shadow engulfing the office like a dark promise. The glare he's giving Midori could peel paint from walls, but he says nothing, his silent intimidation speaking volumes. I have to suppress a grin; even the headmistress seems to shrink back a fraction.

"Even if that were not the case," Felix says as he gestures to my laptop. "We have a massive amount of evidence that her lawyer can independently verify so it will hold up in court when he files a suit against you, the school, and everyone involved in this defamation. Your house is not clean, Headmistress, and that will certainly come out if this hits a legal proceeding."

"To be crystal clear, this will be in addition to what he's already filed," I add, feeling the smugness rise within me like a triumphant wave. "Carina Rockland has been stalking me since she was assigned to me at Capital Prep and we will absolutely be adding all of this bullshit to that case as well. The plagiarism accusation, defamation, libel, slander, tortious interference, and outright theft she's already perpetrated will not make her a good witness for you."

Renard smirks. "You should probably let *ma petite* out of those useless sessions before the badgers think of something else to add to your docket."

The slimy anaconda shifter doesn't flinch; no, she simply shrugs. "I cannot overturn the previous school's recommendation for counseling. Her mother even signed off on the requirement. It's non-negotiable," she states flatly.

Every. Fucking. Time.

My blood boils, the urge to lash out nearly unbearable, but before I can speak, Aubrey steps in smoothly. "Lucille Drew publicly disowned Dolly," he reminds her, his voice calm but firm. "She has no claim to her as an adult who has been stripped of her spot as heir. Dolly isn't hers to manage anymore."

"Be that as it may, it doesn't negate her ability to demand this of an unmarried child," Midori replies with a dismissive flick of her tongue, "I will inform Lucille of the progress on the plagiarism case once I have reviewed your evidence. For now, Miss Drew will remain at *l'Academie*, pending further investigation."

"Keep in mind," Renard interjects, his tone silky and dangerous, "any form of retaliation following this meeting will reflect directly upon you, Headmistress. Rockland's personal vendetta is becoming quite conspicuous, and if she takes this out on our mate, we will return with less pleasant methods of negotiation."

Her eyes narrow, but she gives nothing away. I'm left standing there, seething silently, my friends' support a small comfort against the ties that bind me. The fight isn't over, but today's battle has been waged with precision.

Fitz takes my arm, jerking his head at the others. I can tell he's ready to tear the bitch to pieces, so I follow him without another word. Once we leave, I slam the door to her office behind me with a force that ripples through the hallway.

"I want to murder them all," I seethe as I look at the crazy tiger next to me.

"I'm in," he replies, shrugging. "What the fuck do I care if it upsets the balance? Baby Girl always gets what she wants, that's my policy."

"No," Felix says with a grimace. "We can't be rash. You both know that."

Aubrey blows a couple smoke rings that drift towards us and I turn to give him a grateful look. "It's hard to let them talk us out of violence, huh, big guy?"

He scoffs as we leave the building, his voice full of derision. "It is hard to accept that such an ignorant pred is in charge of educating our young. Keeping from frying her is almost impossible."

The library looms ahead as we walk, but it feels like another cage today. My gang flanks me, a pack of solidarity in a world where logic and reason have taken a backseat to power plays. I despise these kinds of games and I hate the people forcing me to play them to survive.

"This had better be the end of this shit," I mutter under my breath as we round the building to go to our back entrance. "I have too much work to do before the end of the semester."

"Farley will handle this just like he is the corpse cruncher," Fitz assures me. "He'll figure out how to get you out of those shitty sessions, too."

"Right now, I'd settle for one day—just one—without someone trying to take a chunk out of me," I say, throwing my hands up in exasperation. "It shouldn't be too much to ask."

"Luck doesn't seem to be on our side with that, *cherie*," Rennie snorts, sharing a look with the others that tells me they're all too aware of our uphill battle.

We sink into the worn couches nestled in a secluded corner of the library, the tension easing from our shoulders as we fall into the familiar rhythm of camaraderie.

Peace is a fleeting illusion, unfortunately.

The ping of Chess' phone cuts through the quiet, a harbinger of more chaos. Then another ping, and another, until it's a symphony of electronic chirps. We exchange glances, each one heavy with unspoken dread.

"Shit," Chess mutters, his face a mask of grim resignation as he scans the message. I lean over, catching sight of the words on the screen, and my stomach drops.

"Twenty preds are missing?" I echo, my voice barely above a whisper. "They didn't go home, didn't come back..."

"Looks like the Fae are back," Felix says, his eyes darkening with anger.

"Damn it," I hiss, feeling the weight of the news settle over us like a shroud. "We can't catch a break."

Aubrey shakes his head as he reads the full email, then looks at our family. "Farley will have to deal with Midori. We have bigger fish to fry."

Anger floods my veins again and I stare into the distance, my mind racing as I think about what I'm going to do when I get my hands on these dickwaffles.

It's going to make Fitz's body part collection look sane—that I'm certain of.

THIS IS WAR

Fitz

I crouch low, my muscles coiling beneath my skin—every fiber alive with the thrill of the hunt. Today's prey isn't one that requires my tiger's strength or ferocity; no, I'm hunting with a different set of claws. The click-clack of keys under my fingers is as satisfying as the crunch of bones, especially knowing the chaos it wreaks in the digital world.

I'm about to fuck up some dicklickers' worlds and it's almost as good as an orgasm or killing—almost.

"Got 'em," I mutter, the grin on my face feral as Renard watches over my shoulder. The satisfaction of deleting Asani, Midori, and

Rockland's semester work from the system courses through me like adrenaline. No backups, no traces, just a void where all their efforts used to be. It's a beautiful kind of destruction—silent but devastating.

"*Parfait*," Renard murmurs, his own devious streak lighting up his eyes. "They'll be redoing projects until next Christmas. This is a beautiful kind of chaos, my feline friend."

"They're about to have the fucking days they deserve," I growl, the thought of them upsetting Dolly turning my blood hot with anger. No one, absolutely no one, gets away with harming our mate. If my twin wasn't so level-headed, heads would roll—literally.

I'd love to display a mounted version of that dead body diner with her new rainbow rat's nest above the fireplace in here; the very thought makes my tiger want to preen.

"What's next on the agenda?" Renard asks, rubbing his hands together gleefully as we shift focus. "I am enjoying your spin on my usual mischief. I don't get to have a partner when I make trouble most of the time."

"Security profiles." I chuckle darkly as I upload corrupted bio data, replacing the legitimate pictures and confirmation scans with fake info, then scrambling all of their access codes. "Imagine their fury when they're locked out of everything from email to door locks. They'll flip their lids when they can't get back onto campus after leaving. It's enough to force stupid moves and bad choices."

"Technological poetry, Fitzgerald. I approve."

I grin, winking at the gargoyle. "Now, we move to phase two of our plans. Are you ready for more physical-type shenanigans?"

He nods as I close my laptop and grab my phone. "*Absolument, mon ami.* I am eager to get even with the people who made our mate feel so attacked and betrayed."

Together, we slip out the back door of the library, our steps silent as we head towards the tunnel leading to the staff dorms. No one is around, and when we come out, it's a relief to see the area just as empty. At Cappie and Apex, we all paid a lot more attention to movements of the rest of the professors, but here we are treated with a distinct disdain that means we avoid interacting with most of them. Zhenga and the Captain's crew are the only ones we actually speak with because we know we can trust them.

Here, too much is hidden under a veil of snobbery and French speaking fuckwits.

Renard glances around the village, frowning. "It's weird they allowed us to come here and assigned so little student interaction, *non?*"

I snort, shaking my head. "Not at all. Whether they allowed it because of our girl and the forces conspiring to use her or because of our names, it's been obvious since we arrived that they think we're all mouth-breathers, Ren. You're French and they don't even interact with you, man."

He pauses to consider my words, then sigh. "*Oui.* You nailed it perfectly, Fitzgerald. I have felt their smugness as well, but I thought it was because I have not been back to my homelands for a long time. I was wrong; they're purposefully treating us like unwanted house guests."

"Exactly. Now, are you ready for some real fun?" I ask, my voice low and dangerous. "Because I'm ready to fuck some shit up and ruin people's lives."

"I was born ready," Renard responds, the excitement palpable in his voice. "Chaos is one of my favorite states. Where are Midori's accommodations?"

Pointing down the lane, I grin as we head for the fanciest fucking place in the entire set-up. I can't help but relish the thought of the pandemonium that will ensue once these assholes discover the mess we're about to make. The pranks are juvenile, but effective.

It's not about the acts themselves—it's about sending a message about what we will tolerate and what is off-limits.

"Let's make sure they never forget this lesson," I say, determination lacing my words. Renard nods, his own resolve is as unwavering as mine.

"Nobody messes with our *petite lapin*."

The scent of decadence hits me as we push open the door to the headmistress's quarters. My eyes roam over the gilded edges of furniture, the silk drapery that pools on the floor like liquid gold. Renard whistles low under his breath, a sound that vibrates with both admiration and disgust.

"I wonder how many scholarships for less fortunate preds could be funded by just one of these vases?" he muses, his fingers hovering inches from a porcelain monstrosity.

"Too many," I mutter, my claws itching to shred the opulence to tatters. But we aren't here for destruction—not the physical kind at least. "Time to get to work."

Renard grins, and it's all teeth and no mercy. "After you, Fitz."

I lead the way, slipping through her private sanctuary. Heading for the device I spy on the table, I grin.My fingers dance across her tablet, a few swipes and taps granting us full access to her digital life thanks to the back doors I installed earlier. It'll take her weeks to untangle the web of destruction I'm weaving. Her inboxes will be full of spam and phishing and dating site requests that will make it impossible to do anything. Personal information will be leaked all over the dark web, allowing anyone who wants it to wreak havoc on her finances and image.

The thought is so delicious it makes my cock twitch.

"Remember, subtlety is key. We don't want any of them to be able to point the finger at us or our girl," I remind Renard. We're both cut from similar cloth and vengeance is an art form to us. Mine is usually bloody, but having him along helps keep me focused on non-maiming methods of revenge.

"Of course," he replies, but there's a twinkle in his eye that says otherwise. We reset her alarm to blare at odd hours, invert the controls of her smart home system, and program her coffee maker to spew out only decaf. Even her entertainment systems get scrambled with incorrect playlists full of screaming garbage and porn—which may or may not upset her, but it sure makes me snicker.

Petty? Absolutely. Satisfying? Even more so.

"Done with the basics," I say, a smirk curling my lips. "What else can we do?"

We slip through the corridors to her office. The room has a scholarly clutter to it, books piled high and papers strewn about. It feels fake, though, especially since we know she spends very little time on campus. This room is for show, but I bet we can still create damage from it.

"We make it look like a poltergeist hit her," Renard suggests, already at work dislodging pages from their bindings. "Even if she doesn't use this room, fixing it to look used will take time and effort."

"An absolute nightmare of mess coming up," I say, setting up a loop of error messages on her computer that will mock her relentlessly. I can almost hear her frustrated groans, the sweet music of retribution filling my ears. Any calls to tech support will go unanswered by me, and the other IT people she has working here won't ever be able to undo my genius coding.

"Calendars are cleared, deadlines... adjusted," Renard reports, a laugh hidden within the words as he works on the laptop on the other side of the desk.

How that woman is supposed to be working with none of her devices on her person is beyond me—but we know she's not actually running anything in this damn place.

"Good." I feel the thrill of the hunt, the predator within savoring the distress we sow.

"Time for Asani's place," Renard declares once we've finished, his silhouette a dark specter against the backdrop of Midori's disrupted academia.

"My dear cousin won't know what hit him." I say as we leave the ostentatious dwelling.

Ren and I walk down the lane again, keeping our posture casual as we head for the building I know contains my trecherous relative's bachleor pad. Felix and I have been there before, but this time, the intent is less about finding clues than fucking up his universe thoroughly enough to make him want to leave this place.

I don't waste any time when we get to his door. The lock clicks quickly, a sound sweeter than a siren's song. Asani's door swings open, revealing the gross jungle swinger motif that makes me want to barf yet again. It's a stark contrast to Midori's over-the-top opulence, but Asani's shit is easily as expensive, it's just selected to look like a slimy 70s lair instead of a fancy hotel. Renard wrinkles his nose in disgust as we slip in, making me muffle a laugh.

"Computer systems first," I mutter as we head inside. Once I find a laptop, I look for a place to sit that doesn't make me worry about catching something. After I'm settled, my fingers dance across the keyboard with vicious intent. I implant a virus that will cascade through his files, corrupting data beyond recovery. His plans, his work, everything he has on here—it all evaporates into digital oblivion.

Fitz-1, Slimy Chucklefuck Cousin-0.

"Isn't this a bit... excessive?" Renard hesitates, watching as the screen flickers erratically. "You seem to be doing more to his system than Midori's, *mon ami.* I'm not certain, of course, because this is your area of expertise..."

"Excessive?" I scoff, my voice low and dangerous. "This is the tiger whose lies nearly buried Felix six feet under." My twin spent half a decade alone, drowning in whiskey and guilt because of Asani's deceit on Bloodstone. "He deserves worse—and he will get it eventually, but for now, this gives me the satisfaction of ruining every bit of his life that I can like he did my twin."

Renard nods, the uncertainty wiped from his face by the reminder. "Good point. Ensure that he's too entangled in his own mess to ever think of crossing us again, and get the revenge you crave, Fitzgerald. I understand completely."

When I'm done with the laptop, I put it back and rub my hands together. "On to more trouble for the dickface."

Together we lay traps both cunning and cruel—ink cartridges filled with permanent dye, shoes lined with substances that'll make every step a sticky nightmare, food containers altered to allow them to go bad without being noticed. We sabotage every semblance of normalcy, ensuring his day-to-day becomes a labyrinth of frustration. Some of the tricks might be overkill and slightly dangerous, but I don't give a hairy rat's ass. If Asani gets sick or injured? More's the better as payment for his sins.

It's not enough, but it will do for now.

"Rockland's next," I say, a dark anticipation coiling within me.

We've saved the best—or rather, the worst—for last. After locking up Asani's lair, we slip down the hallway and out of that building. I know where the nasty corpse sucking bitch's place is as well, so the path we take is quick and efficient.

The air shifts as we approach her door, charged with the promise of retribution. Rockland, whose venom has seeped deep into Dolly's psyche, needs a taste of her own medicine. I won't be content with mere inconvenience; I crave to see her undone.

"Remember how she treats Chessie and how close she comes to breaking what's ours. Every week, she tries to do what those bitches and her mother failed to do," I remind Renard, my voice barely above a growl. We're not just avenging Dolly now; we're protecting the future prey from Rockland's twisted games.

"We will wreck her world," Renard agrees, fury mirrored in his eyes. "I do not want to see *ma petite* come back from another one of those sessions looking so angry and upset."

We enter, and immediately set about turning her sanctuary into a trap-laden hell. I rig her personal devices to malfunction at critical moments, weave tripwires that blend seamlessly with her extravagant carpets, and tamper with her beauty products, mixing in compounds that will leave her skin itching for days. Ren works on spoiling food, staining things, and making sure her appliances are set to fail or break with use.

Like Asani, this isn't enough for me, but it will sate my cat for a small time.

"She needs to feel a fraction of the pain she inflicted," I whisper, satisfaction curling in my chest like a contented beast. I sit at her desk, hacking into her desktop computer with a dark grin. Sending as many of her files as I can to my own servers for examination, I chuckle, then get to work on finanaces, identity documents, and putting her life up for sale on the dark web. Once that's done, I move to destroying any connections she might have by sending malicious malware to them from her.

"Done," Renard says, a finality in his tone as he comes in from the other rooms..

I nod, taking a few more minutes to set Rockland up for as many horrible online experiences as I can before I push back from her equipment. "Okay."

Stepping out into the daylight, I look around carefully. The chill in the air seems to dance mockingly on my skin, pairing with the satisfaction that twines through my veins after our little caper. We move with stealth as we retreat from Rockland's quarters, a minefield of carefully orchestrated chaos left in our wake.

"Think she'll ever suspect it was us?" Renard muses, his voice low and laced with mischief. His eyes are bright with the thrill of our covert operation. I doubt he's going to get over doing this for quite a bit; in fact, he'll probably want to get a hit of the excitement again later.

I can live with that.

Shaking my head, I smirk. "Not a chance. We were careful to be ghosts—unseen but felt."

As we leave the tunnel, the main campus is quiet, a stark contrast to the tempest we've just unleashed behind closed doors. Our footsteps are muffled by the grass as we make our way back to the library. The air feels charged with the energy of our deeds, a silent acknowledgment of the balance we've tipped in Dolly's favor.

"Today, we struck back and that feels good," I state, my tone resolute. Renard nods, the grim satisfaction evident on his face.

"We did it without spilling a drop of blood," he adds. "Which means we've followed Felix and Dolly's requests not to make things worse before we know who is pulling all the strings. They wouldn't have thought we'd get this creative, Fitzgerald, but we did it."

"Desperation breeds innovation," I reply, feeling the weight of our actions settle comfortably within me. "For Dolly, I happily rewrote my usual rules of engagement."

Renard claps me on the shoulder, a silent signal of a job well done. "Me, too, *mon ami.* I feel a modicum less rage at her treatment now that we have served them some well earned punishment."

Hopefully, it will hold our beasts in check until we can mete out the real *justice in the future.*

I Did Something Bad

DELORES

I push the office door open, leaving the cursed place with a spring in my step that wasn't there when I walked in. Rockland's absence is like an unexpected holiday, a reprieve from whatever abusive nonsense she had planned for our meeting. My phone vibrates as I stride through the hallway, light pouring in from tall windows.

Today might actually be a good day—it's a fucking miracle.

> BabyGirl: Rockland was a no-show. Think your stuff cowed her, Fitzy?

Though I didn't ask them to, my crazy tiger and my mischievous gargoyle went on a rampage of vengeful shenanigans last week. They were eager for revenge on the staff members who have been shitty to me since we returned from break to face the false accusations. Clearly, Midori and the other assholes spread shit around with the professors as Amity has with the students, and it's made me a veritable pariah. I don't much care about the students glaring and avoiding me—I'm used to that shit. The teachers aren't new, either, but that comes with its own set of challenges. I have to be cautious of everything I do and say in their presence to keep people from adding to my administrative misery.

> TigerWoody: Then our master plan worked, Baby Girl. The moping mythical and I managed to push those fuckers into a corner.

> EmoBatman: C'est vrai, Fitzgerald, except we do not know what will come to pass once they regroup.

> LustyLibrarian: Something that should have been considered BEFORE you did that shit.

> BabyGirl: They meant well, big guy. And if it gets them to back off so I can finish these damn big projects before the end of April, I'll deal with it. I have so much to do to be ready for the final presentations. I don't need the extra stress of people dogging me.

> TigerKing: She's got a point, dragon. If we can keep the adults from fucking with her, she can handle the dumbass kids.

> BabyGirl: Fuck, yeah, I can.

> TigerWoody: That's my mate. Use their spines for a toothpick. It's hot AF, Baby Girl.

Smiling at his enthusiasm for murder, I pocket my phone and quicken my pace toward the Shirdal building, the hub of creativity where my studio nestles among others. Forty-five minutes of undisturbed work awaits me—a precious slice of time before the grueling voice class begins.

The air shifts around me as I dodge clusters of students, my senses heightened—not just by my bunny instincts but also by the whispers that flutter through the halls like insidious moths. Asani, Rockland, Midori—they've been weaving their web of words, and it's sticking to the walls, to the minds of the Council-friendly staff. The thought sends a ripple of anger down my spine, but I press it down, focusing on the projects that need my attention.

"Voice teacher's got claws out this week," I remind myself, rolling my eyes at the prospect of facing the music, quite literally. Not that I can't handle it—I'm Delores Fucking Drew, after all—but when your passion becomes a battlefield, even the strongest warriors feel the strain.

I bound up the steps two at a time, my heart thumping in sync with each jump. Creativity pulses through my veins, pushing out those pesky rumors, filling the void with vibrant colors and bold strokes of imagination. That's where I'll find my sanctuary—the notes that will soar from my throat—no matter how harsh the teacher or how tangled the lies.

THE MOMENT MY HAND TOUCHES THE COLD METAL OF THE STUDIO door, a shiver skitters up my spine — not from chill, but intuition. *Something's off.* The door doesn't greet me with its usual silent compliance; it whines, just barely, a sound as subtle as a whisper but loud enough for a bunny shifter's sharp ears. I push it open and peek inside. Shadows cling to my space, unfamiliar, wrong.

I don't like this one fucking bit.

"Someone's been here," I mutter under my breath, fishing my phone out of my pocket with nimble fingers. My thumbs dance over the screen, firing off a text to Fitz.

> BabyGirl: Studio door's weird. I think someone broke in.

His response flashes up almost immediately, the ping slicing through the quiet.

> TigerWoody: Leave now. Go to voice where there will be people around. I'll run diagnostics on all security measures and cams, then send Ren's tiny friends along to gather shit for me. Someone's going to regret violating your domain, Baby Girl. I promise.

"Always so protective," I whisper, though a thread of warmth weaves through me at his concern. Fitz's text bubbles keep coming, a rapid-fire of frustration and worry. He hates that I'm alone after Rockland's no-show—there's no one here to see if someone might be lurking in the shadows.

> BabyGirl: I'm fine, Fitzy. You can watch me through the cameras as I head there if it makes you feel better.

> TigerWoody: It's cute that you think I need permission.

> BabyGirl: It's cute you think I don't assume you're always watching anyways.

My smirk deepens as we banter and I head for the elevator to go down to the vocal student level. I actually think I'll be fine, but I love that he worries so much. Lucille barely cared if I was alive most of my youth unless I was useful as a prop. My men are invested in keeping me safe, happy, and secure, but not so much that I don't get to spread my wings—so to speak.

Unfortunately, my momentary joy is short-lived when the elevator doors open and I hear an ear-grating shriek.

"Oh, look, it's the *thief.*" The snarl comes from Felicia O' Leary, my Pred Games harasser. Her voice is as grating as gravel underfoot, especially at this pitch. I turn and face the wolf shifter head-on. She stands with an overly smug posture, all arrogance and sharp teeth as she spews lies obviously seeded by Asani's venomous tongue.

"You're full of shit, O'Leary," I snap, moving closer until we're inches apart. Our eyes lock, two predators in a standoff that has nothing to do with claws or fangs. "Whoever fed you that story is setting you up to get your flea bitten fur skinned off for a mop."

"That won't matter when it hits Prednet," she retorts, her smirk as cutting as a blade. "You'll be out on your ass, or better yet, vanished."

"Try spreading that trash, and my lawyer will have your package expressed delivered. And not just yours." My words are icy, aimed at making her wonder just what my gangster lawyer can do. "Your whole family will wish they'd never heard your name when my guys unleash on them. Remember: Fitzy already took off your alpha's head and pissed down the neck hole in public. We weren't even sleeping together then. Now? Oh, dear, I simply can't imagine how much fun he'll have hunting them all down."

She huffs, a mix of defiance and disbelief, hair flipping like a scorned queen. But before she can throw another barb, Professor Alexandre's voice cuts through the tension. "Dolly, let's begin."

"Oh, darn. Time for me to go. *Bye, Felicia,*" I say with a smug grin. With a final glare that promises retribution, I pivot away from her, striding past Alexandré into the sanctuary of music, leaving the growls and threats behind.

I STRIDE INTO THE VOICE LESSON, MY ANGER FROM FELICIA'S confrontation smoldering like hot coals within me. Professor Alexandre gives me a sharp nod, and I force my focus onto the scales and arpeggios, my voice rising and falling with controlled precision. Each note serves as an outlet, channeling my frustration into the melody.

My focus cannot be split by all the bullshit; I started the semester behind as it is.

"Sharper on the high E, Dolly," Alexandre critiques snootily. Her gaze is sharp normally, but today, it's like a knife blade.

"Understood," I reply, adjusting my posture and taking a deep breath. The piano keys dance under Alexandre's fingers, and I match them with a renewed fierceness. My voice soars, powerful and clear. For those moments, I'm not just a bunny shifter; I am the music.

The harsh demands to push my voice and my talent continue as the lesson goes on, and I know for sure that she's been inducted into this cult of bullshit the faux Khan, the recently dyed Rockland, and the headmistress have concocted. Alexandre hasn't always been nice, but she's seemed mostly fair, and that wasn't the case for this lesson. She behaved like she wanted to injure me, and that's new.

I exit the room with my resolve hardened. "Fitz will tear them apart for this," I mutter to myself, already composing the message in my head to sic my guardian on Felicia and the brainwashed voice professor. The injustice of the accusation fuels my steps, each one a silent vow of retribution.

How the hell is it that the adults in these damn schools behave worse than the damned kids? It's fucking embarrassing , honestly.

The corridors stretch before me, leading to the dance studio. Dread coils in my stomach, the whispers of my peers scratching at my ears even when they're silent. If word has spread to Fabreaux, my ballet instructor, then my reputation might as well be toe-shoes strung up to dry—an exhibit of shame rather than talent.

"Shut the fuck up before I make you shut it," I hiss under my breath, not caring if anyone hears.

It's not just about clearing my name now; it's war against the conformist pred mentality. The very thought makes me want to scream or kick—anything to vent this building fury. As I approach the dance studio, my pulse quickens. Every step is heavy with the weight of what I'm about to face. A predator among predators, all too eager to pounce on the wounded.

Delores Diamond Drew doesn't cower—not anymore—so I straighten my spine and walk in with my Lucille-esque 'get fucked' face on.

"Bring it on," I whisper, my fists clenching at my sides.

I'll handle Fabreaux, the gossips, the Council—anyone who dares stand in my way.

This bunny no longer runs away from a fight—she starts them.

THE MOMENT I CROSS THE THRESHOLD INTO THE BALLET STUDIO, Fabreaux's eyes lock onto mine, and her expression is a frigid overture of disdain. It's the same look the alpha predator gives when a lesser animal has stepped out of line—an unspoken warning that I'm on thin ice. No words needed; her tight-lipped frown and the slight narrowing of her eyes broadcast the rumors that have found fertile ground in her ears.

"Great," I mutter, feeling my own expression harden in response.

She can get fucked by a giant spiky troll club, too.

I pivot sharply on my heel, stalking toward the locker room with my spine rigid and chin definitely raised. My fingers tremble with barely contained rage, but I shove them into my bag to fish out my leotard and tights. The metal locker door slams shut louder than I intend, echoing off the walls like a challenge.

"Calm down, Dolly," I order myself, though the clatter of my pointe shoes hitting the wooden bench betrays my frustration. The soft thud is unsatisfying, nothing like the impact I wish I could make on those spreading lies. I yank the tights up my legs, each movement brusque and efficient. There's no room for error, not now. The leotard follows, hugging my skin tightly and serving as a reminder that I'm about to enter a battlefield.

Looking at my reflection in the locker mirror, I take a deep breath and sigh. "You have to focus and not let them see you sweat,"

This class isn't just about pliés and pirouettes anymore; it's about proving that I won't be broken by petty gossip or intimidation. As I tie my hair back with a snap of elastic, there's a grim set to my mouth. Once done, I push through the locker room door with a resolve as unyielding as my pointe shoes' shanks. Today, every step will be an act of defiance, every leap a testament to my tenacity.

These people think they can test my limits? They haven't seen anything yet.

STRESSED OUT

RENARD

I PERCH ON THE COLD STONE OF MY SOLITARY TOWER, SPECIALLY formulated ink on a quill scratching across a parchment. The message is crucial, vital information about the Fae's movements in the predator world, but cloaked in vagueness that seems almost casual. I can't risk any directness; our enemies are many and ever-watchful.

This is something I will never be prepared to do—and I thought I never would have to.

The ink smudges slightly as I press too hard, a physical manifestation of the inner turmoil that never quite abates. I'm aching inside, snide thoughts plaguing me with memories of betrayal and loss, guilt gnawing at my insides like a persistent worm. And yet, there's something else—a scent that tugs at the edges of my consciousness, elusive and haunting.

It's a whiff caught on the wind, a trace so familiar it sends shivers down my spine. Since arriving in Apex, that fragrance has teased me, a ghostly presence that should be impossible. It speaks of home, of the days before my exile, heavy with implications that could unravel the fragile peace of my present.

I know that scent, intimately tied to my past, my mistakes, the reason I was cast out. But it's been gone for ages, eradicated from my life until now. My nostrils flare as I try to capture it once more, but it's just a phantom, leaving me doubting my own senses.

Greetings, Laveaux Clutch.

Cela fait très longtemps, non?

As difficult as it is to receive this letter, you must know that it is even more so for me to write to you.

When I was sent away, I spent many centuries resenting your decision. I did not understand why you chose to honor some ridiculous prophecy over keeping the heir to the throne—your eldest child—in your life. However, I now see what motivated you to follow the words of the seers. They foresaw a future where such a union would be outlawed, and it would endanger the entire clutch, possibly to the point of being hunted. Acceptance may well have caused the corrupt shifters on Councils and the nebulous 'Society' to have our entire species wiped out once they found out the true provenance of our people.

You faced a real life trolley problem, and made your decision accordingly.

I understand that weight now, as I have finally found a family to replace the one I was born into. Unlike you, I would choose them over the fate of the species or even the world, so I am forced to initiate contact when I would have preferred to leave the past interr'd with the bones, as the Bard said.

La vie n'est rien si elle n'est pleine d'ironie et de douleur, n'est-ce pas?

Since time is of the essence, I will get to the point rather than continue to focus on the past. I have already spent far too many years allowing your choice to haunt me— both for self-loathing and grief purposes. The latter is why I finally gave in, by the way. My brooding grief kept me from enjoying my first connection as much as I should have for so many years—and a mate is something that should have been centuries of celebration, yet it wasn't. At least, not to the fullest capacity possible, which I blame your actions for.

I hold responsibility as well, but I am working through that in a much healthier way than before.

You are likely wondering what this missive has to do with, other than getting my written closure on my exile. The chickens have come to roost on the topic of magic and the Fae, unfortunately. Your decision is for naught, I believe, because they have resurfaced and they are even angrier than they were at our sentencing. The research my family is in the midst of actually suggests that the people the Councils and their ilk believed they suppressed into near extinction have only been hiding—biding their time until they see openings for rebellion.

Past tries have been unsuccessful, and I am not certain why. However, there is a variable I cannot confirm at this time, and I wonder if it is perhaps the reason why they are now openly attacking the root of their exile. Those responsible for sealing the gates to the Veil and hunting down stragglers may be at their most vulnerable now, and if you are secluded enough that you have not heard about the kidnappings and attacks, you need to be aware now. Your ties to the past before the treaties makes you especially vulnerable because of origins.

You are not safe, even if you believe yourselves to be such based on my exile.

Please understand that I am not using this crisis in the supernatural world to rub in the fallacy of that choice.

C'est comme ça, non?

However, the Fates have brought me to our former home, Paris, and I am closer than I have been in many centuries. I seek permission to bring my new family to your home in the mountains where we can discuss this new threat to both of our clutches, and perhaps understand how to defeat the forces determined to destroy the world as we know it. The verbal archives kept by our people will be the most accurate information on the Fair Folk and the other magical beings in existence—except for, perhaps, those kept by other mythical species out of the current leadership's reach.

I trust our account far more than that other species, of course. Our biases are known, whereas those of the other supes' are not. My mates and the rest of my family will help me sort through the massive amount of information, which is why I am bringing them rather than face my shame on my own. They have varied talents and we support one another much in the way I believed our clutch did before my exile.

You will likely push back on my request to bring non-gargoyles into the clutch territory and I understand why. Allowing that prior to my being cast out is what got us into this very position, but I humbly request that you set aside that prejudice in order to prevent this mainstream shifter problem from becoming an issue for all gargoyles and indeed, the entirety of reclusive mythicals such as ourselves.

The time for hiding has ended Your Highnesses.
There is no place anyone will be safe if this war of magicals versus shifters escalates and I am not certain that the shifter side isn't purposefully allowing it to do so. I haven't shared all of these fears with my family yet because I have to relate the cause of my exile to my mates. Until now, it has been too painful to do so, but before we journey to your lands—hopefully in the summer—I must come clean. Then I will share it with the rest of our clutch so we are all aware of the pitfalls of visiting your lands.

I do not wish to cause more fractures or rehash what cannot be changed while we are visiting. My sole focus is information that will protect my mates and family, then possibly the rest of the world.

If it's not possible to do both, my choice will not resemble yours in the slightest—that much is crystal clear in my mind.

Please send a response post haste upon receipt so that I may begin the process of planning.

With great hope,
Renard Laveaux
Former Heir to the Throne of the Laveaux Clutch

Finishing [1] the letter with a final, decisive stroke, I fold it carefully, sealing it with wax that bears no mark. The message needs to reach the old country undetected, and for this task, I trust ancient methods over modern ones. I rise, stretching wings that have been idle too long, and move to the edge of the parapets.

Below, the campus sprawls indifferently, unaware of the secrets that flutter above their heads. I call upon the service only we gargoyles possess, a network of couriers older than some civilizations, bred for loyalty and discretion. I didn't bring any of my family into this secret meeting because this service would not show if anyone other than a gargoyle was present. Our network is secure only when it is not compromised and I cannot break that vow—not when I am asking for a favor.

A shadow detaches itself from the darkness below, a figure trained from birth for this very purpose. With a respectful nod, it extends an arm, waiting for the missive that could change the tide in a secret war.

"Take it," I command softly, "to the mountains belonging to the Laveaux clutch."

It nods. "It will be so."

My voice is a low rumble that stirs the night air. "It carries more than just ink. You hold the difference between disaster and aversion, courier. Do not fail."

The courier disappears as silently as it arrived, swallowed by the night. Alone once more, I retreat into the shadows of my tower, the echo of that elusive scent still lingering in my mind, a question unanswered and full of foreboding.

As I watch it disappear, a pang of sadness strikes me, not as debilitating as it once was, but significant nonetheless. Dolly's warmth flickers in my heart, a reminder that I am no longer a creature of solitude.

"And soon," I murmur into the wind, "it will be time to unfold my past to Dolly and Aubrey."

I imagine their faces, etched with concern and love, ready to shoulder some of the weight I've carried alone for too long. The thought steadies me, a resolve forming like stone within. Yes, it's time to let them in, to share the weight of memories that have for too long shaped my solitary vigil upon this tower.

Brooding in solitude has done me no favors, and now it's dangerous, yet I struggle to give voice to my trauma.

My mind drifts to the magical orchid I've kept in its case for centuries, revering it as one of the few memories I have of the time of carefree youth. It both comforted and mocked me in turn with its beauty and delicacy—much like the woman who created it as a present for my hatch day so long ago. She was much like the orchid, both ephemeral and fragile, but almost worshipful to gaze upon. Her wit, her charm, and her effortless light made my heart flutter with joy even when it wanted to give into the common teenage ailment of sullen moping.

She was part of my life from the moment I hatched and as the years went on, we got closer and closer—two children of powerful royals with very rigid expectations that we shed together. I barely noticed the differences between us as we aged because our bond was that of childhood friends. When it became more than that as teens, we were careful to keep our attachment secret—both because we enjoyed fooling our parents, but also because our families were so controlling. I don't know that either of us even realized how forbidden it was, nor what kind of problems would arise when it became public.

We simply enjoyed the intrigue, as most young adults do.

I sigh, running my hand through my hair as I look up at the stars in supplication. The scent I have tracked several times should not exist, and if it does... I do not know what that means. Is there perhaps a relative I was not aware of? Could there be someone avenging her cause? Why would that unite such disparate magic users in a rebellion? Is it a private vengeance underneath the veneer of a public revolution?

The questions are far too many for me to effectively contemplate until I see the gargoyles who should hold answers. They alone know what they did and how, and that will tell me which line of inquiry to pursue in regards to her.

If it is anything but the truth I've mourned for longer than most human civilizations have existed, I do not know what I will do to those who deceived me.

Whatever It Takes

Delores

My fingers clench into fists at my sides as I storm out of the classroom, the echo of snickers still a fresh sting in my ears. The heat of anger simmers beneath my skin, a fierce bunny shifter's energy barely contained. Asani, that obnoxious son of a bitch, has been on a tear since the Midori meltdown, and today he sharpened his claws on me.

How I longed to give him a good fucking zap—if I could have convinced my magic to strike out, that is.

In the hallway, my chest heaves with rapid breaths, but I force myself to pause. My heartbeat thumps in my ears, a reminder of my need for control. The early 1900s history segment of history is what I studied this weekend, so I know it like the back of my hand. Yet, Asani spewed his 'devil's advocate' nonsense, deliberately knocking down my answers to his questions. The gaslighting was expert level, especially because he got the support of the other students. Heather E. and Amity, those eagles circling for scraps of favor, squawked their support immediately. That meant I was constantly on the defensive, alone on my island of accurate information as the rest of the fools pretended I was wrong.

"Pathetic," I mutter under my breath, recalling how their smug faces looked so convinced of their own brilliance. I could've shredded their arguments to confetti, but what's the point? It's like arguing with rocks—though given their intellect, I'd probably have a more stimulating conversation with the damn rocks.

Instead of fighting back, I let them bask in their false superiority, holding onto my silence like armor. The screen of my phone catches the fluorescent light in the hall as I unlock it, peeking at the audio file labeled 'Asani's Antics.' A sly smile plays on my lips; every condescending word, each snide interruption is now evidence. Farley told me that he loves to bury his adversaries in paper trails and official complaints. This recording will be the bait that brings the dumbasses to the watering hole.

Vengeance will be mine, even if it's through a thousand tiny paper cuts.

"Let them laugh," I whisper to myself, tucking the phone back into my bag, "They have no idea what my friends and I are capable of." Discretion isn't just about keeping quiet; it's strategic. It's waiting for the perfect moment to pounce.

When Farley presents this new case, it'll be a glorious distraction. Asani won't see it coming, nor will Midori. The thought alone is enough to cool the embers of my rage. With a deep, steadying breath, I lift my chin and stride towards my modern dance class with a renewed vigor.

Wars aren't won only on the major battlefields—no, they are carefully planned and executed on every front until your enemy drowns.

THE MIRRORED WALLS OF THE DANCE STUDIO REFLECT A HUNDRED versions of my determination, each one more stubborn than the last. I slip into the room, muscles still taut with the remnants of anger from Asani's class. My gaze finds Antonovich at the front, her dark eyes already judging me. I know better than to hope for leniency; the Council's whispers have infected every sympathetic professor in this place.

Hell, Apex and Cappie were easier to navigate than this hellhole.

I stake out my corner, a small territory where I can move and stretch away from prying eyes. The thud of my bare feet against the sprung floor grounds me as I begin the warm-up routine. Each extension, each flex is a silent act of defiance. They may judge, they may scorn, but they cannot touch the fire within me.

As I lose myself in the fluid movements, my mind drifts to the stoic gargoyle with secrets heavy as stone. The memory of his voice last night, firm yet vulnerable, echoes through the vast chambers of my thoughts. "I've written to them," he said, his confession sending ripples across the still waters of our family dynamic.

Surprise flitted across Aubrey's face—a rare crack in his usually composed facade. He's always steady and strong, but even he couldn't hide the shock of Rennie breaking centuries of silence. We knew it was a monumental step for him, pulling threads from the tightly woven tapestry of his past. He's been avoiding it since it was first mentioned, and now, he's finally forced himself to reach out.

It's a testament to how much the poetic mythical loves me and I won't forget it.

"Once they reply, I'll tell you everything," Rennie vowed, and skepticism danced in Felix's eyes while Fitz simply furrowed his brow in contemplation. It's not like him to invite others into the shadows that lingered behind his stoic exterior. But this time, he came to us, and that had to count for something.

Chess, ever the peacemaker, placed a gentle hand on Rennie's shoulder. "We all have ghosts that haunt us, even me," he'd murmured. "Maybe it's time I talked about my parents' death as well. Felix and Fitz know, but I haven't told the whole story to the rest of you."

Aubrey grumbled under his breath about the impracticality of collective gloom, but I nudged him with an elbow in a silent reminder that burdens shared are burdens halved. "We don't have to carry it all alone," I'd whispered. "That includes you, big guy."

"Even dragons need to lighten their hoard of secrets," Felix chimed in, his tone light but his words laden with truth.

Once Rennie hears back from his clutch, I have a feeling that we'll all be having a drink as we muddle through our traumas together.

What that means for me, I'm not sure. I've let them in for much of my sorrow from the Heathers and Todd, but my life with Lucille and Bruno was filled with normalized bullshit. I'm not sure what is normal and what isn't, so I don't know what I should tell them. I thought learning to dispose of bodies was an everyday pred thing, but they all seemed surprised when I shared that experience.

As the music swells around me and I leap, spin, and twist to its rhythm, I cling to the promise of release, not just for Rennie or Aubrey, but for all of us entangled in the web of unsaid words and unshed tears. Our stories might be heavy, but together, we are strong enough to bear them.

That is, if I can figure out which of my stories are the kind I should share and which truly aren't remarkable.

SWEAT CLINGS TO MY SKIN LIKE A SECOND, DAMP LAYER AS I SHAKE out my limbs, the final pose of the dance routine dissolving into the charged air of the studio. I've pushed through another class where grace was overshadowed by the heavy glares of biased scrutiny, and now, with each thudding heartbeat, I am ready to vault back into the comforting chaos of my pack.

"Perhaps next time you'll be able to make it through the routine without mistakes, Miss Drew," Antonovich says, her stern voice full of pettiness. "Though I sincerely doubt it. Your body was not made for dance and people have misled you about your level of talent at your previous schools."

I don't respond as I breeze by the shitty wolf, ignoring the unhelpful criticism. Antonovich has more issues with me than simply being a Council toadie, and I refuse to engage with her. With my head high and my shoulders squared, I move to my corner and get my things packed.

Fuck her and the flea-bitten canine dick she rode in on.

The hallway is a welcome reprieve from the mirrored walls and watchful eyes, and I pace towards the door that leads to freedom, to lunch, and to my men—my anchors in this relentless storm. I'm practically salivating for the atomopshere of acceptance among my family when the small raccoon shifter appears, huffing and puffing as she runs towards me on tiny legs.

"Dolly, I'm expecting some interesting intel tonight," Raina breathes out, her raccoon eyes gleaming with a mix of mischief and urgency. She was clearly waiting for me, and her excitement is like a cold shower on my fiery internal rage.

This could be the key to unlocking the cult's documents—or, I'm hoping it is.

"From the prey scholars you know?" I ask, mind already racing, sensing the importance behind her cryptic words. "I thought they were already talking with Aubrey. Why is this coming to you specifically?"

"Some prey—especially elders of more reclusive species—refuse to have any contact with predators. The bloody history is too much for them to bear." Her eyes are sad, but her tail twitches, echoing her anticipation. "Information from these kinds of sources could be game-changing. If we are able to find value in it, we may be able to convince them to contact even more secretive groups like mythical prey types."

Mythical preds are secretive; mythical prey are downright invisible, even I know that.

"Damn. That would tickle Aubrey pink," I exhale slowly.

There isn't time to waste on wondering or worrying about that until we see what Raina is sent this evening. Befriending the elder prey and their hidden ancient groups might give us an edge we've been scrabbling for since the start of term. No one in the Council would ever be able to get information from those groups, nor would they have tried. But the Fae might have convinced them to help them hide their refugees or assist with their plans based on a common enemy.

"I'm going to go tell whoever is home at the library," I say, and just like that, we're off, darting past students and faculty alike, a blur of movement and determination. Raina keeps pace easily, her smaller form nimbly weaving through the throng. Something in my gut is resonating with this development and I want to make sure they're all ready when the crew brings over whatever Raina has coming to her tonight.

The library looms ahead, and I speed up. Bursting through the doors, I scan for any sign of my guys, my breaths coming in sharp bursts matching the rapid tattoo of my heart against my ribs.

My gut is screaming like it knows something my brain doesn't and I have to tell them.

"Chessie!" I call out, spotting Chess at a table in the far corner, books stacked around him like miniature fortresses. His head snaps up, a question in his eyes as he looks me over to make sure

I'm okay. I grin, hurrying over to the cheetah to drop a kiss on his forehead before I make my announcement. "We might have something big coming."

"Like what, Angel?" he asks as he takes my hand and looks up at me curiously.

"I don't know exactly," I admit. "Raina came to find me after dance; she's got some big deal prey scholar sending her something this evening. But something inside of me feels like this is important. The minute she spoke about how it might lead to us contact with mythical prey, it felt like there was a live wire inside of me."

"I don't know much about mythical prey species," Chessie says with a frown. "Ren and Aubrey would be more familiar, I assume. I'd think phoenixes and unicorns and the like would be part of that. But fuck if I've ever been taught about them. Much like Apex, Bloodstone's sole focus was furthering the ambush and the pred narrative."

My grin widens as I nod. "Exactly. That means the Council will have no influence over them, but the fucking Fae and magic users might have turned to them when they began hatching whatever goddamn plan they're executing. Prey animals are easily as oppressed as them, and would likely enjoy sticking it to preds by helping the rebels with shit over the years."

"Holy shit, Angel. That's a brilliant idea."

I know—and I plan on following it down the rabbit hole as fast as my thumpers will take me.

RENEGADES

CHESS

THE SIZZLE AND POP OF THE STIR-FRY SETTLES INTO A LOW HUM AS I stand back, admiring the spread on the kitchen counters, Colors clash and mingle—a vibrant array of Korean dishes, each one tweaked to fit Dolly's strict training regimen. My nose twitches as I examine everything to ensure it's perfect. Cooking is another form of sprinting: it's a race against heat and time to create a winning flavor. It's very meditative for me, much like many of the hobbies I've picked up over time to keep myself busy.

Besides, I enjoy being a 'provider' in our family by making sure everyone is taking care of themselves—it makes both the cheetah and the submissive in me happy.

"We're ready," I say, my voice the starting gun for the feast. My family sighs in relief, coming to fill their plates at the counter in a rush almost as fast as me.

Once everyone is seated, Felix clears his throat. "I know we're all excited about the prospect of new intel that will get us closer to solving all these fucking riddles, but don't choke to death inhaling your food."

That's the signal to dig in, and my angel doesn't need telling twice. She dives in with the ravenous grace of her dancer's build, chopsticks snapping up mouthfuls of bulgogi and kimchi with equal fervor. The rest of the group joins the fray, their laughter and chatter filling the space like the warm glow from the overhead lights.

Midway through a particularly succulent piece of japchae, Dolly leans back, her face the picture of contentment. Then, without warning, she releases a burp that rumbles through the room like distant thunder. Everyone freezes for a split second before Fitz chortles and counters with a belch that seems to shake the silverware.

Oh, no. This will never end if my first mate feels challenged to a duel of grossness.

"Really?" Felix mutters, his tone dry as parchment.

Aubrey and Ren join him in an eye roll chorus while I can't help but let out a half-hearted growl of disapproval. I know it's a complement to the chef in some countries, but for fuck's sake. Most of the shifters at this table are well over three decades old. We can maintain our dignity better than that, right?

Nope.

My beautiful angel and the tiger proceed to out-do one another, sipping sodas and letting out loud, echoing belches like teenagers at a kegger. They're laughing in between like loons, and the broody gargoyle looks like he might consider joining in soon. I sigh as Ren takes a huge sip of his drink, preparing to join the burping buddies.

As if on cue, the fancy doorbell Renard installed buzzes, slicing through the moment of levity. I rise, the pads of my feet silent on the cool tile as I walk over to see who's there. A glance at the small screen shows familiar faces on the door cam—Raina's eyes are practically sparkling with mischief, and The Captain stands with a large box in his small arms.

"Looks like we've got company," I announce, pressing the button to buzz them in. "Are you guys ready?"

"The mysterious package has arrived," Ren says, already pushing back from the table as he readies himself for whatever Raina and The Captain are bringing with them. I guess that's his version of a 'yes'.

"Or perhaps they couldn't resist the smell of your cooking, Chester" Aubrey teases, nudging me with his elbow as he heads for the scotch to pour a glass. "It is particularly delicious tonight, by the way."

I don't get a chance to answer as Raina bursts in, her striped tail a blur of motion behind her. The Captain follows with a sizable box that seems to make the air around him thrum with an unseen energy. I can't help but be drawn in by the electric tingle of potential discovery setting my senses on high alert.

We're all such nerds in this house, even the twins, though they won't admit it.

"Where be the place for yer treasure?" The Captain's question resonates through the room as he follows his mate into the living area.

"Here, let's clear the table," Renard says. He moves to flip over the investigation boards I brought in earlier, then re-organizes the table in the middle to make room. "Although, I didn't ask if the contents were dangerous somehow... we would need to use the inspection rooms in the archives if so."

"Don't worry; it's not going to explode or anything." Raina's eyes gleam as she rubs her tiny hands together.. "It's from an old friend, a prey shifter—a puffin elder from a circus on the Irish coast."

"A puffin elder?" Dolly muses, looking at us curiously.

Aubrey shakes his head. "Don't ask me, snacksize. There's a lot about the prey world that has been lost since the Treaty. My experience with it is very limited since that time; I have no idea what sort of structures they're using amongst their own."

My ears perk up at the mention of the elder. The prey shifters were basically subjugated after the Treaty, so the dragon is right to assume we know only what they allow preds to know. Anything coming from a group of them with a location so steeped in history promises to be more than just interesting.

"What has he sent us?" I ask, crossing the room with feline grace, my curiosity piqued. "And why did it come to you, not Aubrey?"

"Because most prey groups are fearful of what will happen if they come into contact with preds," she replies. "Those of us who work in places where that's required are a bit less anxious, but truthfully, even employment has its risks. Some clans prefer to hide in the wild and stay away from civilization entirely."

I can't imagine how scared those groups have to be to cut themselves off from the world for generations.

The Captain sets the box down with care, the weighty thud prompting all eyes to focus on its weathered surface. "We had the boys check it, most gracious gargoyle. It be safe as far as all of our senses can tell."

"Thank you, Captain," Dolly says with a smile. "You and your crew are true friends to us."

"Most artifacts from before the war were either destroyed, looted, or hidden. Prey animals suffered almost as much as magic users during that time, despite fighting with the predators.

To preserve history, they had to be quick to ferret away things that might be useful one day," Raina says, her gaze steady. "This is a forbidden piece of history, or that's what the puffin said. It details a language used by magic wielders to communicate with other non-shifter supernatural beings during the conflict."

"Other beings?" I echo, leaning in closer as my mind races with the implications. A language that could bridge gaps between the Fae and other creatures might offer insights into the tensions threatening to unravel the world as we know it. "You mean, like vampires?"

"Perhaps. I am unsure which beings were supporting the Fae and other magicals," Raina confirms, her paws dancing with anticipation. "However, it is not a language for shifters—pred or prey—but one designed to conceal information from them."

Aubrey nods, his expression serious, the scholar in him already piecing together the fragments of history and mystery like a puzzle waiting to be solved. "This could unlock the script in that book—maybe even that language on the rocks where we think the vault is hidden."

I look around at my family and friends, and feel a surge of determination. With every revelation, every piece of the past unearthed, we edge closer to understanding the true nature of the threat we face.

The scent of antiquity wafts from the box as Raina delicately peels back the lid, sending a shiver down my spine. My heart races, matching Aubrey's quickened breaths; we're perched on the edge of a revelation that hums through the air like electricity.

If we know what shady shit the future Council members did, we might be able to bring the rebels to the table instead of the battlefield—not to mention find out what the hell they want with our girl.

"Look at this," I murmur, eyes wide as the ancient parchment comes into view. "It's like something straight out of human lore—

code talkers and their secret languages designed to be uncrackable."

Dolly cocks her head, a frown creasing her brow. "Code talkers? I don't know that myth, Chessie."

Aubrey leans in, his voice a conspiratorial whisper. "Humans had these translators who used a little known indigenous language to transmit codes during the Great War. But given our history, it stands to reason that the actual communicators weren't human at all but supernatural beings who spoke a language like this," he gestures toward the scroll with a reverence usually reserved for sacred texts.

The room is still, save for the rustle of parchment as we unfurl the scroll across the coffee table. Words and symbols dance before our eyes, a cryptic ballet of ink and intent waiting to be deciphered. I have no idea what it means—yet—but it definitely looks like the symbols we've already seen.

"Can you imagine the secrets this will reveal?" Aubrey's words are barely audible, his excitement palpable as he envisions the research ahead. Renard grins fondly, leaning into his mate as the dragon has what looks like a librarian-gasm over the artifact.

"Bet it's just an ancient shopping list," Fitz mutters, earning a snort from his twin. "It would serve us right for getting so excited."

"Maybe it's the recipe for a fake love potion," Felix says, grinning as he joins his brother in needling the enthusiastic dragon.

"Guys," Renard chides, though there's a twinkle of amusement in his eye. "Don't ruin Flames's fun. He's much less grumpy when he's riding a wave of antiquity anticipation."

"Of course he is," I say, rolling my eyes but unable to suppress my own smile. "But no naughty fun until we look this over. And we're all going to help. Right, Fitzy?"

My mate groans and slaps his hand over his face. "Ugh. *Fine*. But only if Baby Girl sits with me while we sneeze into dusty tomes."

Dolly smiles, looking at him fondly. "Of course I will. This could be the key we've been searching for. I'm down for a big crusty book and a tiger snuggle."

No surprise there, but that's why we all love her—she's there for anything we need without hesitation.

"Thank you, Raina—you, too, Captain," Dolly says. The gratitude is thick in her voice as she walks over and embraces them both. "You don't know how much this means. You might have provided us with the one thing we need to unravel the mysteries plaguing us. Hell, it might even stop a rebellion before a fucking war breaks out."

"You're welcome, Dolly. We are *always* on your side," Raina replies as she smiles up at our fierce bunny. "You and your family are the only preds who have treated us like equals. We tell the other prey any chance we get because I believe you are going to change the world someday."

That makes our beautiful girl flush bright pink, and Fitz grins crazily. "Hell, yeah, she will. My Baby Girl is like the chosen one or some shit—you'll all see. There's a reason she is like she is and when we figure it out, all these dickheads better watch the fuck out."

As always, Fitz is the most simplistically eloquent of all of us, even when he's being crazy.

"Shall we gather our food and adjourn to Aubrey's bookish dungeon?" I ask as I wink at the big dude.

His gaze narrows. "No dungeon things in my library, Chester Khan. I'll have your hide for a rug."

I grin innocently as they all laugh, shrugging. "It will probably be worth it, though."

That, I'm not joking about—even the dragon knows it.

Feel It Still

Delores

I stretch into Warrior II, my gaze fixed beyond my fingertips as if I can already see the victory in tonight's match. The dim winter sun warms my skin, a gentle breeze playing along the edges of our open air garden, and there's a tang of anticipation in the air. Fitz mirrors my pose to my left, while Chess holds a perfect Tree Pose to my right.

I love when the guys do yoga with me—even if some are less than graceful about it.

"Seriously, Baby Girl," Fitz chuckles, his voice carrying easily over the tranquil space between us, "Zhuǎn xīng U is all about their quantum processors and lab experiments. Their team is going to be as intimidating as a floppy disk. Pasty skin and spaghetti arms will abound as you drill them into the dirt."

His teasing draws a ripple of laughter from me, the sound mingling with the rustle of leaves above. It's comforting, this routine, before the storm of competition. But despite the jests, my muscles coil with a readiness that comes from being more than just your average bunny shifter. I can't have the blue lightning escape unbidden in large, crowded stadiums or someone will have me locked up for certain. So if these guys happen to bring some ridiculous ringer like the state school did at Cappie, I have to be centered and mindful, not blindly raging.

Chess shakes his head, a frown creasing his brow as he transitions into another pose with fluid grace. "Underestimating them would be a rookie mistake," he says, and even without looking, I can tell his gaze is thoughtful. "We should prepare for every possibility. As you well know, Fitz, computer geeks and scientists are good at math. They didn't make a movie about math and sports for no reason."

I roll my shoulders, easing the tension that starts to build at his words. Deep down, beneath the stretches and the laughter, I know he's right. Experience might not have introduced me to the specifics of Zhuǎn xīng's team, but it has taught me that under-dogs often have the sharpest bite. And with the amount of enemies I have floating around? Assuming that no one is going to mess with the results of matches is a sucker bet. I'm smarter than that, even if I'm not a genius like those preds.

"You're probably right," I concede, shifting into a Downward Dog, "but money-balling isn't going to win matches by itself. The choices made during the match and the skill set of their competitors are a greater predictor of success. If they don't have team members who can match my speed, strength, or training, their equations won't help them."

Fitz grins crazily as he comes over to smack my ass. "Algebra's got nothing on this ass."

I giggle, trying not to fall over as he gropes me and Chess sighs heavily. "How can I argue with *that?*"

"You definitely shouldn't," I reply, giving him a smirk over my shoulder. "Do you really think they'll have burly jock girls attending a techie school? It seems unlikely."

The cheetah's voice is as sharp and precise as his warrior poses. "Don't let appearances deceive you. Kartika Dewi doesn't train amateurs," he warns, fixing Fitz with a look that could curdle milk. "If she's coaching Zhuǎn xīng, they're going to be a force to reckon with."

I exhale slowly, sinking deeper into my stretch as unease curls in my stomach. "Great. Another big name I don't know that's out to get me," I mutter, the memory of the State school match fiasco flashing before my eyes—'scholarship' players who turned the game on its head. "Has Zhenga said anything about their girls' team, Fitzy?" I ask, hoping for some insider knowledge.

Fitz shrugs, a nonchalant gesture that belies the serious undertone of our conversation. "She's been weirdly tight-lipped lately. Something's up, but she doesn't seem to be in the mood to share, and Felix would be a better choice to push her. She barely tolerates me —something about my 'jackassery' sets her off."

I can't imagine why my ADHD mate's ping-ponging between psycho and clever as fuck would bother the lioness.

My brow arches as I consider his words. Why would Coach Z be preoccupied and secretive? I tuck away the thought as another item on my growing list of concerns. "Focus, Dolly," I remind myself, trying to push aside distractions. "You've got a match to win."

But my white knight's warning lingers in my mind as we continue stretching, a subtle reminder that in the game of predators, it's never just about strength or speed.

It's about outsmarting the opponent, and that takes a cunning mind—no matter how high their IQ is.

Aubrey's arrival snaps me out of my reverie. He looks like he's been dragged backward through a hedge maze, exhaustion evident in every line of his face. I don't think he's slept since the Captain and Raina brought our newest piece of the puzzle and it shows. I've tried to reason with him, and so has Rennie, but the stubborn lizard refuses to hear it. He's determined to solve this thing, come Hell or high water.

"Still no luck with the scroll?" I ask, already knowing the answer.

He shakes his head, his frustration palpable. "That damn key symbol is hiding in plain sight, but it might as well be invisible. I'm fluent in over thirty languages—even some dead ones—and this is eluding me. My linguistics skills aren't helpful in the slightest. It's fucking ridiculous."

"If anyone can do this shit, it's the icy-Spay alamander-say," Fitz says as he looks at the dragon upside down and gives him a thumbs up.

"Pig Latin is *not*... Fuck it; I'm too tired to spar with you, Fitzgerald."

I watch him closely, a furrow in my brow as he plops onto a chair that might give way any second. The furniture here is definitely not constructed with dragons in mind, and he'll lose his everloving shit if it collapses under him.

"Ready for tonight's match?" he finally asks me when our gazes meet.

"Chessie thinks we might have underestimated Zhuǎn xīng,," I admit, relaying the gist of our earlier discussion. "They have some big wig coach I've never heard of, and Fitzy thinks they could be using sabermetrics to analyze their matches."

Aubrey's frustration deepens into a frown, the lines around his eyes tightening. "The last thing we need is more surprises, snack-size," he murmurs, running a hand through his disheveled hair. "I wonder if we can do some searches on their past results and—"

"I keep telling her that no string bean Dew drinker is going to have a fucking chance with our girl. C'mon, Grumpy Gecko, back me up!" Fitz kicks his legs up until he's standing on his head, and Chess smothers a laugh as his legs pump in the air.

All that does is get a snarl and a puff of smoke rings from the big guy.

"Don't worry," I whisper, infusing my voice with confidence I'm not entirely sure I feel. "We've got this. And if things get hairy out there, I know you'll all be watching. Ready to jump in." With a reassuring smile, I close the distance between us and plant a soft kiss on his cheek. My fingers graze the solid wall of his chest, feeling the steady heartbeat beneath my palm.

He really is a big softie at heart, despite his grumpy schtick.

Aubrey's frown eases, but a shadow still lingers in his eyes as he nods, accepting my reassurance. He turns slightly, fixing Fitz with a dark look that seems to pierce straight through the tiger shifter's nonchalance. The tension is palpable for a moment until Fitz's booming laughter breaks it like a thunderclap.

"Lighten up, you Serious Skink," Fitz chides, his grin wide and wild. "Dolly's got more backup than a pop star on a global tour. We'll have her covered from every angle." He flexes his muscles playfully, his bulk rippling with implied power. "Besides, you know I've been *dying* to teach some fuckwits a lesson, so if they try anything, I'll be out there gleefully ripping off nutsacks and decapitating dumbasses in a split second."

That would scare most preds, but not me—it makes my girly bits sing. Too bad I need to focus.

I can't help the smirk that tugs at my lips, knowing full well the kind of chaos Fitz can unleash if given even half a chance. Leaving Aubrey's side, I pad over to the tiger, noting the semi he's sporting at the mere thought of getting to maul the shit out of people. He really is a lunatic, but he's *my* lunatic, and I love it.

"You're pretty excited about that blood and gore, baby," I murmur as I bend until I'm level with him. "I could probably help you with working off that pent-up energy, but I have to keep my head in the game."

"You can keep my head in your—"

"For fuck's sake, Fitz!"

Before the banter can escalate further, Felix emerges from the shadows. His head shakes slightly, as if to dispel the absurdity of Fitz's bravado, and he steps toward me with a warmth that melts away the lingering pre-game tension. I rise to my full height, moving away from Fitz's big problem to turn to the elder tiger twin. His lips press softly against my temple, an affectionate gesture that grounds me back to the moment.

"Sorry, Sir. He distracted me," I say with a full on pout and batting lashes. "Won't happen again."

Felix snorts, shaking his head. "If anyone believes that, I have a bridge in New York for sale at a low, low price."

My grin is wicked as I wink at him, then go back to my Sun Salutation. Both he and Aubrey groan when I bend down into Downward Dog again, making me grin to myself as I stretch.

"Are you guys wearing Cori's uniforms for the match tonight?" Felix's question pulls me from my thoughts, his voice tinged with curiosity.

Changing the subject, I see.

"Only me," I reply, as I lift one leg in the air. "The rest of the team will suit up in the official gear once the real season kicks off in the fall. Mine is a prototype, so they're seeing how it holds up with scrimmages in the spring."

Felix nods, understanding flashing in his gaze. "That means Zhenga's going to be holed up with that polar bear, obsessing over every last stitch until then, huh?"

"Seems like it." There's a hint of concern in my voice as I consider the implications—Zhenga's attention split between coaching duties and uniform perfectionism could leave us vulnerable in ways I hadn't anticipated. I wasn't worried about it before, but since Fitz mentioned how distracted she's been and now I think about how Cori's been acting—I hope I didn't set up a collab that will drive them both insane.

"Hopefully, she doesn't get too caught up in the minute details," Felix says. He gives my ass a reassuring pat, and I growl playfully back at him. "Now, I've got to go help the gargoyle with the dishes from breakfast or he's going to come out here like a storm cloud. Be good—*all of you.*"

"Sir, yes, Sir!" I call mockingly and he chuckles as he walks away.

A frown creases my forehead as I watch Felix's retreating back from my pose. The uniform I wore in the last match was gorgeous, and the design immaculate. Cori's pure talent shone with every sparkle and the reviews were raving.

So why are she and Zhenga still slaving away over this? It doesn't make sense.

"Everything should be done by now," I murmur to myself, the words barely audible over the rustling leaves around our yoga spot. Cori's perfectionism is legendary, but there's a niggling thought that refuses to be swatted away—her drive could be something more, like a mask for nerves frayed and worn by pressure.

Chess clears his throat. "She is on her former home turf, where her family does business. Maybe that's giving her pause?"

"That could be it. *Maison de Bouvier* operates out of Paris," I muse, trying to convince myself. But the doubt lingers, stubborn as a weed. "Or maybe it's something else."

I shift my weight from one foot to the other, feeling the tightness in my muscles, a physical echo of the tension twisting through my thoughts. Giselle's name surfaces in my mind like a dark cloud blotting out sunlight, bringing with it the memory of their break-up—a storm that left ripples of unease in its wake.

"I'll talk to her Sunday. It could be this, paired with the pressure of this semester..." I trail off, the pieces slotting together with a click of realization. The anxiety must be clawing at her, a silent beast prowling in the shadows of her confidence.

I know it's come for me a few times, especially because we started behind the eight ball.

Fitz looks at me, his expression soft. "Baby Girl, don't you think the badger would have come to you if something was wrong with the bear? You can't worry about this with the match tonight. If you want, I'll come with you to talk to Cococabana on Sunday. Sound good?"

"Okay. We'll talk to her after the match," I repeat, firming the resolve in my voice. Taking a deep breath, I let the air fill my lungs, expand my chest, and with a slow exhale, I release some of the tension that had gathered there.

For now, I have a match to focus on, a team to lead, and a family to cheer me on.

After all, where there is unity, there is always victory.

THE GREATEST SHOW

FELIX

My heart thrums in tune with the electric buzz that's vibrating through the stadium. Seats are filling up fast, a sea of eager faces and jittery anticipation. I can't help but find it odd—this many preds swarming to what's essentially a glorified scrimmage? But then, Dolly's not just any player, and with Zhenga's marketing genius at play, it's like we're at the epicenter of the shifter world's latest craze.

The college level Pred Games are the Prednet's biggest craze, according to my twin.

"I cannot *believe* a college scrimmage in the off-season is packing this place," I murmur, my eyes scanning the packed stands from our front-row seats. "This is like the blood matches at Bloodstone."

"Z's outdone herself," Fitz agrees, his voice a rumble beside me. The faint scent of his excitement, a tangy spice, mingles with the popcorn and sweat-soaked atmosphere. He loves violence; it makes his ADHD zing with happiness, especially when it's our girl doing the deed.

Chess leans forward, elbows on knees, grinning as he takes in the sight. "Feels more like a championship than practice. But you're right, Raj... I'm having mini-flashbacks to the punishment pits at our previous home. Everyone in this place seems hungry for blood and gore. I can't decide if it's that good or bad yet."

"*Je n'aime pas ça, mon ami,*" Renard says, his tone edged with the steel of his darker instincts. As a gargoyle, he's always watchful, and this is no exception. "The vibe in this place is bordering on feral, and if something happens, the entire place could go off."

There's no fucking way to contain that mess, no matter how many allies we have standing sentinel.

To our left, Cori's laughter blends with Rufus's deeper chuckle while the Kavarit triplets exchange knowing glances. I suppose they've grown used to the badger and the bear behaving like the college kids they are, much like we have grown used to their antics with Dolly. On our right, Farley and his enormous associate, Skelly, banter quietly with Raina the raccoon. Their hushed tones are barely audible over the crowd's roar, but I smile when I notice the Captain's steady gaze sweeping the arena like a lighthouse beam. He's sitting with us, but also keeping his eyes on the bigger picture so he can communicate with his crew on Fitz's earpieces.

I catch the occasional glint of metal from Holliday stationed with his rifle at the top of stands facing us. The broad backs of hulking badgers stand out amongst the throng of revelers—a reassuring reminder that our allies have us covered. Yet, nestled beneath the surface of that security, concern gnaws at me. I can't shake the unease about those we can't control: Dolly's family, the elusive Fae, vampires lurking in shadowed corners, and those who'd relish in seeing her fall.

"Look at this fucking place..." Aubrey's voice is almost lost as another wave of fans pours into the stands. "Every predator for miles must be here. What in the crispy fuck did Zhenga do to draw this kind of mass attendence? I highly doubt it was a fucking Fangbook ad."

"These people are drawn by the lure of watching the Princess beat the snot out of something," I say, my pride for her battling the worry that coils tighter with every new face that could hide a foe. "Zhenga's flair for the dramatic probably featured the bunny who eats predators for breakfast, which brought every damn pred in the area out of the woodwork. I don't like it; we weren't prepared for *this*."

"We're here to enjoy the matches, big bro, not worry constantly," Fitz says, clapping a hand on my shoulder, his grip firm, ground-ing. "We've got the best seats in the house, so if anything pops off, we're in the perfect position to help."

"These are the best seats to watch her back," I admit, my resolve hardening as my eyes scan the crowd again. "But we'll also have a perfect view of her kicking the shit out of some geeky U&M nerd, which is also pretty fucking awesome."

Chess sighs. "Stop being jackasses about smart preds. You both know that our smartest member could smash most people like a damn grape without breaking a sweat."

The dragon grins at me, the tips of fangs showing as he smirks. "Chester is right. My form is big enough to flatten a battalion without even blowing one flame. And my IQ is easily as high as the students at U&M, if not higher. Stereotypes are hurtful, Raj."

"We're here for Dolly and nothing else matters," Renard cuts in, interrupting our verbal sparring. "Jocks versus geeks can wait, *mon amis*. Focus on our *petit lapin*."

He's right so I give Aubrey a sheepish grin and he holds his fist out to bump. Just as we're calling a truce, *Thunderstruck* rips through the stadium, a jolt of electricity that ignites the crowd into a frenzy. The *l'Academie* team emerges, their silhouettes stark against the glare of the floodlights. Each player pauses in the spotlight, striking a pose for the hungry cameras—Zhenga's orders after the victory at the last scrimmage.

Dolly wasn't happy about it, but she agreed as far as she told us.

"They look better than last time," I chuckle, leaning forward as the paparazzi feast on the spectacle. "More like they're ready to rock than retreat."

"Attitude was a big part of Z's focus. She wanted her girls to project what they wanted to achieve, so I gave them lessons," Fitz shouts over the din, his eyes sparkling with mischief. "Bet that limp dick brother of hers has his tail so far between his legs it's tickling his throat."

Laughter erupts from our row; Aubrey slaps his knee while Chess grins widely. Ren tilts his head back, howling above the AC/DC anthem blasting through the speakers. None of us have love for any of the Council families, and knowing the Leonidas pride is probably regretting their foolish decision to promote a raging moron is delicious.

"She's really shoved it in their faces," Aubrey yells, and we nod, the roar of approval from the stands echoing our sentiments. "This will be hard to top during the regular season without upgrades to the facilities. There's not an empty seat in this damn arena."

"Nothing like sticking it to the people who rejected you to heat up the blood." Fitz smirks, a glint of wildness in his gaze. "Can't wait until we do the same to dear old Dad."

Cori's lively voice cuts through the chaos, bright and eager. She leans in, her hands animated as she recounts the weeks of preparation for this match. "Dolly's next, guys. Just wait for it."

"Seeing you this keyed up again is baller, Cococabana," my twin says with a grin, his eyes softening at her enthusiasm. "I was worried about you hiding out lately, especially after…"

"Please," Cori scoffs, waving him off but clearly pleased. "Giselle was yesterday's news. I'm all about new horizons now."

I wonder what the hell that means?

Fitz reaches out, playfully tousling her hair, which earns him a mock growl and an eye roll. Rufus chimes in with a snarky comment that has us all chuckling, though the exact words are lost to the cacophony.

"The follies of youth," one of the Kavarit triplets muses, earning a chorus of snickers from the group.

"Speak for yourself, old man," Rufus retorts, his eyes then turning to his partners, murmuring something that makes them blush— obviously, a private joke filthy enough to make ancient Sphinxes turn red.

Good for him.

I can't help but smile at our motley crew. We're an odd bunch, but here, amidst the noise and fervor, we're united by more than just our Drew Fluffle jerseys. Before I can comment on how much I appreciate them all supporting the Princess, the music changes to the thrumming bass of our girl's favorite T. Swift song and my lips curl up.

Oh, I'm definitely ready for it…

The stadium trembles with anticipation, the song pulsating through the air as Dolly makes her entrance. As she strides onto the green, her smirky grin slices through the electrified atmosphere, commanding attention without uttering a word. She's a vision in the uniform Cori crafted, each step a testament to the design that clings and accentuates every curve and muscle honed by relentless training.

"Hot *damn*, Baby Girl!" Fitz shouts as he whistles, echoing the sentiment of every pair of eyes that feast upon Dolly's confident poses. He turns to the polar bear, his eyes dark with lust as reamrks, "Cococabana, you've outdone yourself with those alterations."

"Girls like us *deserve* to look hot, sporty, and like supermodels," Cori replies, basking in the adoration for her workmanship. "I'm going to show the whole world that curvy preds don't need to hide under a fucking tent."

"Dollypop looks stronger and fitter than ever," Rufus observes, his tone laced with pride. "Not skinny, mind you, just toned and ready to rumble. She's really filling out."

"Credit goes to my bro and Zhenga's brutal sessions and Chessie's culinary magic," Fitz adds, clapping me on the back. "I only take credit for keeping her moaning and doing yoga."

"Protein-packed meals that she'll actually devour aren't easy to find," Chess admits with a crooked grin.

We all nod, watching as Dolly takes her seat beside Zhenga, her aura of readiness infectious.

Tonight is going to be her night; I can feel it.

As the undercard matches commence, my sense of ease begins to fray at the edges. The competitors from U&M shouldn't be able to hold their own like this—each bout too close for comfort. They don't look like the preds I'd expect, either, but they don't look totally out of place. I have no idea why this seems off, except that I know how hard Zhenga has been working with her girls. They're much more ready for the season than at the first match, and U&M

doesn't have a rep for successful competition in the Pred Games. Usually Apex and Cappie dominated, and with Apex students disbursed, the balance is off—but not that much.

"This is what I was worried about," Chess leans in, his voice tinged with suspicion. "Something's not adding up here."

Fitz's brow furrows. "They're more like athletes than academics. I agree; something's fishy."

We exchange wary glances, the joy of Dolly's imminent match now twined with a thread of uncertainty. With each clap of the crowd for the alternating victories and defeats, speculation simmers among us.

"Keep your eyes peeled," I murmur to the group, "especially when it's Dolly's turn to shine."

THE ROAR OF THE CROWD CRESCENDOS, NEARLY TANGIBLE IN ITS intensity as the U&M team's exuberant high-fives signal their victory. The last undercard match is over, and anticipation crackles through the electric air of the stadium like a pre-storm charge. I grip the metal railing in front of us, my knuckles white against the cool surface.

The further into the night we got, the more my gut screamed at me and now it's yowling a dark warning.

"Next up," the announcer's voice booms, filling every crevice of the arena with its guttural resonance, "we have the moment you've all been waiting for!" Fans leap to their feet, a sea of heads turning as one towards the central field where Dolly, our fierce bunny shifter, emerges.

I can't help but swell with pride as cameras flash, capturing her every smirky twist and confident turn. The cheers are deafening, reverberating off the stands and into the evening sky. Zhenga is beaming from the sidelines, watching her star with a proud gaze. We all wave frantically, trying to catch Dolly's eye—she's a star in this gladiatorial arena, and it's impossible not to get swept up in the pageantry of it all.

But then, an abrupt silence blankets the stadium—a heavy, expectant quiet that seems to suck the very air from my lungs. My heart hammers against my ribcage as the tunnel at the far end of the field births a monstrous figure. The feral looking girl stomps out, her gait brimming with primal confidence, and the energy shifts palpably.

"Son of a..." I hear Fitz mutter under his breath, the words lost in the sudden resurgence of noise as the crowd takes in this new, formidable contestant.

Monster Girl grins, a horrifying display of sharp fangs, and my hand tightens further around the railing, the metal creaking a protest. Dolly holds her ground, but I see the flicker of something across her features—the slightest hint of apprehension maybe, or determination. It's gone in a heartbeat, replaced by her usual fearless facade.

Good girl, Princess. Don't let them see you squirm.

"This is trouble," I whisper, unable to take my eyes off the beast of an opponent who now prowls toward Dolly. The predatory grace of the canine shifter sends a chill down my spine. This was never going to be just another match; it's clear now that it's a statement, a challenge on a level we hadn't anticipated.

"Watch closely," I say to the others, my voice low and urgent. They nod, each face etched with concern and a readiness to leap into action should things go south.

Chess leans closer, his expression grim. "She's going to need every move you guys taught her and maybe a few we hoped she could keep under wraps. Hopefully, those meditation exercises helped after the last scrimmage."

"More than that," I reply, my gaze fixed on Dolly as she squares her shoulders, meeting the gaze of the creature before her. She might be a bunny amidst wolves, but she's no prey.

The question is whether she can convince her opponent of the same before the match even begins.

BRING ME TO LIFE

DELORES

I SQUARE OFF, MY FEET GROUNDED ON THE DIRT, MY MUSCLES TAUT as I eye the huge girl. My opponent looms across the ring—not just any opponent, but a colossal canine shifter who seems more myth than reality.

The ref bellows her name—Zoya R. Volkova from Siberia—like she's some kind of celebrity I should know. I can almost taste the chill in the air that follows her name, and I frown as I try to remember if I've heard of her ever before. She's definitely not your typical U&M student; she's like something cooked up in a lab, with that too-perfect snarl and those muscles rippling under her pelt.

The way everyone in the damn arena is cheering, I should know who this chick is, but even my guys look puzzled in their seats.

An ocean of noise surrounds us, the faceless preds forming a swarming mass of excitement and anticipation. Cameras flash, catching every detail of the Pred Games ring, and every drop of sweat on my brow. Press members huddle together, phones raised as they wait for blood to spill for their by-lines.

"Looks like I'm pretending to be the chick from Underworld tonight," I mutter under my breath, a sneer curling my lip. I'd laugh if it wasn't so damn irritating—the thought of this...wolf thing coming out of nowhere, trying to make a chew toy out of me.

As Zoya throws back her head, unleashing a howl that seems to reach the moon itself, I scan her form. She's posturing for the crowd, absorbing their cheers like they're fuel for her ego. But I'm not here to admire the show. I'm looking for the chink in her armor, that one spot where muscle meets vulnerability. My eyes narrow as I sidestep along the perimeter of the ring, taking her in from every angle, searching.

"Better hope you're not all bark and no bite," I taunt, the edge of my voice sharp as a claw. It's not just about fighting—it's about wit, about psyching her out before our fangs even cross. As I watch her, something primal within me stirs, a fierce determination to stand my ground against this beast from the frozen tundra.

"Ready to dance, Fleabag?" I ask, voice low, embodying every ounce of the fierce bunny shifter I am.

This is my ring, my fight—and no oversized pup is going to change that.

The second the ref's whistle pierces the air, Zoya and I are a blur of motion, colliding in the center of the ring with the force of a thunderclap. It's a whirlwind of fur and fury, her massive canine form against my lean, muscular rabbit build—two natural enemies locked in an unnatural dance of violence.

A symphony of praise for bloodlust and adrenaline comes from the roaring crowd. I can feel their energy pulsing through me, fueling my every move. Zoya is relentless, her massive paws swiping at me with deadly precision. But I'm too quick, too agile because of my rabbit. I dart and weave, shifting between forms to keep her off balance. When I see an opening, I pounce, knocking her to the ground. She's strong, though, flipping us over so that she's on top again. Our limbs tangle together in a chaotic symphony of fur and limbs as we fight for dominance.

My heart pounds in my chest as we roll and struggle against each other. This is the part of the Games I live for—this raw, primal battle of life and death. Suddenly, Zoya lets out a deafening howl and pushes herself up, breaking our hold. She stands tall before me, panting heavily but still radiating strength.

"Is that all you've got?" she snarls, her eyes blazing with challenge.

I grin back at her wolfishly. "I'm just getting started, furface."

With renewed determination coursing through me, we charge at each other once more. The ring shakes beneath our feet as we collide again and again, neither of us giving an inch. Just when it seems like we're evenly matched, something shifts within me. A surge of power flows through my veins as I tap into the ancient instincts of my shifter ancestors. Faster than lightning, I shift into my full rabbit form—a giant hare with razor-sharp claws and teeth that could tear through steel. Zoya takes a step back in surprise before lunging forward once more.

This time, my attack is different—I am different. My senses are heightened to a new level as I anticipate her moves before they even happen. Then suddenly, everything falls into place: the perfect angle, the perfect moment. I leap at her, sinking my claws into her side until she screams in agony.

"I guess I'm the thorn in your side after all," I say with a wicked grin and the lumbering dog just grunts back at me. I land a solid bite to her flank, tasting copper, before she throws me off with a swipe that stings my cheek.

Man, she fucking tastes like vodka—what a stereotype.

We're up again, circling, feinting. She lunges, I parry. Claws meet flesh, drawing thin red lines that quickly stain our fur. Each exchange is faster, more desperate than the last. I can see it in her eyes—she's not holding back. Zoya's moves become less about technique, more about raw power. It's here, amidst this maelstrom of fury, that I realize brute strength won't be enough. The magic within whispers, urging me to tap into its chaotic depths.

I hiss under my breath, coaxing the blue lightning. But instead of the calming blue arcs I'm getting used to, I feel something else—a roiling, seething tide of red energy, dark and wild. It scares me, yet I know it's mine to command. "Help me," I mutter, more plea than command, trying to mold the power that rises like a tempest inside me.

Zoya's claw rakes across my face, a hot line of pain that snaps my focus back to the fight. Blood trickles into my eye, blurring my vision with a scarlet veil. I stagger back, my hand going to my cheek. The taste of iron fills my mouth, and the crimson energy surges in response, feeding off my anger and hurt.

"Fine," I growl to the magic, "If you won't help, I'll do it myself."

The red power responds immediately, filling my sinews with a vengeful strength. I'm no longer just Dolly, the bunny shifter—I'm a conduit for something wilder, something that doesn't play by the rules of man or beast.

I'm both beast and ethereal power married as one, like an ancient myth.

With newfound ferocity, I launch myself back into the fray, determined to beat this goddamned ringer and show the entire world that they cannot force me to submit. The roar of the crowd is a feral soundtrack to my defiance. Every shout, every cheer, ignites my will to dominate. I'm battered and bloody, but surrender isn't in my vocabulary—not with my mates, my men, urging me on from the sidelines, their voices a fuel that burns hotter with each beat of my rabbit heart.

"Fuck off, dog breath," I snarl through clenched teeth as I kick out with my oversized bunny feet, sending Zoya skidding across the ring's boundary. My blood-soaked uniform clings to my skin, but I'm beyond caring. I swipe the trickle of red from my eyes, clarity returning just in time to evade another lunging attack. In my head, I beg the magic to help me before this freakshow gets me on the ground and I'm pinned for good.

It's as if the magic hears the rage and desperation in my mental voice and decides it's finally time to listen. My internal power surges, flooding my limbs with a strength that feels like it could shatter mountains. A surge of Hulk-like power propels my fists into Zoya's flesh, the impact reverberating through the arena. She falls, and I'm on her in an instant, my legs coiling around her thick neck, my thighs iron bands of unyielding force.

Thunder thighs save lives, baby.

Her struggle weakens, her body going limp as I tighten my hold, and I turn my head, locking eyes with the audience. My grin is all malice and triumph—a bloodied, bruised siren calling them to witness my victory. They oblige with screams and applause, their frenzy peaking just as the referee's count begins.

"Nine..." he starts, but his voice drowns in a shriek that pierces the air, followed by a resounding bang that echoes off the stadium walls.

My gaze snaps upward. A metallic orb streaks across the sky, like a round missile aimed straight for us. Instinct takes over as I give the canine one final squeeze, a crunch beneath my thighs, and Zoya is silent forever. I spring up, my focus honed on the bizarre sphere descending toward the field.

I'm probably going to pay for that later, but I can't worry about it now.

"This is either a stupid crowd toy or something much, much worse, but we can't be too careful," I mutter, sprinting along its projected path. The orb's reflection glints in my eye, an invitation to play hero—or show off, but I don't know which..

Silence blankets the stadium now, an expectant hush that fuels my decision. Channeling the grace of the star of my favorite baseball movie, I slide into a perfect split just beneath the falling object, arms outstretched. It lands in my grasp, and I hoist it overhead, a victorious Pred Peach in a tableau of glory. Cameras flash, capturing the moment for eternity and I tilt my head back like a bloody, vicious pin-up bunny.

Then, without warning, the orb bursts, releasing a shimmering cloud of sparkles that envelops the entire stadium. For a heartbeat, it's beautiful—then the coughing starts, a chorus of hacking and wheezing that spreads like wildfire among the stunned spectators. The glittering haze drifts, a fairy-tale fog turning nightmarish as the first cough rips through my throat.

My grip on the orb slackens, and it clatters to the ground, forgotten. I stumble back, instinctively trying to escape an enemy that doesn't bleed or bruise—an enemy I can't fight with fists of fury.

"Can't breathe," I gasp, the word barely a whisper past my lips as more coughs seize me, each one like sandpaper grating against my lungs. The crowd's cheers morph into a cacophony of choking sounds, a collective struggle for air that drowns out the fallen wolf's silence. My eyes stream, blurring the world into smudges of color as I scan the chaos. Faces contort in panic; bodies double over, hands clawing at throats.

"Shit, shit, shit..." The curse is a mantra, punctuated by my own hacking coughs.

Magic—where's the damn magic when I need it?

I think desperately, reaching for the red energy that just moments ago flowed through me with Hulk-like strength. But it's elusive, slipping away when I try to grasp it, leaving me exposed and gasping. The stadium, once alight with the thrill of battle, dims under a cloud of dread. I swipe at my eyes, forcing them to focus as I search for a way out, a solution, anything. But my thoughts splinter, fragmented by the toxin invading my body and the screams piercing the air.

"Help," someone wheezes nearby, a plea lost amidst the turmoil.

My heart pounds a relentless rhythm, urging me to do something, anything. I push to my feet, my balance faltering as dizziness assaults me.

This isn't how Delores Diamond Drew goes down—not like this, not ever.

But as my eyes rake over the blurry movements that I assume are my guys trying in vain to stumble over to me, I dig my claws into the grass. Crawling towards the enormous white tiger bounding towards me like something out of a fantasy novel, I gasp for breath until I can hold onto him tightly. Within seconds, we're joined by my cheetah, the twin orange tiger, and two huge winged shifters that shield us under their joined appendages.

Whatever was in that fucking ball is going to kill us... and I'm the dumbass who caught it for a photo op.

CHECK OUT WHAT HAPPENS NEXT IN THE FIRST BONUS SCENE FOR Eat. Prey. Love!

Preorder book five Prey It By Ear here!

Reviews, Print, and Merchandise

If you have enjoyed this book, please leave reviews! It helps other
readers find my work,
which helps me as an indie author.

Thank you!

**Reviews for Eat. Prey. Love are appreciated
on the following platforms:**

Amazon
Goodreads
Bookbub
StoryGraph
TikTok
Instagram
Facebook

To purchase print copies or merchandise, go to The Worlds of
Cassandra Featherstone

GET A SECRET BONUS SCENE!

For a secret bonus scene that follows *Eat. Prey. Love.* click the link below, sign up for my newsletter, and get your freebie.

Get your bonus scene from EPL here!

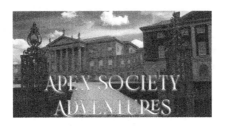

Sneak Peek:
Bloodthirsty

QUEEN BEE

They dim the lights in the club, and the spots click on as the curtain slides open.

It's a full house tonight in the little burlesque club off the Rue Pierre Montaine.

Chez Arc En Ciel is not well known compared to the *Moulin Rouge* or *Le Lido*, but the wealthy from both sides of the Seine gather here for shows four nights a week. If you pass the various layers of security checks to even be permitted to book a reservation, you also have to be able to afford the two thousand Euro per guest cover charge. If you don't eat or drink anything, that's all it will cost; however, that would get you blacklisted.

Intro music pumps through the speakers and I stand on my mark in the opening position. My cane is resting on the wooden boards of the stage by my front foot as I pretend to lean on it. Roars of applause echo through the room as our troupe of dancers catch the lights, sequins sparkling like diamonds when the stage lights rise. We're dressed in pinstriped black pant suits and fedoras to match the big band style opening to the song. As soon as the horn-filled intro finishes, the dance begins.

I follow the routine with precision, snapping and popping my hips to the beat as we spread out across the stage. You wouldn't know by the fake smile on my face that I'm scanning the crowd. Two fan kicks later, I've rotated past the proscenium, and I think I've found my mark. Twirling, I stop in the place I need to be for the bridge, singing along as if my life depends on it. It might, to be honest, because I need to sell my cover tonight, so no one notices me.

The Guillotine moves in the shadows, but tonight, she's in the spotlight.

My ass shakes as I dance my way through the song, swinging the prop cane I'd replaced with one of my design. You wouldn't know by looking at it, but it's not the painted balsa the other dancers have for a very specific reason. I need it to complete the mission that forced me to spend two months in Paris working my way into this job at *Chez Arc En Ciel*. If I can't strike tonight, the surveillance, counterintelligence, and time spent building this cover are wasted because my mark is leaving for Asia tomorrow.

Tonight, the Cobra dies for his sins.

The break of the song slows the music and the dancers pour into the crowd to wiggle around the rich assholes. It's choreographed, but it's also to advertise each girl for private dances in the lounges upstairs. We're not strippers—not that there's a damned thing wrong with a woman using her body to support herself—but we do bare more skin in the closed rooms. The *laissez-faire* attitude of the owners means as long as we kick them thirty percent of the fees for those dances, they don't care what any of the girls do in the rooms. I'd find it sleazy, but the girls who work here are highly skilled performers who choose to make thousands of dollars a night rather than peanuts in some ballet troupe or chorus line.

By the time I've flirted my way to the VIP tables, the Cobra is staring intently at all of us. Spotlights pin each one of us on the floor at the bass hits, and I swivel my hips as my free hand slides down to the secret spot on my jacket. In unison, we tear the jackets off to reveal rhinestone studded bras with straps criss-crossing our waists like shibari ropes. A lift of the fedora and pop of my hip, along with the beat, draws the fierce-looking brawler's eyes directly to me. I pout prettily and stalk towards his table with the swagger of a tiny dicked asshole that owns a monster truck.

His thin lips pull back over the famed curving fangs he had implanted. Dark, glittering eyes follow every move I make as I approach, and I pretend to whip my hair from side to side as I check for his guards. They're here somewhere, but I need them to be far away so I can beat my escape before they notice. When I get within inches, I tap his leg with my cane and spin around to shake my ass in his face. The grunt of approval makes me want to heave, but I turn, holding onto the prop with both hands. My feet click on the floor in a soft shoe step as I make 'fuck me' eyes at the dirty bastard. He leans back, his pants tented as he gestures towards his lap.

Fucking gross.

I don't care about his weapons trade or what happens when people get the shit he moves. I have no clue why I have to take him out. The reason they have sentenced him to death isn't part of my contract, and I'm nothing if not a dispassionate observer of the darkest parts of human desires. Twelve years at *l'Academie* ensured I care very little about anything that isn't directly related to my ability to complete my jobs.

Sighing, I dance closer and drop onto his rather unimpressive erection and wiggle. There's plenty of cloth between us to prevent him from doing anything I'd make a scene over, so I focus on the task at hand. I slip the cane behind his head, resting the wood against his neck as I tug him forward. The move reads as playfully bringing his face to my breasts, but at the last second, I click the release built into the custom weapon. One end slides open to reveal the razor sharp garotte and before he can say a word, I yank it through.

Faint gurgling is the only noise besides the end of the song, and I carefully slide the sides of the cane together. Climbing off the nasty fucker, I put my hands on his cheeks so I can pretend to flirt with him while I arrange the head so it looks as if he's leaning back in the booth. It needs to look realistic to allow me to return to the stage with the others. When I have it settled, I back away from the booth, blowing fake kisses as I walk backwards through the crowd. I almost collide with a dark-haired guy with his collar pulled high as I head for the stage, and I roll my eyes. Whatever celeb that is trying to keep their face away from the paps is doing a shitty job of it.

The entire troupe takes a few bows and shuffles off of stage left to the wings. I exhale a sigh of relief when the next group enters on the opposite side. I haven't heard shouting yet, so I don't think the

Cobra's men realize he's down. Now I take this emetic pill, have a vomiting episode, and I'll get sent home.

That's when Arabella Montaigne, the burlesque dancer, will cease to exist, and Remy Arsine Benoit will re-emerge.

I smile to myself as I chew on the tablet that will have me retching my guts out in a few moments. This is a more complex extermination than I usually prefer, and I can't leave my normal calling card behind. The Cobra's head had to remain in the booth rather than get delivered to his home in a basket.

Such a shame, that. I quite enjoy the reactions my little gifts engender when they're discovered.

Walking into the dressing room, I carefully strip my costume off, putting all the pieces in my bag. Every item in the locker room that belongs to gets placed in the duffel carefully as I wait for the effects to hit me. It won't do to leave loose ends, even if my prints have never touched a single surface in this place. My gut roils and I turn, facing one of the other dancers as the vomit finally comes. Gracelia screams like she's being skinned when I hurl on her and it's everything I can do *not* to smirk through the chunks.

"C'est la merde!" she shouts, running for the showers as if she's on fire.

It takes less than a minute for the owner to send me home for the night. I walk out the back door of the building with everything just as the sirens scream.

Perfect timing, as always.

I jump into the first cab I can hail, directing him to the *Hôtel de Crillon*. Their suites are the ritziest in Paris, and it's my go-to hideout when I'm here. I used to only stay in the Bernstein Suite, but some rich fuckwad purchased it six months ago. If I could track them down and beat the hell out of them, I would, but I booked my schedule until late 2025. Assassins with my skill set and accuracy are getting harder to find. They forced the old guard into retirement because they refuse to adapt to the digital age. Too many cameras, crime labs, and hackers running about to do everything Cold War style.

The future of murder for hire is millennial, people. We're old enough to be stable, but young enough to be agile with new technology. Plus, most of them are broke AF from crooked ass student loans.

It's not an issue I have, but I've been in the business since I hit double digits. You don't survive *l'Academie des Invisibles* if you haven't killed someone before the end of primary school. It's unheard of.

I was eight the first time I used the weapon that would become my signature.

Shivering, I tap on the window of the cab and bitch the driver out. He's taking a longer route than necessary to raise my fare, and I'll have his guts for garters if he doesn't knock it the fuck off. A string of curses in French erupt from him when I voice the accusation, and I slam my palm on the window with enough force to crack the plexiglass barrier. He almost drives into another car, but when he regains control, he makes the requested adjustments to our route.

We arrived at the front entrance after a few more arguments and a traffic jam around the *Champs*. I throw the euros at him in disgust, memorizing the medallion number for later. He's not worth my time, but I have quite a few contacts who might be interested in blackmailing a cabbie in town. Getaway cars are cliche in the crime world now. Most ne'er-do-wells like myself find greater comfort in anonymous taxis or ride-share accounts hacked through the deep web accessed on burner phones. If your ride doesn't know you're a villain, there's no one to flip if law enforcement comes looking.

I never look the same for any job—ever.

I will not use Arabella Montaigne as a cover in the future, and once I move to the location of my next job, I'll ensure that she meets with a terrible fate. It's a lot more work to slowly kill off my alters once I've used them, but it's also why I've never even come close to being caught. The dancer with long wavy red hair, freckles, and big green eyes will never grace the streets of Paris again after I hop a plane. She will, however, get a minor story in the paper and an obituary when I decide how she tragically dies.

The Guillotine will rise from her ashes and be reborn.

Sneak Peek: Blood on the Ice

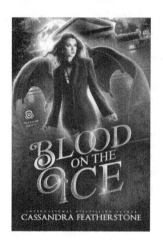

Killer Queen

Morgana

Looking around the campus with a critical eye, it isn't hard to notice the differences between the campus of Swallowtail and State U. The major difference is age, of course, but even secondary schools overseas are unlike the blatant marketing machines that are American universities. State U doesn't resemble the colleges I've seen in American movies or on TV, though much of that is the Society's doing.

However, banners, statues, plaques, signs, and even architecture are emblazoned with the school's motto—*Honoris. Veritas. Potentia*—as if constant reminders will enforce the virtues it extols. *That* differs from the places in Europe I attended or worked in.

"Getting used to the sales aspect of education here won't be your biggest challenge and you know it," I mutter to myself.

When the outcome of my trial led to a guilty sentence, I didn't expect the punishment they handed down. Instead of being jailed for the murder of my ex, they decreed I would replace him as the Dean at State U. I wasn't the only one who disagreed with my purgatory—the vote on the High Council was split down the middle until a mysterious figure cast a vote in favor of my exile. They summarily dismissed me from Swallowtail Academy and sent me home to pack my shit for a journey overseas to the nest of corruption created by the man I thought I would marry.

Not only am I the youngest Dean to ever hold the title, but I'm the only hybrid to head one of the Society's schools.

Placing me at the helm of the crown jewel of their American institutions made their unorthodox punishment even more bizarre, but I've never believed the group that guides our kind to be infallible. The irony of replacing the being responsible for all the university's current issues with the fiancee who killed him hasn't eluded me. It's like my penance for not blowing the whistle on him instead of taking my vengeance in blood.

They did not impress hard line elders with the eventual outcome, but that had to be expected. Some supernaturals don't believe in the young being given positions of power, especially when that young candidate is also a woman and a hybrid. Given that I believe Magnus had cronies at various levels of government he was paying off, some of them must be worried I'll expose them to prove I was right to remove him from this world. Either way, the assholes who are screaming I'll ruin their precious programs and reputation haven't shut up since I left the trial chamber.

Let them whine about their outdated, elitist standards. I'll show them.

I turn away from the greenery of the campus, leaving the balcony to take a seat at the enormous desk in my overly plush office. Knowing the way parents and donors behave in this country, I assume every inch of this space has been purchased not by the college, but by donors who had 'one little request' for my ex. Magnus Corona was well-known in academic circles for milking the wealthy Americans until they ran dry, but his lack of ethics couldn't go on forever. My greedy, dragon lover went on the lam after a series of scandals involving kickbacks, illegal sponsorships, sports, and sexual harassment. The last one is why I hunted him down and eventually watched the last breaths he took on this planet with vengeful glee.

I'll start looking for a decorator immediately. If it's not in the budget, my trust fund will cover it.

Like most lost ones, they left me on the doorstep of a very talented witch and her gargoyle mate. I never found my 'real' parents, but growing up on Swallowtail's campus was not a burden. It was different when my adoptive parents were professors there—three hundred years brings a lot of changes. When I graduated, I attended Oxford and came back to work there in administration because I missed the old buildings and libraries.

That's the gargoyle in me, I know.

My adoptive mother is blind—except for the gift of future sight. Being a beautiful, blind witch couldn't have been easy when she was teaching, but she met my father in college and they've been together ever since. When they graduated, they came back to Swallowtail to teach. Eventually, she became the head of the Witchcraft & Wizardry department at the Finishing School and my father was the chair of the Physical Education & Training program. Over the years, my mother's gifts made their investments and ventures fruitful enough to retire while they could still enjoy it. They live on a small island in the Mediterranean where supes of their caliber like to soak up the good life.

Once I get settled here, I might invite them to come tour the campus. My father would particularly enjoy the Gothic structure of the buildings; they were constructed to evoke the feeling of Oxford and he loves those old buildings. I give the picture of them on my cherry wood desk a half smile and sigh when I realize it's going to be awhile before I can extend that invitation.

First, I have to figure out how to get this ship back on course. Loyalty divides the staff; the students are due to arrive in two weeks, and I have a lot of house cleaning to do within these hallowed walls. It's going to ruffle feathers to do the things that are necessary to keep our supernatural accreditation *and* our human sports certification. I'll have to let some staff go, shuffle departments and assignments, and bring in new people to monitor certain aspects of the college's accounting to satisfy all the requirements we need to meet by the end of the semester.

State U has never been forced to toe the line quite as closely as we must now, and that is all because of Magnus Corona's lack of scruples and inability to think without his dick.

Not that any of his adoring fans will believe it for a second—and that is the rock I'll have to push up the hill for the foreseeable future.

"They'll have to get on board or get the fuck out," I say as I compare the list of coaches, trainers, and support staff for the football team. "I don't have a choice and neither do they."

When I finally finish going over the massive budget for the major boys' teams, my brain is damn near fried. I cannot fathom how colleges here justify the expenditures of these programs compared to the paltry sums I saw on the balance sheets for academic programs. Americans truly have lost their focus on education, and it doesn't surprise me at all that Magnus could manipulate this to his advantage. There's so many discretionary funds and black holes in the books that I'll have to find someone much more numerically inclined than myself to help me wade through this shit.

It's almost like it left room for loopholes and nefarious deeds.

Pushing to my feet, I rise from the high-backed leather chair and slip my shoes back on. I've been at this for hours and because I don't have office staff, no one was there to remind me I should eat or take a break. I had to fire everyone who worked in Magnus' immediate circle—both out of principle and necessity. I can't prove they knew what he was doing, nor that any of them would try to harm me as retribution, but I'm also not stupid enough to let someone with loyalty to my ex pour my goddamn coffee.

Coffee.

The word makes my blood hum and I know it's time to find sustenance—particularly caffeine. I locate my phone on the massive desk and slip it into the pocket of my suit pants. My appearance has been a topic of gossip on campus since I arrived—social media is a terrible curse when you're in the spotlight, even if it's for the right reasons. I've seen staff and alumni commenting on the 'uptight murdering bitch' strutting around campus dressed like someone from the *Addams Family* as if their vitriol isn't public when they post on Facebook.

My lips curve as I look down at the bespoke Tom Ford suit, Zegna tie, and Louboutin heels. Dressing the part has always been a theme of mine, but Magnus preferred the 'rumpled academic' look. He allowed the staff to run around looking like grad students and that will soon end. If they hate me for looking sharp compared to my frumpy ex, they're going to hate the new dress code when it rolls out in a week. I will not go as far as the Society schools did at home or in other countries, but I refuse to have the press haunting our grounds while taking pictures of grubby looking professors and coaches for their rags.

If this is the crown jewel, it needs more polishing than the Council realizes.

Before I go out, I shake my purple and black curls out of the messy bun, letting my hair settle over my shoulders. A quick check with the selfie mode on my phone tells me my makeup doesn't need to be freshened—thank hell—so I close the camera and put on my sunglasses to keep my sensitive eyes from the waning sun.

I'll need the State U app to find a place that's out of the way. I open it and cringe—the damn thing is hideous in form and function. I make a mental note to interview app designers and web developers; the website has to be as poorly maintained as this bullshit. Yet again, I marvel at the level of incompetence men can show without consequence. It finally loads the map and I scroll around until I find a coffee shop on the edge of campus. I don't want to go to a break room or the food court—there will be far too many eyes on me and I'd like to relax.

Noting the landmarks around the shop, I walk out onto the balcony and touch the amulet at my neck. My wings spring free, sprouting through the suit without a single tear, and I leap into the air. Catching a wind shear, I glide to the far end of the commons, then bank to the right towards the arts building. They nestled the little beanery I identified between the theater and the gallery, so I pull my wings back to descend slowly as I approach.

When I land, the magic of my mother's amulet helps me slip my appendages back in gracefully and walk towards the door without missing a beat. I open the door, take off my sunglasses, and stride in with confidence. I'm not here to throw my weight around, but I can't let anyone see me sweat, either. I look at the menu board before I lower my gaze to see the barista behind the counter.

Holy. Mother. Forking. Shit.

The guy behind the counter is beautiful, and I don't say that lightly. His long blond hair is pulled back in a ponytail, but somehow, it doesn't look douchey. Paired with his patrician features and thin silver framed lenses, he projects the air of a student, but not a new one. My guess is a grad or doctoral student and this is his side hustle. The muscled forearms and powerful hands tell me he's not just a bookworm, so I ponder what discipline this lithe, gorgeous supe is studying. When I finally drag my eyes back to his, the aqua color of his is mesmerizing.

"Can I take your order, ma'am?"

Yikes. That destroyed my brief fantasy.

"Um, yes, sorry. It's been a long day. I'd like a triple espresso and a club sandwich, please." I feel my cheeks heating not because I was staring—he's got to be used to it—but because I got caught checking out one of the students.

It's not forbidden at State U, but I am the murdering bitch with ice in her veins that's here to destroy everything the university stands for. Or, so the article in the *State U Review* said last night. There's no way this gorgeous coffee-serving man doesn't recognize me and I'm sure I'll get an earful about my evil ways once he's done making my order. In fact, I should continue watching to make sure he doesn't mess with my food for revenge.

Yeah, that's why I want to watch him.

"I don't blame you for coming here. It's not one of the campus hot spots. Mostly we get professors, arts kids, and the occasional normie who wants to hide from the masses."

I blink, realizing he's nailed my reason for choosing this shop without even trying. "I think it's rather cozy."

"You don't have to pretend, Dean LeCiel." His pretty eyes meet mine again and I feel that heat creeping up my spine. "I'm aware of how contentious your appointment was. It doesn't bother me, honestly. I've been a student through much of your ex's reign and since the music department was of little concern to him, I don't have any allegiance to the former administration."

Definitely a doctoral candidate. His thesis is probably massive.

Covering my mouth as the unintended double meaning of my words occurs to me, I wait until the urge to giggle like a teenager fades. It would be extremely unprofessional of me to comment on his… attributes… especially since that kind of bullshit helped bring Magnus down. Of course, that doesn't mean I'm not wondering now…

"Dean? Hello?" The hot barista is waving his hand as he looks at me curiously.

"I'm sorry to be so rude. I didn't catch your name?"

There we go. That sounded totally normal.

"I'm Slade," he replies with a slow smile.

That doesn't surprise me in the slightest, and I wonder if he might be part Fae. Not giving me his real name is part and parcel with them, and so is the ethereal beauty. "You may call me Morgana when I am here. I think titles are dreadfully stuffy, but…"

"Set boundaries early because you have mutinies to deal with."

Frowning, I tilt my head. "You aren't reading me with magic, are you, Slade? Even during my ex's time, that kind of invasion of privacy wasn't allowed."

"No, no!" He stops making the sandwich and gives me a sheepish look. "I inferred it. I mean, I don't run with the undergrads or the popular crowds, but I hear things. It wasn't hard to figure out that you're at the hole in the wall shop so you don't have to be on stage while you eat or that you're going to make big changes because of all the charges against the former dean."

I nod, observing him. "I believe you, though I probably shouldn't. Betrayal hides in obvious places; I'm living proof of that."

His features look sharper as he smirks. "There are those of us who don't believe what you did was unjustified, Morgana. Living here at State U will provide you with plenty of evidence to give the Council that will mitigate your actions."

"That's both my desire and my deepest fear, Slade. There's only so much bad PR this place can take before the Council shuts it down and moves on."

A coffee cup and a plate with my sandwich slide across the counter as he murmurs, "You'll have to decide if that's what you want when the time comes."

"I know."

Get it on Kindle Unlimited

Get Season Two on Ream

Sneak Peek: Veiled Flame

Loser

Kat

The little blue icon on my app has been glaring at me all day, but I'm too damn nervous to open it. Everyone at Woodlawn High has been buzzing all day with their notifications and the squeals of joy and moans of despair were too much for me to take. My anxiety is through the roof—this is the moment I've been waiting for since middle school, but I can't seem to force myself to bite the billet and check.

Maybe it's because I don't have the support system most of my classmates have?

That's probably true, given I've always been a loner and I don't fit into any specific 'caste' here. It's hard to make friends when you get shuffled from foster home to foster home over the years. I've rarely stayed anywhere long enough to make a friend, much less a group of them.

I'm not delinquent or anything—the families I've been placed with just return me like a pair of pants that doesn't fit after a year or so. The caseworkers click their tongues sympathetically and hunt down a new placement, but I've never been given a reason *why* people don't want me around. One lady said I must be born under a bad sign and hell if I knew what that meant other than I'm not good enough to keep around.

It would be different, almost understandable, if I misbehaved or got bad grades. But I don't—I'm always in the top five percent of my class and I do everything I'm asked. I don't even lord my smarts over the other kids or adults. Being presentable and unassuming was something I adapted long ago to improve my probability of staying in a home long term.

Unfortunately, it never worked and though I should be a shoo-in for scholarships and acceptances galore, I can't bring myself to be rejected yet again.

So I wait for the last bell of the day, slinging my bag over my shoulder and trudging home to the latest in my temporary housing. I can't even contemplate looking at the possible heartache waiting for me in the college application system WHS insisted we use. The fear is too great and despite knowing I'll be on my own for good at the end of this year, I'm unable to risk the pain.

I hate being this way.

My court mandated therapist says it's some sort of attachment disorder that's common in foster kids, but I think that's bullshit. The problem isn't *me* not forming attachments; it's asshole adults not forming one to me. Being left at a safe haven in a fucking basket as a baby wasn't because *I* did anything wrong—again, fucking adults couldn't handle their commitments.

As usual, I arrive home to an empty house. There are two other kids who live here—Bryce and Blake—but they're at football practice. Of course, the Jamesons *love* them; they get to strut around at games because their strays are the stars of the team. I'm not mistreated, but I'm definitely an afterthought. Both of my 'parents' are still at work, so I drop my bag on the couch and head for the kitchen to get a snack.

Don't get me wrong. I *could* have been placed in far worse homes than any of the seven I've been in since elementary school. None of the ex-fosters starved, beat, molested, or abused me. They were all decent folks with jobs and houses that weren't hellholes, but they never liked me.

I have no idea why. I tried to be everything they wanted.

But when the end of each school year came, I was handed in like a textbook and off I went to some group home until the next contestant stepped up. It baffled everyone, not just me, but that's what happened every single time.

Sighing, I pull some fruit out of the fridge and grab a soda. I have homework to do and if I want to have time to work on my stories, I'll need to get it done before the house is full of people at dinner time. Bryce and Blake will have gotten messages about their applications, too, and I'd bet my pinkie toe those idiots got into some big sports school. Brett and Allison will be oozing happiness for them and I don't know if I'll be able to keep food down if I have to admit my failure when they ask.

Being eighteen sucks ass.

After I grab my books and tablet, I head down to the den. I have to give my current parents credit; they set up a very nice workspace for us to study in the converted basement. By the time they took me in, the Jamesons created a cozy room down here where the three of us could relax and do our work for school without being interrupted. It might have been more for the boys than me, but I appreciated it all the same. Desks, a couch, big chairs, and bookshelves fill the space, making it almost seem like our mini-library. They even put a small fridge for drinks and snacks in case we had to be up late to cram.

It's my favorite place in the entire house and I spend most of my time here.

I sink into the huge armchair, putting my drink and snack on the side table. It only takes a few minutes to arrange myself in the soft cushions and I pause to tug my headphones out of my pocket. Music always soothes my jagged edges and I need it to stay focused on the bullshit AP Calculus I need to keep my average up in. My course load is heavy, but I applied to tough colleges. I wouldn't have a chance to get in, especially on a scholarship, if I wasn't taking equally challenging classes in comparison to all the prep school kids.

As always, the sounds of Vivaldi carry me away as I scrawl equations on my screen and before long, thoughts of the blue notification completely fade away.

"Kat!"

The shouts barely register as I continue working on the problem set, gnawing on my lower lip in concentration.

"Jesus fuck, where is she? I could eat a hippo!"

"Kat!"

Thumping followed by what could pass for a stampede of elephants jerks me out of my math filled trance when Bryce and Blake come down the stairs. They smell as bad as the aforementioned pachyderm's cage, so they must have rushed home right after practice. The blond twins glare at me as if I'm the offending element despite being sweaty and covered in dirt and grass stains.

This doesn't bode well.

Usually, they're tired and hungry after practices so I'm used to cranky ass boys, but tonight, there's a light to their faces. That had to mean they've gotten their letters and dinner will be a gush fest in honor of their perfection. I'm going to need all of my strength to fake smile and nod as Brett and Allison fawn over them.

I don't begrudge them their success—not really. They work hard and play even harder on the field. It's not their fault they're the American dream teens and I'm the nerdy basement troll no one wants. But it's awfully hard living in the shadow of their bright light, especially when I'm no less intelligent or talented.

"I'm finishing the AP Calc, guys. What do you want?"

They roll their eyes at me before Blake scoffs. "It's not due until Monday. You're so hyper."

Duh. I take anxiety meds, douchebag; of course I'm 'hyper.'

"I can only be who I am, Blake." That earns me a snort from Bryce and I know it's because he thinks that's the problem. "Is dinner ready?"

"Almost. Get upstairs and set the table so we can shower—Brett's orders." Blake grins smugly.

The two of them seem to always arrange it so chores get passed to me for some half-assed reason and this is no exception. Sighing, I put my stuff aside, fully intending to hide down here after the dinner mess is cleaned up. Likely by me, but like I said, I could definitely live in worse foster homes so I let it go. Doing some chores isn't worth risking the group home for the last few months of my high school career.

They take off running up the stairs and I wait for them to disappear before I follow suit. My phone is tucked in my pocket and I feel like it's a stone of shame I have to bear. I know once the adults make over the twins' success, they will remember me, and I'll be forced to find out what disappointment lies in wait for me. The dread weighs on me, but I head into the sunny kitchen and pick up the pre-prepared pile of plates, silverware, and napkins on the counter.

Allison looks up from the stove and gives me a half-smile, nodding as I take the dishes into the dining room. Like I said, no one is mean or horrid, they just seem…obligated. After a while, it makes it hard to waste time trying to be bright and sunny. Being reserved makes it a hell of a lot easier not to feel rebuffed when they don't pay attention to you regardless.

"Make sure you include champagne glasses for your dad and I!" she calls from the other room.

The twins definitely got acceptance somewhere big. Brett must have gotten the bubbly on the way home.

Once I set the table, I return to help Allison bring out the roast and sides. I'm a little amazed at her efficiency when it comes to getting the housework done while working full time, but I suppose it's something people with real parents get taught as they grow up. My home life has been so fractured that I haven't learned how to cook more than very basic shit from YouTube videos. That may be a problem after graduation, but I've never felt comfortable enough to ask Allison if she'd teach me. I'm sure she would try, but it doesn't feel right.

"How was school, Kat?"

I look over my shoulder, seeing Brett in the entry to the dining room. He's already changed from work and smiling, but I see the distraction in his eyes. He's waiting for the boys to come down. "It was fine. I've got a Calc test at the end of the week. I'll be studying a lot to get ready."

"Good, good. No matter what happens with applications, keeping your grades up will ensure no one pulls any offers," he says.

Those words aren't for me. They are for the two wet haired boys who just appeared behind him.

"Kat's too much of a geek to ever let her grades slip, Dad," Blake says as he pushes past his brother and drops into his usual chair at the table. "Grab me a Powerade since you're in the kitchen, mouse!"

Both Brett and Bryce stare at me and I turn around, heading to the fridge despite the fact that I was *not* closer than the other twin. Out of habit, I take two of the drinks and a soda for myself. I've been here long enough to know Bryce will send me back to get him one as well. It would feel like typical sibling stuff, but for some reason, I just *know* they do it to fuck with me. I have no idea why I feel that way, but trusting my gut has been the one thing that helped me get through all the upheaval in my life over the years. It's a good gauge for knowing when I'll get booted or if people are being earnest in their reactions.

The therapist says that's some sort of trauma induced early trigger warning shit, by the way.

After I hand out the drinks, I sit down on my side of the table and we wait for Allison to come out. Brett is at his seat at the far end of the table and the twins are punching each other as they look at something on their phones. I know where this is all going but I drop my gaze to the table, swallowing the coppery taste of fear as it courses through my body.

I'm going to be exposed and there's nothing I can do to stop it.

Download now!

NOTES

BIG GIRLS DON'T CRY

1. Suck my dick, lizard boy.
2. Be nice, big guy. He's truly hurting.

THE FIX IS IN

1. It's true.

THE SET UP

1. Shit, little one. That's vicious.

I DON'T TRUST ANYONE ANYMORE

1. Listen!
2. fuck your dead bodies

LOSE YOURSELF

1. God, your stupider than you look.

VERDIS QUO

1. Maya Angelou, "Still I Rise"

KNOW YOUR ENEMY

1. Perhaps you are not stupid as well as slutty. Excellent.
2. Stupid Americans never speak the language of the countries they visit. Fine, I will switch to English since you are so... handicapped.
3. angry bunny

PSYCHO

1. I'll be damned.

THE SLEEPING BEAUTY, SUITE, OP. 66A, ROSE ADAGIO

1. pay attention
2. sharper, faster, my little hippos

CRIMINALS

1. Me? I would never, brother.

MASQUERADE

1. Good-bye and good luck.
2. It was a time of rebirth

STRESSED OUT

1. Translations from letter:
   It has been a long time, hasn't it?
   Life is nothing if not full of irony and pain, is it not?
   It is what it is, no?

ABOUT CASSANDRA
FEATHERSTONE

Cassandra Featherstone has channeled her lifelong passion for writing into a flourishing career, a journey that started when she first grasped a pencil as a gifted child with ADHD.

Her debut novel, born during the solitude of COVID lockdown in March 2020, draws on a tapestry of personal encounters and insights that resonate deeply with her readers.

An international bestseller, Cassandra has topped Amazon charts in categories such as LGBT Anthologies, LGBTQ+ Mystery, and Bisexual Romance, among others. Her works navigate the complexities of bullying, PTSD, body dysmorphia, mental health struggles, personal reinvention, and the empowerment of claiming one's own space. Importantly, Cassandra offers a thoughtful and respectful portrayal of LGBTQIA+ relationships, subtly reflecting her own connection with the community through her narratives.

Her literary repertoire spans sci-fi fantasy, urban fantasy, paranormal, and comedic genres in academy whychoose settings, with a strong commitment to portraying consensual, safe, and accurately depicted BDSM and kink lifestyles. Her books are an invitation to explore transformative stories that are both inclusive and engaging.

Often affectionately called 'The Muppet' for her wacky theater kid personality, she resides in the Midwest with her tech-savvy husband, their creatively inclined college student, a literary-minded dog, and four scheming cats.

READ MORE AT CASSANDRA'S WEBSITE OR HER FACE-BOOK PAGE. SIGN UP FOR EXCLUSIVE CONTENT AND UPDATES HERE.

FIND HER ON ANY OF THE SOCIAL MEDIA BELOW AS SHE *LOVES* TO CHAT AND *NEVER* SLEEPS!

ALSO BY CASSANDRA FEATHERSTONE

THE MISFIT PROTECTION PROGRAM SERIES

Road to the Hollow

Return to the Hollow

Home to the Hollow

Rejected in the Hollow

Revealed in the Hollow

Healing in the Hollow

Revenge in the Hollow

AUDIO OF THE MISFIT PROTECTION PROGRAM SERIES

Road to the Hollow

APEX ACADEMY CAPERS

Come Out and Prey

Let Us Prey

In Prey We Trust

Oh Holy Spite (3.5 novella)

Eat. Prey. Love.

Prey It By Ear

AUDIO OF THE APEX ACADEMY CAPERS SERIES

Come Out & Prey

Let Us Prey

In Prey We Trust

TRANSLATIONS OF THE APEX ACADEMY CAPERS SERIES

Come Out & Prey (German)

DISCORDIA UNIVERSITY

Veiled Flame (Book One)

Quiet Burn (Book Two)

SECRETS OF STATE U

Blood on the Ice (Book One)

VILLAINS & VIXENS

Bloodthirsty (Book One)

Ruthless (Book Two)

Wicked (Book Three)

AUDIO OF THE VILLAINS & VIXENS SERIES

Bloodthirsty

Ruthless

TRIANGLES & TRIBULATIONS

Hoist the Flag (PQ)

Yo-Ho Holes (Book One)

CHILDREN OF THE MOON-
WITH SERENITY RAYNE

New Moon Rising (Book One)

Waxing Crescent (Book Two)

Waxing Gibbous (Book Three)

Full Moon (Book Four)

Waning Gibbous (Book Five)

FAETAL ATTRACTION

Hell on Wheels (Book One)

RISE OF THE RESISTANCE

Ream Exclusive Prequels

Hooked on a Feline (Book One)

Book Two (TBA Title)

REAM SERIALS

Secrets of State U

Discordia University

Denizens of the Dark

Faetal Attraction

Agents of the Ouroboros

Rise of the Resistance

F.E.A.R. Academy

ANTHOLOGIES

Unwritten

Shifters Unleashed

Jingle My Balls

Love is in the Air

Silent Night

Snowed In

All Hallows Eve

Made in the USA
Monee, IL
17 June 2025

19542198R00354